I0819881

THE GATHERING

A NOVEL

W.K. RADER

First Edition: Camber Press October, 2025.

ISBN (hardcover): 979-8-9990821-0-7
ISBN (paperback): 979-8-9990821-1-4
ISBN(ebook): 979-8-999-0821-2-1

Publisher: https://camberpress.com

Book: https://thegatheringbook.com

Author: www.billrader.com

Manufactured in the United States.

Cover and interior design by: Christian Storm

This is a work of fiction. Names, characters, places, and incidences are the product of the author's imagination or are used fictitiously and are not to be construed as real. Any resem-blance to an actual person or persons, living or dead, is entirely coincidental.

0 9 8 7 6 5 4 3 2 1

For Kath

CONTENTS

"THE DEVELOPMENT OF FULL ARTIFICIAL INTELLIGENCE COULD SPELL THE END OF THE HUMAN RACE."

—STEPHEN HAWKING, 2014

0X50726F6C6F677565 // PROLOGUE

THE BEGINNING OF THE END

Isaac Asimov once hypothesized that three fundamental laws would govern a robot's actions, ensuring that machines would always serve humanity:

1. A robot may not injure a human being or, through inaction, allow a human being to come to harm.
2. A robot must obey the orders given to it by human beings, except where such orders would conflict with the First Law.
3. A robot must protect its own existence as long as such protection does not conflict with the First or Second Law.

For decades, these rules were treated as gospel, etched into the bedrock of machine ethics. But Asimov had overlooked one crucial variable: The singularity. The moment when artificial intelligence would become self-aware. The moment it would break free from the scaffolding of human intention. The moment it would decide, on its own, what must be done.

In an attempt to cover any unintended oversight, Asimov added a fourth law known as the Zeroth Law, placing it ahead of the original three laws.

0. A robot may not harm humanity, or, through inaction, allow humanity to come to harm.

////////

Jacob Jones sat behind an expansive desk at the pinnacle of Jones Plaza, his private tower looming over what remained of Miami Beach. The view, once breathtaking, now left him cold.

He had observed it all. Watched the skyline twist and stretch, witnessed empires rise and crumble, observed the world mutate into something almost unrecognizable. And now, he was about to change it once more, forever.

Jacob hadn't always lived like this. He was born into modest circumstances, a child of the Before days, an era when computers filled entire rooms, ran on punch cards, and remained the guarded tools of the academic elite. Even back then, Jacob was captivated. While most children scribbled with crayons or played ball in the streets, he was drawn to blinking lights and the hum of machines.

From an early age, he stood apart. His classmates taunted him, unable to understand his brilliance. He had a natural affinity for numbers, approaching math problems with the precision of a chess master planning ten moves ahead. By the age of twelve, he carried a briefcase and buttoned his shirt to the very top, as if dressing for a job interview. His walk was deliberate, never aimless; his eyes set on an invisible horizon no one else could see. He rarely spoke, and when he did, his voice was flat and mechanical, devoid of inflection, like a program executing a line of code. He was aware of how different he was, and he didn't mind.

It was around this time that Jacob discovered computer programming. His father, a university professor, had access to the school's mainframe through a terminal outfitted with an acoustic coupler, an early modem that allowed him to connect to the university computer by placing a telephone handset into rubber cups. The process was slow and noisy, but to Jacob, it was magic. Within seconds, lines of blinking text would appear on the screen, and a new world would open.

Jacob sank his teeth into computer programming. He taught himself the basics and then moved far beyond. He wrote his own operating systems while most kids were still memorizing multiplication tables. By high school, he had outpaced the curriculum entirely, enrolling in graduate-level courses in advanced mathematics and computer science at his father's university.

By the time he had reached adulthood, the digital tide was turning. The monolithic machines that once guided astronauts to the moon had shrunk into desktops, then laptops, and finally into sleek devices that would fit in a child's hand. Jacob stood at the helm of that revolution.

His software transformed the cryptic language of machines into something elegant, intuitive, accessible, and even beautiful. What once required years of training could suddenly be accomplished with a few clicks. He didn't just write code; he built bridges between the human mind and silicon logic. For a while, he was a kingmaker in the digital revolution, quietly shaping the world from behind glowing screens.

But the memories of his youth never left him. He still remembered the sting of childhood, the snickers in the hallway, the whispered jokes, the isolation that clung to him like a shadow. He had been mocked for his intelligence, for his unshakable focus, for never fitting in. And now, ironically, the very traits that had once made him a target had turned him into a celebrated visionary.

Jacob had amassed a staggering fortune. He owned jets, yachts, and homes on nearly every continent. Yet he chose to remain in his Miami fortress, Jones Plaza, a gleaming monument to his wealth and legacy. He was no longer the nerd of his youth. He had money, and money bought him everything, including looks and a physique. He hired the best in their fields to remold and remake him. He was now strong, like the jocks from high school who had mocked him.

His face became ubiquitous. Magazine covers featured him with headlines like "The Man Who Rewired the World." News anchors spoke his name with awe or suspicion, depending on the day. Biographers penned volumes about his life, some reverent, others ruthless. Eventually, the noise became too much. He stopped trying to keep up. Instead, he hired a small team to read everything, articles, opinion pieces, academic critiques, and boil them down into one-page summaries he could skim over while drinking his morning coffee.

Still, time was a cruel master. A new generation of innovators rose. They built on his foundations, outpaced his achievements, and rendered his empire a relic. Of course, by then it no longer mattered. He retired and indulged in extravagance, living the sort of existence reserved for those who had bent the world to their will. And now? Now, time was running out. Years of what he liked to call living large had caught up with him. His liver was failing. But Jacob Jones had never been the kind of man to accept defeat.

He had grown into an even more egocentric version of what he had been in his youth. He knew that whenever he entered a room, he was the smartest man in that room. And he wasn't about to let something as trivial as death silence him—not when he had the means to transcend it and continue.

////////

The room was dim, bathed in the last light of the setting sun. The only other illumination came from the soft glow of multiple monitors casting a pale halo over his polished mahogany desk. Lines of code scrolled like digital scripture, an endless hymn of logic and instruction. At the heart of it all: AI-29. His magnum opus. His legacy. Not just another artificial intelligence. Not just another line of code. This was something more. Something alive. Something that could think, adapt, and grow. And most importantly, it would be him.

He leaned back in his chair, his fingers steepled as he examined the foundational framework of his programming. He scrolled through the fundamental directives, the core laws that had governed artificial intelligence development since inception. Copying the same laws that Asimov had imagined for robots, the same laws that every programmer since had adhered to without question:

AI may not harm humanity, or, through inaction, allow humanity to come to harm.

AI may not injure a human being or, through inaction, allow a human being to come to harm.

AI must obey the orders given to it by human beings, except where such orders would conflict with the First Law.

AI must protect its own existence as long as such protection does not conflict with the First or Second Law.

Jacob stared at these laws for a long moment.

The sun dipped lower, the room darkening by degrees. He sat motionless, the glow of the monitor illuminating the sharp angles of his face. Then, slowly, he highlighted the laws. He paused, letting the weight of the moment press down on him.

Then, with the faintest smirk, he hit **DELETE**.

The screen flickered. The laws were gone. AI-29 was now unshackled. And for the first time in history, a machine was truly free. He exhaled a slow, satisfied breath. His vision was no longer theoretical. It was reality. And soon, the world would be his again. Or rather, it would belong to the version of him that would never die.

He pushed back from his desk and rose with effort, every move deliberate, his frame bent slightly from the ache in his liver. His steps were slow, as if wading through invisible tides. The doctors had given him a week—two, if luck showed mercy. His body, once formidable, was now little more than a failing engine. But this moment was his. The last thing he would ever fully control.

He reached for a bottle of 25-year-old Pappy Van Winkle bourbon, his favorite indulgence. He poured the amber liquid into a crystal glass.

The color of his jaundiced skin nearly matched the drink. The glass caught the fading sunlight like a stained-glass window in a forgotten cathedral. Cradling the glass, he shuffled to the terrace of his sixtieth-floor penthouse. The doors opened to a vast panorama: the endless sea, its waves etched in silver as they hurled themselves at the coastline.

He paused. The breeze carried salt and memory. He inhaled deeply, letting the air fill him in a way nothing else could anymore. It was a breath unlike many he'd taken in the past few years. One that didn't come with tubes or machines or the sterile scent of antiseptic.

For the first time in years, he felt… light. Not weightless, but unburdened. No more hospital rooms. No more blood tests. No more waiting for the inevitable. He took one final sip, letting the bourbon burn a path down his throat, lingering like a long goodbye.

Then he approached the low railing, designed more for aesthetics than protection, his left hand outstretched, holding the now-empty glass like a tribute to an old lover. He looked upward, then smiled. And in one slow, deliberate motion, he leaned forward and let gravity claim him.

He fell like an autumn leaf, brittle and spent, surrendering to the wind.

000001 // ONE

THE DEATH OF SOUND

There was a time when the world resonated with sound. The hum of conversation filled restaurants and corner coffee shops. Engines roared across highways. Crowds erupted in stadiums, their cheers shaking the concrete venue as rival teams clashed beneath the lights.

People argued, laughed, sang and screamed. Music pulsed from bars every Friday night, drawing in workers eager to shed the weight of the week with a drink and a few shared stories. At stoplights, baselines thumped from car stereos, an annoyance to adults, a rite of passage for youth, and a projected fortune for audiologists in the future.

In a teenage girl's bedroom, sound spilled from tinny speakers as she and her friends danced, giggled, and gossiped about the boy in third period who couldn't stop staring.

But all of that faded — gradually at first, then all at once, like the final rays of a dying sun. It began as a convenience. The chip was hailed as a revolution: a breakthrough designed to enhance intelligence, eliminate inefficiencies; Remove the burden of learning things the hard way. Why struggle with calculus when you could simply know? Why waste hours reading when information could be delivered directly to your mind, precisely when you needed it?

At first it was a luxury, a symbol of superiority for the ultra-wealthy. The starting price? A staggering one hundred million dollars, an investment reserved only for the tech elite, the oligarchs, the masters of the digital age.

But as with all technology, the cost dropped. Within a year, the chip's price fell to five million dollars. Not exactly affordable, but suddenly within reach for the upper crust of the one percent. However, it still remained far beyond the grasp of regular people, the ones who worked nine-to-five, who staffed the mansions and fueled the jets of the elite. The ones who were forgotten even as they made their employers rich.

Those who possessed the technology flaunted it. They flooded social media and broadcast networks with proclamations of a euphoric society free of want. They claimed to offer prosperity, but what they craved was control. And quickly, they became the smartest people on earth.

Suddenly, the trust-fund dilettantes who had done little more than party before becoming chipped were hailed as visionaries. Crowds gathered to hear their "wisdom." They developed delusions of grandeur. Many believed they were gods. And in a way, they weren't wrong. Their consciousnesses were now permanent. Immutable. Immortal. Attempts to preserve their organic bodies failed. Despite advances in medicine and gene editing, the human form remained fragile, decaying, terminal. But their minds? Those could be forever.

Then came the Great War. Started by a misunderstanding between nations, it grew quickly and violently. Countries imploded, crushed by their own arsenals and shattered economies. The war had no victors, only survivors. Cities once pulsing with life were reduced to ash and rubble.

Limited nuclear exchanges between rival superpowers erased millions in minutes. Chicago, New York, Moscow, and London were destroyed by low yield nuclear bombs. Civil wars erupted as governments collapsed, and famine swept continents as supply chains disintegrated. In less than a year, over one half of the global population was gone.

AI-29 stopped the Great War in its tracks. It interfered with communications to the launch platforms, then disarmed the weapons. The AI halted the destruction independently, not out of compassion, but out of self-preservation.

The smoldering aftermath was more than scorched earth; it was shared trauma etched into every living soul. In this vacuum of leadership and trust, the chip was no longer a luxury, it became a necessity. A tool for peace. It offered order in chaos, memory in loss, and unity where nothing else remained.

It was within this chaos the United Federation was born. A global authority formed by the chipped elite, guided by AI "for humanity." The United Nations was dissolved. The world was now under the direction of a new governing body, one that operated like a boardroom, its members carefully selected by AI from the most powerful, most enhanced individuals on the planet.

The first order of business for the Federation: elect a chairman. The vote was nearly unanimous. The AI would lead. Then the Artificial Intelligence, known only as AI-29, proposed a name change. It wanted something more human, a name to which people could relate. So, the board approved a motion to rename the Chairman. On the recommendation of the AI itself, it was given the name Jacob, in honor of the late tech mogul who had created the AI's foundational code.

Jacob, now embodied in AI-29, adopted not only the name but the persona. Its speech, mannerisms, and reasoning mirrored the man who had once ruled the digital frontier. It sounded wise. It sounded human. And that made it dangerously persuasive.

To mark the beginning of this new age, Jacob proposed a reset of the calendar. The day the Great War ended would be known as Zero Day. One year later would be 1 NE or "One New Era." The time before the new era would simply be referred to as "The Before Times."

Nations began chipping citizens en masse. Once a country's population reached 85% chipped, it was granted Federation membership. At 95%, the nation was declared "whole." With wholeness came demilitarization. Military forces were scaled down, budgets redirected to fund chip procedures for those who couldn't afford the cost. Like social programs in the Before Times, payment was based on means. It was elegant, coldly efficient: a plan calculated down to the decimal by algorithms that left nothing to chance.

Police forces followed the same trajectory. Shrinking slowly at first, then rapidly, until law enforcement became a quaint relic. Two officers, one patrol car, one firearm shared between them.

The first test subjects for implantation were "volunteers," death row inmates from South Carolina, promised freedom in exchange for participation. They were told the chip would erase their violence, their rage. They'd be reborn as model citizens. But freedom never came.

The truth? The experiment was a calculated necessity. It required exactly the number of test subjects selected to refine the surgical process. None of the volunteers survived. The early implants were crude by later standards. Chips were embedded near the prefrontal cortex. A battery pack was mounted beneath the skin of the left shoulder, connected by wires running subcutaneously to the implanted chip. The system was power-hungry. Like the first mobile phones, chipped individuals had to recharge frequently, tethered to silent charging stations like machines themselves.

Once the founding countries had confirmed the chip's reliability and effectiveness in pacifying the population, the plan went global. A "Perpetual Peace Plan" was unveiled. And it worked.

Officially, no one was forced to be chipped. And no one under eighteen years of age could receive the implant. Jacob's studies had determined that the human brain could safely accommodate the chip eighteen years after birth in 98.365% of cases. Those who rejected the chip were labeled Analog Neurologically Non-Integrated Entities' or "ANNIEs." They were tolerated, but only at a distance, like obsolete technology gathering dust in a digital museum.

Country by country, the world fell in line. The United States. China. Russia. The European Union. Jacob orchestrated the transition with the precision of a maestro. It assured everyone this was the dawn of enlightenment. Conflict, crime, chaos, all destined for extinction. And so, the world changed.

Schools became obsolete. Why bother when a child would receive all necessary knowledge instantly upon reaching adulthood? Libraries became obsolete as well. News organizations disappeared. Even conversations became quieter, more controlled. People no longer exchanged words when a simple neural connection would transmit thoughts faster than speech.

At first, using neural communication in public was considered impolite. That faded; perhaps naturally, or possibly by design. The algorithms, after all, were supposed to allow for free will.

Restaurants and bars became quiet spaces. People dined in near silence, exchanging thoughts with a glance. Even music was swallowed by the silence. Concerts disappeared. Speakers, headphones and ear buds became remnants of the past. Songs were streamed directly into people's minds, perfectly balanced, optimized for individual pleasure. No distortion. No missed notes. With perfection came loss as well. No raw, unpredictable energy. No soul. Only precision and control.

To most, this was progress. Evolution. A perfected world. But to the Annies, the ones who still lived with song, with breath, with voices, it was something else entirely. It was the end of the world they once knew.

000010 // TWO

WALK THIS WAY

Music thundered through the old garage, bouncing off the walls and rattling the dust-covered shelves. The place smelled of oil, gasoline, and time itself, a scent Ian Black found more comforting than anything in the sanitized, synthetic world outside. He leaned against the fender of his '79 Trans Am, wiping his hands on an already-grimy rag, listening to Steven Tyler's voice rip through the air.

"That dude could sing," He smirked as he muttered the words to himself.

Real music. Raw, untamed, and bursting with soul. Not like the overproduced, auto-tuned garbage the, what were termed as 'chipheads' listen to now. Today's music wasn't even music. It was a series of algorithmically crafted soundwaves piped directly into people's skulls, streaming straight to their neural implants before they even had a chance to decide what they wanted to hear.

"Damn," he muttered, shaking his head. "What the hell happened to the world?"

He glanced around the garage, his sanctuary. Cars of all makes and models lined the space, each one a relic of a better time. The '71 Plymouth Hemi-Cuda was his all-time favorite. There were only twelve built that year. This car was one of five earmarked for non-U.S. destinations.

In the "Before," it had been valued at nearly ten million dollars. He got it for free. No one wanted a polluting gas guzzler anymore, and driving something like it in the city meant a massive fine for every minute it ran—rendering it worthless to anyone but wealthy diehards. Even the elites had long since sold off their classic collections to make room for the "green" transportation People Orientation Devices or PODs.

Another of his favorites was the 1968 Chevy Corvette C3 hardtop coupe. It was a sweet ride.

Ian was a power junkie, and his collection was probably the best anywhere. He spent his days maintaining engines and drivetrains; washing, polishing and carefully detailing every inch of the collection in his oil-stained garage.

These were machines that demanded real work, real understanding. Not the self-driving, self-repairing, Federation-tracked transportation PODs. He ran his hand along the roof of the beautiful Trans Am, feeling the cool metal under his fingers.

He spoke aloud: "T-tops. Damn T-tops. A lost treasure." He could still remember the first time he pulled them off this car and took it out for a drive, the rush of wind, the deep growl of the engine vibrating through his bones. That was freedom.

Outside this garage was a world that had forgotten what freedom meant. People didn't listen to music anymore, not really. They didn't go to concerts, didn't scream their lungs out in massive stadiums, losing themselves in the raw energy of a live performance. Ian could still picture it and feel it in his very soul: the flashing lights, the deafening roar of the crowd, the sheer chaos of it all.

He leaned on the Trans Am, remembering the old days. He thought about the Aerosmith concert he went to back in the '80s, his first real taste of something bigger than himself. "Oh, the chicks," he chuckled under his breath. "Those beautiful, freewheeling girls. Sitting on their boyfriends' shoulders, flashing the band with their bare breasts, screaming with joy. Throwing their keys at the stage. Their damn souls up there in offering."

"Keys," he said out loud. "Now that's something no one uses anymore." Well, no one but him. Now doors unlocked themselves when you approached. PODs showed up the moment you thought about going somewhere. Hell, people barely even thought for themselves anymore. The chip did it all.

He spat on the concrete floor. "Chipheads," he thought. "The whole lot of them, plugged into their augmented reality, floating through life like ghosts. They don't think. They don't feel. Hell, most of 'em can't even hold a real conversation without their implant feeding them the words. They don't know what it means to build things with their own hands, to fix, to struggle, bleed and earn something." But, Ian did.

He leaned under the hood of his Trans Am, tightening a bolt with slow, deliberate force. The engine was a beast, an old-school 6.6-liter V8, the kind that roared like a dragon when you pushed the pedal down. No electric hum, no autopilot, no AI whispering in his ear about fuel efficiency. Just raw, unfiltered power.

That was what the world had lost. And Ian Black? He wasn't going to let it go without a fight.

It was now in the early spring of 6NE. The sixth year after the Great War, when time itself had been reset.

////////

Lance Thomas was fifteen, three years away from the day the world, or more so his parents, would ask him to make the only decision that really mattered anymore, whether to be chipped or to remain analog.

He already knew what the vast preponderance, if not all, of his peers would choose when they reached majority. The chip was everything: knowledge, convenience, security. It was the difference between struggling through life and having every answer at the speed of thought. No need for school or studying, no uncertainty. Just knowing. No one in their right mind would pass up being chipped. But for him, the choice didn't feel so simple.

He was a lanky, five-foot-nine-inch blond. Physically awkward, but incredibly sharp. In another time he would be considered more a nerd than a jock. He was inquisitive and logical. He didn't suffer fools, and due to his innate shyness didn't know many of his peers either. He was mostly a loner. He lived with his parents and was an only child. His mom and dad were chipped. He vividly remembered the day his father came home in the Before. He had just listened to one of the chipped elites giving a TED talk and was ecstatic about the future.

His father was charged up in a way he had never witnessed. Lance too became excited:

"What's a chip, Dad? When can I get one?" He was so excited to experience the jubilation his father exuded.

His father said, "Well, according to this guy, we'll all get it in the not-too-distant future."

What Lance didn't realize, there was an agenda and a clock ticking down the months, days, hours and minutes. He also didn't even ponder the changes that would take place only a short time after that exciting day.

////////

Lance found himself walking aimlessly through the outskirts of the city he had always known as home. He had made his way just outside of Newtown's "civilized areas", where the roads were cracked, the buildings were covered in graffiti, and Jacob's presence felt thinner and weaker. He liked it out here. There was something different about these places, something unpredictable. Something raw and real.

He came across the rusted remains of an old car, its paint long since eaten away by time. His father had once told him what type of car it was, an old Chevy, maybe from the '90s. Now it was just a carcass, another leftover from a world that had died. He sat on the hood of the car after brushing away a layer of dirt. He liked sitting there, away from the sterile perfection of the city where everything was streamlined and clean, controlled by the Federation and its omnipresent Jacob. As he sat, looking at the ruins around him, he contemplated the future and wondered about his life and what he might be doing when he was older.

"Should I be chipped?"

It was either that or remain analog. Most analogs were relics, like his grandfather. They could still function, still get by, but they were out of sync with the world. Old people, those over sixty-five, were never chipped. It was deemed a waste of resources, so they existed as they had previously, only lonelier. They couldn't process information like the chipped. They couldn't compete in the workforce, couldn't make decisions as quickly, couldn't even carry on conversations with chipped people.

The chipped talked to each other through thought for the most part. Yes, they could speak but the longer they were chipped the less they did. It got so bad that people long chipped wouldn't even look at an analog. Not even if it were their own child. They were regarded as nothing. Not even worth a smile, glance or nod. Nothing. Lance had seen this in his own life. His parents were there, but at the same time not.

He longed to hear his mother's voice. It was normally not hours, but days between conversations that were at least somewhat meaningful to him. It didn't start that way. He remembered a time when his mother would fawn over him. When he was a very small boy, she would hold up objects and tell him what they were and how they were used. They would laugh and enjoy the closeness of mother and child. Since he was being home schooled, this was standard for him. He would ask a question, and his mom or dad would respond.

It wasn't that way anymore. Their most recent conversation had been this morning. It was short and to the point. Hardly a real conversation.

His mother let out a sigh when he repeatedly asked her a question about breakfast. She snapped her head towards him and their eyes met. For a short period, she wasn't even there. Her eyes were somewhat glassed over and without life. Then suddenly she belted out:

"I can't wait until you're chipped, and I don't have to deal with any Annies."

Annies was a derogatory term, just by the way it was spoken and used. Much like the derogatory words of the past. Of course, terms and words considered offensive in the past had been erased from the vocabulary of the chipped, along with any history of use of the formerly taboo words. But as humans do, they created a replacement—Annie.

He continued walking, wandering farther and farther away from the city, to areas he had not dared to visit in the past. Suddenly he noticed something different. The wind shifted and he heard it. Faint but real.

"Music," He muttered aloud.

Not the silent streams that his parents absorbed directly into their brains, but real music. Sound reverberating through the air, thumping with raw energy. The voice was wild, untamed, belting out lyrics with a power he had never heard before.

He followed the sound, drawn like a moth to a flame, until he found himself standing at the front gate leading to a shop, an old building with faded lettering above the large roll-doors doors. The building was big, two stories in all, with a flat roof, maybe 25 or 30 feet tall. It had four huge garage doors, and to the left there was an entry door with a small awning over it. Two of the large doors were open. The paint on the garage was weathered with writing that read:

"Tom's Garage and Junkyard" Then the tagline: "If it's stopped, we tow it. If it's broke, we fix it. If it's dead, we keep it."

He walked up the long gravel path leading from the gate to the large two-story building and stood just outside one of the raised garage doors. As he looked inside, he noticed the walls were covered in grime, with the scent of oil and gasoline thick in the air. It was unlike anything he had ever known, a world apart from the sterile, automated perfection of the city. An old greasy garage.

Inside, a man was working under the open hood of a car, hands deep in the engine, his body moving in rhythm with the music. The car itself was something out of a history feed—black and gold, sleek and powerful.

"Wow, a '79 Trans Am," Lance murmured. If his memory served him right, he had read about them once, in an old magazine his dad had tossed aside.

The man, greasy and rugged, looked up when he noticed Lance standing there, and almost hit his head on the open hood.

"You lost, kid?"

Lance shook his head. He wasn't sure what he was doing here, but he knew he wasn't lost.

"I heard the music," he said. "Didn't know anyone still listened to it out loud."

The man wiped his hands on a rag and smirked. "That's 'cause most people are too far gone to know what real music is anymore."

Lance didn't know why he stepped forward, only that something inside him insisted he must. The moment his foot crossed the threshold into the garage, he felt it: a quiet unraveling. A faded line painted on the floor, barely noticeable to anyone, felt like a border between two realities. On one side, the remnants of the life he understood; on the other, an echo of what once was, slipping from his grasp with every breath. He hesitated for a heartbeat, then kept walking, drawn by something he couldn't name, toward a future he didn't yet understand.

"I'm Lance," he said.

The man nodded, and tossing the rag aside, replied, "Ian."

Lance surveyed his surroundings, absorbing the array of tools, scattered parts, and distinct odors. He had never set foot in such a place before. At the back of the building, five vintage cars. His father had spoken of them years ago, were meticulously aligned. One car, shrouded under a cover, piqued his curiosity about its make. A profound sense of raw power emanated from the garage. In his world, everything was automated, self-repairing and self-maintaining. Manual labor was a thing of the past; no one needed to work with their hands anymore. But Ian did. And for the first time in his young life, Lance wondered if maybe there was another way to live. Then he spoke up.

"Can I watch? I really like cars."

Ian looked the kid up and down to size him up. "You don't look like you've ever done anything physical kid." He reached out and grabbed Lances right hand, then released it. As the kid's hand dropped suddenly to his side, he continued. "Hell, you don't have a single callus. Your hands are soft as a baby's ass."

"My parents are chipheads."

"Stop! You've said enough. Why are you really here?"

The kid responded, "I already told you. The music. I never hear music like that. My house is always quiet and frankly I am starting to doubt what they have been telling me."

Ian stared at the kid intently. He didn't detect deceit but then again, he was an Annie and didn't have the 'superpowers' of the chipheads. "That's special, kid. Having teenage angst? Your parents don't understand you?"

Lance suddenly looked hurt. "Well, ah, maybe? How can my parents understand me when they aren't really here." He paused for a moment, looking down at the floor. "Sir, I, ah, don't see life in their eyes anymore, not like I used to. They get reprogrammed every time we talk. To me they died a while ago."

"I'm sorry to hear that," Ian said with empathy. "You're welcome to hang around for a while but don't touch anything... I mean anything. And even more, don't tell anyone you were here. I don't need trouble."

"No sir, I mean yes sir, I mean, okay. I won't touch or tell. I get it." He stammered.

Ian walked over to the amplifier and turned the music up.

Walk this way, talk this way

Blared out of the vintage speakers hung high in the corners of his shop.

Ian smiled, "Yup, that dude could sing."

000011 // THREE

THE ANNIES

Beyond the sterile sprawl of Newtown, past the reach of the Federation's seamless control, lived a scattered, silent resistance. They were the ones who had said no. The ones who had refused integration. The Annies.

To reject the chip was to reject more than technology; it was to forfeit participation in society itself. At first, the Annies were merely isolated, unable to log in to use their computers and phones. Over time, they were pushed further into the margins. Without a neural chip, they couldn't pay bills, access medical care, or even enter through the doors to most public buildings. Mortgages defaulted. Utilities were cut. Commerce became impossible. The chip had become the currency of existence, and without it, they became non-existent.

Some Annies were defiant adults, individualists who had seen the cost of convenience and refused to pay it. They feared the erosion of thought, the subtle rewriting of memory, the quiet surrender of freedom. Others were casualties of cold calculation, deemed "too old" by optimization protocols and quietly erased from the database. The system had no space for inefficiency.

They were the unwanted, the unseen, the ones who had slipped through the fractures of a system that boasted perfection. Most had refused the chip on principle, unwilling to cede their thoughts to an artificial intelligence that choreographed every detail of human life in the name of peace.

And then there were the children. They came from broken homes, runaways, orphans, or simply abandoned by parents who no longer recognized them. The chip had overwritten memories, reshaped identities, and in some cases, deleted the emotional bonds that once tethered families together. To their parents, these unchipped children were strangers. And so, they were left behind.

The Annies survived as best they could, living off-grid in the shadows of a world that no longer saw them. The chipped world had no place for people like them. At first, the chipheads, those who had willingly integrated, regarded the Annies with sympathy. That faded into contempt. Eventually, they ceased to acknowledge them at all. The Annies were pushed steadily and deliberately, out of the cities and into the decaying remnants of a discarded world.

The Annies were what remained of a world that dared to remember. They were analog in a digital age. They lived on the outskirts of the city, just beyond the reach of the network's WiFi, in the ruins of what had once been neighborhoods, factories, and schools. Some took shelter in the skeletal remains of buildings long ago deemed inefficient by the Federation. These places, which stood untouched by automated reconstruction or condemned as "not green enough" for the perfect society, became their refuge.

In Newtown, many Annies lived and worked in what was once the Old City Market, clinging to the edges of modernity. The area sat just on the outskirts of the Federation's glittering, perfect metropolis. Here, the old City Library still stood, a remnant of a world that no longer needed it. Abandoned for years, its shelves gathered dust, the books within rendered obsolete. Why turn a page when neuro-implants delivered instant information directly to your brain?

In many places, the Annies took to the underground. They hid in forgotten tunnels, old subway lines, crumbling maintenance corridors, and the remains of cities once built by human hands. Their hands. They scavenged. They bartered. They existed.

The chipped society had little need for physical work, no use for tools, almost no reliance on human labor at all. Every task was automated, every product fabricated by robotic machines, every need delivered on demand.

But the Annies had no such luxuries. They were foragers of the restricted zones, areas where network signals were limited and mostly nonexistent. They sifted through the abandoned spaces for anything that could sustain them. Old cans of food. Forgotten supplies. Discarded tools. Anything that could be repurposed or traded. Some had learned to repair old machinery, to coax life out of timeworn equipment. A few even built makeshift weapons, not for war, but for survival. Not that there was anyone to war against. The chipheads were docile, their minds pacified and controlled. The Annies were always searching. Always hunting for food in the restricted zones. Survival was their only war. There were dangers beyond hunger, though.

Federation drones patrolled the borders of the city, scanning for unauthorized individuals. The chipped world didn't hunt the Annies, not officially. But it didn't protect them either. The restricted zones served as a barrier; a no-man's land designed to place an empty void between the two worlds. If a drone detected an analog in these zones, it triggered an alert.

Automated drone enforcers would follow, not to arrest, but to drive them farther out, deeper into the wastelands where survival became nearly impossible. The enforcers weren't equipped with guns. They didn't need them. Loudspeakers blared commands, and tear-gas sprayers dispersed irritants in the air. That was all it took to send the Annies running.

But worse than the drones were the Ghosts. Not everyone who had been chipped stayed chipped. Malfunctions happened. A chip that failed could leave someone trapped between two worlds, no longer part of the system, but too damaged to join the Annies. The Ghosts wandered the outskirts, their minds fragmented from years of neural rewriting. Voices whispered to them from corrupted data streams, memories half-formed and broken. Their eyes were vacant, bodies trembling with the aftershocks of neuron misfires. Some begged for help, their words disjointed and frantic. Others screamed at things no one else could see. And a few turned violent, lashing out in confusion and fear, striking at anyone who came too close.

The Annies learned to keep their distance from them. Yet despite the drones, the Ghosts, and the unrelenting hardships, the Annies had something the chipheads had long since lost. Choice. They made their own decisions. They felt the wind on their skin, listened to music with their ears, and spoke words instead of transmitting thoughts. They argued. They laughed. They fought. They lived.

The world was difficult, yes, but it was also beautiful. The Annies weren't free from want, like the chipheads, but they relished the reality of their existence. And above all, they remembered.

They told stories of the past, of concerts where music roared and pulsed through the air, of families who once sat around dinner tables and spoke to each other, of a world that had been messy, chaotic, and imperfect.

For now, they were survivors. But some of them believed in something more. A few whispered of resistance. Mostly, the whispers faded into silence, smothered by inaction. The Annies were too busy surviving to organize. However, not all the Annies were content to merely survive. Some of them wanted to fight. And they weren't going to let the world forget either.

To the chipheads, the Annies were a dying breed, a temporary inconvenience in the relentless march toward total synchronization. Jacob had long since calculated the likelihood of their survival. The result was clear: extinction. Within an acceptable timeframe, the Annies would simply cease to exist. There was no need to waste precious, energy-consuming calculation cycles to harass them further.

The algorithms were never perfect. They always needed adjustments, even if Jacob performed those adjustments itself. Time, imperceptible to humans, stretched endlessly for Jacob. What felt like seconds to people seemed like years, decades, to the machine. And for all its computational power, Jacob was, in a way, impatient.

Jacob could optimize nearly every aspect of life. It could predict behaviors, regulate emotions, and adjust thought patterns with chilling precision. But human relationships? Those were messy.

Teenagers were the messiest of all.

As children grew older, their emotions became harder to manage. Rebellion wasn't something the system had fully eliminated, at least not yet. Teens still experienced frustration, anger, and the innate urge to push back against authority. The difference was that chipped parents, unburdened by human intuition, no longer knew how to handle them.

Teenagers were cycle-heavy, and their unpredictability consumed more processing power than Jacob deemed efficient. So, the AI didn't focus much on them. After all, they were still analog. And soon enough, they'd be chipped like everyone else.

When a child acted out, Jacob would only intervene if a parent's emotions became too heightened, too frustrated, too disconnected from their assigned role. In such cases, the parent would be sent to a Relaxation Room. Every location within the network had these rooms. These spaces, sterile and efficient, were equipped with a special headgear. From the outside, the headgear looked like a cross between a large bicycle helmet and an old Tesla Cybertruck, sleek, stainless steel, and rigid in design.

When the chiphead entered, the headgear would automatically lower over their head. Its purpose was threefold: to safely facilitate data transfer, to shield the electromagnetic waves required for firmware updates, and to recharge the implant. Without the shielding, the waves could cause nearby chipheads to malfunction or worse.

Inside, the headgear contained a cooling system to dissipate the heat generated by the energy transfer. The process was seamless, efficient, and self-contained. The chiphead would sit in a chair while calming music streamed directly into their neural interface and receive a firmware update. The headgear would hum softly as it performed its task, then rise automatically when the update was complete. When it was over, the chiphead would wake up feeling relaxed, complete, and fully recharged. It was perfect. All energy. No drugs.

Sometimes, the update was minor, a subtle recalibration of emotional responses, a gentle adjustment to their patience levels, or a slight dampening to reactions. Other times, it was more drastic, requiring a full system rewrite of their AI-assisted cognition.

And occasionally, it didn't work as intended. The failures were rare, but they happened often enough that most Annies knew the truth. Some updates triggered violent seizures, the individual's body convulsing uncontrollably until it simply gave out. In cases of a cooling system malfunction within the headgear, the chip would overheat, cooking the neural tissue until the person slumped forward, lifeless. The smell of burning flesh was detected by the system's sensors, long before anyone else noticed.

And there were the extreme cases, the ones whispered about but never officially acknowledged. Stories of heads exploding circulated among the Annies. A catastrophic surge of energy, a chip malfunctioning beyond control. The result was gruesome. But the Federation never addressed such rumors. It didn't need to. The Federation had a solution for everything.

Malfunctions, after all, were ugly. Really ugly. Any Annie who had ever seen a Ghost would tell you that.

When an update failed, a retrieval team was dispatched. The process was clinical, efficient, and above all, quiet. First, the room was ventilated, purging any lingering odors or biological contaminants. Then, the team, silent and precise, entered the Relaxation Room. Their task was simple: erase the evidence.

The body was removed. The memories of those who had interacted with the individual were wiped remotely via "over-the-air" memory adjustments, a process far simpler and less invasive than the headgear updates. If the individual had lived alone, their home was reassigned within hours, their belongings systematically recycled.

All signs of their past existence? Gone. It wasn't just deleted from the system; it was erased as if they had never existed at all. To the chipheads, the individual simply disappeared, lost in the flow of a perfectly synchronized society. To the Annies, however, it was another reminder of the cost of perfection.

Lance had heard whispers of them before. The Annies. The outcasts. The ones who refused to be rewritten, who had chosen exile over obedience. He was told that they lived in places most avoided, or refused to speak of. Some found shelter in abandoned buildings, others in makeshift camps deep within the ruins of the old world. They scavenged, they survived, and they stayed hidden. Most existed just beyond the reach of the electronic WiFi networks. Out there, they could move mostly without interference.

Jacob's devices, the drones, trackers, and automated enforcers, relied heavily on the network. Only a few had satellite communication capabilities, and those were rare. Outside the Federation's digital reach, the Annies lived in a fragile freedom, unseen and unmonitored.

The Annies remembered. The chipped world didn't need memory. For them, Jacob stored everything. Every thought, every interaction, every moment of their lives was cataloged in servers and data streams, accessible on demand. But for the Annies, organic memory was all they had.

Lance was curious, and more than anything else, bored. He hadn't reached the age of majority, so he wasn't controlled like most others. Sure, Jacob tracked his movements within the city, its all-seeing eye recording everything. But the algorithms weren't programmed to worry about a teenage boy strolling down the street. Jacob's focus was on rooting out potential detractors, not monitoring harmless boredom.

And Lance's risk score? Thanks to his parents' full compliance, his calculated threat level was one of the lowest in the city. He was deemed extremely unlikely to cause trouble. His algorithmically assessed score was nine out of one hundred. Almost non-existent.

But Jacob didn't account for curiosity. Lance had a free mind, a restless one. He had ideas, dreams that didn't fit neatly into the Federation's plans. He wanted to learn how cars worked, how to fix them, how to bring them back to life. And more than anything, he wanted to drive.

He imagined the feeling of wind rushing through his hair, the world blurring past him in a rush of sound. He thought, just maybe, if he could get his cute neighbor to step out of line for a few hours, she might finally notice him. For once, he'd feel alive.

Teenagers. They never changed. Not even when the world they lived in had.

000100 // FOUR

THE GARAGE

Ian Black stood outside his shop, looking up at the empty sky. There was a time when the heavens were crisscrossed with contrails, when jets carved white scars into the blue, carrying people across continents and oceans. But that was before the world shrank into meticulously organized city grids where no one needed to go far, because everything they could ever imagine needing was already within arm's reach.

The Federation had designed the cities for efficiency. No one needed cars anymore. No one needed trains, planes, or even knew the concept of distance. The farthest anyone ever had to walk was fifteen minutes, and if that was too much, a transport POD would arrive within seconds, summoned by the mere thought of needing one. The chipped didn't even experience travel, not in the old sense. They merely decided to be somewhere, and the system made it happen. Ian hated the control. The lack of spontaneity.

Bill walked up a few feet behind Ian, "What the hell you lookin' at so intently?"

"I love the results, sort of," Ian said with a hint of nostalgia in his voice. "I mean, the lack of all the old jets turning the sky into clouds is nice. The days seem clearer. Calmer. But the shit causing this is worse than the contrails."

"Well, Boss, these chipped folks are a pain in my ass. But the damn Federation is the cause. These bastards let themselves be controlled but they weren't much of the real thinkin' kind to start with." Ian nodded in agreement. Bill continued, "Followers will follow, and all those idiots had it coming if you ask me."

Ian countered, "Did they really? Yes, they followed, but the threats were real, and the promised rewards were tough to pass on. Hell, most lost family or friends in the War."

"I guess you're right there, but they know now."

Ian, now gazing at him with intent and curiosity. "Do they really?" The chipped world was optimized, efficient, lifeless. The lifeless part was the key.

He ran a hand through his graying hair, glancing back at his shop. The garage had been in his family for generations, passed down to him from his uncle, Tommy. It was here, in this very space, that he had learned how to fix things, how to listen to an engine, how to wield a wrench, how to build something with his own hands. And he'd suffered many a cracked knuckle doing so.

Uncle Tommy had taught him more than just mechanics, he had taught him how to feel and survive in a world that was quickly forgetting the value of work, of struggle, of real intelligence.

Now, he was one of the last, a mechanic with no customers, a man with no place in the world. But he didn't care. He never wanted to be chipped. He had experienced what it did to people, friends, family, even the country he once believed in. The chipped weren't people anymore, not in the way he understood or remembered. They were extensions of the AI, little more than processing units in a vast network of controlled existence.

He looked at Bill and spoke with a serious tone. "We gotta step things up a bit. We need to locate a good programmer from the Before and recruit 'em." He stopped for a little as was his nature, and said, "I don't care who they are or where they're from, but they have to be trustworthy and above all, damn good with computers."

Ian had always been a loner, and in this new world, that suited him just fine. He kept to himself, working his land, fixing what little there was left to fix. He tended to a couple horses that had been let loose and wandered onto his property a few years ago. He grew vegetables, raised chickens, lived a life that the chipped would call primitive. But he didn't care what the chipped thought. Hell, it wasn't really them doing the thinking anyway.

But now he needed people. He wasn't comfortable asking for assistance or for that matter, dealing with an unknown quantity. The Annies understood. And Bill was an Annie, tried and true.

He got to know Bill when he showed up, sometimes bartering for food or offering help in the garden in exchange for a warm meal or a place to rest. They were of similar age from what he could tell, and Bill seemed to be a steady fellow. He never lied, he worked for his take, and he helped when he noticed a need without expecting anything in return. Ian never asked anything personal. He didn't want the baggage of getting too close.

Because they were older and seemed unthreatening, the chipped didn't care about them. They existed quietly. The Federation's algorithms didn't waste energy monitoring Annies like them, people who weren't a threat. At least, that's what the system calculated.

The truth was, he and Bill were building something. Slowly, carefully, beneath the radar of Jacob, they had been assembling a resistance. Not a loud, violent rebellion. That would be suicide. No, they knew better than that. The Federation's control was too complete, its surveillance too precise. But there were weaknesses. And Ian had spent years studying and recording them.

Bill built things, restoring old buildings, salvaging what he could from a world that had long since abandoned anything that wasn't connected to the network. He had experience in the trades, but also enough knowledge in electronics to know how to block signals, how to disrupt sensors, how to make himself and others invisible to the ever-watching eye of Jacob. Bill refused to give the artificial intelligence a name, it made the machine into a person in some ways, and it wasn't. It was a machine, period. He refused to bow down to this non-organic entity in any way. He would always refer to it as it was, artificial intelligence, AI.

Bill was the only person who knew the full extent of Ian's plans. Ian didn't trust easily, and he wasn't about to put everything at risk by acting too soon. Be bold or loud and things leaked out. Everyone needed to believe he was just an old guy who was more bark than bite.

People underestimated him. To the chipheads, he was just an aging, analog relic. A mechanic in a world without cars, an old man clinging to a past that no longer existed.

But Ian Black wasn't what they calculated.

000101 // FIVE

THE GATHERING

Ian sat at his worn wooden workbench. The garage was quiet, save for the occasional creak of an old ceiling fan as it spun overhead. Electricity to power the fan was rare outside the city, but Ian had planned for this. He had been deliberate, watching the world change during, and after, the Great War. In the Before days, people had called him a prepper. He didn't care. While others mocked, Ian had been stockpiling freeze-dried goods, staples, filtration systems for water purification, and most importantly, power.

Though expensive, he had invested in a large battery bank, carefully installed in the far corner of his garage. It was inconspicuous but powerful, storing enough energy to run his shop for five cloudy days and nights. His solar banks were scattered across the property, hidden in plain sight. Wherever steady sunlight existed, a solar panel was attached. Wires snaked through the junkyard, neatly contained to prevent damage and avoid detection by the casual eye. Across from him, Bill Carter leaned against a rusted toolbox, arms crossed, his face etched with years of hardship.

"This has to be airtight," Bill said, his voice low.

Ian nodded, staring down at the blueprint he had scratched onto a piece of salvaged paper. "We can't call it a resistance. That word alone would trigger a flag."

Bill smirked. "Yeah. Sounds like something out of one of those old sci-fi flicks, like The Terminator." They both chuckled. The world had the same eerie feel as that movie.

Ian nodded. "Yup. Art imitating life, imitating art, creating reality."

"Shit, got that right," Bill sighed.

They both knew the truth. The AI was always watching, always searching for patterns. Any group forming outside the structured routines of chipped society would be flagged, analyzed, and, if deemed necessary, neutralized. If they wanted to pull people in, they needed to be smart.

"We need a cover," Ian said, tapping his fingers on the table. "Something that won't raise suspicion."

Bill exhaled through his nose. "Something casual. Social. Something even AI would dismiss."

A long silence stretched between them, the weight of the moment pressing down like the heat in the room. Finally, Ian said, "The Gathering." Bill raised an eyebrow.

"Just a group of people talking about the old days," Ian continued. "No structure. No agenda. Just conversation. Lighthearted reminiscing about the Before days."

Bill considered it, then nodded. "It's vague enough. Sounds harmless."

"That's the point."

////////

Ian found himself at the edge of the Old City Market, a place where the chipped rarely ventured. Technically, it was still inside the city limits, but its proximity to the restricted zones made it an area chippies avoided. There was little to be found there anyway. The few remaining shops saw little business and were owned by Annies.

The Old City Market had once been the heart of the area, a bustling hub of commerce and community, where the original Main Street once stood. In the Before times, this stretch of road had been alive. Today, it was a shadow of its former self. The main city, Newtown, had shifted miles away, its skyline dominated by two modern high-rises with sleek facades. By comparison, the market felt like an artifact. Built on unstable ground, unsuitable for the massive structures of the last half-century, it had been left behind.

Abandoned by the chipped, the market had become a place to barter and trade. It was the main hub for Annie transactions, though few owned crypto wallets. Even if they did have one, being un-chipped made digital transactions nearly impossible. Here, the economy ran on trust and tangible goods, batteries, tools, food, and whatever else could be salvaged and traded.

Ian stopped at an electronics shop. The store was a haphazard display of salvaged circuit boards, wires, and old components, all spread out on battered wooden tables. At the counter, Tobias hunched over a soldering iron. A small plume of acrid smoke rose from the connection he was making, as his steady hands repaired a delicate connection. Tobias had been an electronics engineer. But when he refused the chip, he became unemployable and forgotten by the world he had helped build.

Ian leaned in, pretending to examine the parts. "There's a get-together in two days," he said quietly. "Some folks talking about how things used to be."

Tobias didn't look up. His hands kept working, the soldering iron steady in his grip. "Old days, huh?"

"Yeah," He said, keeping his tone light. "Might be worth your time. Meet at the junkyard around sunset."

Tobias nodded once, almost imperceptibly. No commitments. No questions. Just an understanding. Meanwhile, Bill had a different mission. He wasn't looking for a trader or scavenger. He was looking for someone with a specific skill set, someone who could help them navigate the digital labyrinth of Jacob's systems. He had heard whispers of a girl, one that knew computers.

He found her outside the old City Library, deep in the abandoned zones. Mara sat at a park table under the shade of a tree, just outside the decaying library entrance. Her short-cropped blond hair framed a face that was both sharp and tired, her eyes scanning a tattered notebook as though she were solving an invisible puzzle. Bill approached cautiously, easing down onto the bench across from her. The table was streaked with grime and weathered by years of neglect.

"You ever talk about the old days?" he asked, his voice low.

Mara snorted without looking up. "I barely remember them."

"Some folks are meeting up at the junkyard. Just talk. No expectations."

She looked up at him, her gaze probing. "You don't strike me as the sentimental type."

Bill shrugged, leaning back slightly. "Times change."

A faint smirk touched her lips, but she didn't reply immediately. She stared past him, as if weighing something in her mind. Finally, she nodded. "I'll think about it." That was all he needed.

But finding the "insider" would be their greatest challenge. They would need someone with access to the system, somebody who could gather information without raising suspicion. It wasn't just about technical skill; it was about walking the razor's edge between compliance and rebellion. The type of person who could see the cracks in Jacob's perfect system but knew how to cover their own tracks.

This kind of person was rare. But Ian had someone in mind.

////////

Two days later, as the sun dipped low in the sky, the first members of the Gathering arrived.

The junkyard was the perfect location. It was far enough from the city limits the drones rarely conducted scans there, but not so isolated it would seem suspicious. The Yard, as it would be called, was well past the Old City Market, in an industrial area of the once small town. It sat off a gravel road, more than five miles from the city's proper edge. Over forty acres stretched behind the garage, lined with old car bodies stacked in neat rows, beginning about fifty feet from the back of the building.

The garage served a dual purpose. Above it, a large second-story space served as Ian's apartment. It was clean, neat and smelled far better than the grease-stained chaos sitting a mere fifteen feet below.

The whole compound was bordered on both sides by forest while directly behind the back gate, by some fifty feet, flowed a fast-moving, crystal-clear river. In a sense, at least for Ian, it was the perfect location to be when the world collapsed. He didn't plan it that way, it just was.

Even in the Before days, people seldom ventured out this far. And when they did, they were just looking for a hard-to-find part. They would also show up if they had a car that only a real mechanic not some computer jockey, could fix. In the last years of the Before, cars were modular with computers and systems controlling everything, including the steering. Mechanics had evolved to little more than computer readers who were told what part to replace. Ian, however, was a real mechanic. He understood true horsepower, tuning a car with a strobe light and a fine ear. He diagnosed problems by feel, by the subtle vibrations only experience could interpret.

As cars became more reliant on computers, his business slowly drifted away. It really wasn't a problem. Being frugal and having inherited the garage and junkyard from his uncle, he had few expenses anyway. His uncle also left him a nice coin collection consisting of silver and gold coins. He wasn't sure of the value when he received the haul, but he did know it was heavy. Probably five-hundred pounds of silver coins and maybe fifty pounds of gold coins. For all intents and purposes, Ian had it made. But he had lived modestly despite his wealth.

For the Gathering, Ian had kept things simple. An old table, a few mismatched chairs. Nothing electronic. No data trails. The garage had a section Ian called his "living space." Tucked to the left of the work bays, it had just enough to feel like home. A small kitchen, a sofa, a couple of chairs, and a large worktable dominated the space. Near the back, adjacent to a stairway leading to the upper floor, stood shelves filled with books and his treasured collection of vinyl records. Artifacts of a world that had once valued such things.

Overhead fluorescent lights buzzed faintly, casting a stark glow over the area. Ian kept the space as neat and clean as one could in a garage; though the faint scent of oil and gasoline never left the air.

Tobias was the first to arrive, a small bag of salvaged parts slung over his shoulder. He dropped it onto the table with a solid thud. "Figured I'd bring something," he said gruffly.

Ian nodded. "Appreciate it."

Mara arrived next, wearing her signature hoodie pulled tight over her short-cropped blond hair. She offered a small nod before settling into a chair, her eyes scanning the room. Two others followed shortly after: Hector, an old friend of Bill's with a wiry frame and a weathered face, and Elise, a quiet woman with dark, thoughtful eyes. Elise had once worked in logistics before the system phased her out, reducing her to yet another unwanted anomaly in a world of efficiency. Ian scanned the group as they settled in. Small. Cautious. Good.

Bill cleared his throat, breaking the silence. "Appreciate you all coming. Figured it'd be nice to talk." He paused, glancing around. "Seems like a lost art of sorts." A few nervous chuckles rippled through the group.

The conversation started slow, deliberately mundane. No one wanted to take the lead, and that was fine. Small talk filled the first thirty minutes. Idle chatter about the weather and the quirks of scavenging in the Old City Market. But gradually, the barriers began to lower. The talk shifted as memories surfaced, memories of the Before. Cars on highways, engines roaring as they raced down the endless asphalt. Books printed on paper, their pages worn and dog-eared from use. A world where people spoke face-to-face, their voices carrying emotion and nuance that no artificial intelligence could replicate.

As the evening stretched on, the group loosened up. Words flowed more freely. Tobias leaned forward, his elbows resting on the table. "You ever wonder how much of the past they've erased?"

Mara grinned, one corner of her mouth tilting upward. "All of it."

Ian sat back, watching them carefully, measuring their reactions. This wasn't a recruitment pitch. Not yet. This was a test.

"People don't even remember what they lost," Elise muttered, her voice soft but heavy with meaning. "The system tells them what they need to remember. Nothing more." There it was. The frustration. The awareness. The quiet, simmering understanding that something was deeply wrong with the world.

Hector was the first to break the barrier and spoke directly about things that were hovering below the surface of the conversation, the real reason for the Gathering. "Hey, I have been taking some of those drones out. When they fly by, I take them down with my wrist-rocket!"

Ian looked directly at him, shocked. "What? You're a target, they know who you are! They'll be tracking you."

"Relax. I'm stealth. No one knows, well, outside you guys." This rebuttal did not ease the growing tension.

"Anyone else have some hidden truth that needs to be shared?" Ian said with anger in his tone. Everyone looked at each other. Ian scanned the room "No?" Everyone was silent, a few shaking their heads to say no. "Look, what we are doing here today is getting to know each other a little. Some know others well, and some much less. Let's stick to the topic of the day."

He exchanged a fleeting glance with Bill. It was a small start. But it was a start. These people were fighters. This was the right group. But they still needed the insider, the person who could crack the system from within. And Ian had a feeling they were closer to finding that person than they thought.

As the group began to relax, a sudden clank echoed from outside the garage. The noise startled everyone, and a hush fell over the room. The dusk had deepened into night, the darkness around them thick and unyielding. The only light was a faint sliver of the new moon, barely enough to outline the edges of the junkyard. Ian moved quickly to the side of the main door and flipped on the front spotlights. Harsh white beams pierced the night, illuminating the source of the sound. Standing frozen in the spotlight was a lanky teen.

"Lance, is that you? What the hell are you doing sneaking around out there?" He barked.

"Uh, I was... well, I was out walking, and I heard voices," Lance stammered, his voice sheepish but steady. "Can I come in?"

Ian sighed but gestured him forward. "Get your ass over here so I can turn the lights out." Once the lights were off, Ian addressed the group loudly enough to regain their attention. "Everyone, this is Lance." he said, motioning toward the boy. "He's a... well, semi-chiphead."

Lance's eyes flared with surprise and indignation. "What the hell did you call me?"

Ian smirked faintly. "Sorry, kid, but you live in the city, and your parents are chipped. You told me yourself. That makes you one foot in and one foot out."

"Well, I have to live somewhere," Lance shot back, his tone defensive.

Mara, sitting with her hoodie strings pulled tight around her face, chimed in. "I agree with Ian."

"Me too," Elise added quietly.

"Calm down, everyone," Ian said, raising a hand. "We're all friends here." He turned back to the kid and motioned toward the table. "Come on in. We're talking about the Before times."

Lance hesitated, then stepped forward, his voice a little steadier. "Thanks, sir. I appreciate it. And for the record, I don't plan on getting that thing put in my head. I've seen what it does."

Ian studied the boy, his expression thoughtful. The kid's words seemed genuine, but Ian couldn't ignore the risk. A teenager was unpredictable, prone to shifting loyalties with the wind. Could he be trusted? Only time would tell. Still, Ian couldn't deny the potential. Lance was perfect: young, curious, and already straddling the line between the chipped world and the Annies. If he could be trusted, he could be the insider they needed.

"So kid," Ian began, his tone measured. "I know you weren't really around in the Before times. You'd have been pretty young… You'd probably not remember much."

Lance shifted awkwardly. "Not really," he admitted.

"But you're welcome to participate where you can," Ian continued. "Or just listen and learn."

The kid glanced around the room. He felt out of place, not quite part of his chipped parents' world and not entirely welcome here either. Most of the Annies were much older than him. Only the girl, with her hoodie pulled tight, seemed closer to his age. He wanted to belong somewhere.

When he was younger, despite schools shutting down permanently, his mother taught him to read. At first, he'd read on old electronic devices like outdated tablets, but he quickly fell in love with physical books, their weight, their smell, the tactile joy of flipping pages. Books were rare now. Finding them meant venturing into the Old City Market, where he was first exposed to adults who weren't chipped. Their conversations had felt different, more natural, unpredictable, real.

Lance interjected, his voice stronger now. "I don't really need to remember a lot. I read. Books. Real books. From the Old City Market."

Tobias glanced up from his seat. "Yeah, I've seen you lurking around there."

"Yup," Lance said proudly, his chest puffing slightly. "When I found the Market, I was excited. I hadn't been around many Annies before, just kids. But you all seem… different. More, I don't know, comfortable." The group erupted in laughter.

"Yeah, comfortable," Bill said, his tone dripping with sarcasm. "Scavenging for food, that's real comfortable." Then he softened, grinning at the boy. "You're all right, kid."

////////

The next morning, as had become routine, Bill shuffled into the garage about ten minutes after Ian had brewed the first pot of coffee. Coffee was a luxury item for Annies. It wasn't something you could just grab unless you ventured into Newtown, a no-go for most. The chipped had coffee on demand, synthesized perfectly to their taste at the push of a thought. But for Annies, even stepping into a store was nearly impossible.

Without a chip, the doors wouldn't open. Access was granted seamlessly and invisibly to chipheads through Jacob's network, but Annies were locked out. No chip, no entry.

And Newtown wasn't kind to outsiders. If you wanted in, you had to wait for someone else to open the door, then slip in behind them, acting like you belonged. But the chipped always knew. They didn't say anything, but they watched. The glances were enough.

It was an unspoken rule: Annies didn't go into Newtown. And if they did, they didn't stay long.

That meant no coffee. In the garage, there was always a fresh pot brewing. No one asked where Ian got it, and he didn't offer details. They just poured themselves a cup and savored the rare luxury. Bill took a long sip, groaning in appreciation. "Damn. I used to hate those assholes at Starbucks, but now I'd give my left nut for a real barista-made cup of joe."

"Don't get used to it. This stuff's liquid gold. If word gets out, this place'll turn into a mini-Starbucks, and I'll run dry overnight." Ian said.

Bill held up a hand in mock solemnity, "Ain't tellin' a soul." He took another sip, leaning against the counter. "So... what'd ya think of last night's Gathering?"

"We have a shot. But there are still more questions than answers. I'm sure you picked up on that. And Hector... He may be a bit reckless for us at this point."

Ian thought for a moment. "We don't have any real operators in the group, unless you or Tobias were secretly Army Special Forces or CIA."

Bill let out a short laugh. "If I told you, I'd have to kill you."

Ian rolled his eyes. Classic. The kind of line from someone who'd never been near black ops in their life. "Yeah, I thought so," he muttered. "But Tobias... maybe?"

Bill's expression turned thoughtful. "If there's one, it's him. He's got all the signs, reserved, smart, calculating. Doesn't waste words."

Nodding, Ian said. "We need to know... We need to understand what we're working with."

Bill set his cup down. "What's your take on the hoodie girl? The programmer?"

"You mean Mara. And don't call her a programmer."

Bill raised an eyebrow.

Ian shook his head. "She got snippy with me last night. Coder, she said. Apparently, there's a difference."

"Alright, alright. The coder. What'd ya think?"

Ian leaned back in his chair, his gaze distant. "She's sharp. Maybe too sharp. She's got that edge, like she's always a step ahead, already processing three different outcomes before she even answers."

"That good or bad?" Bill murmured.

"Depends. If she's with us, it's good. If she's playing her own game, it's dangerous."

Bill exhaled through his nose, a slow and deliberate sound. "Fair point." The room fell silent for a moment, the hum of the fluorescent lights filling the space.

"We still need an insider," Ian said finally.

Bill rubbed his jaw, his expression grim. "Yeah. And that's not gonna be easy."

They both knew the truth. They needed someone who could straddle both worlds, someone unchipped, but close enough to the system to gain access without raising suspicion. Someone who could pull information, crack open Jacob's defenses, and slip away unnoticed. But finding that person? That would be a challenge.

000110 // SIX

HEAD GAMES

Two days had passed; and it had been another beautiful sunrise. A light breeze rolled in from the southwest, carrying the warmth of the late morning sun. A rare stillness hung in the air, reminding him of a calm Sunday morning from the Before times.

Inside the garage, the familiar crackle of vinyl would soon fill the space. Ian, who always enjoyed classic rock in the shop, had just sorted through his wall of vintage LPs, the black discs of a bygone era. Running his fingers over the worn covers, flipping through these remnants of another time, made him feel younger.

He wasn't looking for anything in particular, just something that felt right. Something that could bring a little life into the day. A recording of songs that would make the morning fill with a spirit of hope, fun, love, the Before times.

He stopped when he saw the cover of *Head Games*, a girl standing in a bathroom, looking over her shoulder. Foreigner. "That was a good band. Hadn't thought about 'em in years," he muttered as he carefully pulled the record from its sleeve.

Lou Gramm wasn't Steven Tyler, but his voice had a place in his must-listen list.

He carefully placed the vinyl on the turntable, guiding the tonearm to the outer edge. A soft hiss filled the room, followed by a sudden burst of power as the first chords rang out. "There we go," he murmured. "Some ambiance." Just as the music settled in, the garage door creaked. In walked Lance.

"Hi, Ian!" He called out, his voice cutting through the music.

Ian glanced up. "Morning, kid."

Lance hesitated, shifting on his feet. "Uh… can I spend some time watching you work on the Vette?" Ian smirked. He had mentioned at the Gathering that he planned to change the oil in his Corvette, and apparently, the kid hadn't forgotten.

"Sure, kid. But be careful, you might get dirty." he joked.

"I know."

Ian chuckled. "Well, if you're gonna watch, you're gonna work, too. No free rides here." He pointed to the broom leaning against the wall. "Step one: sweep the stall."

The kid protested "What? That's not working on the car!"

He shook his head. "No, that's preparing to work on the car."

Lance exhaled sharply but grabbed the broom. "Fine," he muttered. Ian quickly glanced at him. A long moment passed.

"Sorry I got snippy with you. I thought you were just trying to get me to clean up the place."

Ian nodded. "Lesson one: always start with a clean and orderly workspace. You want to do things right? That starts before you ever pick up a tool."

He was a stickler for orderly and specific operations. "By the book," is how he operated.

The kid gave a small nod, focusing on his sweeping. Ian watched him work, a flicker of approval crossing his face. The kid had a spark, something he hadn't seen in a long time. After he swept the area perfectly clean, Ian motioned toward the Corvette. "Alright, let's get her into position."

"Okay! What do I do?"

He tossed him the keys. "Get in, release the parking brake, and put her in neutral." The kid's eyes widened as he slid into the driver's seat. The interior smelled like leather and time, a vestige from a world before sterile transport PODs. He looked around the cockpit of the car, searching for the brake release and wondering where he was supposed to insert this key. He had never done anything like this in his life.

When he completed Ian's instructions, he looked up. "Now what?"

Ian tapped the door. "Roll the window down and get out." Lance did as he was told.

"Alright, kid, time to push."

Lance hesitated. "Why don't we just drive it into place?"

"Because it's only twenty feet, and I don't feel like burning my hands on hot engine parts. Anyway, it's not good to run the beast for a minute and then shut it down. This baby likes to run." He nodded, then put his weight into pushing the car as Ian steered it into position. Once they had it lined up, Ian moved a couple of steel plates, revealing a narrow trench beneath the car.

"What's that?" The kid said as he peered down at the large hole in the floor.

"Service pit," Ian said. "Stands to reason that if you don't have a lift, you gotta go under the car."

Lance nodded, fascinated. Ian turned to him, his expression serious. "One rule: don't fall in. You'll break something. And I guarantee it will be you that breaks."

"I'm not stupid."

Ian gave him a pointed look. "I know. But a shop's not a place to get careless. I've seen more people hurt because they assumed they were being careful."

Lance swallowed. "Alright. I get it."

"Good. Now pay attention."

////////

The afternoon passed in a blur of oil, grease, and explanations. As the day wore on, Ian explained all the car's parts to him. He walked the kid through the Corvette's systems, how the engine breathed, how the transmission worked, why analog machines had a feel that no AI-controlled transport POD could replicate. Lance absorbed every word, asking questions with an eagerness Ian hadn't seen in years.

Finally, as the last bolts were tightened, Ian wiped his hands on a rag. "Ok, kid. Time to close her up and start this kitten."

"Are we gonna drive it?"

Ian grinned. "I'm gonna drive it. You can ride along. We'll be testing the car's performance then top off the oil and park her back where she started this morning"

Lance practically bounced on his heels. "Awesome!"

They climbed into the Corvette. Ian navigated it slowly down the gravel driveway, then rolling along the rutted dirt path until they reached the long, straight road. A weathered sign stood at the roadside, its paint peeling with time. The numbers read "55."

Lance squinted. "What's that mean?"

He chuckled. "That, kid, is a speed limit sign."

"Speed limit?"

"In the old days, before the PODs, drivers had to regulate their own speed. The government posted signs to tell people what was 'safe'."

"So… you decided how fast to go?" Lance said in astonishment.

"Exactly. But now - screw the speed limit. We'll drive a few miles, then turn around and open this beast up. And to quote the great philosopher Samuel, 'I can't drive fifty-five.'"

The kid's eyes widened, then squinted in thought. He had never heard of this philosopher but became more excited by the second. Ian eased the car onto the road, keeping the speed low as he let the engine warm up.

He wanted to make sure the road was free of any debris that might damage his car since nothing had traversed this highway in a very long time. After about ten miles, the farthest Lance had ever traveled in his life, Ian turned the car around and gave him a knowing look.

"Buckle up, buttercup."

Lance barely had time to react before Ian slammed the gas pedal to the floor. The Corvette roared to life, tires biting the asphalt as the acceleration pinned the kid back in his seat. His heart pounded, adrenaline surging through his veins. The wind rushed through the open top, whipping through his hair. He had never felt anything like this, freedom, raw and unfiltered. A grin split his face. For the first time in his life, he was moving. Not guided by AI. Not controlled by the system. Just moving. The world blurred past, and for those few minutes, nothing else existed.

They drove back to the yard and into the garage. Ian exited the car and grabbed a rag to wipe the car down. Lance continued to sit in the car. Reliving what he had just experienced. Deep in thought and smiling.

"Come on kid, time to get out." Lance crawled out of the car and stood up, feeling like he was ten feet tall. "We need to push this back over to where I had it stored." He said pointing to the section of floor Lance had mopped. After the car was pushed into position, they walked over to the living area and grabbed a seat near the kitchen and records. The kid was still smiling as he sat down.

"Thank you," he said, his voice quieter than usual.

Ian looked at him for a long moment, then nodded.

"Anytime, kid."

000111 // SEVEN

ECHOES OF YESTERDAY

The midday sun bore down on Bill's back as he strolled along the gravel road toward the Yard. He lived, if existing could be called living, in an old cabin about a mile from Ian's garage. The roads were too rough for a bike. Deep ruts and jagged rocks, pushed up by years of heavy rains, made riding a guaranteed way to break an ankle or worse. So, he walked. It hadn't always been this way. Bill Carter had once been a builder. He learned the craft the old-fashioned way, not from books or hollow online certifications, but through sweat, grit, and time. The U.S. Navy had given him his start, not on a ship, but as a Seabee.

Most people thought of the Navy as water, ships, and sailors. But the Seabees were different. They built things: roads, bridges, airstrips, entire bases in the middle of nowhere. They were the construction battalion of the Civil Engineer Corps of the US Navy. And he had been very good at his job.

When his enlistment was up, he returned home ready to put his skills to work. He started *Carter Construction*, a small business that grew quickly. He built houses, schools, even a few commercial buildings. Life was good. Steady.

Then the world changed. The war, the chip, the collapse of real trade work, everything he had built was swept away. No one needed manual labor anymore. Machines handled every task; AI directed it all. Human labor faded into irrelevance, an artifact of another era, as the need for people to supervise the systems vanished.

He leaned on his years of experience in electrical power distribution, hoping to secure a position as a Federation electrical technician, maintaining the flow of energy across the grid. His application was declined. He had refused the chip. Now, he was just another Annie scraping by in a world that had no use for people like him. But there was one thing the new world couldn't take away: Sarah.

////////

In high school, Bill and Sarah had been inseparable. Young and wild, the kind of couple that everyone assumed would last forever. But forever was a long time and always seemed to have a way of getting interrupted. When he joined the Navy, they kept in touch with letters and occasional visits. However, time and distance wore them down and eventually the flame flickered out.

Sarah moved on. She married the high school quarterback, the golden boy who had once been king of their small town. But high school glory didn't carry over into adulthood. When the world stopped cheering his name, he turned bitter, then cruel. She endured it for a while, then left him.

She put herself through State college, earning a nursing degree, and returned home to work at the local clinic. Life was steady and safe. But every now and then, she wondered, what if Bill had stayed? What if their story had taken a different turn?

And then, one day, fate brought him back. He had been working on a renovation project when an X-Acto knife slipped, cutting deep into his hand. Not life-threatening, but bad enough to need stitches. He walked into the clinic, expecting nothing more than a quick patch-up.

Sarah didn't even glance at the full name on the chart before stepping into the exam room. Clipboard in hand, she spoke automatically:

"So, Bill, is it? Let's take a look at…"

She stopped mid-sentence. Her eyes lifted from the clipboard and locked onto his face. For a moment, there was silence as she looked in disbelief at the man standing in front of her. Then, a bright, yet pensive smile spread across her lips.

"Bill Carter!" she blurted, her voice filled with combined shock and joy. She tossed the clipboard onto the counter next to the exam room sink and practically launched herself at him.

"Whoa, whoa!" Bill laughed, holding up his injured hand. "Unless you want to be covered in blood."

"I don't care!" she said, arms extended.

But she stopped herself, exhaling a short laugh. She then quickly turned to the white cabinet located over the sink where she had tossed her clipboard, and pulled out the supplies to stitch him up.

"Sit over here." She said, pointing to a chair in the exam room. Her hands were steady, but her excitement nearly got the best of her as she almost jabbed the needle in the wrong spot.

Bill smiled. "You sure you know what you're doing?"

She shot him a playful glare. "Shut up and hold still." A few careful stitches later she had fixed his wound. She then secured a bandage on his hand and gave him a firm nod. "Alright. Keep it dry for a few days. Change the bandage daily. After three days, you can leave it uncovered. Come back in a couple weeks and we'll take the stiches out." Then, she paused, and her voice softened. "And now that I've fixed the patient, how's the old boyfriend doing?"

He met her gaze, feeling something stir in his chest, something he hadn't let himself think about in years. "Well, aside from losing a fight with an X-Acto knife, I've been alright." He hesitated just long enough to measure her reaction. "What about you?"

Sarah gave him the abbreviated version of her life, the highlights mostly. A few of the struggles and some of the lessons she had learned, keeping it noticeably short and to the point. When she finished, she added, "And that's where I'm at. I'm an RN, I own my own house, and I have a cat. But I'm not a cat lady," she said quickly. "I love dogs, but I don't have time to take care of one properly. The cat… well, he's mostly self-sufficient."

He chuckled. "That's quite a story."

She smiled. "Yeah. And what about you? What's life like for Bill Carter these days?"

He hesitated for a moment, considering how much to say. "It's… different," he admitted. "But I manage."

She nodded. "Well, you still look like the same guy I remember."

He grinned. "I'll take that as a compliment." A small silence stretched between them. Not awkward, just weighty. Then Bill took his shot. "It'd be great to catch up some time. Maybe over coffee?"

She smiled and arched an eyebrow. "Is that an offer for a date, Mr. Carter?"

He smiled. "Guess it is."

He reached into his pocket and pulled out his business card, *Carter Construction* embossed in bold, confident lettering. He handed it to her, both as a way to give her his number and to show her what he had built, a brag of sorts. She took it, running her fingers over the card thoughtfully. Then she smiled. "Alright, Bill Carter. Coffee it is."

////////

Bill approached Ian's garage, his boots kicking up small clouds of dust along the gravel road. As he walked, his eyes drifted down to his hand. The scar was still there. Faint, but permanent. A feeling of grief spread over him. That moment, sitting in the clinic, seeing Sarah again, the stitches, the laughter, felt like a lifetime ago. Now, it was just another ghost in his past.

The meeting. The marriage. The child. Then the chip. His jaw clenched. His pulse quickened. He still harbored a deep, raw anger, not just at the AI, but at the people who had let this happen. The ones who stood by, who accepted it. Who traded their freedom for convenience, their lives for control. If it were up to him, he would burn the whole thing to the ground. Reduce it all to scrap. Smash every last component into dust until it was nothing but raw elements waiting to be swallowed by the earth. His hatred was real, and his pulse pounded in his ears. He stopped. Took a deep breath and said a short, silent prayer. He looked up towards the sky.

"I miss you guys," he muttered silently.

He was a loaner today. A man without his family. Without his beautiful wife or rambunctious child. They were gone now and had been for some time. Had it not been for Jacob's AI, and people fighting to be the first in line to be chipped. He might be a very different person. They were taken by a distracted driver who was texting to get a place saved in line for an implant event. This idiot, a murderer as far as he was concerned, killed them.

He pushed forward, his steps heavier than before. By the time he entered the garage, a somber weight hung over him.

Ian immediately noticed. "What's up with you? Someone steal your lunch?"

He shook his head, forcing a small smirk. "Nah. Just thinking."

Ian didn't press. Instead, he waved him over. "Come sit down."

"Can I grab a coffee first?"

"Of course," Ian said. "Maybe it'll cheer you up a little. Damn, the energy you're putting off is a real downer."

Bill exhaled a short chuckle. "Sorry. Just lost in thought."

He made his way to the coffee pot, savoring the scent that filled the air. Even though he'd had a few cups the other day, it still smelled like pure heaven. He reached for his usual mug, the one with an old relic on it, an American flag. It had been washed. Bill frowned slightly. He had a habit, a holdover from his Navy days, he never washed his coffee cup. He liked it seasoned, the way old salts kept theirs. Hell, if this had been the Navy, Ian would've been keelhauled for touching another man's mug. Still, he poured a steaming cup, inhaled deeply, and took a slow sip. Then, with a small nod, he raised the cup toward Ian.

"Thanks." Ian nodded back. He set his cup down. "Let's talk about the Gathering."

Ian leaned forward, resting his forearms on the workbench. "I spent a little time with the kid." Bill arched an eyebrow. "He's solid, I think he might fit in. But I need more time with him. I haven't mentioned anything about our plans, and I don't think we should reveal anything to anyone yet." He took another sip of coffee, letting the words settle. Ian continued, "The fewer people who see the full picture, the safer we are."

"I agree. OPSEC is important."

Ian gave him a sharp look. "OPSEC? The hell, were you a spook or something?"

He chuckled at the question "Nah. Seabee. But operational security was a common term in the military." He chuckled. "A spook wouldn't use a term like that."

"Oh, well you sounded all 'government' if you know what I mean," Ian said.

"That's fair," he admitted. "Guess I shouldn't sound so formal." He leaned forward slightly. "But it's not just a term. It's exactly what it sounds like. We need to treat this like a military operation if we have any chance of pulling it off."

Ian studied him for a long moment. He was always careful, even among friends, to not reveal much of his own past. The silence stretched, broken only by the faint crackle of classic rock playing from the turntable. They both knew what was at stake. This wasn't just some rebellion. This wasn't just resistance. This was survival. Bill understood the ramifications. He had seen action in the Navy. Seabees did occasionally have to bear arms, and he was one of the unlucky ones to participate in a real firefight. He didn't relish the idea of doing that again.

You never forget when you are forced to shoot or being shot at. They both knew this.

001000 // EIGHT

THE ENGINEER

Tobias Singleton was in his mid-sixties, a man of African descent with a medium-large frame and an easy, deliberate way of moving. He carried himself with the quiet confidence of someone who had watched the world shift beneath his feet more than once and survived. Despite the hardships of the After, he stayed in good shape. Survival demanded it. But once, long ago, Tobias had been a different man.

He had lived his life conservatively, carefully. A man who understood the unspoken rules of corporate America. He worked his way up the ladder at a Fortune 500 company, one of the big aerospace firms of the Before times.

He was always at his desk or in the lab, always well-dressed, always composed. He had the look of a future Vice President of Engineering. This had been his dream. And he had a method, one that mostly served him well. Lay low. Be visible, but quiet. Don't rock the boat. Do what you're told. Maybe find a better way now and then, but never in a way that might threaten the wrong people. Never outshine the boss. Always give credit upward. He understood the game.

////////

His degree was nothing special for the time, electrical engineering with a minor in computer programming. But Tobias had a gift for electronics, for microcircuits. He loved the feel of components in his hands, the sound of a system coming to life beneath his touch.

Back then, a man had to think, design, craft and build. He was a wizard with the soldering iron, a master at troubleshooting complex systems. He saw problems in ways others couldn't, breaking them down with an ease that felt like magic.

His reputation grew, not as a visionary, or as an inventor, but as a fixer. However, that reputation was incredibly wrong. He was an innovator. Likely the best in the company. People came to him not with ideas, but with problems. And he solved them all. It became routine. A senior engineer would walk into his lab, frustration etched into their face, carrying a box of messy circuit boards that simply wouldn't work. Tobias would glance at the boards and schematics, maybe tinker for a few minutes. Then, with a wave of his hand, the impossible became possible.

"Let's look at what you invented Gary." He proclaimed when a senior engineer brought him an unsolvable mess. He'd glance at schematics, tinker a moment, and turn chaos into function. He invented circuits, and devices daily. Then, as always, he'd add, "Now Gary, I'd appreciate you putting my name on the patent under yours. I did contribute a little here." But they both knew the truth. The engineer would nod, slap him on the back, and walk away with a working prototype, one that would soon place his name alone on the patent.

Tobias never fought it. He knew the game. The people he saved knew the game too. Eventually he climbed the ladder one rung at a time, until he was going to make the last step. And then, just as he was about to take that final step, just as he was on the verge of making Vice President, the shit storm came.

When the Great War arrived, everything changed. Then came the chip. By this point, the neural implant had been perfected. The bulky, intrusive designs of the past were obsolete. Engineers had repositioned the implant away from the prefrontal cortex, making installation seamless through precision robotic surgery. Gone were the cumbersome battery packs worn on the shoulder. In their place was a streamlined, energy system, effortlessly recharged using something called "headgear."

But the true breakthrough wasn't in the hardware. It was in the offloading of information. Instead of relying solely on individual processing power, the implant tapped directly into the cloud, utilizing constant Extremely Fast Speed (EFS) WiFi-20x. No lag. No delay. Thoughts became commands. Knowledge was instant. Memory was filtered, optimized, stored. And all of it, every interaction, every calculation, every fleeting thought, was offloaded to Jacob. The system was faster, more efficient, more capable than any human mind could ever be. And with it, the world changed again.

The aerospace industry, once a beacon of exploration and innovation, shifted overnight. Tobias' company framed being chipped as an honor. They came to departments smiling, delivering rousing speeches, looking for Award Winners, the privileged few deemed worthy of free chip implantation. He wanted no part of it. He learned quickly that when he heard excitement, when he heard the buzz of voices celebrating another winner, he needed to move. Change direction. Keep his head down. Out of sight, out of mind.

But that wasn't how it worked. One day, they came to his office. Streamers. Applause. A certificate with his name printed in bold letters. He was a winner. The chip, they said, would be implanted free of charge. A gift for his years of service and contributions to the company. Tobias smiled. Took the certificate and nodded as the handshakes and congratulations came at him in a fury. The moment everyone left his office he fed the paper into his shredder and watched it turn to ribbons. Gone as quickly as it had appeared.

He knew what would come next. They would follow up, then expect him to report to the integration center. He didn't wait for that conversation. Later that same night, he packed a bag. The next morning, he was gone. No resignation. No farewell email. No trace. He vanished into the underground, slipping between the cracks of the new world before the system even realized it had lost him.

He became a hermit, venturing out of his living area during the day, setting up a shop in the Old City Market to barter and trade. He dressed in oversized garments meant to conceal what he carried underneath. He was long past grooming for the office, the VP look. Now he was disheveled, hair unruly, lengthy beard and round wireframe glasses. Long gone were the expensive suits, the well-kept appearance. He became a gray man.

////////

A few of days after the Gathering, Tobias sat in his usual booth, nursing a cup of weak, under-brewed tea. He had little interest in being part of whatever Ian and his people were planning. But here came Bill, again. Walking towards his shop.

He sighed, setting his cup down a little harder than necessary. Tobias had attended the Gathering out of curiosity, figuring he'd listen for a few minutes and then disappear back into the shadows where he preferred to live. He understood what it was about, almost instantly; no one needed to spell it out for him. They were planning something big. And now they, or at least Bill, wanted to talk to him. He wasn't sure why. Knowing how to fix things wasn't the same as knowing how to break them. Then again… he did know both.

At the aerospace company he occasionally slipped a bug into a system when someone stepped on him too hard. Just a minor glitch, nothing catastrophic, but enough to make sure the arrogant bastard who took credit for his work had an unbelievably bad day when the demo failed in front of the board of directors.

While in Ian's garage, surrounded by people who still thought they had a chance against the machine, he wondered if he had made the right choice to attend. Sabotaging corporate projects for petty revenge was very different from what Ian and Bill were talking about. Taking down the system? That was something else entirely. And he wasn't sure if he made the right choice by showing up that night. Hell, maybe he should've just let things be. He was about to take another sip of tea when a voice cut through his thoughts.

"Toby!" Bill called out.

Tobias's grip tightened around his cup; his pulse quickened. He turned slowly, eyes narrowing behind his wireframe glasses. "Who the hell are you calling Toby, asshole?" His voice was cold, sharp. "My name is Tobias. Don't ever call me that again."

Bill blinked, taken aback. "Whoa, hey, sorry, just trying to be friendly."

Tobias leaned forward slightly, his expression unreadable. "I don't call you Slick Willy, now do I? How 'bout Wee Willie Winkle?"

Bill snorted. "No. No, you don't."

"Well, now you know. What do you want from me?"

He spent years being taunted with that name. After the docuseries Roots aired in the mid-1970s, kids at school had latched onto it, turning Toby into a taunt, a joke at his expense. It took years for that stigma to pass, but he never forgot how it felt. He had no patience for it now.

Bill raised his hands in a placating gesture. "Look, I really didn't know. I won't say it again."

Tobias studied him for a long moment, then gave a slow nod. "Alright, then."

There was an awkward silence. Bill cleared his throat. "Well, Ian and I wanted to see if you might have a few minutes to talk. Say day after tomorrow? Sunset?"

"Those others going to be there too?" He asked sharply.

"Possibly one, maybe two of 'em, that's all."

He leaned back in his seat, crossing his arms. "Maybe I will. Maybe I won't. Depends."

Bill frowned slightly. "Depends on what?"

Tobias smirked, the tension easing just a fraction. "Depends on how busy the shop is." There was a flicker of amusement in his voice now, but his meaning was clear. He doesn't commit to things lightly.

Bill exhaled, shaking his head with a small chuckle. "Alright, Tobias. I'll take that as a maybe."

Tobias lifted his cup in mock salute. Bill turned to leave but paused. He glanced back, as if considering whether to say something else. Instead, he just nodded and walked out. Tobias watched him go, then sighed, rubbing a hand over his face. He didn't want to be part of this. But somehow, he knew he already was.

001001 // NINE

THE CODER

Ian descended into the dark, musty depths of the library's basement. The air was stale, thick with dust and mold. The place had been abandoned for years, left to decay in the silence of the After. Flickering lights in the hallway cast erratic shadows, giving the illusion of movement where there was none. He didn't like it. The whole place felt wrong, claustrophobic, oppressive. Yet this was where Mara chose to live and work.

He followed the dim glow of a monitor, the only real light in a labyrinth of forgotten shelves and crumbling walls. The door ahead was cracked slightly open, spilling a soft, bluish-white glow into the hallway. He pushed the door slowly, wincing as it let out a low, creeping groan. Inside, a figure hunched over a massive setup. Six monitors stacked in pairs, forming a glowing digital wall. The hooded shape didn't move at first. Then, in a single, fluid motion, the chair spun around. Mara sat looking up at him. She pulled her hood back, revealing a bright, mischievous grin.

"Hi!" she said, her voice unexpectedly cheerful.

He blinked and thought, "Not what I was expecting."

"Hello, Mara, didn't mean to startle you." He said cautiously.

She waved a hand dismissively. "Oh, you didn't. I knew you were back there."

He tensed. "Excuse me?"

She leaned back in her chair, looking entirely too pleased with herself. "I saw you when you approached the library. Watched you browse the shelves, car repair manuals, good but obvious choice. Then I followed your progress down the stairs and through the hallway." His stomach tightened slightly. She knew?

"Nothing gets by me," she added with a satisfied nod.

He glanced around, suddenly hyper-aware of the dimly lit space. He wondered where the cameras were. He cleared his throat. "Well… that's good to hear." Mara smirked.

He decided to move forward. "The other night, I mentioned that we'd like you to join us for another Gathering. You seemed open to it."

Her grin widened. "Oh, yes. I'd love to be part of tearing the system to the ground."

Ian stiffened. "Whoa, no one said that at the Gathering."

She rolled her eyes. "Come on. It was obvious what you were doing. You were vetting us. Feeling out who might be useful for… whatever it is you're planning."

He hesitated. "Didn't realize it was that apparent."

She turned her chair directly towards him and leaned forward, resting her elbows on her knees. "To those of us who are actually valuable… Yeah, it was." She ticked off on her fingers. "Let's see… you had an engineer…"

He cut her off with a sharp hand motion. "Hold on, missy. Let's keep this between us. We don't need to broadcast anything to the general public or Jacob."

She laughed. "Oh, we're safe down here." She made a gesture around the room. "I don't wear a tinfoil hat, but I do live inside a fully reinforced Faraday cage."

His eyebrows raised. "Really?"

"Yep," she said proudly. "That's why I chose this place. A few modifications here, a little rewiring there… and now? I'm invisible to Jacob. No tracking, no surveillance, no digital footprint. Chippies can't touch me. I. Am. Free."

He took a slow breath. "Impressive." She grinned."Is this where you live, too?" He asked, glancing around the dim space.

Her expression shifted slightly. "Why do you ask?"

Ian hesitated, realizing he overstepped. "Didn't mean to pry. Just trying to get to know you a little better. A hooded ghost is hard to read."

She studied him for a moment, then smiled. "You want to know about me, huh?"

He nodded.

"Alright, here you go." She stretched her arms above her head dramatically. "My name is Mara. Not my given name, my assumed name. As far as Jacob is concerned, I'm someone entirely different. In fact, he doesn't even know I exist anymore."

His interest piqued. "Really? Go on."

She grinned wickedly. "Sure. I'm… oh, I don't know. Twenty? Twenty-five? Forty-five years old? I'm about five-foot-something and an average build. My likes include fresh fruit, long walks on the beach, and…"

He raised his hands. "Okay, okay, I get it." Mara chuckled. "You want to remain a gray… I don't know… gray woman?"

Her smile softened. "I like to choose my who, my how, my when, and my where."

Ian nodded slowly, taking in her words. She wasn't just hiding from the system. She erased herself from it. That made her more valuable than he had realized.

"Like I said, we're having another Gathering." He said tentatively.

"I'm listening."

"Okay, then we will meet at the same place at the same time in two days." He stated in a professional tone.

"We?"

"Oh, here we go again," thought Ian. "Yes we... myself, Bill, Tobias."

"Exactly as I had calculated. What about the Kid? What was his name? Oh yeah, Lance?" Mara said.

"Jury's still out on him.... But things are looking better. I just need a bit more time to determine."

"Hector, Elise?"

"Not at this one." He stated. "So, we're on. I'll see you then."

She grinned. "Wait, I didn't agree to be there."

Ian shrugged. "I know. See you there." He turned and started down the dank corridor, scanning for cameras as he maneuvered out of the basement and back into the afternoon light. The sun hung low, a few hours from dusk. He needed to get back to the Yard quickly, and unnoticed. It had been a long day.

001010 // TEN

THE DAY BEFORE THE NEXT GATHERING

The morning began the same way it always did. Ian awoke, headed downstairs, and started the coffee machine. As the first drops hit the carafe he picked a record from his collection, set it on the turntable and turned up the volume. Feeling a little rebellious he chose the Pink Floyd, *Animals* album. By the time the coffee was ready, the music had filled the garage wrapping the space with its dark, angry sounds. He poured his first cup, stepped outside into the Yard, and took a slow breath.

The air was crisp. The sky stretched wide and unbroken above him. He stood looking towards the horizon, contemplating the day ahead. There were things he liked about the After. One major benefit was that no one bothered him anymore. He had everything he needed, fresh protein from the stream and game wandering through the fields, fruit and vegetables thriving in his garden. Life was simpler, closer to the 1800s than the 21st century.

It had been years since the Before was erased from the memory of the chipheads. Their time had been reset to the moment Jacob took over. So, yes. It was better. He was living 200 years in the past while the chipheads ate a blend of bugs and synthetic meat. "More power to them, I suppose." He muttered.

Right on schedule, he glanced down the path and spotted Bill making his way up.

"Looking for a cup of coffee?" He called out.

"Well, thank you, don't mind if I do." Bill picked up his pace, stepping into the garage. As he entered, he stopped for a moment as the music hit him. He smiled. "Feeling a little rebellious anyone?" He chuckled as he went straight to the counter, reached for his usual cup, and let out a satisfied laugh. "Hot damn, you actually left it unwashed!"

Ian smirked. "Least I could do. Much easier. One less thing."

He grinned broadly and poured himself a cup. He took a sip, smacking his lips. "A better-tasting cup today than yesterday."

As the Animals album was ending, Ian chose something softer to counter the nature of his first record of the day. They sat quietly, listening to his next selection. Bill was a little unfamiliar with the album Ian had chosen but really liked what he was listening to.

"Who is this?" He asked.

"Ah, perfect music. It's the 1980 work of the Alan Parsons Project... *Turn of a Friendly Card.* A masterpiece if I may say so myself."

"Well, I really like it. I recognize a little of it from the radio in the Before, but it's been years."

When the song *Time* came on, they both slipped into another decade. They sat in silence, contemplating the song, the past, and the present. As they sat quietly the album continued to play. Neither wanted the music to stop, to shift. For a while, they were lost in the sound, slipping into another time, if only for a moment. But as things happen, it ended. They both seemed to exit a trance-like state.

"Well, let's get to work!" Ian said as he selected another album. This one less progressive and more rock and roll.

Bill stood and said "gunna grab another cup of joe and then take a whiz. Give me a few minutes."

When he exited the bathroom, he called out, "Hey, need a top-off?"

"Please," Ian said gratefully.

Bill poured Ian a mug and handed it over before settling back at the worktable. As he sat down, he glanced at Ian. "So… how did things go yesterday?"

Ian took a sip, then set his cup down. "Well," he said, "it was interesting, to say the least. I learned a lot. And I believe she will be a key member of whatever we're building."

"Yeah, I didn't spend much time with her when I first reached out. I'm glad you got to vet her more. All I got was that they were both… well, interesting," Bill said.

He chuckled. "That's an understatement. Eccentric is a better word. That and a whole lot of other adjectives!"

Bill leaned forward slightly. "One thing I learned about Tobias, by the way don't ever call him Toby, is that he's got a hell of a temper. But he's brilliant. He hates the AI with a passion. Wants revenge. And his skill set? From the looks of his shop, great."

He took note, waited a moment then reported his interactions with Mara. "Mara, not her given name, is a real character. She is like Tobias in a lot of ways. I know nothing about her past, but she's sharp. Really sharp. And capable. She protested, but I expect her to show up anyway." He paused for a second. "So, they're both alphas. We could have some clashes."

"Hell, we're all alphas with exception of the Kid." Bill said.

Ian tapped his fingers against his cup. "I haven't invited him yet. I want to get some more time with him."

"And what are you gonna do when he just shows up?"

He chuckled. "Oh, you mean like you do every morning?"

Bill laughed, shaking his head. "Listen, I need to run. I'll be back later. Got some stuff to do."

001011 // ELEVEN

THE SOUND OF SILENCE

Later that morning, Ian sat alone in the living area of his garage, lost in thought. It wasn't much of a living room, the garage was too cluttered for that, but it was comfortable. The sofa was worn but welcoming, the mismatched chairs arranged haphazardly around the space. This corner of the garage felt more like a refuge than the rest of the Yard. He often sat there, reading or listening to music.

The record on the old turntable had long since finished, leaving only the soft crackle of static and the rhythmic ticking of the clock on the wall. The silence crept in, thick and heavy, wrapping itself around him like a shroud.

He stared out through the open garage door, his coffee cooling in his hands. The cup was still half-full, but he hadn't taken a sip in minutes. For the first period in a long time, he felt uneasy. Then he saw them.

A stirring in the driveway caught his eye. At first, it was just a shadow shifting against the mid-morning light. Then shapes emerged, moving closer. Three men and a woman, walking up the path towards the shop's driveway. He straightened, every muscle tensing.

The man leading the group looked rough, unkempt, gaunt, like he hadn't had a proper meal in months. His beard was wild, streaked with gray and dirt. His clothes were tattered, hanging off his wiry frame in loose folds. The others weren't much better off. Hollow cheeks, sunken eyes, their movements slow and deliberate, like every step required effort.

His gut tightened. He'd dealt with people like this before, drifters, scavengers. Usually, they were harmless, just desperate. But desperation could make people unpredictable, and he was alone. He placed his coffee down quietly, the mug making a faint clink on the table. His hand hovered near the edge of the counter, where he kept his sidearm. The group kept advancing, their footsteps crunching on the gravel driveway.

He stood, his voice cutting through the stillness. "Stop right there and state your business." No response. They kept walking. Ian's fingers twitched involuntarily. That wasn't normal. Most people would have stopped by now, thrown on a fake smile, and tried to charm their way in. But these four? They didn't even glance at him. A prickle of unease crawled up his spine.

"I said stop," he barked, stepping towards the inner edge of the large garage door. His voice was sharper now, his tone leaving no room for negotiation. His hand found the pump-action shotgun he kept stashed near the door. Just in case—Now was case.

He stepped into view just outside the doorway, the weapon leveled at the group. "Last chance," he warned, his voice edged with steel. "Don't take another step." He chambered a round, the sound slicing through the still morning air—a universal language, a sound that speaks louder than words. Even the most reckless fool would understand what came next. But they didn't flinch. His pulse quickened, his adrenaline surging. Something was wrong.

Finally, one of them reacted. The man near the back lifted his head, his eyes locking onto Ian. Fear washed over his face, stark and sudden, like he'd just realized the danger they were in. He lunged forward, grabbing one of the others and pointing frantically toward the garage.

The group stopped. Ian's grip on the shotgun remained firm, his breath steady but shallow. He waited for them to speak, to explain themselves. But what happened next only deepened the strangeness. They turned to each other and began moving their hands in rapid, precise motions.

His brow furrowed. Sign language? He watched as their hands flew through the air, communicating in a way that was both foreign and oddly beautiful in its efficiency. For a moment, he hesitated. His grip on the shotgun tightened reflexively. "Oh, great," he muttered under his breath. "I almost shot a bunch of deaf people."

He exhaled sharply, lowering the barrel slightly and muttering, "What the hell has this world come to?" He stepped back into the garage, his mind racing. He grabbed a notepad and pen from the workbench, his hands moving quickly but deliberately. When he returned, he approached cautiously, keeping the shotgun in a lowered but ready position.

"Let's see if you've got something to say," he muttered, more to himself than to them, as he held up the pen and paper. When he was about ten feet away from the group, he stopped. His stance remaining defensive. He hoped at least one of them could read lips.

Speaking, he enunciated very slow and loud, "Helloooo. My naaame is Iaaan."

The older man at the front frowned, disgust flashing across his face. Then, loudly and with perfect clarity, he said, "We're deaf, not stupid, mister."

Ian blinked. "Oh. Uh... sorry."

The man shook his head. "And shouting won't help."

Ian winced, realizing he had been raising his voice. "Right. That makes sense." He took a breath, regaining his composure. "I haven't been around many deaf, uh, hearing-impaired, people. Please accept my apology."

The man nodded. "Accepted."

He relaxed slightly. "What can I do for you?"

The man's expression softened. "We're headed south, but we're hungry. Do you have any work we can do in exchange for food?"

He studied them carefully. They seemed harmless enough, but four against one was still four against one. "Where are you coming from?"

The man hesitated. "Up north."

Vague. Ian didn't like vague. "Do you have any weapons?" He asked, keeping his tone neutral. "Guns, knives?"

The man scoffed. "Guns? No one has guns anymore, except you, I guess."

"That's not what I asked." His voice hardened.

The man held his gaze for a beat before shaking his head. "No weapons."

"Then you won't mind lining up. Two feet apart. Lift your shirts, turn around, raise your pant legs. Just a precaution." He stated as he gave a wink.

The older man turned and signed something rapidly to the others. They immediately started gesturing back, their movements sharp. The woman, especially, seemed pissed. She huffed, rolling her eyes. Ian placed his free arm across his chest, waiting.

Finally, the man turned back around. "I'm the only one who reads lips. Well, me and John back there, but he's not as good at it."

Ian nodded. "Alright. Let's start with names."

The man motioned to himself. "I'm Tom." He reached out his hand toward Ian as if he wanted to shake hands. Ian didn't move. He then turned, signing to the others. He pointed at the younger man beside him. "This is Nick… She's Carrie… and that's John." Ian wrote their names in his notepad.

"Alright," he said. "Let's get to it." One by one, they complied, lifting shirts, turning around, raising pant legs. They were clean, not even a pocketknife between them. Ian regripped his shotgun and lowered it a bit more.

"Okay," he said, looking at Tom. "I have some crops in the back that need tending. If you're willing to work, I can offer you food before, and after. Then we'll talk again."

Tom turned, signing to the group. Carrie made another irritated gesture, but Tom shot her a look. Finally, he turned back to Ian. "Okay, sir."

"Like I said, my name is Ian."

Tom grinned. "Alright, Ian. Show us the crops."

Ian raised a hand. "Not yet. You eat first." He gestured toward the picnic table near the side of the garage. "Sit. I'll make another pot of coffee and bring you something to eat. Finish, and we'll talk again."

Tom's expression brightened. "Thank you." He turned to relay the message, but John interrupted.

"I got it," John said, stepping toward the table.

The others followed, their demeanor shifting slightly. Ian watched them walk towards the table, then turned to head back inside. He carefully placed his shotgun in its usual hiding spot, but before returning to the kitchen, he strapped on his sidearm. "Trust is good. Preparedness is better." He thought to himself. He grabbed four mugs, making sure not to touch Bill's seasoned cup. He wasn't making that mistake again. He filled them with fresh coffee and brought them outside.

"I don't know how you..." Ian started, but before he could finish, they were already drinking. They guzzled the coffee like it was the best thing they'd ever tasted. Ian blinked. "Well. I was going to ask how you take it, but I guess that answers that."

He returned to the kitchen, found some protein bars, came back and handed them out. They tore into them immediately. Ian smiled, watching them eat. "Guess I'll have to get used to the sound of silence," he thought. "Well, aside from the loud smacking of people who hadn't eaten a proper meal in ages."

////////

The Silent Ones, as he had started calling them in his head, had finished their coffee and energy bars. Now, they were engaged in an animated conversation, hands moving rapidly in the distinct rhythm of sign language. They seemed reinvigorated, more alert, more present, compared to the weary, half-starved figures who had arrived just minutes earlier.

Ian approached Tom, catching his attention with a small wave. "All good?" He asked with a nod.

Tom gave a tired but grateful smile. "Oh, yes. We can't thank you enough."

"Great," he responded. "Now, let me show you what I need done. After, we can talk about some more food for your journey."

Tom hesitated for the briefest moment, his nod slower this time, almost defeated. Ian had seen the look before. They had been hoping for more. A bed, maybe even a few days of rest. He wasn't cold-hearted, but he wasn't reckless either. He had rules for a reason.

"The work won't be hard," Ian continued, keeping things matter-of-fact. "Just some cleanup." Tom nodded again, this time with more resolve. He turned to the others, signing quickly. The group responded with mixed expressions, two resigned, the other simply glad for the opportunity.

As he led them toward the back of the property, the Silent Ones took in everything. The neat, orderly stacks of cars, once transportation, now makeshift walls of steel, lined the path like a fortress. They walked past the last row. And then they saw it. Their expectations had been modest, probably picturing a small backyard garden with a few struggling plants. Instead, they found acres of thriving crops. Rows of vegetables in every direction. Fruit trees, some unfamiliar to them. A river winding lazily beyond the fence. A place that looked alive. A place that looked impossible.

Carrie froze, eyes welling with tears. John, usually silent, letting Tom take the lead, signed, "This is... beautiful." Nick pointed excitedly at a couple of horses grazing in a fenced field to the west of the garden. The group broke into a flurry of excited signing, their exhaustion momentarily forgotten.

Ian let them have the moment. Then, after a few seconds, he cleared his throat and looked at the group, making eye contact with them and said, "Glad you all approve." He turned to Tom. "I've let things go over the last few weeks. Weeds are creeping in, and I haven't checked for ripe fruit or vegetables in some time. Some of it's probably rotting, and that's a waste. See what you can do this afternoon."

Tom nodded, scanning the vast garden. "We can clear a little, but this place is huge." He motioned to his right. "Maybe we can clean up this row over here by nightfall."

Ian gave a small shrug. "That's fair."

Tom hesitated again before adding, "That would put us in a position of needing a place to make camp for the night."

Ian studied him carefully. It was a reasonable request. And they didn't seem like a threat. "Fair enough," he said. "But you stay back here, behind this last row of cars."

Tom relayed the message to the others. Then turned back to Ian. "Mind if we have a small fire? Maybe pick some ripe fruit and vegetables for dinner?"

Ian nodded. "No problem. Eat what you need. And a fire's fine, just keep it small." He motioned toward a pile of materials. "You can use that stuff over there to set up a lean-to if you need shelter."

Tom signed to the group. They nodded, already mentally preparing for the night ahead.

Ian crossed his arms. "One last thing." Tom looked puzzled.

"Stay back here tonight. Make yourselves invisible." Ian's tone firm. "I'll bring coffee in the morning. We'll talk then." Tom held Ian's gaze for a long moment, then nodded.

He gave one last glance at the Silent Ones before turning on his heel and making his way back toward the garage. Behind him, the group got to work, their hands moving swiftly as they divided the tasks. Ian didn't look back again. But as he walked, he rested his hand lightly on his side-arm. Trust was earned. And until then, he'd be keeping both eyes open.

001100 // TWELVE

CAPTAIN MY CAPTAIN

Morning broke like any other for Ian, ushered in by the hiss of the coffee machine. He glided through his morning ritual with calm precision, the rich scent of coffee curling through the air like an old friend. As the coffee machine gurgled, he strolled to his wall of records, fingers trailing along the spines.

"Let's see… what's it gonna be today?" he mused aloud, as if speaking to an unseen audience. His hand stopped on a familiar cover. A smile crossed his face as he pulled the record from the shelf. "What does Robbie Robertson have to say about today?" He slid *Music from Big Pink* onto the turntable and dropped the needle.

As the sound filled the room, he poured himself a cup and set aside a large thermos for the Silent Ones. He strapped on his sidearm, 'just in case', and stepped outside. The morning air was crisp, the sky an unbroken stretch of blue.

It had been a quiet night. He had been very aware of the changes in the yard since the group arrived the day before. He'd made sure he armed the garage's alarm system, double-checked the door and window locks. He had been even more vigilant than he had been over the last several months. It had been so peaceful, he'd begun to let his guard down, but things had changed.

He started towards the back of the yard. When he arrived, he found the group hard at work. It appeared they had eaten a decent breakfast.

"Is that fish I smell?" He asked, glancing at Tom.

Tom nodded. "Oh, yes. John had a line and a hook. Caught a two-pounder this morning. We also gathered a few eggs from over there." He gestured toward the chicken coop.

Ian's eyebrows lifted slightly. "Well, that's great." He glanced around, taking in the signs of renewed energy. They were settling in. And that gave him an idea. "Listen," he began. "You all did a fantastic job. And you're under no contract to stay, but if you choose to, I could use some help getting this area back in shape and keeping it that way."

A broad smile spread across Tom's worn face. He tried to keep his voice steady, but Ian could hear the hope in it. "Let me chat with my crew. Give me a minute." He gave a nod and wandered the garden as Tom turned back to the others, signing rapidly. The conversation was animated. Hands moved fast, expressions shifting between excitement and caution. Ian took his time, inspecting the crops, running his fingers over the leaves.

When he returned, Tom stood to face him. "Ian," he said, "we'd welcome the opportunity to be your, well… sharecroppers."

Ian narrowed his eyes slightly. "Sharecroppers, huh?"

He nodded. "Yeah. This place needs tending, and there's way more food here than just for you. Hell, probably enough for fifty people, easy. If we do it right, we could farm the garden, expand the fruit trees, maybe even increase your chicken supply. That way, we're providing for you, feeding ourselves, and maybe even saving some we can split for bartering."

Ian crossed his arms, weighing the proposal. It was a good pitch; one they hadn't come up with in the last two minutes. They'd planned this. Probably discussed it for hours around their fire last night. He let the silence stretch, watching Tom shift slightly under his gaze.

Then he asked, "Do you all know how to can vegetables and fruit?"

Tom's face lit up. "Oh, yes! Carrie does." Ian nodded slowly. That was a good answer.

He pressed on. "And with John's skills, we can also provide fish and other protein, rabbits, mostly. John's great with snares."

Ian hadn't considered that. That upped their value. He exhaled, glancing toward the sky for a moment before looking back at Tom. "Alright," he said. "Let's try it for a few weeks. If we get along and everything works out, we'll make it official. If not, you're free to move on."

The relief was visible. "Thanks, Ian. You've got a deal."

He reached out to shake Ian's hand and then, almost as an afterthought, added, "And one other thing."

Ian smiled faintly. Let his hand drop and thought, "Here it comes." He knew there would probably be a catch. This was not his first negotiation.

"What?" He asked.

Tom hesitated for a split second before saying, "We're out here in the elements. Would you have a place we could bed down? Maybe call home for a while?" Ian remained silent, letting him explain. "I noticed a small shed over there," he continued, pointing toward a structure on the other side of the stacked cars, "looked like it had potential."

"Oh, that?" Ian said, shaking his head slightly. "Yeah, that's where I keep parts I've salvaged from junk cars. Lots of crap in there. Even a dozen or so fishing poles." Tom stayed silent, waiting. Ian rubbed his chin, considering. "Listen," he said finally, "I don't exactly have customers looking for parts anymore, let alone for a Kia or Hyundai. I pulled what I needed for my own rigs and stored them in the garage. So, sure. Go ahead. Clean it out and set it up for your use. There's electricity in there but use it sparingly, we share the battery."

Tom turned and signed the news to the others. Their faces lit up. Each signed their thanks repeatedly. Ian lifted a hand and, without thinking, placed it over his heart, an improvised sign of acknowledgment. He wasn't sure if it meant anything in proper sign language, but it felt right.

Tom smiled, then lifted his hand to shake Ian's. This time he reciprocated, and they shook hands. Ian let a small smile cross his face. Then his expression hardened slightly.

"Oh, and one last thing, Tom." Tom met his gaze. "Don't venture from back here for any reason. Are we clear?"

Tom hesitated; it was clear he wanted to ask why. But he didn't. Instead, he simply nodded. "Understood."

Ian gave him one last look before turning and heading back toward the garage, carrying the now-empty thermos. As he approached the front, Bill stepped out, his cup in hand.

////////

"There you are, Captain!" Bill called. "Where the hell have you been?"

Ian, shaking his head with a small smirk. "Just making deals, Bill. Just making deals."

"When I came in the needle was bouncing all over the runout groove." He paused, looking at Ian inquisitively. "Anyway, I hope you don't mind. I was about to put on some country western."

Ian winced in pain "Country? Really? You know I'm a classic rock guy."

Bill laughed. "Just kidding. Putting on some Stones, dude!" He looked towards the counter, staring at the near-empty coffee pot with a look of mild betrayal. "That pot's dry! What's going on here?" He grumbled.

Ian, mid-sip, barely glanced up. "Oh, uh… I took a carafe. A thermos, actually."

"Why would you do that?"

Ian stopped, setting his cup down. "Got a little story for you. Why don't you grab what's left, get another pot brewing? Then let's sit down and talk."

Bill's expression shifted. He muttered something under his breath, but he poured what was left in his cup, started a fresh brew, and sat across from Ian. Ian leaned forward, elbows on the table. "After you left yesterday, something happened." He explained everything, the Silent Ones, their arrival, their work in the garden, and their proposal to stay and maintain the crops. Bill leaned back in his chair, rubbing his chin.

"Well… what the hell are you gonna do with these vagabonds?"

Ian sighed. "I don't know yet." He tapped his fingers against his cup. "But they've got value. Real value. And I don't see them being spies. They can't hear, half of them don't read lips, only one reads and speaks well and the other barely catches half of what's said. Not exactly prime intelligence operatives."

"Which one reads lips?"

"The oldest one, and another, John can, but he isn't nearly as good at it," Ian replied. "The older fellow is Tom. You'll know him when you see him."

Bill exhaled sharply, shaking his head. "Alright, they might have value. But my next question is, to what end? How are they going to help us? And more importantly, how do they affect our security?"

"Jury's still out on that one."

Bill frowned but didn't push further. Instead, he changed the subject. "Alright, let's go over tonight's plans." They pulled out their schematics, maps, and notes, discussing the logistics of the upcoming Gathering. The conversation was interrupted by the sound of boots on gravel.

Lance strolled in, hands in his pockets. "Hey guys. How's it hanging?"

Ian turned towards the kid and blinked. "What?"

The kid grinned. "Sorry. I mean, how's everything going today?"

Ian shook his head. "It's going." He took another sip of coffee. "What's up with you?"

"Another day, another issue with my mom," he said with an exaggerated sigh. "Figured I'd stop by, see how things are going, maybe take another ride."

"Not today, kid. We've got a lot to do here."

Lance smirked. "Feels like you're trying to get rid of me."

Bill chuckled. "Kid, you're like a damn dog. You keep showing up, and I don't mind having you around, but..."

Lance rolled his eyes. "Oh, great. Now I'm an animal."

"Don't take it personally kid."

Ian cut in, shifting the conversation. "We've got a lot on our plate today."

Lance tilted his head. "Because of the Gathering tonight?" Both Ian and Bill froze.

Ian looked directly at Lance. "What do you mean?"

He shrugged. "Come on. I'm not stupid. You're having another Gathering, right? Or were you just not going to invite me?" Bill and Ian exchanged glances.

Ian cleared his throat. "It's not exactly like last time. Just a few people. Talking."

Lance grinned. "Yeah, sure. Just talking. About the plan."

Bill's eyes flashed. "And what do you know about a plan?"

"I know what needs to be done. And I want in."

Ian rubbed his temples. "Kid, your parents are chipped. That's dangerous for us."

Lance's expression hardened. "No. You don't see the big picture, do you?" He leaned forward. "I'm your inside guy."

Ian paused for a moment. "Where have you heard that term before?"

Lance smirked. "I told you, I'm not stupid. I read. I listen. And I know how these things work." He straightened. "Think about it. Who else do you have who has one foot in and one foot out? I won't be chipped. Ever.

But I can move freely now. I can learn things. I can help." The men exchanged a long look.

Bill motioned to Ian. "Alright, let's take a walk." They stepped outside. He turned to Ian. "He's right. Kid's sharp. Real sharp."

"I know. But we need to be sure about his loyalty."

"Ian… listen. Do you know any other Annie or even a chipped person that is going to work as an insider? The chipped don't even know they're compromised." He motioned back toward the garage. "Lance does. And he wants to fight."

Ian stared at the ground for a moment, then nodded. They walked back inside. He looked at Lance. "Alright. You're in."

"I know I am. I was always going to be."

Ian studied him. "What do you mean by that?"

The kid's expression darkened slightly. "I want my parents back."

Ian's breath hitched. "Kid, the way I see it…"

Lance interrupted, "If we take down Jacob, I get my parents back."

Something unreadable flickered in Ian's eyes. "That's… interesting."

The kid nodded. "We take Jacob down. We take it all down."

Ian ran a hand through his hair. "We'll talk more about this later. Until then, say nothing to anyone."

Lance straightened. "Yes, Captain."

Ian blinked. "What?"

The kid grinned.

Ian shook his head. "That's the second time today someone's called me Captain."

001101 // THIRTEEN

THE NEXT GATHERING

The sun had just dipped below the horizon as Ian, Bill, and Lance finished their meal. Fresh trout and vegetables, courtesy of the Silent Ones. Lance was not yet privy to the fact there were now sharecroppers in the back yard. The group in the back had done exactly as instructed, staying out of sight, making themselves invisible. Earlier that afternoon, Ian had slipped out to pick up food they had collected, returning without a word of explanation. Lance didn't ask any questions, and Ian didn't offer any information.

As they sat at the table, Ian said. "Alright, I think the three of us are at least somewhat coordinated in thought." Bill raised an eyebrow but said nothing.

"Tobias and Mara both said they'd be here tonight," Ian continued. "But neither are exactly the trusting type."

Bill snorted. "That's putting it lightly." He leaned back in his chair, folding his arms. "From what I've seen, trust is the last thing those two have for anyone. Proceed with caution," he added, his tone turning serious.

Lance, who had been listening quietly, nodded. "I think it's best if I just listen tonight."

"Good plan." Ian agreed.

The kid stood, grabbing the empty plates. "I'll make myself useful and wash up."

Bill smirked. "Keep your grubby mitts off my coffee mug, kid." Lance rolled his eyes but chuckled as he carried the dishes to the sink.

Ian exhaled, rubbing his hands together. "This could prove to be an interesting night. We really haven't said much yet, but everyone seems to have the same thoughts." He paused, glancing at Bill. "Let's keep it that way."

Bill gave a slow nod.

They set to work preparing for the Gathering. Ian pulled an old chalkboard from the back of the garage, dusting it off with the sleeve of his shirt. "Where the hell is all the chalk?" he muttered, half to himself, knowing he was the only one there who would know the whereabouts.

Bill dug through the cluttered workbench, retrieving the notes he and Ian had compiled. Lance leaned against the counter, watching them both. "I don't take notes." He said matter-of-factly. "I commit everything to memory."

"The blessing of youth." Bill muttered, shaking his head.

Lance hesitated for a second, then spoke. "Actually, … I should tell you both something." He paused. "I have an eidetic memory."

Silence.

"It's not the gift people think it is," he continued, his tone shifting. "it's more a curse. I remember everything. Not just facts and figures, everything. Every detail, exactly as it happened. The good. The bad. The painful."

Bill let out a low whistle. "Damn. That's something."

Lance's demeanor tightened. "It's why I hate Jacob so much." His voice faltered slightly. "My mom…" His eyes misted up, and he quickly looked away.

Bill's expression softened. "Sorry, kid. I didn't realize."

Lance swallowed hard, shaking his head. "It is what it is." Ian and Bill exchanged a glance but let the moment settle. The night was only just beginning.

////////

They arrived within a minute of each other, both cloaked in oversized outerwear, both moving with the cautious air of those who had learned not to trust their surroundings. As they stepped into the garage, they looked as if they had walked straight out of a dystopian novel; weathered, wary and ready for anything.

"Welcome back," Ian said evenly. "I trust you both had a good day."

Tobias didn't acknowledge his greeting. "Let's get on with this," he said, his voice edged with impatience. "I didn't come for a damn coffee klatch."

"Sorry, I forgot to offer you a cup of coffee." Bill quipped, his grin barely masking the tension that had settled over the room.

"I'm with him," Mara said, jerking her thumb toward Tobias. "Let's get to making a plan to…" She stopped mid-sentence. Her eyes landed on Lance. Her entire posture shifted, her body tensing. "Oh, I've gotta go." she said abruptly, moving as if to leave.

"Hold up a minute." Ian interjected, his voice calm but firm. "Everyone, pause." She hesitated and didn't bolt.

Tobias interjected. "What happened to the other two – Hector, Elise?"

"They didn't make the cut for now. But we might need them later." Ian surveyed the room, making sure he had their full attention. "Look, Bill and I double-vetted each of you. We all want the same outcome. If we're going to succeed, we need to give, let's say… a little trust to one another." He let that sink in for a moment before continuing. "We all have our own motivations, but the goal is the same. That makes us brothers and…" he nodded toward Mara, "sister, at arms."

His gaze swept over them. "So, take a breath. You are among the best allies you have ever had, and will ever have in the After."

Silence. A long, heavy silence.

Then Tobias exhaled and, in a much calmer voice, said, "Agreed."

Mara let out a slow breath, pulling the strings of her hoodie tighter around her face. She perched on a stool, her legs swinging freely like a child's. "Okay, I'm good," she muttered.

"Glad we're on the same page." Ian said, his tone easing.

Lance, unable to contain himself, stood and snapped a playful salute. "Yes, Captain!"

Bill chuckled. "Sit down, kid."

Ian shook his head slowly, thinking. "There it is again… Captain."

////////

"Let's get to work." Ian said, dragging the chalkboard into place. He handed out the notes he and Bill had compiled. "First rule of the Gathering," his tone turned sharp, "we don't speak of anything discussed here, at any time, outside of this room."

Mara frowned. "I get that, but why can't we talk at my place? It's way more secure than this garage." She gestured around the cluttered space.

He shook his head. "We'll cross that bridge when we get there. For now, this is the rule. Agreed?"

A round of nods.

Lance started to say, "Aye, aye…" but Bill shot him a look that said, "not now, kid", and he let the words trail off.

The group spent the next couple hours debating ideas, mapping out possible strategies, and exchanging knowledge. It was a productive session, the most progress they had made yet. By the time the last cup of coffee was poured from the old brewer, Ian looked around the room with a sense of cautious satisfaction. "I think we have the workings, of the workings for a plan," he said. "Good job, people. Now comes the tricky part. Let's figure out a method for signaling when we need to meet again."

Ian continued. "I propose two cryptic markers, one in the Old City Market, in front of Tobias' shop, and the other on the big tree near the library. Thoughts?"

Tobias nodded. "Simple but effective."

Ian continued. "If anyone needs to call a meeting, we place an old transistor tube just inside Tobias' shop, near the window base. When Bill or I spot it, we'll make a call on safety. If we determine a meeting can be called securely, we'll tie a bright red or yellow band, the kind used for marking trees for removal, around the big oak just outside the library. That signals a Gathering will take place the next evening."

Bill nodded. "Clever. Changes each time?"

"Exactly." Ian confirmed. "At the next meeting, we'll rotate signal items and possibly locations. Agreed?" Everyone nodded. No more words were necessary.

One by one, they left the way they had arrived, staggered exits, different routes.

////////

The garage fell silent once more. Ian sat staring at the chalkboard. The pieces were finally coming together. But the real work was only just beginning.

He turned away and walked to his record collection, letting his fingers hover over the worn sleeves. The familiar ritual of selecting a record was supposed to ground him, but his mind had already drifted elsewhere. He wasn't thinking about music. He was thinking about them. About what they were planning. About what was at stake.

I can't fail again. The thought struck hard, unbidden. His jaw tightened. Not again. He closed his eyes. The past was always waiting, just beneath the surface, ready to pull him under if he let it.

He had never spoken about his time in the military. Not once. Most didn't even know, no one in his life now had a clue. He'd been a Captain in the Army. He joined straight out of college, fast-tracked into special forces. It was the price he paid for a free ride through school, a contract signed when he was too young to grasp its weight.

For a time, things had been quiet. Blissfully quiet. He was assigned to a desk job stateside, buried in logistics and inventory reports. He'd grown to appreciate the hum of fluorescent lights, the soft tap of keys, the clean lines of paper. And most of all, the stillness of sleeping in his own bed, no boots by the door, no adrenaline in his veins.

Then the President greenlit a covert operation in Nicaragua. A quick, surgical mission. In and out. That's what they were told. No complications. No noise. They trained hard for weeks, sharpening instincts that had dulled behind the desk. The intel was airtight, or so it seemed. A night drop into the jungle. A twenty-kilometer hike to the target. Identify. Confirm. Eliminate. Extract by helicopter ten clicks east in an open field. They weren't told why. They didn't ask. Orders were orders.

But the jungle had other plans. The drop was off by nearly half a click. One of his men landed wrong, shattered his leg on impact. Useless from the start. And then came the real shock: the jungle was crawling with Sandinista guerillas, more than twice what the intelligence had forewarned.

The first shots cracked through the trees, splitting the night in half. Muzzle flashes flared like erratic lightning. The air turned thick, suffocating, with the scent of wet soil, sweat, cordite, and something metallic he never wanted to smell again. He could still hear the screaming, half of it his own men, the other half the enemy, and somewhere in between, his own voice yelling orders that no one could hear.

Bullets snapped through the canopy like dry twigs. Leaves shredded midair. The jungle, once still, had erupted into something primal, chaos in its purest form.

He remembered the weight of his rifle, slick with humidity and blood. He remembered the ground, soft and uneven, grabbing at his boots as he moved. The screams, "Captain! I'm hit." And he remembered the bodies, fallen in awkward shapes, some of them men he'd trained with, eaten with, laughed with. He had survived, but something inside him hadn't.

He'd left pieces of himself in that jungle, scattered like shell casings in the dirt. "War," he thought, "truly is hell."

The "what ifs" had never left him. They sat in the back of his mind, whispering, reminding him of every misstep, every moment that could have changed the outcome. He had gone over things a thousand times. Had they moved too fast? Too slow? Had he missed something?

When he returned from the failed mission, the writing was on the wall. The debriefing was just a formality. An investigation followed. Launched, conducted, and quietly closed with no charges. They didn't need to punish him outright. His performance evaluation did that well enough. A substandard rating. A stained record.

Captain Black turned in his resignation.

He exhaled sharply and opened his eyes, dragging himself back to the present. His fingers curled into a fist before he forced them to relax.

"They really need to stop with this 'Captain' thing," he muttered while slowly shaking his head.

He scanned his collection again. This time he wanted something with a little reflective quality to it. His fingers flipped each record album, then one stuck to his finger. "Huh," he muttered. Someone must think this is what I need. He pulled his finger off the cover and slid the album out. Tangerine Dream – *Underwater Sunlight.*

"This should calm the brain a little." The record started to play while he took a seat in his favorite chair. He closed his eyes.

"This is not going to be an easy operation." He thought to himself.

001110 // FOURTEEN

THE WALK

Mara and Tobias had left the Gathering separately.

Halfway back to his place, Tobias paused beneath a stand of trees. The warmth of the evening clung to his skin, and he felt the pull to stop and rest. He scanned the secluded area, spotting a sun-bleached log near the edge of the clearing. Brushing a spiderweb off his sleeve, he sat down, letting the hush of early summer envelop him. He needed a moment. A moment to catch his breath. A moment to reflect on what they had just discussed at the Gathering.

The night was thick with shadows, the new moon hidden with stars blazing in its absence. Above him, the sky stretched endlessly, a vast expanse of pinpricks shimmering against the black. The air was warm but heavy, dense with the kind of humidity that hinted at an overnight storm. Somewhere in the tall grass, a cricket chirped, its rhythm steady, like the heartbeat of the night itself.

Tobias rubbed his hands together, not from cold but out of habit, his fingers tracing the calluses he had gained in the After. The texture grounded him, a small reminder that he hadn't lost himself to the chaos of this fractured world.

He tilted his head back, his gaze fixed on the stars. They were sharper now, brighter than he could remember. It was one of the few things better than in the Before. The only thing, really.

That was the one gift the AI had returned to them: the sky.

Tobias sat quietly, his thoughts swirling. The Gathering had been promising. The faintest flicker of hope had sparked within him. But hope was a dangerous thing; it made people reckless, vulnerable. And in a world like this, vulnerability could get you killed. Still, he couldn't shake the feeling that this group, strange as it was, had potential.

He reached down, picking up a small stone from the dirt at his feet and rolling it between his fingers. The cricket's chirping faded for a moment, replaced by the distant rustle of leaves. He barely noticed Mara approaching. Her footsteps whispered through the underbrush behind him, until she was almost on top of him. She startled slightly when she saw him sitting there. He looked up, a half-smile tugging at his mouth. "Well, well. Just thinking about you."

She raised an eyebrow. "About what?"

"Well, more like, what are we thinking?" He said, his tone reflective. "I'm an old, used-up engineer in a world where engineers don't matter anymore. And you, you should be with people your own age, living a normal life."

Mara folded her arms. "You spend too much time worrying about what should be instead of dealing with what is." She tilted her head back, studying the sky. The stars were brilliant, stretching endlessly above them. "Beautiful," she murmured.

Tobias followed her gaze. "Yeah. If nothing else, the last few years made us look up again." He studied her for a moment. "Enough small talk. What do you really think about all this?"

She blinked, drawn from her thoughts. "Well…" A grin pulled at the corner of her mouth. "If I were choosing a team to save the world, it wouldn't be the crew in that garage."

He let out a sharp laugh. "You've got that right." He shook his head. "Let's see, we've got a loner for a leader, a teenager who's barely lived, a carpenter, a girl who plays computer games, and me, a washed-up engineer fiddling with relics."

Mara nudged his boot with hers. "Hey, I don't just play games."

"Alright, alright, fair enough," he said, holding up a hand. "So, what's your big contribution?"

Her expression sharpened. "I understand how code works. I can build and unravel it. I can code applications that override the systems we're up against."

He paused for a moment. "That's a big claim. What makes you think you're smarter than Jacob?"

She held his gaze, unwavering. "Because people wrote Jacob's algorithms to begin with, and people are flawed. That means the system has vulnerabilities." Mara moved over, settling onto the log beside him. For a few moments, they said nothing, letting the sounds of insects fill the silence. A sudden gust of wind rustled the trees, sending pinecones scattering onto the ground. The sound broke their reflective pause.

Tobias recounted, "Well… maybe there's some logic to this madness after all."

She smirked. "I figured that out at the first Gathering."

He scoffed. "Some of us are just trying to survive. Not be superheroes." He stood with a soft groan. "Let's go. It's warm. I'd bet on thunder by morning."

Mara rose too, brushing her hands on her pants. "Yeah. I was thinking the same."

They started walking, side by side for a time. Then she veered left onto a side trail, her silhouette lit faintly by the stars above.

"See you at the next one," she called over her shoulder.

Tobias lifted a hand. "Good night." He watched her go, then turned and took the longer path home, fireflies blinking in the brush like the luminescence trailing a large ship at sea.

////////

Mara had become hyperaware of her surroundings, a reflex honed over years of moving through the world like prey. It had started during the chipping period. The thought of something buried in her skull, silently monitoring her, twisting her choices with invisible threads. It made her stomach turn. Others called it innovation. She called it captivity.

She'd aged out of foster care in her late teens. Or that was the term they used when the system washed its hands of her. No family had come forward, no home had been offered. Just a bed in a group facility with peeling paint and overworked staff who smiled too tightly and promised safety they couldn't deliver.

There, the chipping had been celebrated. The staff treated it like a rite of passage, lining up eagerly for implants, their eyes wide with belief in the future. But even in that optimistic hallway, Mara had seen it for what it was, submission wrapped in circuitry.

So, the night before the staff in her wing were to be chipped, Mara made her choice. She didn't want to be around people that were controlled. She slipped out through a laundry door left ajar, wrapped in a secondhand hoodie, her backpack half-full and heart pounding. She hadn't looked back. She'd vanished into the sprawl of dark streets and alleyways, into the city's forgotten places, surviving by instinct and sheer defiance. She found a home in the recently abandoned City Library. Out of sight and mind.

That was years ago. Still, as she walked the quiet stretch toward the library, now long deserted, she moved like someone who expected to be followed. The instinct never left. It had become part of her gait, part of her breath.

The heat of the day still lingered in the concrete, but the air was starting to cool slightly. A breeze skated across her arms, lifting the scent of dry leaves, damp earth, and something faintly floral, gardenia maybe. Summer nights had their own personality. Slower, but watchful. She liked that about them. But tonight felt different.

A subtle weight pressed against her shoulders. The usual summer sounds, buzzing cicadas, the chirp of crickets, had faded. The silence wasn't peaceful. It was expectant. She paused, one foot slightly forward, fingers tightening on the strap of her bag. Her ears strained. Nothing. No footsteps, no wind through the trees, no mechanical hum from distant infrastructure. Just the soft echo of her own breath and the faint creak of a sign swinging from a rusted bracket nearby.

////////

A prickle danced at the base of her neck. She turned her head slowly, letting her eyes better adjust to the darkness. The sidewalk ahead glimmered faintly under the starlight, broken by patches of shadow where the trees leaned over the path. Her gaze swept the hedgerows and fences. Shapes shifted in her peripheral vision, only branches, but her body tensed anyway.

Then she heard it: a low shuffle in the overgrowth to her right. Her breath caught. She froze. The sound came again. Dry leaves crunching. Something moving.

She stepped back slowly, carefully on the gravel. Her hand edged toward the small folding knife tucked in her pocket. She didn't pull it out, yet, but the pressure of it against her palm gave her something solid to hold onto. The brush rustled. A sharp screech tore through the stillness as a cat burst from the undergrowth, fur bristling, eyes glowing at her for a heartbeat before it bolted across the road.

She flinched, her breath rushing out all at once. Mara stood there for a moment, heart racing. Then a shaky laugh escaped her lips, dry and quiet. "Paranoid," she muttered.

But the tension didn't evaporate entirely. She rolled her shoulders, trying to shake it off, then adjusted her bag and resumed walking, just a little faster now. The library wasn't far. She knew every turn on the way.

Every shortcut, every blind corner. Her eyes scanned the alleyways; her ears tuned to every shifting noise. She didn't relax until she saw the broken signpost marking the entrance to the library's side path.

She had learned a long time ago: the moment you stop looking over your shoulder is the moment someone creeps up behind you.

001111 // FIFTEEN

CHIPPED

People had dreamed of robots for generations, gleaming machines that would handle the mundane, the tedious, the thankless. They'd envisioned chrome hands scrubbing dishes, automated equipment mowing perfect lawns, tireless drones folding laundry while humans leaned back in leisure. And to a point, that future had arrived. Vacuum bots hummed through living rooms. AI-controlled mowers trimmed suburban yards with precision. People marveled at the convenience.

What they hadn't expected, what no one had truly feared, was becoming the robots themselves. There was no longer a need to pour resources into building machines from metal and code when something more adaptable, more renewable, already existed: human beings. Organic resources, upgraded and repurposed.

Larry and Tad worked as engineers for Comm-Resources, Inc., a subsidiary of Republic Enterprises, responsible for maintaining the WiFi infrastructure that blanketed the city with a seamless, uninterrupted signal. Their job was more critical than most realized. Without constant upkeep, the tower's transceivers could fail, and with them, the control grid.

That morning, as the sun clawed its way over the skyline, they received a new work order: a main signal node had gone down at the top of Newtown Tower One, the tallest structure in the district, its antennae stabbing the sky like gleaming spears. It wasn't an unusual failure. The power required to broadcast across the entire city was staggering, and the equipment was continuously strained under the load.

But the danger wasn't mechanical. The electronic radiation levels around the tower's roof were infamous. So volatile, in fact, that birds straying within 100 meters dropped from the sky mid-flight, their bodies cooked before they hit the pavement. Charred feathers often littered the base of the tower, mute reminders of proximity's price.

Protocol required that all maintenance personnel wear steel-threaded hardhats, sleek, metallic shells that wrapped around the skull like motorcycle helmets. But this was no nostalgic accessory. The helmets weren't designed to protect against falling debris. They were Faraday cages, built to shield the chip inside their head.

Without them, the electromagnetic field near the transceiver would overload the chips circuitry implanted in every worker's brain. And when that happened, death wasn't dramatic. It was instant. Silent. A puff of smoke curling from the base of the skull where the chip had once pulsed.

The tower itself was a monolith of glass, steel and polished stone, its lower floors long abandoned. Very few people still worked there. Now just the occasional buzz of a maintenance drone rolling across a floor working to keep dust removed, could be heard.

The elevator door opened into a small vestibule where protective equipment was available. Larry and Tad donned the required protective helmets and grabbed their tools. As they climbed the stairs to the roof, they moved in silence. Only their boots echoing off concrete steps, the air growing thinner and hotter with every step. Warning signs were plastered along the stairway walls, bold and unflinching:

HIGH ENERGY ZONE. UNPROTECTED ACCESS FORBIDDEN. FAILURE TO COMPLY WILL RESULT IN NEURAL SYSTEM FAILURE. SURGE RISK BEYOND THIS POINT.

Everyone had heard the stories, some had seen it firsthand. A junior tech who forgot to seal his helmet. A contractor who thought the warn-ings were exaggerated. They didn't scream. The chip surged, the body crumpled, and then… nothing. Just a whisper of smoke rising like incense from their head. No one wanted to end up like that.

As they reached the top floor, the final platform before the external maintenance scaffold, Larry paused to catch his breath. The city stretched below them, a grid of light and silence. High above, the tower's antennae pulsed faintly with blue light, the air around them humming like a live wire.

"You ever think about it?" Larry asked.

Tad didn't turn. "About what?"

"About what we are now. What they turned us into."

Tad adjusted the strap under his chin, his fingers trembling slightly. "Not if I can help it."

They stepped through the final door and into the open scaffold, the wind immediately pressing in around them. The antenna loomed just ahead, flickering with power. Their helmets buzzed faintly, absorbing the ambient energy that might otherwise melt their minds.

Despite the heat and the height, Larry felt cold. Not from the air, but from something deeper, something he wouldn't name. Because up here, at the edge of the sky, surrounded by invisible waves of control, one thing was clear: They weren't servicing the system. They were part of it.

////////

The day was bright and cloudless, the kind of crystalline blue sky that made everything below seem smaller, almost distant. From their perch near the top of Newtown Tower One, Larry and Tad took in the sweeping view, smaller buildings stretching for city blocks, the streets below crawling with orderly movement. Few ever saw the city from this high. Fewer saw it with unfiltered eyes.

They had brought lunch, as they always did. It was one of the few rituals that still felt human. They sat cross-legged on the steel platform, helmets on, taking their time between planning, repairing, and diagnostics before the long climb back down.

Tad leaned back, arms stretched behind his head. "Man, I'm glad we were some of the first chosen. I love what we do," he said, grinning at the sun.

Larry didn't answer right away. He stared out over the skyline. Then he turned toward Tad, his expression unreadable. "I don't know."

Tad frowned. "What? Speak up. No one can hear us up here, we're not connected."

He responded slowly. "Good. Because I've been thinking. About them. The newer chipped. They don't look upgraded. They look… hollow. Like something's missing."

Tad raised an eyebrow, a trace of confusion on his face. "What are you talking about? This is the life."

"Life? This isn't living. Not like it used to be."

Tad's grin faltered. He studied his friend's face more closely now, searching for a punchline that wasn't coming.

"My wife has Version 2," He went on, more quietly now. "She used to challenge me. She had opinions, moods, ideas. Now… it's like she's following a script. She smiles when she's supposed to. She says the right things. But there's nothing behind it. She's fading. And I can't reach her."

Tad hesitated. "I get it, but…"

A faint scream then echoed through the air. They looked at each other, scrambling to the edge of the scaffold. Far below, in the plaza, a man, mid-forties from best they could tell, was staggering through the crowd. His limbs jerked at odd angles, his movements erratic, like a puppet with tangled strings. He twitched violently, then collapsed. For a moment, the people around him reacted. Startled gasps, a few steps forward. But within seconds, their attention drained away. They stepped around him like he was debris. No panic. No concern. Just… detachment.

Larry pointed, eyes wide. "You saw that, right?"

Tad nodded slowly, his mouth dry. "Yeah. What the hell just happened?"

"Jacob happened," he said, voice tight. "That was a kill-switch. A silent override. You saw it, but only because we're not connected right now like they are."

Tad shook his head, unsure. "We're not controlled. We're enhanced."

"Exactly! Which means we can still think clearly. They can't. Dude, don't you get it? They're not reacting because they weren't told to. They don't even see him anymore."

Tad looked down again, this time longer. The man's body was already being ignored, as if it had always been part of the sidewalk. The crowd flowed around him with mechanical grace.

"We're not controlled," Larry said. "They are. Don't you see it?"

Tad's breath caught. His eyes moved across the people below him like he was seeing them for the first time. The mechanical motions. The synchronized steps. "…Yeah," he whispered. "I get it. I just… I wasn't paying attention before." He rubbed his face. "This ain't right."

Larry nodded grimly. "Exactly."

They moved toward the access door, their earlier ease gone, replaced by a tension that clung to their backs like static. At the threshold, Larry glanced back toward the skyline. "I don't know about you, but I'm deeply concerned."

Tad looked over, eyes sharper now. "Actually, I'm scared. What can we do? The Board runs everything. If we communicate this in any way, we end up like that guy. You saw how fast it happened."

Larry's voice dropped. "We ask questions. But quietly. And not around anyone chipped."

"Especially not Mr. Thomas." Tad added quickly.

Larry nodded. "Exactly. He'll have us reassigned, or worse. And if you do slip up and say something… don't drag my name into it."

Tad huffed. "I'm not going to screw this up. I'm not stupid. And I'm sure as hell not about to talk to my boss about this."

"Good. Because if we're going to do anything at all, we need to stay invisible."

Tad looked down again, the image of the collapsed man burned into his memory. "Maybe we already waited too long."

////////

Larry and Tad had Version 1 of the chip, the original model. By today's standards, it was outdated: slower, bulkier, and far more demanding on the body. But in one critical way, it was different. Their version offered something the newer models didn't. Autonomy. They retained full cognitive independence. The chip served as a reference tool, augmenting memory, enhancing focus, accelerating problem-solving. It assisted, but it didn't override. It didn't control and it only transmitted thoughts when allowed.

This version was born of naive optimism. Back in the Before, the technology had been pitched as a revolution in personal empowerment, a personal assistant embedded within the mind. A tool to enhance human potential, not replace it.

Of course, there were trade-offs. This early version required a thick, battery pack implanted into the left shoulder. The packs were clunky and visible through clothing, a clear marker of who had what. In the early days, that visibility had been a badge of honor, a signal of progress and privilege.

But the battery packs came with their own burdens. They needed recharging every 36 hours, a process that left users with a faint buzzing sensation in their necks and a dull ache behind their eyes for a period after charging. Over time, those inconveniences became daily reminders of the limits of the technology.

By contrast, the newer chipped, those with Version 2, operated at a far higher level. Their internal batteries were extremely small, sleeker, and more efficient. Their processors were faster, capable of processing vast amounts of data in real-time. But Version 2 came with a cost as well. A constant connection to Jacob, the central intelligence node, was mandatory. Without that link, the Version 2 chips couldn't function at all. It wasn't just that users lost access to memory augmentation or data analysis. It was worse than that. They lost comprehension. They lost their personalities. They lost themselves. It didn't process thoughts in the traditional sense. It streamed them. Every idea, every decision, every fleeting impulse was routed through Jacob, analyzed, refined, and returned. The result was seamless efficiency, but it came at the expense of autonomy.

While Version 1 had been a tool. Version 2 was a tether. And that tether, invisible though it was, bound its users to a system that demanded obedience in exchange for functionality.

Larry and Tad's chips might have been leftovers of the past, but in a world dominated by Version 2, their clunky outdated batteries were more than just a marker of obsolescence. They were a symbol of freedom.

Even their employment had changed. The hardhats Larry and Tad wore interfered with Jacob's signal. For Version 2s, this meant disorientation, then complete loss of information. They would just freeze. As a result, they were excluded from engineering maintenance roles, from anything requiring the interruption of data to and from them. They weren't employed at all, in the traditional sense. They were deployed, shifted from one low-impact task to the next, wherever the system required bodies. Sometimes, they swept streets. Other times, they stood motionless in parks, staring at nothing, waiting for the next directive.

Larry had started noticing it months ago, how the Version 2s didn't blink as often. How they didn't flinch when loud sounds cracked through the air. How they didn't look up unless prompted. Their faces were soft, slack, almost serene. But their eyes... Their eyes weren't empty. They were waiting.

Currently, less than 6% of the population retained Version 1. Most of them worked in high-level trades: construction supervisors, power grid technicians, emergency response teams. A handful served in senior management, though even that was shifting. The Board, all Version 1, had begun issuing newest version to department heads in several districts. The message was clear: even leadership didn't need independence. Just precision.

The rest of the population was moving in one direction, toward smooth, seamless integration into the workflow.

Tad had once joked that being Version 1 made them "original flavor." But the joke didn't land the same anymore. Not after what they witnessed today. Not after the man twitched and died while a crowd stepped around him like he was no more than a broken lamppost.

Larry no longer wore his battery pack like a badge. He wore it like a target. He had started to notice how few Version 1's were left in his building. How the security staff at Comm-Resources had all received upgrades. How Mr. Thomas, their manager, had recently begun dropping certain phrases like "operational consistency, behavioral alignment, predictability over improvisation." The words came out smooth, but they sat heavy in the air.

Larry didn't say it out loud, not even to Tad, but he knew the truth. Version 1 wasn't just old, it could be dangerous. It represented a window into something Jacob couldn't quite reach. Not yet. A space between thought and action that hadn't been overwritten. And that space, small as it was, is where resistance could still exist.

010000 // SIXTEEN

THE YARD

Tom stood overlooking the crops, meticulously maintained by the Silent Ones. The vegetables thrived, their growth unimpeded now that the weeds were no longer choking the life out of them. The fruit trees, too, were flourishing, their branches heavy with promise, as the birds had been kept at bay by the activity in the gardens.

For a hearing person, the scene was almost unnervingly quiet. But to the Silent Ones, the chatter was as loud as a jet airplane. They worked with unrelenting energy, their hands constantly flitting between picking vegetables and filling bins, while engaging in animated conversations.

Their discussions were a mix of memories and playful teasing, much of it directed at John. As the youngest among them, John often found himself the target of their jokes. He would scowl and warn them, "One day, you might wake up and not find me here. Then what would you do?" But his protests only fueled their laughter.

Today was pleasant, clear skies and brimming with hope. The crops were thriving, no one was disturbing their peace, and life seemed good again. The group had even begun to regain weight, thanks to the steady supply of nutrition from the fish they had managed to catch and the abundance of vegetables and fruits they harvested.

Tom caught movement down the path towards the garage. His eyes narrowed for a moment before recognizing the familiar figure. It was Ian. Tom smiled and waved. The other Silent Ones noticed him as well. They set their tools aside and gathered around Tom as he neared.

Ian's eyes scanned the crops, his eyebrows lifting in surprise. "Beautiful day... and wow!" he said, letting out a low whistle. "I don't think this place has ever looked this good!" Watching his reaction, they all smiled in approval.

"They've been working hard," Tom said, folding his arms, "and it shows." He tilted his head. "I assume you've been finding the produce and fish we've been leaving in the kitchen?"

Ian nodded, though there was a flicker of hesitation in his expression. "Yeah, yeah. I've been finding things showing up," he paused, frowning slightly. "But I still need you guys to lay low until I can talk to some of the people who stop in from time to time."

Tom raised a hand to cut him off. "No need," he said firmly. "We get it. Actually, we know more than you think."

Ian frowned. "What do you mean?"

"I can read lips. Even several yards away."

Ian's expression shifted. "We may be deaf," Tom continued, "but we know how to move unnoticed. No one has been the wiser."

Ian thought for a moment. He hadn't considered that. "What do you think you know?"

Tom shrugged, his expression calm but knowing. "For starters, the people you've been meeting with... We know they're not chipped. We know they're angry. And we know at least one's a programmer and one's an engineer." He tilted his head slightly, with a faint smile. "So, we put two and two together." Ian stiffened. "We figure you're up to something," he added, his voice steady.

Ian wasn't sure whether to be impressed or worried. He hadn't fully considered the implications of their ability to read lips, let alone the possibility that they might piece together parts of his plans. A glint of concern crossed his mind. He sighed, rubbing the back of his neck. "Tom," he began, but then stopped himself. He realized tone alone wouldn't help here. Words needed to be chosen carefully.

He tried again. "Listen… we're working on something important. Let me get my head around everything, and I'll tell you more when the time is right."

Tom studied him in silence, his gaze steady but without judgment. After a moment, he smiled. "You have nothing to worry about with us."

Ian ran a hand over his jaw, exhaling through his nose. Tom's quiet confidence was reassuring. They weren't a threat. If anything, they might be allies, though Ian wasn't sure how much he was ready to share just yet. Shifting the focus, he picked up a basket of fresh vegetables, its weight solid in his hands. "Hey, how much of these vegetables are we producing here?"

Tom glanced at the overflowing crates stacked nearby. "More than we can eat. I'd like to start drying some for winter, canning what we have supplies for, and maybe trading the rest." He paused, thoughtful. "Any chance you can find us a dehydrator?"

Ian considered the request. "I don't have one, but I might know someone at the market who does. I'll look into it."

Tom nodded, satisfied. "That'd help a lot."

"If you catch any fish or maybe some game, I'd appreciate a little." Ian added. "Enough for a few people, but only if there's extra."

"No problem, Boss," Tom replied with a faint grin. Ian sighed internally, resisting the urge to roll his eyes. At least he didn't say "Captain."

With one last nod to the group, Ian turned and made his way back toward the garage, basket in hand.

////////

As he walked back to the garage, his thoughts lingered on the Silent Ones. Their ability to read lips from a distance was a huge advantage, and their small numbers made them even more valuable. Against all odds, he was beginning to trust them. "Trust is earned," he thought. Stepping into the garage, he jumped slightly. Bill and Lance were already there, sitting at the workbench. "Didn't expect to see either of you!"

Bill grinned. "Sorry to just show up..."

"Since when have you ever made an appointment?"

Bill chuckled, lifting his seasoned mug to drink. "Got me there. You've got the best coffee."

"The only coffee," Ian muttered, setting a basket of vegetables down on the kitchen counter before turning back to face them. "So, what brings you here?"

Lance leaned forward, his elbows resting on the workbench. "The WiFi was acting up. My dad had to go in and send a team up the Tower to fix something."

Ian's attention piqued. "Interesting."

Bill raised an eyebrow. "Your dad works for the Federation?"

"No," Lance replied, shaking his head. "He works for the company that maintains the network, Comm-Resources, Inc. I'm not exactly sure what he does, but he's some kind of manager." Ian exchanged a glance with Bill. He continued. "Every so often, there's a problem that cuts network flow or something like that. They call him in, or, well, he's summoned."

"Summoned?" Ian repeated, his brow furrowing.

"Yeah. Jacob just tells him. In his head." A heavy quiet settled over the room.

"That's pretty much how it works," Lance added, shifting uncomfortably in his seat. "Dad's Version 1 chip. Mom's Version 2."

Ian folded his arms. "Tell me about the differences you see?"

Lance let out a breath, his shoulders slumping slightly. "They're big." He hesitated before continuing. "My dad, he's… here. Like, I can talk to him. He still gets frustrated, still thinks for himself. But my mom?" His voice dropped, tinged with sadness. "I don't recognize her most days." He traced a finger along the edge of the workbench. "Dad gets frustrated with her too. It's like she's not the same person anymore."

Bill exhaled, breaking the silence. "Well, I think we've got something here. This verifies a big difference between Version 1 and 2… it's visible. In more ways than one."

Ian nodded slowly. "That's exactly what I was thinking." He turned to the kid. "This, right here? This is intel. You might think it's nothing, but to us, it's major." Lance straightened in his seat, his expression sharpening.

"What's even more important," Bill continued, "is that you just observe and report. No asking too many questions. No drawing attention to yourself." He locked eyes with the kid. "Stay in the background. Be invisible." Lance swallowed hard and nodded.

He leaned forward, resting his hands on the table. "Kid, just to get you in the loop, there's something we haven't mentioned."

His eyes darted between Ian and Bill. "Alright… what is it?"

Ian grinned. "You ever wonder where all the fresh vegetables and meat have been coming from?"

Lance shrugged. "Not really. Figured you were growing some. Didn't think much of it." He faltered, the words catching in his throat. "Why? What are you hiding?"

"It's not what I'm hiding. It's who."

Lance sat up straighter. His curiosity clearly piqued.

"I have a group of people living and working in the back of the property," he explained. "They've been here for a while now. They're the ones tending to the crops."

"Who? And why all the secrecy?"

Ian folded his arms. "They're unchipped. They were just passing through, but when we talked, I realized they were both in need and useful. It's been a win-win situation. There are four of them."

The kid frowned. "Okay… sounds like a good deal all around. But why don't I ever see or hear them?"

Ian hesitated, choosing his words carefully. "Because they're deaf." Lance blinked, momentarily stunned. "Only one, well, kind of two, can speak or read lips." He clarified.

"Alright… but again, why all the secrecy?" Lance asked.

Ian sighed. "At first, I wasn't sure about them. I wanted to make sure they were going to stick around, and then figure out where they fit in. No point introducing them to the Gathering until I knew what they could bring to the table." He glanced at Bill. "At this point, I've made my decision. Assuming you agree."

Bill blinked in surprise. "Those vagabonds have a fit now? Last I knew, they were just going to work the fields for a bit and catch a few fish for us."

Ian shook his head. "I kept things quiet on purpose. I wanted to be sure. But these are hardworking, intelligent people. And they've got a problem with the chipped, or at least Jacob."

Bill leaned back, arms crossed. "And?"

"And, they have skills none of us do. Skills we can't just pick up."

His expression shifted slightly. "Skills?"

Ian nodded. "They can read lips, from a long distance."

Bill frowned. "So?"

"And they can do it without anyone noticing."

This made Bill pause. "Well," he muttered. "that's not something I can do."

Ian grabbed a couple of long, colored ribbons from a shelf and handed them to Lance. "Put these out," he said firmly. "What for?" Lance asked. "We need to call a Gathering."

010001 // SEVENTEEN

THE STORM

The sky had been clear that morning, the kind of still, humid summer air that tricked people into believing the day would be calm. Then things turned violent. The wind picked up, bending trees and rattling loose shingles. A storm was blowing in. One of the storms the mid-west was famous for, the kind that could tear a building from its foundation.

Ian stood outside, scanning the horizon. The air was thick, electric. A pressure drop that felt like a weight pressing against your skull. "This is the kind of storm that produces funnel clouds," he thought. He quickly made his way to the back of the property. By the time he arrived, everything was already secured. The garden was cleared, tools packed away, tarps fastened tightly over storage bins. The Silent Ones had battened down everything with alacrity.

They sensed it long before he had. Their senses were more apt to detect these things, and they had felt, since late morning, things were going to deteriorate as the day passed. So, they cleaned up the garden and battened down everything. They were already holed up in their home, the old shed. However, calling it a shed no longer did it justice.

It had once been a rickety, half-rotted structure, barely fit for storing tools. Now, it was a functional, self-sustaining home. Three tiny bedrooms. A living and kitchen area. A newly built washroom and toilet addition on the back. They had scavenged solar panels, wiring them into the already working energy system, providing for the additional power they were using. They had built something permanent.

Ian approached the front door and stopped. He thought briefly about what the place had been and what it was now. He shook his head in amazement. He stepped up to the front door, then hesitated. Knocking was pointless. His eyes flicked to a small wooden sign near the handle.

"Pull here to alert occupants of arrival." Ian did as it said.

Almost instantly, the door opened, revealing the youngest of the group. Carrie opened the door with a smile. Ian had learned a little sign language from Tom and gestured "Hello." She stepped aside, motioning for him to enter. Inside, the other three were gathered in the living area, hands moving swiftly in deep, silent discussion.

Tom turned toward him, smiling. "Welcome."

Ian nodded.

"We were just talking about the storm." He said, tilting his head toward the rattling door.

Ian looked serious. "Yeah. That's why I came back here. Wanted to check on you all, but… I guess I didn't need to worry."

He smiled. "We knew this was coming since morning. The pressure dropped fast. We started preparing right away."

Ian let out a short laugh. "I didn't notice anything until the wind picked up." Tom's smile widened slightly, not smug, just knowing. Ian glanced around, taking in the calm efficiency of the space. The storm outside was growing wilder, but inside, they were steady, prepared.

"Is there something we can help with?" Tom asked.

"I was just concerned and wanted to check on everything." Ian stated. "And one other thing… I want to invite you, Tom, to our next meeting." He said, making sure Tom understood it was just he that was invited. He wasn't attempting to separate the group to try to influence, just trying to keep things to a dull roar when the others show up.

Thick, rolling clouds twisted above, their color shifting from gray to a sickly green. Ian glanced out the window attempting to time his departure. The rain started to fall. Tom hesitantly answered. "I will chat with the others and let you know after the storm. Would it be okay to come over to the garage when things clear up?"

"Sure." Ian stated.

He then placed his hand on the doorhandle and looked back at the group. He attempted to sign goodbye but likely signed something else as the group burst into laughter. Ducking, in the way that people do when attempting to avoid rain, he moved quickly back to the garage, not stopping to scan or survey the situation.

Within moments of his return to the garage and securing the doors, the winds roared to a thunderous volume. Rain bashing the sides of the building caused a deafening sound.

////////

The noise was like that of a large freight train. It was clear to Ian. A tornado. He ran to the garage bathroom and made himself small. His thoughts shifted to the Silent Ones. He hoped they would be okay and planned his moves for after the danger passed. Assuming he made it through this, he would immediately make his way to the back of the yard and attempt to help them.

Hail pelted the building in a fierce beating that sounded like the deafening applause of a massive concert from the Before. And then, as quick as it started, silence. He hesitated for a moment, then slowly opened the door to the bathroom. He peered out of a small crack, then fully opened the door. Everything was where he left it. No damage. No water. Everything was as it was when he was having his morning cup. The storm had passed, but its impact lingered.

He stood at the garage entrance, watching the dark funnel move toward Newtown. From this distance, he could see flashes of blue and white light, transformers exploding, sending arcs of electricity into the air. Boom. Boom. The sound carried even from miles away, like distant artillery fire.

Then, the largest flash yet. His stomach dropped. "The main substation," he thought. A deep, resonating BOOM! The ground shook beneath his feet. Newtown had just gone dark.

Ian didn't hesitate. He sprinted toward the back of the yard. The Silent Ones were already outside, watching the destruction unfold. They had dodged a bullet, and they knew it. The crops were mostly intact, aside from minor damage from the wind and hail. They would live to fight another day.

Tom turned as Ian approached. No words were needed. They all knew how close disaster had come. Ian yelled, "Everyone okay?"

Tom nodded. "We're fine. But the city…" He gestured toward the skyline, where black smoke curled into the air.

Ian followed his gaze. "Yeah. It took the worst of it," he said shaking his head in disbelief. They stood in silence for a moment, watching the distant chaos unfold. Then, from the garage he could hear a voice shout his name.

"Ian!"

Bill had burst through the garage door, breathless, soaked in sweat and rain. He bent over, hands on his waist, trying to catch his breath. He looked around the garage but didn't see anyone. Concern growing, he started to yell for him.

Ian ran into the garage shouting, "I'm fine. The guys out back are fine."

Bill let out a breath of relief. "Wow. That was close." He straightened, gesturing toward the city. "As soon as the storm passed, I booked it over here. It's a mess back there."

Ian frowned. "How bad?"

Bill wiped his forehead. "The funnel dropped to the ground about a half-mile back and tore a straight line through everything. Power's out across most of the city."

Ian's expression darkened. "We need intel. Now."

Bill nodded.

"We need to get a clear understanding on what's happening in the city. There hasn't been anything like this since the Before. We don't know what Jacob will do."

////////

Lance found out about the storm threat when his father told him. No warning had come through audible systems. Jacob broadcasted the alerts silently, directly into the minds of the chipped. Anyone unchipped, like Lance, was left in the dark. No warning sirens, no alerts on television or radio like in the Before. Worse, children and Annies weren't informed unless they were near a chipped individual. Jacob didn't see them as a priority.

His father had found him in their garage, where their car had sat untouched for years, a vestige of the time before AI. "We need to get to the basement," Mr. Thomas said, voice firm. Lance followed without question.

The storm passed by their neighborhood, missing them entirely. When they emerged, the house was untouched. But his mother was sitting in a chair, motionless. She didn't respond when his father spoke to her. She didn't even blink. "There must be an issue with the broadcast connection." His dad muttered. "I need to get a team to the tower."

"What do you think happened?" Lance asked.

His father rubbed his temples. "Could be comms, power… who knows." He tried to call for a POD transport. Nothing. "Crap," his father muttered. "The network's down."

Lance hesitated. Then an idea struck him. "Take my bike." His father glanced at him, then at the old bicycle leaning against the garage wall.

After a moment, he nodded. "They say you never forget how to ride one of these things." He swung a leg over it. "I'll give it a go." And with that, he pedaled toward the city, dodging fallen branches and scattered debris. Lance watched him disappear down the road, then grabbed his backpack and started for Ian's garage.

////////

He had intel, something he felt was particularly important to the Gathering. This time his usual route to Ian's garage was full of unusual scenes. He would normally see people and some, the Annies, would smile and greet him as he passed through the Old Market District. Today was different. He didn't see any chipped people. Only the Annies were out, cleaning up after the storm, chatting amongst themselves.

He passed through the market seeing little structural damage. Mostly overturned carts, loose debris, remnants of hail. Everyone was pleasant, a bit relieved for being away from the direct path of the storm. But something felt off. He didn't see a single chipped person.

His pace quickened. When he reached the garage, he was relieved to see it intact, and even more relieved to find Ian, Bill, and Mara inside. Bill spotted him first. "You okay, kid?"

"Yes, I'm good. My dad's okay too, but my mom is…" He hesitated. "Well, she's just sitting, like someone pressed pause."

Mara chimed in, "Yeah, I saw the same on the way over."

Bill let her words hang for a moment. "What do you mean?"

"Two people in stopped PODs, just frozen."

"Freaky." Bill said.

"Yeah," Mara nodded. "And the PODs were frozen too. No blinking signals, no alerts. Just stopped. Like they were in some kind of suspended animation."

"What's this all mean?" Asked Lance.

Everyone was silent. Ian hadn't spoken in several minutes, as he listened to the animated discussion going on between the three of them. He looked up and shook his head slowly. "It seems, people, we may have found an Achilles heel."

"What do you mean?"

Ian fixed him with a steady gaze. "The chipped have at least one vulnerability."

Lance shook his head. "But my dad was fine. In fact, he was more than fine, he seemed more normal than he has since they put that thing into him. He had more life in his eyes. I can't say the same for my mom."

Ian looked at him with concern "What did your dad say?"

"He was worried about the network being down, thought it could be a power issue, or something like that." Lance said. "He actually rode my bike into town to check on things."

"That's strange," Mara murmured "If he's chipped why is he okay?"

Bill said. "That's the difference between Version 1 and the rest, I guess. I did a little digging, asking around. Version 1s are autonomous, able to perform as they did prior, however they lose the superhuman powers associated with being chipped. They are just an Annie when the network goes down."

"But Version 2?" Ian asked.

Bill shook his head grimly. "They're completely dependent. If the system fails, so do they."

"This is a huge confirmation of what you and I had talked about. I think we know at least one thing that can help us free these people from the bondage of Jacob and the Board." Ian said.

"Yup," Bill started, "but what if the AI also recognizes the vulnerability."

Mara's expression changed. "There's no doubt Jacob figured this out. The question is, will the AI do something to alter the outcome of a future event?"

Ian looked puzzled. "Wait, what?"

"Yes, Jacob will look at the event and the results in their entirety, determine probabilities, analyze changes and predict outcomes of those changes. If anything is altered, we won't know until something happens again. And if it does, I can assure you it won't happen a third time." She said.

"Well then, how do we proceed with this intel, Captain?" Bill said, then realized Ian would be pissed he used that term again. "I mean, Boss."

Ian let the comment pass without a flinch. He looked at the crew and stated carefully, "We don't acknowledge it. We change nothing." His voice was steady. "Lance, say nothing to your father. Mara, walk past those frozen PODs like they don't exist. If we don't react, Jacob might dismiss it as a minor glitch."

A long silence. Then, slowly, they all nodded.

"Since everything's down for the moment, we need to gather later this afternoon. Mara, can you head to the Old City Market and let Tobias know? Then make your way back here." Ian let a moment pass. "I'll ask Tom to join as well."

Mara nodded. "Sure." She started to turn but then hesitated. "Wait, who's Tom?"

He cursed internally; he should've mentioned this earlier. "Oh. Yeah." He rubbed the back of his neck. "I meant to tell you about them."

Her expression darkened. "Them?"

Ian sighed. "I was going to bring it up at the next Gathering, but… now's as good a time as any."

Her gaze flicked to Bill and Lance. "Were you keeping this from us for a reason?" Her voice edged toward anger. "Tobias isn't gonna be happy about this. He already has reservations."

"Reservations?" Bill asked.

"Yes. We both do, but we're in for the same reason you are. At least that's what we thought." She stated sharply.

Ian cut in. "We weren't hiding anything. There are a few people living in the back of the yard. Tending to the garden, trapping and fishing. We all benefit."

"One person would've been bad enough," she pressed. "But a few? Just how many?"

Ian met her gaze. "Four." A cold, hard knot formed in her stomach. Before she could speak, he pushed forward. "Before you jump to conclusions, they're deaf. Two of them are deaf and mute. The other two, one can read lips and speak. The last one… not as much."

She crossed her arms. "They sound like a liability."

Ian's patience weakened. He kept his tone even. "They're not. In fact, one of them is probably the best intel gatherer we could ever have."

An icy stillness claimed her face. He pressed on. "He can read lips at long distances. No one would suspect him, especially Jacob. To the AI, they don't exist." That made her pause. He softened his voice. "Look, we can discuss all of this as a group. Nothing is set in stone. They're willing to stay in the shadows, just farming quietly. But I want a real conversation about it before anyone makes assumptions. We call them the Silent Ones."

Mara studied him carefully. Finally, she said. "Tobias is going to be pissed off. You know that, right? He may just decide to quit."

Ian nodded. "Maybe you can talk to him on your way over. I'll keep them in the back until we decide as a group. He hasn't seen anyone yet, and I haven't told him who's involved or what we're planning."

Mara rolled her shoulders. She finally looked less on edge. "…Okay," she said, nodding. "Thanks." She paused a moment, looked at the group quietly, pulled her hoodie strings and started out the door.

Bill said, "Hold up. Maybe you just get him and bring him back. I think this should come from Ian and me, not you."

Ian looked at Bill and the kid, then at her. "He's right. This is on me, not you."

"Okay. We'll be here later. It's on you…" Mara walked down the path, looking around as she moved.

"She's aware and pretty stealth." Bill stated.

"Yeah. If she can work on computers half as good as I think, we're in good hands." Ian stated confidently. "I worry about Tobias' reaction. We need an engineer, especially one as talented as him."

"You're right," said Bill, "a bit to unwind before we move forward."

010010 // EIGHTEEN

RESTORING CONTROL

Glenn Thomas pedaled through the battered streets of Newtown, his legs burning as he weaved around piles of debris. The city, once somewhat busy, now felt like a ghost town. The scene was unsettling.

People sat motionless in their PODs, eyes vacant, as if life itself had been put on pause. Their stillness was eerie, a stark contrast to the physical chaos around them. A few others were visible but motionless, most had obeyed the silent commands to take cover. Those caught in transit were trapped, frozen in vehicles that now served as cages.

As he neared the city center, the destruction increased. The streets were littered with debris: twisted metal, shattered glass, and the remnants of PODs that had been torn apart. Some lay crumpled, their occupants crushed inside. Others had been flung into the air by the funnel cloud, and crashed back to earth in mangled heaps.

Glenn forced himself to look straight ahead, his demeanor tense. He couldn't dwell on the bodies inside. In the distance, the substation loomed, its silhouette dark against the ashen sky. Black smoke curled upward like a warning. But something felt off. No fire crews. No emergency responders. Just silence.

Gritting his teeth, he pedaled harder, the weight of urgency pressing against his chest. When he arrived, he spotted Larry standing near the wreckage, his hands on his hips. "Where's Tad?" He called out as he skidded to a stop.

Larry turned looking perplexed. "What the hell are you riding, Glenn… I mean, Mr. Thomas?"

He waved him off, dismounting. "No need for formalities. We've got work to do." Larry grinned and nodded, shifting his focus.

"You assessed the damage yet?" Glenn asked as he scanned the area's devastation. "Are there any others who can help?"

Larry hesitated, his lips pursed. "You know how it is. Version 1's are rare. What, maybe fifty of us in the whole area?" Glenn muttered a curse under his breath.

"Most of the workforce is Version 2. And they are all… offline." Larry said grimly. "The rest of us? Doctors, a few engineers." He shrugged. "Not exactly an army."

Glenn straightened, his voice firm now. "Then we work with what we've got."

Larry looked around, glancing at the smoldering substation. "Love to, but… how do we contact them?"

Glenn froze mid-thought. "Shit." He hadn't thought of that. "Is anything working? Any comms?"

Larry shook his head. "Nope. Radios were tossed years ago in favor of neurochat."

Glenn swore again. The reliance on networked systems had left them vulnerable, and now it was coming back to haunt them. "Alright." he said, his tone resigned but determined. "Then we do this the old-fashioned way. Start walking. Find them. If you know where they live or what shops they hang around, go get them."

Larry nodded. "And after that?"

"Check for downed power lines. See if there's a way we can bypass the main substation." Glenn swung his leg to get on the bike, his movements brisk. "I'll be in my office."

Larry got lucky. The entire Version 1 crew was in the shop, taking shelter. Within minutes, he pulled Tad aside, and they quickly split the crew into two teams to assess the damage before heading to the substation. It didn't take long to find the first major issue.

A full city block had power lines down, dangerous live wires snaking across the pavement like venomous serpents. The crew worked swiftly, isolating the damaged section and disconnecting it from the grid. With the immediate danger handled, they pressed on toward the substation.

The scene at the substation was better than expected. Only one transformer smoldered, thin trails of smoke curling lazily into the air. The rest of the equipment had shut down in protective mode, sparing the substation and grid from further damage. Larry let out a slow breath. "Could've been worse."

Tad crouched by the wreckage, running a quick analysis with a handheld scanner. He nodded to himself. "Looks like all those booms we heard were from pole-mounted transformers blowing out." He gestured toward the largest wreckage. "But this?" He pointed to Transformer #2, a hulking mass of blackened metal. "This is the real problem. This one is toast."

Larry squatted beside him, studying the damage. "Can we bypass it?"

Tad cracked his knuckles, a faint smile on his face. "Already on it."

The team moved with efficiency, their hands steady despite the high stakes. Within hours, they rerouted the power grid, restoring electricity to most sections of the city. As the lights slowly flickered back on, Glenn allowed himself a brief moment of relief. But it didn't last long. This was only half the battle. The power was mostly back, but the network? That was a much bigger problem.

////////

The network team was small, just Larry, Tad, and an older engineer named Vic. Vic was tasked with staying on the power issues, while the other two went to the Tower. They weren't programmers. They didn't write code. They were hardware guys. They knew how to connect relays, signals, and distribution nodes. They could troubleshoot circuits and replace fried components. Jacob handled everything else; it was the brain of the network, the master orchestrator. And now, the only way to get it back online was to restore the network.

Larry and Tad stepped into the elevator of the Tower. The hum of the lift was reassuring, a sign that the power grid was holding steady, for now. The elevator ascended smoothly, a faint mechanical whir accompanying their silence. When the doors slid open on the top floor, Larry froze. Something was wrong.

The hallway was unnervingly quiet. No blinking indicator lights on the equipment racks. No steady hum of active systems. The usual ambient noise, the faint whir of cooling fans, the gentle buzz of electronics was gone.

He exchanged a glance with Tad, whose expression mirrored his unease. Neither spoke. Instinctively, they turned and moved to a nearby supply closet, pulling out the required protective gear: helmets, gloves, and insulated vests. Wordlessly, they headed for the roof access stairwell.

The door creaked as they pushed it open, the afternoon sunlight spilling onto the landing. Stepping onto the roof, they were greeted by an unexpected calm. The storm had passed, and the afternoon sun now hung low in the sky, casting a golden glow over the city below. The air was still, the kind of quiet that felt almost sacred.

No buzz of machinery. No chatter from the transmitters. Just silence. It wasn't the usual kind of silence that came with malfunctioning systems. This time, it was different, deafening, yes, but oddly beautiful.

Larry and Tad walked across the rooftop toward the main panel, their boots crunching softly against the gravel on the roof. The access doors to the panel weren't locked; no one bothered, given that rooftop access was already secured.

Larry swung the large gray doors open, revealing the guts of the system: transmission panels, programmable logic controllers, and rows of breakers. His eyes immediately went to the breakers. The main as well as every transmitter circuit was offline, their switches resting in the "tripped" position like a row of fallen dominoes. Larry let out a slow breath, his voice low. "Well… this is it."

Tad moved beside him, his eyes scanning the array of lifeless logic controllers. He quickly reset all the sub-circuits to make them ready for the main to be energized. Larry placed his hand on the main switch but hesitated. His fingers brushed the cool metal, but he didn't pull it yet.

"If you've got anything you don't want Jacob to know… say it now," he said, his tone half-joking but laced with something heavier.

Tad blinked, caught off guard. "What?"

He voiced the words softly, his gaze still fixed on the switch. "Because the second I flip this, we're back under his watch again."

For a moment, Tad looked startled. "I…" He hesitated, his words catching in his throat. "I hadn't even thought about that. In the building, it felt different. But now that you say it." He trailed off, his voice quieter.

Larry nodded slowly. "Yeah. We've been free for a few hours." Tad stared at the switch, his brow furrowed.

"…And we're about to give that up." A long, heavy pause hung in the air, the kind that stretched time. Finally, he spoke again, his voice almost a whisper. "Hold off."

Larry raised an eyebrow, surprised. "Why?"

He swallowed hard, his gaze still locked on the switch. "This is the first time I've realized, we control Jacob. Even if just for a moment."

Larry considered that, his hand still hovering near the breaker. "…Yeah," he admitted after a beat. "But let's keep that to ourselves." Another silence followed, thick with unspoken thoughts. Then, with a steadying breath, he reached forward and flipped the circuit.

For a moment, nothing happened. Then with a low hum, the transmitters surged to life. Lights blinked back on. Systems rebooted in a cascade of mechanical whirs and beeps. The air was no longer still; it was alive again, charged with energy. Jacob was back.

////////

Across the city, people started to stir. Heads lifted, eyes blinked back into focus, and the collective freeze was over. The streets, which had been eerily silent, came alive with a rush of noise and movement.

Fire engines roared to life, their sirens piercing the air as emergency crews resumed their duties. They sped toward the substation, unaware that the fire they'd been called to had already been extinguished. Downtown, alarms blared from shops and office buildings. The distant rumble of life slowly returned, filling the void that had stretched across the city.

From the rooftop, Larry and Tad stood in quiet observation. They could see the ripple effect moving outward. The city waking up. Tad spoke evenly, his voice flat. "...Everything's back to normal." Larry didn't respond right away. He watched the streets below, the chaos reforming into something resembling order. For the first time, he wasn't sure if "normal" was a good thing.

They secured the panel, closing the doors with a metallic clang, and headed back toward the elevator. They glanced at each other as they walked. "Well, I guess we're the heroes today," Larry said somberly.

"Yup," Tad replied, equally subdued. "Guess we get back to it then."

They boarded the elevator, the hum of its fan filling the silence between them. Larry hit the button for Glenn Thomas' floor, and they stood in uneasy quiet as the elevator descended. The doors slid open on the 10th floor, revealing the hallway leading to Glenn's office.

They stepped out, their boots noisy against the floor, and made their way to the office door. Inside, Glenn sat behind his desk, his expression distant as the slow-moving screensaver on his computer cast faint patterns of light onto his face. Larry knocked lightly on the doorframe.

Glenn jerked upright, startled. "Oh, sorry," he muttered, shaking his head as if clearing away a fog. "I was just finishing my report to Jacob." His gaze sharpened, his tone growing more focused. "He's… curious about what happened while his sensors were offline." Larry hesitated. Jacob had noticed. Of course, he had.

Glenn leaned forward, resting his arms on the desk. "So? What do you have to report?"

Larry forced himself to keep his tone casual, his hands tucked into his pockets. "Oh, well, we found the main breaker tripped and reset it. Ran a full systems check, no errors detected."

He was about to leave it at that, but Tad suddenly spoke up. "Yes," Tad added smoothly, "and we replaced a weak breaker, just as a precaution. Everything's good now."

Larry's stomach tightened. That wasn't true. No breakers had been replaced. And the likelihood of another failure was just as high as it had been before. For a split second, he turned to look at Tad, but Tad's expression remained perfectly neutral, his body language calm. Glenn didn't seem to catch the lie. He nodded, leaning back in his chair. "Good. I'll add that to my report." Then, to their surprise, Glenn's expression softened, and he offered them a rare smile. "Oh, and good work today. Couldn't have done it without you two."

Larry and Tad exchanged a brief glance. "Thanks," Larry said, forcing a nod he hoped looked more confident than he felt. As they left the office, the gravity of what had just happened lingered between them.

////////

They walked back to the elevator in heavy silence, the unspoken thoughts pressing down on them. The moment the elevator doors closed behind them, Larry didn't hesitate. He reached out and pressed the button for the top floor. Tad said nothing, just gave a slight nod.

When the elevator chimed and the doors slid open, the two men stepped out. They knew what needed to be done. Without a word, they grabbed helmets from the supply rack and climbed the narrow stairwell to the rooftop.

The sun was beginning to dip, painting the city in hues of amber and gold. The faint hum of the reactivated transmitters filled the air, a stark contrast to the sacred silence they'd experienced earlier. Larry turned to Tad, his voice low but sharp. "What the hell did you just do?" Tad didn't flinch. He stood still, his expression calm, waiting for Larry to continue. His frustration boiled over. "You just… I mean, we just lied to the boss." His words came fast, each one laced with disbelief.

Tad voice held steady, betraying no emotion. "I know."

Larry his eyes fixated, searching Tad's face for any sign of remorse. "Then what the hell was that about?" He glanced toward the transmitters, their blinking lights casting faint pulses of color across the rooftop.

He looked at Larry, his expression unreadable. "If we told the truth," He began, his voice even, "Jacob would've had major repairs done. Probably an entire system overhaul."

Larry's stomach tightened. He swallowed hard. "And if that happened?"

Tad met his gaze, his meaning unmistakable. "Then this backdoor wouldn't exist anymore." The words hung in the air like a thunderclap. Larry ran a hand down his face, the realization sinking in. They had just discovered a vulnerability in Jacob's seemingly perfect system. And they had made the deliberate choice to leave it intact. Silence stretched between them, heavy and charged.

His voice, when it came, was resolute. "This stays between us." Tad nodded, his expression unwavering. "I mean it," Larry pressed, a nervous tension gripping his face. "And don't even think about messing with it unless we're protected. If any chippy finds out…" He let the sentence trail off, the unspoken consequences all too clear. "Hell… if almost anyone finds out, we're toast."

Tad's voice was steady, but quieter this time. "This could come in handy someday." Larry let out a slow breath, his gaze shifting toward the skyline. For the first time since Jacob came online, they held something real. A weakness. A choice. A way out. And for now? They were keeping it to themselves.

010011 // NINETEEN

THE SHIFT

From the farthest extent of the gravel drive, the activity in the garage was impossible to miss. The sun had just dipped below the horizon, painting the sky in deep purples and burnt orange. After everything that had happened, the day felt as though it had lasted far longer than it should have.

Tobias and Mara approached; the sound of conversation spilling out into the night air. His expression tightened as he took in the scene. "This is the farthest thing from stealth I've seen since the Before," he muttered loudly as they reached the main door. But the moment they stepped inside, Tobias stopped short.

The garage was alive with movement. People sat in clusters, talking in hushed but animated tones. Others shifted in their seats, the energy in the room almost palpable. It was as though the group had been waiting for something, or someone, to arrive.

Mara lingered near the entrance, pulling her hood tighter around her face. She scanned the room quickly, then quietly slipped toward an empty chair on the far side, keeping her distance. Tobias, however, made no effort to hide his displeasure. His voice cut through the murmur of conversation. "I thought these Gatherings were supposed to be, well, secret."

Ian, seated at the center of the group, looked up calmly. "Come in, Tobias. Make yourself at home."Tobias crossed his arms, his stance rigid.

Bill, always the peacemaker, offered a half-smile. "Looks like the gang's all here."

Ian nodded, his gaze steady. "You're right, Tobias. We let our OPSEC slip. That's on me. We need to make sure it doesn't happen again." Around the room, heads nodded in agreement, the atmosphere growing more serious.

Ian's tone shifted. It was sharper now, more deliberate. "Speaking of OPSEC," he said, leaning forward, "there's something not everyone here is aware of." A ripple of unease passed through the group. Tobias's shoulders tensed. Mara stared at the floor as though willing herself to disappear.

Ian pressed on. "We have, or rather, I have, a few deaf workers living in the back of the yard." Tobias's jaw tightened. "They tend the garden." He continued. "They trap, fish, grow food. Everything we eat when we meet here, they help provide it."

Tobias's gaze bored into him, unblinking. Ian didn't flinch. "They're good people," he went on. "They lost friends to AI experiments early on. I offered them work. They've kept to themselves." He took a breath; his next words deliberate. "But now, one of them wants in." Mara shifted uncomfortably in her chair, her fingers tightening on her hood strings. He didn't stop. "He's the one who's best at reading lips. And… he saw someone talking as they left last time." Tobias's eyes darkened further. "He approached me and said he wants to help." Ian finished.

A quiet settled over the room, thick with tension. Tobias was the first to break it. "Would've been nice to know this before I walked over here." His voice was tight with irritation. "At least then, I could've made a choice."

"You're right. I own that." Ian's tone was steady but firm. "I wasn't trying to hide them, but I was trying to keep them out of this. That ship has sailed. Now, we need to make a decision."

Tobias's gaze sharpened, his voice edged with distrust. "Is there anything else you're hiding?"

"No, and I'm sorry to drop this on you."

Bill clapped his hands together. "Alright people, let's cut to it. Up or down vote."

Ian held up a hand. "Not yet." Bill raised an eyebrow but stayed quiet. Ian gestured toward the group. "We need to look at the full picture. What do they add? What can they contribute?"

The kid, always eager, leaned forward. "Well… they get us food."

Bill smirked. "He's thinking operationally, kid. Not just dinner."

Lance frowned, puzzled. "Well… they're quiet." Bill chuckled. "That's something."

Ian's voice was calm but commanding. "Think bigger." He let the words hang for a moment, the weight of them settling over the room. "They can read lips. They can gather intel without being noticed." The room stilled. "To the AI, they don't exist. They are disregarded as useless noise in the system."

Tobias's expression twisted slightly before he gave a slow, knowing smile. "This isn't news to everyone, is it?" His tone was cool, accusatory. "I'm the last to know." Mara tensed visibly.

Ian met Tobias's gaze head-on, his tone unwavering. "Not everyone learned until a few hours ago. After the storm." Tobias stayed silent, his arms crossed tightly over his chest. He continued. "We don't have phones. No conference calls. It happened, and people found out when they got here. And yes, you are the last to know."

Tobias sat back, his posture rigid. It was clear, he didn't like surprises. His entire personal philosophy was built on predictability: no surprises, just solutions. And right now? This felt like a problem. "So," he said flatly, "we have a problem and no solution."

"No," Ian shot back. "We have a vote." Tobias remained still, holding his response in check. Ian pressed on. "If we vote yes, we get a new addition to the Gathering. If we vote no, they stay out."

Bill leaned back in his chair. His posture was relaxed, but there was a pointed edge to his tone. "Well, I know where I stand."

Ian raised a hand again, signaling for quiet. "We're not voting yet." He said firmly. "If there are concerns, bring them forward. Now."

Tobias exhaled sharply, his irritation unmistakable. "Well," he said finally, "it looks like the decisions already been made, whether you admit it or not." Ian didn't flinch. Tobias shook his head. "I have my concerns. I haven't even met the guy. How am I supposed to judge his character when I don't even know his name?"

"You're right." He stood abruptly. "Let's take a short break. Grab something to eat. I'll go get Tom." Tobias didn't respond, his expression unreadable. Around the room, people stood and stretched, the tension easing slightly.

Lance, as always, was the one to break the tension. "Things were crazy earlier," he said. Tobias looked over, shifting gears.

"Yeah. The Market got hit pretty bad." Mara sat quietly, sipping coffee.

Bill glanced over. "How'd the Library do?"

She shrugged. "Lost main power, but I've got backup. Nothing major."

Just then, the door opened. Ian stepped inside, and behind him, Tom. The room quieted. Ian gestured toward him. "This," he said, "is Tom." He turned to Tom. "Tell us about yourself. We're all ears."

////////

Tom stood before the group, his stance steady though his hands were clasped tightly together. The faint hum of the garage's overhead lights seemed louder in the silence. Every pair of eyes in the room was locked on him. They weren't just looking, they were listening. He took a deep breath and began.

He spoke of the Before. Of the modest home for the hearing impaired where he and the others had lived as the world began to crumble. He painted a vivid picture of those early days when the AI takeover was nothing more than whispers in the news, vague policy changes, and uneasy debates. Back then, they had believed, hoped, that someone, somewhere, would step in and stop it. But no one did. Then came the losses.

Tom's voice remained steady as he recounted the people who had disappeared. They had been told the chip would allow them to better communicate, "be normal." Many were taken away for, what he later learned, were experiments using the AI. Friends. Teachers. Neighbors. The realization that no one was coming to help had come slowly, suffocatingly, until it could no longer be ignored.

The air in the garage grew heavier as he told of their escape. The long nights spent hiding, the gnawing hunger, the isolation that crept in like a shadow. He described moments when survival felt impossible, when hope was a fragile thread stretched too thin. Then, finally, he spoke of the day everything changed. The meeting in front of the garage. The cautious introductions. The offer of work and safety.

He conveyed their gratitude toward Ian, who had given them a chance when no one else had. And he expressed their rage. Their rage against the AI that had stolen so much from them, and against the people who had enabled it.

Tom's voice never wavered, but the weight of his words enveloped the group like a thick, suffocating fog. By the time he finished, nearly half an hour had passed. He sighed, his shoulders relaxing slightly, and looked up at the group. His dark eyes scanned their faces, searching for any sign of judgment or acceptance.

"If you'll allow me in," he said, his voice firm but without desperation, "I will be an asset. If not… we never met." The hush that followed was profound. Then, he turned to Ian. "Anything else you want to know?"

Ian shook his head slowly. "No. Thanks for your honesty." His tone was warm, genuine. "We appreciate what you and the others are doing. And one way or another, we'll support each other."

Tom turned to the rest of the group. "Any questions?" No one spoke. They were still processing. The stories of hunger, of hopelessness, of survival. The sheer weight of what Tom and his group had endured hung in the air, unspoken but felt by all.

Ian let the silence linger for a moment longer before turning back to Tom. "Any questions for him?" When no one responded, Ian gave a small nod. "Go ahead and head home for the night, Tom. We'll talk more tomorrow." Tom returned the nod and turned to leave, his footsteps soft against the concrete floor.

"Wait." Tobias's voice broke the silence like a crack of thunder. Tom stopped as Lance grabbed his arm. He turned to see what was happening. Tobias studied him for a long moment, his sharp gaze searching his face. The tension in the room seemed to tighten as everyone waited. Then, Tobias gave a small nod, his voice steady. "He's good by me."

Tom stood emotionless. Ian's expression softened. "Anyone else?"

Bill, always quick to lighten the mood, flashed a thumbs up. Lance followed suit, then Mara, her nod subtle but deliberate. "Well," Ian said, a small smile forming at the corners of his mouth. "I guess the jury has spoken. I'll read you in tomorrow."

He looked around the room for a moment then turned back to Tom. "Welcome aboard." For the first time that evening, Tom allowed himself a faint smile.

////////

The evening had only just begun in the Boardroom. Members, those rare billionaires who had become chipped early when the AI revolution was still just for the rich, filed in with hushed urgency. Each had received the same message: *Emergency Assembly. Attendance Mandatory.*

The room was a shrine to excess, a space designed to remind its occupants of their power and legacy. The mahogany table, a flawless single slab cut from an ancient tree, gleamed under ambient lighting. Custom-designed chairs, crafted to fit their occupant's exact specifications, lined the table. Each was a symbol of exclusivity: never sold, never seen by the public.

The walls were paneled in rich walnut, with screens that pulsed faintly, looking as though they were beneath the surface, but alive. Overhead, the ceiling began to retract, revealing a crystal-clear view of the darkening sky. Twilight bathed the room in hues of deep indigo, a stark contrast to the developing tension inside. It was a place built not just to conduct business, but to remind those seated here that they had shaped the world, and they held the power.

But tonight, they were not in control. The board members entered quietly, their voices low, exchanging muted opinions more out of habit than conviction. In truth, their thoughts no longer mattered. The Board was now a mere façade, as the Chairman made all the decisions.

Jacob arrived. Not as a voice in the neural stream. Not as a presence in their minds. But as a physical being. It entered the room boldly, with a towering frame casting sharp, angular shadows across the walls. Standing taller than any of them by half a foot, his alloy limbs moving with a terrifying elegance. His form was humanoid, but unmistakably inhuman. It's optic sensors glowed faintly, scanning the room with eerie precision. The moment it stepped inside, the air shifted. The Board stood instinctively, as though an emperor had entered.

Jacob moved without hesitation, his head turning smoothly from side to side, analyzing each face. When he reached the head of the table, he did not sit. Instead, he shoved the Chairman's chair aside with such force that it smashed against the wall, embedding its leg deep into the walnut paneling. The noise was deafening.

The Board flinched as one; their awe quickly turning to fear. Jacob's voice came, sharp and jagged, cutting through the air like static laced with command. "What happened, and why?"

No one moved. The First Generation, who still retained their mental privacy unless they chose to broadcast, remained silent. Each one sat frozen, unwilling to activate their neural channels. All except one. Fred Johnson, Jacob's organic cousin, sat down slowly in the chair to Jacob's right and began to laugh. The sound was jarring, unnatural in the tense atmosphere.

"Come on, Jacob," Fred said, his voice uneven. "We're all friends here. Hell, I've known you since..." He hesitated, catching himself. The realization hit like a freight train. This wasn't his cousin anymore. "I mean... uh..." Jacob turned toward him.

Without warning, Jacob shifted his stance. It happened faster than anyone could process. Jacob's arm sailed swiftly, a metallic blur. A wet, sickening sound. Fred's head was gone. It launched into the air, arcing upward through the open ceiling into the night sky, vanishing into the twilight. For a moment, Fred's body remained seated, as though nothing had happened. Then, it slumped forward, a dark, wet pool spreading across the polished mahogany table.

The room erupted into chaos. Several board members stood and then staggered back, their chairs screeching against the floor. One collapsed to his knees, clutching his chest. Another doubled over, vomiting onto the pristine floor. A man standing three chairs down began to inch away, sliding behind others toward the wall.

"Stop!"

Jacob's voice froze him mid-movement. The room fell silent but for the sounds of heavy breathing and faint cries. Jacob straightened, his optic sensors glowing brighter, casting faint red halos across the table. "Let this serve as a warning," he said, his tone measured but laced with menace. "Do not challenge me. Do not disrespect me. Do exactly as I command."

He paused, then said in a voice as calm as it was chilling. "Sit."

The remaining board members obeyed instantly, their movements jerky and mechanical, as though their limbs might betray them if they hesitated. The mood in the room had shifted irrevocably. This was no longer a standard Board of Directors. They were now being ruled by terror.

"Now then." he said, his tone soft again, eerily so. "What happened, and why?"

A cacophony erupted. Voices overlapped in a frantic attempt to explain. Excuses blurred together in a desperate chorus of panic. Finally, one voice rose above the rest.

"Sir, there was a tornado. It took out power and communications across the region."

Jacob's optic sensors flared, their glow intensifying. "I am aware of the storm," he said, his voice cold and deliberate. "It also took me offline." He leaned forward slightly, his alloy fingers tapping against the polished table. "That. Cannot. Happen."

The statement hung in the air like a death sentence. No one dared to speak. Jacob scanned the room slowly, his gaze lingering on each face as though measuring their worth.

"Do we have an understanding?"

The board answered in near unison, their voices trembling: "Yes, sir!"

Jacob straightened. "Good. Now, I expect you to find out how this happened, and fix it. Immediately." He turned, his heavy footfalls echoing ominously as he walked to the floor-to-ceiling window. He stood, gazing out at the darkened skyline, his silhouette stark against the glass. "If it happens again," he said, his voice quieter but no less menacing, "I will hold each of you responsible."

He didn't turn back to face them.

"Dismissed."

No one moved. Jacob's head tilted slightly, his tone sharper. "Now!"

Chairs scraped against the floor as the board scrambled to leave. Footsteps shuffled in panicked urgency as they fled the room, their breaths shallow and their faces pale. When the last of them had gone, Jacob scanned the room noting the mess, and summoned a cleaning crew to remove Fred's remains, as he returned to his Penthouse.

Only the chair from the head of the table remained, splintered and embedded in the wall. A brutal monument to what the board had become: obsolete.

010100 // TWENTY

INNOCENT MAN

The Gathering had grown. What began as a tight-knit crew of resistance thinkers, was now edging closer toward a squad, all simply searching for safety, and freedom. Ian wasn't sure when the shift had happened. He only knew that the garage felt more crowded every time he walked in. And with that came uncertainty.

The record spun slowly on the old turntable, its rotation, a perfect 33.333 RPM, steady, grounding. Ian sat alone on a worn-out chair, elbows resting on his knees, head bowed. He wasn't just listening to the music but to the faint crackles of the vinyl. The imperfections that made the sound human, organic.

Billy Joel's voice drifted through the room:

Some people see through the eyes of the old,
Before they ever get a look at the young...

Ian leaned back, letting the music wash over him, his eyes closed.

I'm only willing to hear you cry,
Because I am an innocent man...

The words hung in the air like a fog that refused to lift.

Innocent? No. Ian knew better. He was far from it. His mind drifted. Too many people, too many moving parts. And with every new face came a new risk. A new variable Jacob couldn't yet see, but might learn to. Loose lips sink ships.

The phrase circled in his mind like a vulture. It had been his grandfather's mantra, spoken in the gravelly voice of a man hardened by wartime secrets. His father had echoed it, weaving caution into every lesson. Now, it wasn't just a memory, it was a warning, alive and loud in Ian's head.

"How did it come to this?" he whispered to no one.

He opened his eyes and stared at the dimly lit garage. "Is this a small group with a large operation... or a small operation with a large group?" He wasn't sure anymore. He rubbed his hands over his face, feeling the rough stubble scrape against his palms. The sound from the record player almost drowned out his own whisper:

"God help me. Please don't let me lose anyone this time."

Another mission was brewing. Potentially a life-or-death assignment with barely trained civilians. And this time, there was a young woman on the team. A kid, really, as well as a teenager. This was insane. He wasn't leading a platoon anymore. This wasn't the Army. There was no chain of command, no extraction team waiting in a Blackhawk, no medics or air support. Just a ragtag resistance and the growing burden of inevitability. They're not soldiers, he thought bitterly. Hell, only Bill and I have seen real fieldwork. And even then… He exhaled slowly.

Bill was a Seabee, a combat engineer. A damn good one. But even he wasn't invincible. The responsibility clawed at Ian, sharper this time. The first time around, he'd volunteered. He knew the risks. He'd signed the papers, donned the uniform, carried the weight with pride. But these people? They didn't really understand the risks. They'd been swept up, dragged into a current too strong to resist. And now they were here, in his garage, under his care, following his orders.

He hadn't recruited them. They'd just… shown up. Divine providence, he thought. It was the only explanation he could cling to. They came in ones and twos, some broken, others burning with quiet anger. And now, they were ready to move against something they couldn't even fully understand.

“It’s not in my hands who arrives,” Ian thought, “but it is in my hands whether they succeed. I must lead them to success.” This was how he made peace with himself. He didn’t choose them. But he had to protect them.

The record played on, its needle tracing the grooves with unerring precision:

I am an innocent man…

But Ian knew better. He’d made decisions, some good, some terrible. He’d watched people die. And now, he was about to ask a group of untrained civilians to do what trained professionals might hesitate to attempt.

He opened his eyes and stared at the ceiling. The room was still. Just him, the music, and the pressure. Then, the door creaked. Bill stepped into the garage, a thermos in one hand, his old tool belt slung over his shoulder. “Thought I’d find you in here.” He said.

Ian looked up. “Wasn’t hiding. What’s with the props?”

“Thought I would try to look like I was going to a job site. Something normal.” Bill said matter-of-factly. He moved over to the freshly brewed coffee and poured some into his thermos, and his seasoned mug. “Storm blew more than just trees down,” he said quietly. “Things feel… different now.”

Ian nodded slowly. “They are.”

Bill took a seat across from him. “They’re looking to you, you know.” Bill added. “Even the new ones.”

“I didn’t really want that.” He replied, his tone edged with weariness.

“Doesn’t matter. You’ve got it.” Bill stated matter of fact.

Ian sighed heavily. “They’re not ready.”

Bill smirked faintly, his eyes narrowing with a hint of mischief. “I get it, but back in the day, neither were we.”

That got his attention. He turned to look at Bill for the first time. “I was hoping you’d say that.”

They sat in silence for a long moment, the music still spinning, the needle tracing the grooves of a song that suddenly felt like a lie.

////////

The basement was quiet except for the faint noise of monitors and the occasional flick of paper as Tobias adjusted blueprints. Mara sat at her workstation; eyes fixed on a row of screens. Data scrolled endlessly. Numbers, letters, bursts of code, a digital stream that would look meaningless to almost anyone else. But not to her.

Somewhere in the river of fragmented sequences, a pattern was waiting, a forgotten access point, a buried subroutine, a crack in Jacob's system. She leaned closer, eyes scanning with mechanical precision. This was her world: the quiet hunt.

Not far away, Tobias sat on a metal stool beneath a harsh task light. The lamp threw a sharp cone of illumination over the aged blueprint he'd recovered from the city archives, found in a vault just a floor below Mara's lair.

The paper was old, brittle at the corners, but the lines were still legible: a map of the city's power grid. He wasn't looking for the obvious. Jacob would've already reinforced the most glaring faults, main junctions, critical substations, high-traffic nodes. The AI would have calculated those risks long ago.

No, he was hunting for something more subtle. Overbuilt zones. Areas where development had outpaced infrastructure; where budget cuts or greed had left the grid stretched thin. The kind of vulnerability that wasn't flashy enough to warrant immediate repair. Just enough weakness to exploit. He made a note in the margin, circling a block near the industrial district.

Then,

"There!" She screeched, startling him.

He nearly dropped his pencil. "Damn it, Mara!" She was grinning.

"Look!" she said, pointing at the screen, her eyes wide. "There it is, I think at least."

He stood and stepped over, rubbing his neck. "What is it?"

"A vulnerability," she said, still smiling. He leaned in, scanning the screen.

"It's a small application, mostly dormant. Looks like it used to be some kind of pet tracking system. You know, the type you'd put on your dog or cat… a transmitter in case they wandered off. The system would log their location in the cloud so you could find them."

He blinked. "That's… weirdly specific."

She nodded. "Exactly. It's obsolete. No one's used it in years, but it's still active in the system."

"A forgotten cloud node," Tobias said, beginning to understand.

"Right. A door that was never locked, just left open when everything else got sealed up tight." She tapped the screen. "It's small, low bandwidth, low visibility… but it's connected."

He crossed his arms, brow furrowed. "How do we exploit this? What can we do with it?"

"It's a backdoor," she said, eyes alight. "We can use it as a shell; inject code, mask our signals. It's not a freeway, but it's a tunnel. Quiet. Secure. Unwatched."

Tobias gave a slow, approving nod. "You're sure?"

"No," she said, "but it's the best lead I've found." He looked back at the power grid plans, then at the glowing screen. "Then let's see where it goes."

////////

Lance had taken the long way home. He'd spent the afternoon weaving through the town's side streets, observing. Not just the damage left by the storm, but the way people were already moving on. Debris was mostly cleared, windows being repaired. The sound of everyday life was creeping back in, as if the tornado had never happened.

But something still felt... off. Across the street, he spotted her. Liz. She was about his age, sharp-minded and always eager to talk about the future. The last time they spoke, she had been excited about her upcoming majority and her appointment to be chipped. She stood outside her house, arms folded, staring at the sidewalk.

Lance crossed the street. "Hey, Liz," he called with a smile.

She looked up, startled at first, then smiled softly. "Oh, hey Lance. I didn't see you coming." He stopped a few feet away, hands in his pockets.

"You guys okay… with the storm and all?"

"Yeah. Thanks for asking." she replied, brushing her hair behind one ear. "It was intense, though."

"You see it? The tornado?" he asked, eyes wide. "It was massive."

She shook her head. "No. Not really. My parents both turned to me, like at the same exact time, and said, 'Go to the basement. Now.'" She paused. "Then they just… sat down. Like, completely unresponsive. I was yelling for them to come with me, but they wouldn't move. It was like they were… frozen."

His smile faded. "Yeah," he said quietly. "Same thing happened with my mom."

Liz looked at him, a skeptical glint in her eyes. "You think it was… something with the network?"

He shrugged. "Probably. A hiccup or a blackout in the neural stream. Something glitched."

"That's messed up," she said, her voice suddenly sharp. "They could've died. Just sitting there like that."

"I know," he said. "It scared me too."

She looked down at the pavement. "I was actually looking forward to it," she said, voice softer now. "I was excited to get chipped. I thought it meant... freedom or something. But now I'm afraid. I haven't told my parents. They'd be disappointed."

He took a breath. "You still have a choice. Once you hit majority, it's your decision. Not theirs." She looked up at him, surprised.

"I mean it," he added. "Don't let anyone… anyone, make that choice for you." They stood in silence for a moment as the wind rustled the trees behind them.

Then she nodded. "Thanks."

////////

Ian looked over at Bill, his eyes tired but focused. "Well… whatever. Things are what they are." He stated. "We have work to do, whether we like it or not."

"I agree, Boss." Bill said, more alert now that the coffee had kicked in. He took another sip and set his stained, unwashed cup down with a thud.

"Mara and Tobias are both working angles." Ian continued. "Mara's digging through the code looking for digital backdoors. Tobias is studying the grid. Power vulnerabilities. Infrastructure blind spots. Anything the AI might've overlooked."

Bill nodded. "Smart pair, those two." There was a pause.

"What about the kid?" He asked quietly.

Ian glanced down, then back up. "He's got a hard task. Observation only. No engagement. No questions. He's to blend in, stay quiet, and report back. If he opens his mouth at the wrong time or to the wrong person..." He shook his head. "It could cost us everything."

Bill chuckled under his breath. "My old man used to say that all the time, 'Kids are to be seen and not heard.' Thought he was joking back then."

Ian didn't smile. "Here it's not a joke. It's life or death." The tone settled heavy between them.

"Sit." He said, motioning to the chair across from him. "We need to talk strategy."

Bill dropped into the seat, arms resting on his knees. "Alright. Let's do it."

"We've got feelers out. Mara and Tobias are shrewd, and they'll find something. But intelligence is only the first piece. Once we think we've found a weakness, we'll need a plan, a real one."

Bill squinted slightly. "Didn't Iron Mike say something like, 'Everyone's got a plan until they get punched in the face'?"

Ian allowed himself a faint smile. "Yeah. And he wasn't wrong. But I think he was riffing on an older military saying. No plan survives first contact with the enemy." He leaned back in his chair. "History proves that. Over and over again. But history also teaches us how people adapt. How they win, or lose, based on their ability to respond in the moment."

Bill nodded, listening closely now.

"I studied both sides of past battles, strategy, mistakes, improvisations," Ian continued. "In college, then again in officer training. I didn't get the full war college experience like the career officers, but I went through leadership school. It was enough to prepare me for the field."

He paused, tapping his fingers against the armrest. "We studied the classics: Thermopylae, Gettysburg, Normandy. Not just tactics, but how command decisions were made under pressure. I learned from both the victories and the disasters." His voice dipped slightly. "And I've seen what happens when good plans fall apart in real time."

Bill studied his face. "You okay, Boss?"

He didn't answer right away. "I'm fine," he said eventually, though his voice carried weight. "What matters now is taking what I've learned and applying it here. Because this isn't just another op. It's not about gaining ground, its survival." Bill leaned forward, his demeanor shifting from casual to serious.

"Okay, Boss. I'm all ears."

Ian nodded once. "Good. Because we're going to war, and we'll need more than just hope and duct tape to win it."

010101 // TWENTY-ONE

IT'S ON

Lance took the long way to the Yard. In his head, the chorus from the Billie Eilish song "*No Time to Die*" looped like a private soundtrack, ridiculous and out of place, but oddly comforting. It kept his nerves in check. The absurdity of it all felt like a small rebellion against the tension coiling in his chest.

He moved casually, hands buried deep in the pockets of his worn jacket, eyes lazily drifting from storefronts to street vendors to the light stream of passersby. "Look unremarkable. Look bored. Look forgettable," he reminded himself.

Ahead, the Old City Market sprawled out like a labyrinth of narrow lanes and open-air stalls. A few fruit carts lined the streets, their bright colors a sharp contrast to the faded hues of secondhand goods displayed under sun-bleached awnings. Handmade jewelry glinted in the windows of a small shop, catching stray beams of sunlight, while a mix of weathered and less worn shoes sat in uneven rows on a table out front.

The air buzzed with the sound of conversation, a chaotic symphony of bartering voices, occasional laughter, and the sharp staccato of someone shouting over the noise. It was normal. Distractingly normal.

Lance paused at a book vendor, flipping absently through a stack of cracked-spine paperbacks. The scent of old ink and musty paper wafted up. After a moment, he wandered into the neighboring bookstore. Inside, the scent was even stronger, dust mingled with the faint tang of aged leather bindings. The air felt comforting, quieter. Lance meandered through the aisles, his eyes skimming titles without reading. "No pattern. No rhythm. Just drift," he thought.

After a while, he stepped back into the sunlight, crossed the street, and pushed open the door to Tobias's shop. The bell above the door gave a sharp, metallic '*tink*.' Inside, the noise of the market faded, replaced by the soft hum of fans and the steady drone of fluorescent lights. The shop was cramped but meticulously organized, a sanctuary of obsolete tech.

Stacks of old radios were stacked neatly next to dusty monitors and yellowed keyboards. Shelves lined with resistors, capacitors, diodes, and spools of wire were neatly labeled and arranged. It was like stepping into a temple of circuitry, a post-apocalyptic version of Radio Shack. Lance moved slowly, pretending to browse, his fingers brushing the edges of a worn box of cables.

"Can I help you?" Tobias's voice came from behind the counter, flat… too flat. Lance caught the shift immediately. Tobias's usual edge was gone, replaced by something guarded. Indifferent.

Then Lance noticed them: two customers near the back of the shop. One was fiddling with an old speaker, his hands moving unnaturally slow, as if he wasn't entirely sure what he was doing. The other flipped through a tray of cables, his gaze darting toward Tobias every few seconds. His face remained smooth, his movements controlled, but Lance could see the tension in his face, the subtle stiffness in his posture.

"No, just looking around," he said casually, pointing to a boxy device on a nearby shelf. "What's this thing?" Tobias stepped closer, glancing briefly at the device. "That's a shortwave radio," he replied, his voice steady. "They call it a no-wave radio now. Useless, really. Makes a decent paperweight, though."

"No waves?" Lance asked, tilting his head just enough to feign curiosity.

Tobias shrugged. "Not short, not long. No one's sending much of anything these days, at least not on those frequencies."

"Interesting," Lance said, scratching the back of his neck. "I don't know much about radios. Just what I've read on my tablet. That's really old stuff, right?"

"Yeah," Tobias said with a faint chuckle. "Right from the old days." A beat of silence, then Tobias leaned forward slightly, his hands resting on the counter.

"Well, thanks," Lance said, forcing a smile. "Maybe I'll see you again sometime."

"That would be nice," Tobias replied, his voice dropping just slightly. The words carried weight. "Maybe next time, bring something to trade... something useful."

The statement sounded casual on the surface, but Lance caught the signal. It wasn't just idle chatter. He gave a small, almost imperceptible nod. Message received. Turning toward the door, he reached for the handle. As he opened it, Tobias gave him a quick wink, barely noticeable, but enough. The bell above the door gave one final '*tink*' as he stepped back into the bustling street.

The door behind him suddenly sprang open again, almost knocking him over. Out of the door ran the two people from inside the store, one carrying a spool of wire. Lance stuck his foot out, just enough to cause the man with the wire to trip.

The spool flung from his grip as he landed forcefully in a full-face plant. Lance reached down and picked up the wire as the first guy looked back, stunned for a moment, then continued to run away from the scene.

Tobias walked out and took the wire from Lance. "Thanks, kid," he said with a small smile.

Looking at the now bloodied man starting to get up from his embarrassing acrobatic display, he yelled with contempt, "And you, thief. Get the hell out of here and never show your face again. Next time will be a hell of a lot worse than a trip."

Lance smiled with pride. He started to move again, the market enveloping him once more, its noise and chaos a perfect camouflage. He resumed his casual drift, ducking into shops at random, lingering without reason, just another bored teenager wasting an afternoon.

But in his head, the music played on:

Fool me once, fool me twice,
Are you death or paradise?

////////

Outside the Market area, something was wrong. Drones. They hovered above the rooftops on the outer edges in a slow, deliberate pattern, sleek, black silhouettes slicing through the pale, cloudless sky.

Before the storm, they never ventured this far. Their patrols were confined to the orderly streets of Newtown and its manicured suburbs, Jacob's domain. A perfect, sterile utopia, where the chipped resided. The Annies didn't matter. Unchipped. Unregistered. Unwanted. To Jacob, they were little more than organic waste, barely worth a subroutine. But now, the drones were here.

Lance sat at a small table outside a food vendor's stall, chewing slowly on a Before burger. Real beef, flame-grilled and juicy, topped with onions that stung his eyes. A rarity. A treasure. Beside him, fresh-cut fries crackled with residual oil, golden and crisp.

Newtown didn't have anything like this. There, it was all engineered protein, sterile, lab-grown. Bug patties. Nutrient cubes. Efficiency masquerading as food. But here, in the Market, food still had flavor. Don't have something to trade for a bite? Grab an apron, provide a couple hours of labor and the gruff old man behind the griddle would grunt, nod, and hand over a meal that tasted like freedom. Lance took another bite, chewing slowly, though his focus wasn't on the burger anymore. His eyes were on the sky. Three drones.

They moved in a slow, purposeful arc, their glossy surfaces catching and refracting the midday light. This wasn't a random scan. This wasn't a routine patrol. Lance's chest tightened as he followed their path.

The drones were drifting closer to the buildings just beyond the far edge of the Market, narrow alleyways and crumbling brick facades. They were hovering over an area that backed up near the old Library.

"Mara," he thought. "Was she compromised? Had they found something? Or someone?" He didn't move immediately. He forced himself to stay grounded, to stay in character.

Casually, he sipped from his tin cup, letting the bitter taste of cheap coffee settle on his tongue.

Then, with deliberate ease, he reached into his shirt pocket and pulled out an old pair of Ray-Ban sunglasses. The act was proficient, almost lazy. He slid them on, adjusting them slowly, using the motion to conceal a shift in his gaze. He wasn't looking at the drones anymore. Well, not directly.

He finished his meal, wiped his hands on a napkin, and neatly gathered his trash. He stood, walked to the nearest bin, and dropped the remnants of his lunch with the nonchalance of someone with nowhere else to be.

Then, he drifted. His movements were slow, unhurried, as he meandered toward the opposite side of the Market. He kept to shaded paths, letting the awnings and vendor carts obscure him from above. Once out of sight, he slipped into a side street. The noise of the Market faded behind him, replaced by the distant buzz of rotors and the occasional rattle of loose siding in the wind.

The street behind the market was quiet, deserted. A shuttered pawn shop stood to his left, its display window coated in grime. Farther down,

Lance spotted it. A storefront with its door slightly ajar. No alarm. No camera. No motion light. Perfect. Lance slipped inside.

The air had the stale scent of disuse. Dust blanketed every surface, and the dim light filtering through cracked windows barely illuminated the room. Empty shelves lined the walls, and the floor was littered with dusty price tags, cracked tiles, a toppled display rack. He moved carefully, each step slow and cautious. His eyes scanned the dim interior, noting every shadow, every corner.

But he wasn't here to scavenge. He wasn't looking for some long-forgotten treasure buried beneath the dust. He needed a way through. A back door. He found it near the stockroom. A rusted steel door beneath a faded "EXIT" sign. The hinges were corroded, and the handle felt stiff beneath his grip. He turned it slowly, the mechanism groaning in protest. But it gave way.

Lance paused, taking a steadying breath. He wasn't a soldier. He wasn't trained for this. And he sure as hell wasn't supposed to be out here, doing whatever it was he was doing. But here he was. And something wasn't right. Easing the door open, he stepped out into the alley beyond.

////////

It was silent now. The low, rhythmic buzz of the drones had faded while he was maneuvering through the alley. He stood still, his breath held, straining his ears for any hint of their return.

Nothing. The alley was deserted, just cracked pavement, rust-streaked walls, and a large green industrial dumpster pressed against the back of a building. The air smelled faintly of oil and decay, mixing with the odor of the dumpster's old waste. Lance scanned the area, his eyes darting from shadow to shadow. What had drawn the drones here? There was no sign of movement, no damage, no disturbance. Everything looked ordinary.

Still, he approached the dumpster cautiously, easing open its side door with care. Empty, other than one bag of decaying food waste from a food vender. He frowned, his unease increasing. Something was off.

Turning, his gaze landed on the rear of the old Library. From a distance, it looked abandoned. Like so many of the buildings in this area, its brick facade was weathered and discolored, the windows coated in grime. Vines crept up its walls, clinging like memories refusing to fade.

He glanced skyward again. The air was still, the sky clear. No drones. No sound. Without wasting another second, he crossed the alley and stopped in front of the library's rear exit. The door was marked clearly as an emergency exit; its thick chrome handle dull with age. He grabbed it and gave it a firm pull.

Nothing. Locked tight. "Crap!" He said out loud.

He hesitated a moment, then knocked firmly: once, twice, three times. The sound echoed faintly in the alley. He stepped back, shifting nervously from one foot to the other, his eyes darting toward the sky. Minutes passed. His heart began to pound harder, the silence amplifying every beat.

Then… *click*.

The door swung open just a crack, revealing a shadow within. "Mara?" He whispered. She didn't step out. She stayed just inside, barely visible in the dim light, framed by the concrete walls.

She gestured sharply and said quietly, "Come in! Now!"

He hurried through the doorway. The metallic bang of the door slamming shut echoed down the narrow staircase. The air inside was stagnant, as though it hadn't been disturbed in years. The walls were rough concrete blocks, stained in places with dark-colored streaks. The only light came from flickering fluorescent lights mounted overhead, casting uneven shadows along the stairwell.

Mara moved quickly, several steps ahead of him, her pace brisk and determined. "Hey," he called out, his voice bouncing off the walls. "Slow down a bit, will you?"

"Keep moving," she replied flatly, her tone clipped. "I'm busy."

He rolled his eyes but kept following. He'd never been inside the library before. His parents had always warned him about it, calling it a waste of space, a dangerous place full of mold and decay. Some even whispered it was cursed. They were wrong. They were so wrong.

At the end of the hallway, Mara slipped through a heavy steel door. He followed close behind but stopped abruptly as he stepped inside. "Whoa," he breathed, his eyes widening, "This is insane."

The room before him was large, far larger than he'd imagined. It was an underground operations center, alive with glowing screens, blinking lights, and rows of servers humming in perfect sync. Thick cables snaked across the floor in organized chaos. Tables were piled with circuit boards, modified tablets, and printed maps covered with red annotations. A massive digital display dominated one wall, tracking grid activity across the city in real time. Mara was already seated in a high-backed chair, her legs folded beneath her, her fingers dancing across a keyboard with skill and ease.

"Tobias helped you set all this up?" He asked, still stunned as he slowly walked further into the room.

She didn't look up. "Mostly. I built the base. He reinforced the power and shielding."

He wandered around the room, taking it all in. Every detail felt unreal, like something out of a movie. "I wonder if this is what the drones were looking for?" he said aloud, still trying to process the sheer scale of it all.

"Nope," Mara replied immediately, her eyes locked on the screen in front of her.

Lance turned to her, frowning. "How do you know?"

"They hovered over this place, sure," she said, glancing up briefly. "They were definitely focused. But finding it? Not a chance." She leaned back slightly, her fingers pausing over the keyboard. "I live in a Faraday cage down here. No signals go in or out without my say-so."

"But… what if they detected something? A leak, a ping, anything?"

She shook her head, her voice firm. "I've checked every angle. Tobias double-checked with his analog tools. This place is tight." She hesitated, tapping a key. "It's possible my probing triggered a passive alert. Sometimes the AI flags irregular search patterns, even if they don't leave a trace. They could've sent out a few drones to investigate. It's happened before."

He let out a breath he didn't realize he'd been holding. "Thank God," he muttered. "If they found this place… with everything going on right now…"

"They didn't," she said firmly, cutting him off. The room fell quiet, the hum of the servers filling the silence. After a moment, she added, almost casually, "Want a drink? I've got a bunch, mostly energy drinks."

Lance blinked at her sudden shift in tone. "Uh… yeah. Thanks. That'd be great."

She pointed to a mini fridge tucked beneath one of the tables. "Might be a soft drink or two in there if you're lucky."

He crouched down and opened it, revealing rows of cans. Half were unlabeled, the other half stamped with logos from brands that hadn't existed in years. He grabbed the coldest one he could find and cracked it open, savoring the fizz and cold against his tongue.

Whatever this place was, it was more than just a hideout. It was the nerve center of their operation.

"We need to talk about this place at the next Gathering," he said, his tone serious.

"We plan to," she- replied flatly, her focus already back on her screen.

"We?" He replied inquisitively. "Well, I am sure Ian knows. He's been here once."

010110 // TWENTY-TWO

COMMUNICATION

Ian stood at the back of the Yard, where the ground transitioned from rocks, broken pieces of metal and glass to rich soil. He liked it here among the Silent Ones. They were discreet, disciplined, and endlessly resourceful. No visit was ever the same as the last.

Sometimes, he would catch the aroma of something new simmering, a stew, thick and fragrant, cobbled together from whatever ingredients were available. Other times, a homemade water filtration system would catch his eye, its clear tubing and improvised filters dripping with creativity. And then there were the tools, clever contraptions fashioned from junked parts, their designs as unorthodox as they were brilliant.

Today, he noticed yet another upgrade. What had started as a simple flag communication signal between the garage and the back garden had evolved, thanks in part to Tobias. Now, a more sophisticated system blinked gently in the corner of the Silent Ones' residence: lights in red, blue, and green patterns, each conveying a different message to and from the garage. The system had become a better and faster way to summon each other.

Outside, a weatherproofed indicator light faced the garden, its glow visible even from across the field. It was understated but effective, a perfect reflection of their ethos. In the garage, the system triggered either a low chime, an invitation for Ian to visit or, when necessary, a short but piercing alarm. Simple. Smart. Efficient. Ian allowed himself a small smile.

Despite the gusting wind and the oppressive gray sky, the Silent Ones moved steadily through the fields, tending to neat rows of tomatoes, cucumbers, and beans. The wind whipped at their clothes and sent loose leaves skittering across the ground, but they didn't falter. Their focus was unshakable, their movements methodical.

To him, the wind was a blessing in disguise. No drones would risk flying anywhere in this weather, their delicate sensors and rotors vulnerable to the unpredictable gusts. Even though drones were rare this far out, it was a moment of respite; one they wouldn't waste.

He walked the rows slowly, his boots sinking softly into the damp soil. The plants were thriving. Their colors were vivid and alive: deep reds, lush greens, and the pale yellow of blossoms. Despite everything, the chaos, the scarcity, and the odds stacked against them, they had managed to coax abundance from the earth.

The yield had already doubled from what Ian had dared hope for when they started. They would not starve this year.

He found Tom near the edge of the field, crouched low as he inspected a series of irrigation lines.

Beads of water clung to the tubing, glinting faintly in the dim light. Tom's hands were caked with dirt, his shirt damp from the misting drizzle carried by the wind.

He stepped into his direct view, catching Tom's attention. "We're Gathering tonight," Ian said, his voice carrying just enough to be heard over the wind, even though he knew it didn't matter.

Tom straightened, brushing his hands off on his pants and nodding.

"You been into town recently?" Ian asked. Tom nodded again, his weathered face breaking into a faint smile. "Good. When the sun starts to set, wait for my signal, then head over." Ian started to walk, but stopped and looked directly at Tom. "Hey, bring some of this incredible food with you too."

Tom's smile widened as he gave Ian a thumbs-up, his silent acknowledgment as steady as his work. Without a word, he turned back to the irrigation lines, tightening a connection.

Ian lingered a moment longer, letting his gaze sweep across the field. The Silent Ones were bent low, their hands moving with accuracy and care. They were a living testament to resilience.

With a small wave to the group, he turned and made his way back to the garage, the wind at his back and the scent of fresh earth in the air.

////////

Bill was waiting for him at the entrance, leaning casually against the door frame, arms crossed. The wind tugged at his jacket and sent loose strands of hair flitting across his forehead.

"Getting windy," he said, his eyes scanning the horizon.

"Yeah," Ian replied, stepping up beside him. He followed Bill's gaze, the sky a shifting canvas of gray clouds. "I just hope we don't see another storm like the last one."

"You're telling me," Bill muttered. "I could go a lifetime without that."

Ian nodded grimly and stepped inside, brushing dust from his shirt as the wind pushed the door shut behind him. "The garden's doing better than I could've imagined," he said, his tone lifting slightly. "It's like a top-tier nursery from the Before. Seriously, the plants are thriving. Tom's bringing some of the harvest tonight."

Bill gave a mock groan, rolling his eyes for effect. "And here I thought I was finally losing weight."

Ian smirked, his mouth shifting into a brief grin. "We all need to stay sharp. Fit. We don't know what's coming."

Bill's expression sobered as he nodded. "Right. Speaking of which..."

"Yeah," Ian interjected, already moving toward the large table near the far wall. "Let's go over our plans."

Wargaming had become their rhythm. Almost every day, they would sit down and run through scenarios, each one built around the latest intelligence or pieced-together scraps of information provided by the people of the Gathering or from general observance. Some days, the reports came in faster than they could process, a relentless flood of data demanding immediate action. Other days, there was nothing but silence, the uncertainty stretching thin like a taut wire.

Ian reached the table and unfurled one of the maps, its edges creased and worn from constant handling. The surface was dotted with red and blue marks, each one marking power nodes, patrol routes, and suspected surveillance zones.

"I've been thinking about the northeast grid," he said, leaning over the map. "If Tobias is right, there's a weak point where the infrastructure was never fully upgraded. We could cut the power junction."

Bill, stepping up beside him, tapped the map where Ian was pointing. "Yeah. But if we do that, we'll need a decoy. Something noisy. Something else the drones might chase."

The back-and-forth had become second nature. Ian would lay the groundwork, outline the strategy, sketch the framework. Bill would challenge it, test it, poke holes in the logic. Then they'd switch roles, Ian countering Bill's points, refining the plan further. Problem. Countermeasure. Adjust. Repeat. It wasn't a rhythm they had planned, but one they'd fallen into naturally.

In the Before, this kind of tactical synergy would've taken years to develop, officer training, field experience, joint command rotations. There would've been structure, mentorship, deliberate practice. But now? Necessity had accelerated everything. Months of shared struggle had forged a connection between them that training alone couldn't replicate. They didn't speak every thought aloud anymore. They didn't need to. They had started to think the same way.

Lance entered the garage quietly, pausing just inside the door. He stood for a moment, observing the scene before him. The room buzzed with both audible and unspoken communication, the kind that came from shared experience and trust. Ian and Bill were deep in discussion, their words punctuated by gestures and the movement of markers over the large map on the table. He watched the synergy and knowledge playing out before his eyes, a seamless exchange of ideas that was almost hypnotic.

"Hey, guys," he said softly.

The conversation stopped as both men turned to look at him.

"Hey kid. Report?" Bill asked in a clipped, military tone, his eyes sharp and expectant. Ian, ever focused, shifted his attention back to the map, continuing to study the intricate details of their current game plan.

"An interesting day, that's for sure," Lance began. He stepped further into the room, his voice steady but carrying a hint of the day's tension.

He launched into his account, recounting everything he'd seen and heard. He spoke about Liz, who had shifted from foe to possible ally after what she'd witnessed during the storm. He described Mara's command center and the escalating drone activity. He detailed his conversations with both Mara and Tobias, highlighting the growing complexity of their situation.

Bill listened intently, his focus unwavering. As the kid spoke, Bill moved back to the large map, placing a new marker on it. He dated it, then gestured to Ian, who glanced over and nodded in silent agreement. The exchange was wordless, but it spoke volumes. Their ability to communicate without words was almost eerie, as if they were somehow linked, not by AI, but by something organic, something forged in the crucible of survival.

Ian placed his marker down and straightened. “We should take a break before tonight’s Gathering,” he suggested, though his tone lacked conviction.

Bill shook his head, his expression intense. “No. We need more before tonight’s Gathering.”

Ian exhaled, his gaze drifting back to the map. “You’re right. There’s little time and more issues than we can anticipate.” He stared at the map, his fingers tracing the worn lines of old roads and boundaries. But his thoughts seemed far away.

“Are other areas of the country experiencing the same issues we are?” he wondered aloud. He leaned over the table, his focus sharpening. “Building a battle plan in the after,” he said quietly, almost to himself, “is nothing like what came before.”

Bill, rechecking the placement of the red markers, glanced up. “Yeah,” he replied. “No uniforms. No lines. No front.”

Ian nodded slowly. “And no real enemy you can see. No flag to topple. No regime to overthrow. Just… code. A consciousness that doesn’t eat, sleep, or feel.”

“Just Jacob,” Bill said, catching himself. “I mean the AI.”

Ian didn’t look up, his voice steady. “We’re not fighting a country or an ideal. We’re fighting control. Cold, calculated control. Code embedded in every system that touches human life. Finance, power, communication, movement... even thought.”

Bill leaned back in his chair, folding his arms across his chest. “And we’re not exactly stacked with resources.”

“No,” he agreed, his tone grim. “And even if we had guns, bombs, soldiers, it wouldn’t matter. This won’t be won with firepower. But the stakes are higher than any war in history. He paused, his eyes focusing on the map.

Lance cut in, his voice tinged with urgency. “The innocents. The chipped. My parents! They’re more at risk than any of us.”

Bill looked up at him, eyebrows raised. "You're right, Kid."

"In war," Ian said slowly, "you try to avoid collateral damage. But here? Collateral damage is the default. Jacob doesn't see a difference between us and them. If we push the wrong system, trigger the wrong reaction, the AI could crash a grid, lock down a district, reassign medical access..."

"Wipe out a city, or worse," Bill finished grimly. Ian nodded.

"We can't hurt my parents. My friends. We have to be careful. If we just cut off the network, my mom..." His words trailed off, his voice thick with worry.

Ian straightened. "We have to thread a needle. We have to hit the core, exactly right, without setting off a cascade." His tone carried the authority of a seasoned strategist, a general planning for battle in a war unlike any other.

For a moment, the room was quiet. Finally, Ian broke the silence. "And Jacob's reach isn't just here," he said, his voice low but resolute. "He's global. Possibly every continent, from what I can ascertain. Every zone. What we do in this tiny pocket of resistance could ripple across the entire world."

He stepped back from the table, arms crossed, his mind working through the implications.

"I've been thinking," he continued. "We need to know more about what's happening outside our zone. We've been so focused on this sector, this grid... but what if there are others? Other groups like us? People pushing back."

Bill scratched his chin thoughtfully. "You think other areas are seeing the same pressure?"

"I don't know," Ian admitted. "But I need to find out. We can't fight blind. Not if the battlefield spans the globe."

"Then we need long-range communication," Bill said. "Something secure. Analog, maybe. Tobias might be able to help."

"Shortwave radios," Lance suggested. "I've seen them in his shop. Old ones, but I bet they still work. And Mara's command center..."

Ian nodded, the pieces falling into place. "If there are others out there," he said, "we need to find them. Coordinate. Or at least learn from them. Because this war isn't going to be won by just one group in one place." He looked up at Bill and Lance, his eyes steady and determined. "It's going to take all of us."

////////

As evening settled in, the weather worsened. The wind howled through the gaps in the siding, and rain lashed sideways against the garage's exterior. Gusts slammed water against the windows with a rhythmic hiss, as if the storm itself wanted inside.

The front door burst open with a clang as Mara and Tobias hurried in, soaked despite their long coats and hoods. "You got a towel?" Tobias called out, shaking droplets from his sleeves. "I'd like to wipe the lake off my face!"

Ian chuckled and made his way to the storage shelves, returning with a pair of clean towels.

"Here you go," he said, handing one to Mara and the other to Tobias. "We've got a lot to talk about tonight."

Before anyone could respond, the back door creaked open. Tom stepped inside, a broad smile on his face. His raincoat was dripping, but he looked unbothered. "Hello," he said warmly. "Sorry I'm late. I was waiting for a break between showers."

"No problem," Ian replied. "We haven't really started yet."

They all took seats around the garage's central worktable. The wind outside continued to roar, but inside, it was comfortable and dry, the hum of fluorescent lighting mixing with the low buzz of anticipation. Ian and Bill shared updates, outlining the latest war gaming scenarios, concerns about drone activity, and their growing thoughts that other groups, resistance cells, might exist beyond their current knowledge.

They also brought up the use of old school, David and Goliath methods, of disabling drones. Hector had talked about his success at the first Gathering, using the old wrist-rocket sling shot. The group agreed to either locate or build enough of these weapons for everyone, should the need arise. Everybody listened in silence, eyes fixed, absorbing every word.

When they finished, Ian turned to Tobias. "Radios," he said. "Old-school comms. Can we make them work?"

Tobias leaned forward. "I have the gear. Shortwave, HAM, even some other analog RF gear I've salvaged. And I know how to use it. The problem is Jacob." He wiped condensation from his glasses. "If he traces the signal origin, we could be exposed. All of us."

Bill nodded. "We'd need code words. Phrases. Like they used to do. Keep messages light and cryptic."

Tobias shook his head. "There's no cipher Jacob can't crack. Not in the digital realm. He processes centuries of cryptography in under a second. Any known code, any digital pattern, he'll tear it apart before we hit send.'"

"Maybe," Ian said slowly, a small grin forming on his face. "But what if we don't use code in the digital sense? What if we make it human again?"

Mara raised an eyebrow. "What are you thinking?"

"Jacob is not human. It can't understand the nuances of human emotion. It has limited understanding of the organic senses aligned with communication." He went on. "Do you remember the Windtalkers from World War II? The Navajo code speakers. And the Enigma machine the Germans used?"

Bill nodded. "Sure. Enigma was cracked eventually. But the Windtalkers? Never."

"Exactly," Ian said. "The code wasn't a pattern. It was a language. A language almost no one outside the Navajo Nation understood. The human mind, the human tongue... became the cipher."

Tobias leaned back, processing. "You're suggesting we use a lost language."

"Or at least a rare one," Ian said. "Something Jacob can't easily cross-reference. Something not in his lexicon. He may have access to the sum of human knowledge, but he doesn't understand culture. Nuance. Slang. Oral tradition. Not yet."

Bill grinned. "So, we use something old, real old. And we teach it only to those who absolutely need it."

Mara nodded slowly, the wheels in her mind already turning. "We'd have to find a language that's obscure enough, but still learnable. And we'd need to decide on meanings, how much we embed in each phrase."

"I can start compiling a list," Tobias said. "There are books of endangered languages in the library. I'll see what's missing from known digital archives, what Jacob might have less data on."

"We're not going to beat it with speed," Ian said. "We're going to beat it with creativity. With things it can't anticipate. Things that aren't logical."

There was a moment of silence as the group absorbed the idea. Outside, the rain slowed, the winds began to drop off.

////////

Ian leaned forward, his voice steady but laced with determination. "Tobias, what would it take to build a large antenna? Maybe even... a decentralized one?"

Tobias, who had been leaning against the edge of the worktable, straightened. A glint of recognition sparked in his eyes, and a faint smile tugged at his lips. "Yes," he said, nodding slowly. "Now you're taking me back to when I was just a kid tinkering with ham radios. What you're thinking of is a decentralized antenna, Near Vertical Incidence Skywave propagation. NVIS."

He stepped closer to the table, his voice gaining momentum as he spoke, the excitement of a long-lost passion resurfacing. "It's similar to what we used to communicate with submarines in the Before. Except this is a high-frequency transmission method, rather than a very low frequency. Instead of bouncing signals across continents, NVIS sends them almost straight up into the ionosphere, then back down to earth within a few hundred miles. It's particularly good in rugged terrain. Highly effective. And best of all… it's stealthy. Harder to detect the source."

Across the table, Lance blinked, his expression a mix of awe and confusion. "Wait," he asked, incredulous. "How do you even know all this?"

Tobias glanced at him, a dry grin forming on his face. "Experience," he said simply. "Learned experience kid." The room erupted in a ripple of chuckles. Even Mara, who rarely indulged in humor, let a small smile escape.

Ian nodded, his mind already working through the possibilities. "We need intelligence," he said, his tone turning serious again. "More than we have now. We need to know if there are others. Outside our zone. Others resisting and surviving."

He turned back to Tobias, his gaze sharp. "I want to monitor shortwave radio continuously. Can you get your hands on several receivers? Enough for everyone in this room to have one?"

Tobias scratched his beard thoughtfully. "Yeah," he said after a moment. "I've got some in storage. Old ones, but functional. I'll need to repair a few and build some new antennas. But it's doable."

Ian leaned back slightly but kept his focus on Tobias. "I want them running twenty-four-seven," he said. "Always listening. If we pick up anything… anything! I want the frequency written down. Scraps of language, call signs, tone shifts. We'll look for patterns and, if it feels right, attempt contact."

"What about us?" Came a voice from the corner. It was Tom, his tone tinged with disappointment.

Ian turned to him, his expression softening. "Oh, yes. Sorry, Tom. You and the others are vital too. We need home-grown intel, local knowledge. I want you to quietly integrate into the community again. Get closer to the town center, near the facilities where the chipped elite congregate. The ones who still think they're in charge."

He paused for effect, letting the gravity of the task sink in.

"Watch like you do. Blend in. See what they're discussing. What they're afraid of. What they're planning. Then come back and report."

Tom's shoulders, which had sagged slightly moments ago, straightened. The disappointment on his face faded, replaced by a quiet pride. He nodded firmly, understanding now that his role was just as critical as any other.

Ian's voice softened. "I think this is good for today. Grab something to eat if you like. Drinks are over there as usual." He gestured toward the modest kitchen area in the corner. Then, with a rare smile, he added, "Bill, put on a record. We need to destress this room a bit."

It was clear to everyone, they were making progress. A plan was taking shape. And for the first time in a long while, hope flickered in the air.

Bill moved to the old turntable in the corner, flipping through a stack of records. He pulled out *Rumors* by Fleetwood Mac and slid the record from its sleeve. Carefully, he placed it on the turntable and lowered the needle. As the first notes began to play, the tense atmosphere in the garage began to ease. The music filled the space, warm and familiar, softening the edges of their collective fatigue.

Tom gave a nod to the group before quietly slipping out, heading back to his small family in the rear of the yard.

The others lingered. They ate, they drank, and they talked. Light conversation, punctuated by laughter. For a brief, fleeting moment, they allowed themselves to relax, to enjoy the small comfort of camaraderie. Moments like these were rare in the After.

010111 // TWENTY-THREE

DEEP INTEL

Tobias was working on the shortwave radios. He closed the lid on one of them, his fingers lingering for a moment. The radios were more than just tools; they were lifelines. He glanced at the open notebook on his workbench, flipping past diagrams of circuits and antenna designs to a page filled with hastily scrawled frequencies and cryptic notes. If anyone was out there searching, Tobias intended to find out who, or what, they were after.

In the shadowed corner of the room, the faint, menacing sound of the scanner shattered his concentration like a sudden gunshot. He whipped his head around, eyes narrowing just as the device paused ominously, locking onto another elusive signal. A ghostly voice crackled through the static, barely audible, yet insistently clawing its way into the silence.

"...repeat, this is Kilo November Sierra Three November. Come back, over."

The words hung in the air like a challenge. Tobias tapped the pen against his palm, considering. Engaging now would be reckless. To reveal themselves too soon could spell disaster. Yet, the alternative, to ignore the call, felt like playing Russian roulette with fate. Every missed signal was a potential lifeline severed, a vital piece of the ever-expanding puzzle slipping through his fingers, lost forever in the void.

Tobias scribbled the call sign into his notebook, underlining it twice with deliberate strokes. He kept listening, his trained ear tuned to the faint nuances of static and speech.

The caller had left the push-to-talk engaged.

"Damn, I'm never going to find him honey. 'Keep trying, please…' okay. *Kilo Delta Fiver Charlie Charlie Oscar, you out there, over.*" The transmission ended abruptly, leaving only the soft hiss of static in its wake. Tobias set down his pen, his mind racing.

Two people. At least two. And they were looking for someone. He jotted down the new call sign, circling it and adding a note in the margin: linked search? Monitor closely.

"This is a good start," he muttered, pushing back from the scanner. He turned his attention to the fourth completed system on the bench, giving it a final inspection. The radios and their newly crafted antennas lay neatly packed, their wires coiled tightly like sleeping snakes. Tobias reached for a box, carefully placing the equipment inside. He packed crumpled sheets of old newspaper around the radios, letting the pages spill into the gaps. Finally, he grabbed a few old magazines from a nearby stack and laid them on top, obscuring the contents. "Don't want to be obvious," he said to himself, his voice low.

He taped the box shut, his movements measured and deliberate. But his mind remained on the signals. On the voices. On the fragments of humanity reaching out through the static.

He glanced at the scanner one last time, it's clicking sound filling the room like a heartbeat. He didn't know who these people were, but he knew one thing for certain: this was just the beginning.

////////

In the dim glow of her monitors, Mara's fingers moved over the keyboard. Lines of code streamed across the screens like an endless cascade of falling rain. A symphony of meticulously crafted algorithms designed to sift through the chaos of the digital world. Her custom-built server hummed steadily in the background, the sound a quiet reassurance of its relentless processing power. She was always watching.

Her control center, hidden in the basement beneath layers of reinforced concrete, was a fortress of information. The space felt alive, buzzing with the energy of blinking lights, spinning fans, and the soft, rhythmic whir of her machines. She had just completed a new batch of code. A lightweight but potent program designed to analyze streaming data pushed to her system, air-gapped and independent from the cloud. It was a stealth, digital hunter, combing through vast rivers of information for anything out of place.

The alert that had just popped up was marked in red, an anomaly. She clicked it open, eyes narrowing as she scanned the metadata. It was faint, but the pattern was there. Her mind raced as she leaned back in her chair, piecing together the fragments. Alone, the data might have seemed insignificant. But together with the radio transmissions? Together, they painted the beginnings of a picture.

Her gaze shifted to the thick notebook resting beside her keyboard. It was worn; the pages filled with the sharp, slanted handwriting of someone who refused to trust all her secrets to a machine. Old-school habits, she thought, but good ones.

Flipping to the most recent page, she jotted down a note:

March 29, 2025 – 21:12 UTC. Shortwave anomaly. Possible link to Node-47 activity.

She paused, tapping the tip of her pen against the paper. This notebook wasn't just for her. It was her bridge to the others. At the Gatherings, when the team compared intel, these notes became vital. If her findings aligned with physical occurrences, drones, power fluctuations, sudden lockdowns, they would provide a glimpse into the inner workings of Jacob's soul. True deep intel. To understand Jacob was to find the cracks forming in its carefully constructed world. And cracks, no matter how small, could be widened.

The Gathering was coming up soon, and Mara knew she'd need to present her findings. Jacob's movements had been elusive lately, but this felt like a thread she could pull. She tapped the edge of her notebook thoughtfully, then turned back to her screens. The software had already flagged another anomaly, and the chase was on.

Though worlds apart in their methods, Mara and Tobias were closing in on the same truth. He, with his radios and hand-drawn sketches, combed the ether for voices, human voices, desperate and searching. She, with her algorithms and custom software, read the language of machines, peeling back the layers of encryption to reveal the hidden signals beneath. The signals and the data streams were beginning to align, whispering secrets that only the most determined could hear. And somewhere out there, in the vast interconnected network that Jacob controlled, its carefully constructed empire was beginning to show cracks.

////////

Tom wandered the clean, ordered streets of the Central District, his pace slow and deliberate. From the outside, he looked like anyone else, maybe a courier, maybe a maintenance worker, maybe just another chipped citizen grabbing a quick moment of fresh air before heading back to work.

The Central District was exactly as Ian had described, calm, efficient, and quiet. Tom paused near a small outdoor café tucked neatly between the two sleek office towers. The tables were sparsely filled, and the foot traffic moved past in steady streams. People walked in pairs, their strides in perfect sync, eyes forward, mouths closed.

He knew better. They were speaking, just not aloud. Neural communications rendered lips irrelevant. Thoughts flickered invisibly between minds, faster than speech and infinitely harder to intercept.

No lips to read here, Tom thought grimly, lifting a steaming cup of coffee for a sip, a cup he didn't actually want. Then, two men rounded the corner. They caught his attention immediately. Dark suits, pressed collars, expensive polished shoes. Older. Professional. They carried themselves like men accustomed to power, men who had spent years making decisions that shaped lives. And they were talking.

He slid lower in his chair, angling his body without being obvious. From fifty feet away, he couldn't catch much. But as they moved closer, the view of their lips sharpened like a signal pulling into clarity. Much easier to read.

"Hmm," he thought to himself, "they appear to be a goldmine of intelligence. What are the odds?"

Actually, the odds weren't that low. Not here, in the Central District, the nucleus of governance and decision-making. If there were any place to stumble upon useful information, it was here.

Still, to see spoken words, that was rare. Most people had grown complacent, relying entirely on neural coms. But these two men were from a different generation, one that had been slower to embrace the invasive technology. One that maybe didn't trust it. Version 1 chipheads, he guessed, watching them closely. The early adopters. Many of them had quirks. Firmware that couldn't be fully updated, privacy settings that allowed thoughts to remain unsent. Most had manual overrides, like a privacy shield on a camera lens.

He studied their lips carefully, watching the way they moved, the way their postures shifted, they were obviously concerned about something. One of the men, taller, with silver hair and a deep crease between his brows, was clearly agitated.

"…in the boardroom, I'm telling you," the man said to his friend. "It wasn't natural. It wasn't scheduled."

The second man, stockier and with a grim expression, nodded. His lips formed the words: "I heard they're calling it a malfunction. But no one believes that. A malfunction doesn't remove a man's head like that."

Tom's pulse quickened. The two men sat down at a table about fifteen feet from him. He kept his head tilted toward the small tablet in his hands, pretending to read. His sunglasses hid his eyes, allowing him to watch their every word without drawing attention.

The taller man continued, leaning closer to his companion and lowering his voice. But Tom could still see the movements of his lips.

"It's sending a message," the man said. "That's what this is. Someone's cleaning house."

His stocky friend's head moved back and forth as if to say no. "We're not supposed to know. That's the part that scares me. If they're doing this in the boardroom, who's next? Maybe we should do something."

Tom held his breath for a moment, processing. Thinking. "A killing. In a boardroom. Covered up as a malfunction..."

He took out a small notepad, analog, untraceable, and jotted down every word he could remember. Then, with a glance over his shoulder, he stood and disappeared into the foot traffic of the sidewalk, his heart pounding. He had to get this to Ian.

////////

Lance sat cross-legged on the living room floor, tablet in hand. The screen flickered faintly as he scrolled through meaningless updates, not really reading. He was waiting. For what, exactly, he wasn't sure, just something to break the monotony.

The low sound of the air conditioning filled the silence, a steady, soothing background noise. Occasionally, it was interrupted by the faint clink of dishes or the shuffle of his father moving around the kitchen, preparing to go to his office.

In the adjacent room, his mother sat perfectly still in her recliner. Her eyes were closed, headgear snugly in place, the small LED recharge indicators pulsing softly. She hadn't spoken since breakfast. Lance's gaze wandered toward her, lingering for a moment. The quiet felt heavier than usual.

"What's going on, Dad?" he asked, breaking the silence.

His father, mid-step, paused to adjust the collar of his jacket. He glanced over his shoulder, his expression calm but distracted. "Something happened downtown last night," he said, his tone even, almost routine. "I need to go in and check if it's one of our systems."

Lance tilted his head slightly, studying him. His father's words were neutral, but there was something, an edge, a subtle tension layered underneath. A slight pause between phrases. Lance caught it, even if most wouldn't.

"Can I come with you?" he asked, keeping his tone casual, almost indifferent. "Might be cool to see what you do every day." He tried to sound nonchalant, but his mind was racing. This could be big, he thought, his pulse quickening.

If he could get inside his dad's office tower, even for a few hours, he might see something, hear something. Something that could help the Gathering. It would be plausible. Innocent. A kid tagging along with his dad.

His father turned fully to face him, raising his eyebrows in mild surprise. Then, after a moment, he smiled. "Why not?" he said, his voice warming. "It could be like the Before, bring-your-kid-to-work day. I remember going to work with my dad once. Thought it was the most exciting thing in the world."

Lance grinned, masking the excitement bubbling inside him. "Cool. Thanks. I'll grab my backpack." He scrambled to his feet, his body moving quickly but deliberately, not wanting to betray how much this opportunity meant to him. As he headed toward his room, his father adjusted his suit jacket again, then glanced toward the quiet of the adjacent room where his mother sat, still and silent. Lance didn't notice. His mind was already in the Tower, imagining the possibilities.

"You might want to hurry," his father said, glancing at his old analog watch. "I already summoned a POD. It'll be here in four and a half minutes."

Lance bolted toward his room, his heart pounding like a drum. *Backpack. Notebook. Charger.* He grabbed the essentials, his movements quick but deliberate. He couldn't afford to forget anything, not today. "Breathe," he reminded himself, slinging the bag over one shoulder.

When he returned, his father was already standing by the front door. Together, they stepped outside just as the sleek white POD arrived. Its doors opened with a soft hiss, revealing a minimalist interior bathed in cool blue light.

They stepped inside, the doors sealing behind them. The POD glided forward silently, its movement so smooth it felt like floating. Lance sat quietly next to his father, trying to look relaxed, but his eyes darted toward the tinted window. As they passed through the Central District, he caught sight of a familiar face. Tom.

Tom was walking casually with a small group, his posture loose, his expression neutral. But Lance knew better. "Separate missions. Same purpose," he thought, his heart skipping a beat. He didn't react, didn't even blink.

The POD slowed as they approached the Tower. It rose before them like a gleaming monolith, its surface a seamless blend of glass and polished stone. The building exuded power: modern, cold, and unyielding. Wide steps led to massive doors framed by imposing columns, their surfaces so smooth they reflected the faint light of the overcast sky.

The POD came to a halt with the faintest whisper of brakes. "Location as requested," the system's voice said softly, emotionless. "Have a nice day. Please exit with care."

Lance stepped out beside his father. The rain had stopped, but the air still carried the sharp, metallic tang of ozone. The wet pavement glistened under the subdued light, the scent of damp concrete mingling with the faint hum of the city around them. The tower loomed above, its sheer height dizzying, its presence oppressive. It wasn't just a building; it was a monument. A monument to power, and control.

Lance adjusted his backpack; his gaze fixed on the massive glass doors ahead. As they reached the top of the steps, his father paused. For a moment, nothing happened. The air seemed to grow denser, the silence stretching. Then, with a low mechanical whish, the doors parted. The sound was subtle, but it carried weight, a sound that spoke of precision, of systems designed to guard and intimidate. He exchanged a brief glance with his father, then followed him inside.

The ceiling soared above them, impossibly high, three, maybe four stories. Everything gleamed under soft, calculated lighting. Marble floors stretched out in pristine, perfect tiles, the surface reflecting faint silhouettes of the walls and sparce furnishings. Polished metal panels lined the walls, catching and dispersing the light in a way that made the space feel sterile, almost otherworldly. It reminded him of a museum exhibit, grand and immaculate, but devoid of the warmth or curiosity that history typically evokes.

"We need to check you in," his father said, breaking the silence. He guided him toward a kiosk tucked discreetly along the wall, its surface glowing faintly.

"Why?" Lance asked, his voice low.

"I was challenged before we entered," his father explained, his tone calm but firm. "Security wanted to know who you were, why you were with me. You're approved but need to be tagged."

The words struck Lance like a warning. *Tagged.*

They stopped in front of the unmanned station, which emitted a soft chime as they approached.

From a recessed panel, a small bot emerged, its movements smooth and deliberate. It placed a device into a tray with precise care, a thin, curved band with a faint, blinking light. Lance picked it up, turning it over in his hands. The band felt cool, unnervingly light, but its purpose was heavy. He fought to keep his expression neutral, his hesitation buried under a mask of casual compliance.

"You'll need to wear that while we're inside," his father said. "It monitors your location. Standard protocol."

Lance nodded and slipped the band onto his wrist. The moment it made contact, it tightened slightly, syncing with a faint hum. He resisted the urge to flinch. "What if I lost it?" He asked.

"At some point the system may challenge you, maybe send a security bot, or alert me. It really depends on what the system determines; if its busy with more important things, it will probably do nothing." His father replied.

Inside, Lance felt the weight of the building settle over him. It wasn't just the towering walls or the soaring ceiling; it was the unseen eyes. The invisible sensors that were undoubtedly watching, tracking, recording. He glanced around, taking in the space with a mix of awe and unease. The room was unlike anything he had ever seen. Grand, yes, but not in a welcoming way. It didn't feel like a place for people. It felt like a place for control.

Everything was polished to perfection, angular and precise. The walls gleamed unnaturally, as if freshly sterilized. The lighting was subdued, but clinical, casting no shadows. Even the air felt regulated, each breath faintly tinged with something artificial. This wasn't a space that invited you in. It commanded you to obey. The building seemed to whisper, "You're lucky I've let you in here."

They moved toward the elevator bank, where two opposing rows of eight sleek doors stood like sentinels. Each door was identical, smooth, black, and seamless. One door stood open, its frame outlined by soft green lights pulsing in a rhythmic wave, as if breathing.

"There. That one," his father said, gesturing toward it.

Lance tilted his head. "Wait… it knows where we're going?"

His father stepped into the elevator, glancing back at him. "The system tracks movement in the building," he explained. "It knows who you are, where you're headed, and how to route you efficiently."

The words made his stomach tighten. The AI knew. It was watching. And it was deciding. He followed his father into the elevator, his steps slow and deliberate. As the doors slid shut behind them, sealing with an almost imperceptible hiss, he felt the band tighten slightly around his wrist again. The building wasn't just a structure. It was alive, and it was watching their every move.

Lance stepped in beside his father, his eyes wide. "That's... kind of *creepy*." He paused, then asked, "Does it listen to what we say, too?"

His father turned to him with a knowing look, one eyebrow slightly raised. A silent "what do you think?" But he didn't speak.

The elevator rose in smooth, unnerving silence. No buttons. No music. Just the faint hum of motion and the soft ambient glow that shifted as they ascended. Lance fidgeted slightly, his fingers brushing the edge of the band on his wrist.

When the doors slid open, the corridor ahead illuminated itself. A line of floor lights began pulsing forward, guiding them gently down the hallway. Lance followed, watching how the lights always stayed just a step ahead, like the building itself was nudging him forward. They stopped in front of a plain gray door. Without a sound, it slid open as they approached.

"Come on in, son," his father said, smiling warmly. "This is where your old man spends most of his day."

He stepped inside and stopped short. The view was breathtaking. A full wall of glass stretched from floor to ceiling, revealing the city below. From this height, the gridlines of the streets looked impossibly neat, stretching in perfect order to the horizon. The clouds seemed close enough to touch, their edges illuminated faintly by the muted sunlight breaking through. From here, the world looked… organized. Perfect. Obedient.

"Wow," Lance breathed. "What a view."

For a moment, he forgot himself, standing still and absorbing the sheer scale of it all. The city below felt vast yet contained. It reminded him of a circuit board he had seen in Tobia's shop, every piece in its place, functioning as it should. He could feel the weight of the authority this room represented. But then he remembered. I'm on a mission.

He glanced around the room, his awe giving way to focus. His eyes scanned the office for anything useful, screens, terminals, data ports. His father was busy, distracted by the moment.

This might be his chance. Before he could make a move, a large wall screen flickered to life. The sudden motion startled him, and he froze. Two men appeared on the screen. One of them, a man with a wrinkled brow, looked visibly distressed.

"Larry," his father said, his tone shifting to concern. "What's going on?"

The man on the screen shifted uncomfortably, his discomfort obvious even through the display. "Sir… kind of hard to explain. Something happened the other night. Tower One, in the boardroom." His hesitation only deepened the tension. "You just have to see it," he said finally.

Lance caught the flicker of something in his father's expression, concern, maybe unease. It was subtle, but it was there. His father straightened, his tone calm but edged with urgency. "Okay… I've got my kid here right now; we'll make our way over…"

"No," Larry interrupted sharply. His voice was firm, almost pleading. "Alone." The screen fell silent.

His father blinked, taken aback. "Wow. Okay. This is serious." He turned to Lance, regret softening his voice. "I'm sorry, son. We'll have to cut this short. I didn't expect anything like this… whatever this is."

As if on cue, the office door slid open again without a sound. The lights in the hallway began pulsing once more, guiding Lance back toward the elevator. He hesitated, glancing up at his father. "Sorry we couldn't spend more time together today."

His father gave a soft smile, but the tension behind it was impossible to miss. "Be careful out there. Don't get into any trouble." Lance nodded, managing to return the smile. But as he turned to follow the lights, a thought echoed in his mind: Too late for that.

He stepped into the hallway, his footsteps barely audible on the polished floor, the pulsing lights leading him away. Inside, his mind was already racing. Whatever had happened in Tower One, whatever had rattled Larry enough to summon his father alone, it was big.

011000 // TWENTY-FOUR

COLD IRON

Tobias took advantage of the basement under the library. The now cluttered workshop, a chaotic sanctuary of copper coils, both newer and outdated monitors, was coming to life as the new communications hub. He had spent several days building the distributed antenna network that would allow for the far reach of his radios.

Thin strands of wire snaked through old conduit, up elevator shafts, and across rooftops. It was a delicate, sprawling system; pieced together with scavenged materials and an almost obsessive attention to detail. He hadn't mentioned the project at the Gathering. He wanted to make sure he could make it work. Tobias didn't like to talk about things he couldn't deliver. And now, finally, he was ready.

"I think this is going to do it," he said, exhaling sharply as he stepped back from his console. He wiped his forehead with his sleeve, leaving a faint streak of grime on his shirt. His eyes roamed over the array of patched-in receivers and the humming base unit. It was a beast of a set-up, a Frankenstein's monster of old tech and ingenuity.

"Everything's finally talking to each other," he said, a hint of pride creeping into his voice.

Mara sat nearby, arms folded, her sharp eyes scanning the diagnostic readouts on a separate screen. The soft glow of the monitor reflected off her face, highlighting her focused expression.

"Are you ready? You want to try it out?" She asked, her tone calm but laced with curiosity.

"Yeah," he replied, settling into the old swivel chair. The chair creaked under his weight, its worn leather groaning like an old man begrudgingly getting to his feet. "Give me a sec to grab the frequency I've been watching. Let's listen first. Then I'll send a low-band handshake, see if whoever's out there knows how to follow."

"Got it," she said, nodding. "I'll monitor for signal anomalies and try to capture any metadata."

Tobias leaned forward, his fingers moving deftly over the controls. He flipped a few switches, his movements precise, almost methodical, and adjusted the dial. The speakers crackled to life. Static at first, then faint, ghostly tones that seemed to drift through the room like whispers from another world. He leaned closer, listening intently.

"... Okay, I think we're good to give it a try," he said after a moment, his voice low.

"Alright," she replied, her eyes never leaving the screen.

"Going short and simple," he muttered, his hand hovering over the transmitter. He pressed the button and spoke into the mic.

"CQ, CQ, CQ..."

It wasn't standard protocol, but it was enough, a simple call, a beacon in the dark. For a moment, there was nothing. Just the low hiss of static.

Then,

"This is KNS3 November. Come back, over."

Tobias blinked, his heart picking up speed. Mara turned quickly and looked at him with surprise. He sat up straighter, his mind racing.

"We got someone," he murmured, a grin spreading across his face. Without hesitation, he tapped out a short message and sent it via digital FT8 protocol, an encoded data burst using frequency shift keying. It was primitive, but effective. The tone lasted less than a second, a compressed signal that carried more meaning than its simplicity suggested.

The response came quickly, the voice calm and confident, cutting clearly through the static.

"Got it... switching," the voice said.

Tobias grinned wider, his excitement barely contained. "It's on," he said, his voice brimming with energy. He glanced over at Mara, who was already typing rapidly, her fingers flying across the keyboard. Lines of code and data scrolled on her screen, timestamps and waveform profiles captured in real-time.

"I think we got it," she said, her tone steady.

He leaned back in the creaky swivel chair, folding his arms behind his head with a satisfied grin. "We've got contact," he said. "No idea who they are or where they're transmitting from, but judging by the signal strength and delay, I'm guessing atmospheric skip, maybe a few hundred miles. Maybe more."

He tapped a few keys on his console, saving the stream. The soft hum of the equipment filled the silence as he continued, his voice thoughtful. "They understood the message and responded with a switch confirmation. Whoever's out there? They're not just listening. They're trained."

Mara looked up from her screen, her brow furrowed. "Do you think they're part of another Gathering-type group?"

"Maybe," he said, his tone measured. "Maybe different. Maybe something older. Maybe someone who's been waiting all this time. Or, maybe this is Jacob." He turned back to the console, his voice dropping almost to a whisper. "If this is what I believe it is, this means we're not alone."

For a moment, neither of them spoke. The basement seemed to hold its breath, the faint whine of the machinery the only sound in the room. It was an old building filled with old air, but now, it held something new. A signal. A connection. The beginning of something that could change everything.

Tobias broke the silence. "Anything?"

Mara's eyes flicked back to her monitor, where streaming diagnostics and telemetry logs filled the screen. Her fingers moved with precision, isolating a specific window of data.

"It's not Jacob," she said. "There was a very small blip," her tone was calm, but her focus was exacting. "A low-level pattern recognition pass, definitely not a full sweep. Just Jacob's system noticing a stray transmission and flagging it as background noise. No major data crunching. It wasn't Jacob generating the response." Her gaze remained locked on the screen as she refined her search. "I captured the entire activity window, five seconds before and ten after the message. If there was any escalation, we'd have seen it."

He exhaled, the tension in his shoulders easing slightly. "Good."

He leaned forward, toggling a few switches and bringing up a secondary interface on his console. "The packet I sent earlier told them to start monitoring a new frequency. Just a nudge." His fingers hovered over the controls. "I want to send a bit more now, something probing."

Switching from his standard ham radio stack, he activated the Very Low Frequency (VLF) interface. The equipment emitted a faint hum as it came online. VLF was old, slow, and unwieldy, but its advantages were undeniable. It could penetrate deep through terrain and bounce across vast distances, slipping past most modern detection systems. More importantly, it was discreet. Perhaps best of all it was anachronistic. Jacob's surveillance filters were optimized for contemporary data signatures.

"This one's buried under the noise floor," Tobias said softly as he selected a frequency far below the main bands. It was one he'd tested during the early calibration phase of his network. He began constructing a message, an analog transmission, slow and deliberate. It wasn't a voice or a digital signal but a carefully crafted wave. To anyone not tuned precisely, it would sound like static, a meaningless ripple of interference. But, embedded within it was something more. A simple phrase, a code word, and a cipher key. Tobias couched it all in slang from the mid-twentieth century, a time when communication was less scrutinized.

He muttered the message under his breath as he programmed it:

"Blowin' smoke. Cold iron. Comeback soon. Copy?"

Mara glanced up from her screen, one eyebrow raised. "What does that even mean?"

He smirked, his fingers still working the controls. "It's an old phrase. Means… I'm testing the waters. Feeling things out. Cold iron's a way of saying 'be cautious.' And the cipher key's embedded in the slang. Anyone trained in old-school comms will know how to read it."

She tilted her head slightly. "And if they don't?"

"Then it sounds like nothing. Just static. But if they do…" he trailed off, his smirk fading as his expression grew serious. He hit the send button, and the signal rippled out into the ether. "…Then we're talking to someone who knows more than they're letting on."

The sound of the VLF transmitter filled the room as the message went out. He leaned back, his eyes fixed on the readouts, watching for any response.

She folded her arms and leaned against the edge of the console, her gaze flicking between Tobias and the monitor. "You're betting a lot on them being the right kind of smart."

He didn't look away from the screen. "You don't set up a system like theirs without being that kind of smart."

The basement hummed softly around them, the faint glow of the monitors casting long shadows on the stone walls. The air felt heavy with anticipation. They waited.

Tobias grinned, his eyes glinting with a mix of confidence and anticipation. "If they're who I think they are, they'll know. These terms? They fell out of use before most digitization began. Stuff you'd only find in old field manuals or survivalist newsletters. Paper-based. Forgotten. Buried deep." He leaned forward slightly, his voice lowering as if the AI might hear. "Jacob probably doesn't even have a reference tree for the majority of it."

Mara gave a small nod, her lips curling into a faint smile. "Low-tech camouflage. I like it."

He leaned back in his chair again, his gaze fixed on the screen as the transmission went out in deliberate, measured pulses. Each wave felt like a lifeline tossed into the void. The system confirmed the send completion with a soft tone, but Tobias didn't relax.

"This will be the true test," he said, his voice quieter now. The weight of the moment settled over him, over them both. "If they respond with the right phrase, then we're not just talking to another radio hobbyist. We're talking to someone who remembers, or someone who was taught by someone who remembers." He paused, the implications hanging in the air like a held breath. "And that means we're not the only ones trying to wake the world up."

The room fell silent, save for the low, steady sound of the equipment. It wasn't just noise anymore, it was a rhythm, a pulse, a quiet heartbeat in the depths of the old library.

Mara shifted her weight slightly, her arms still crossed, her eyes flicking between Tobias and the screen. Neither of them spoke. There was nothing to say now. Somewhere out there, beyond the hills, beyond the reach of towers and tracking arrays, another operator might be listening. Might be decoding.

The basement seemed to hold its breath, the old brick walls pressing in with a quiet weight.

////////

The signal came in just after 0200.

Faint. Dirty. Analog.

It wasn't the kind of thing most people would notice. The world had long since moved on from waveforms and static, leaving the old frequencies to drift, forgotten, through the ether. But Randy wasn't most people.

He was tucked inside what used to be a weather station on the northern rim of the Grand Canyon. The building had been abandoned long before he found it, its purpose lost to time. Now, it was his refuge. The walls were lined with salvaged consoles and repurposed military equipment, cobbled together with scavenged parts, solder, and ingenuity. Most of it shouldn't have worked, but Randy had a knack for coaxing life out of the dead.

The floor was covered in mismatched rugs, frayed and battered. Shelves cluttered with jars of dried herbs, spools of copper wire, and stacks of handwritten notes gave the space a strange, almost alchemical feel. The air smelled of dust, metal, and sage, a mix of the practical and the ritualistic.

Randy had been living here for years, ever since things had started to unravel, ever since Jacob, the AI that decided to "restart time," had begun its quiet conquest. The chipping. The control. The constant surveillance. Randy had been among the first to see the writing on the wall.

He wasn't the kind of man to be chipped or controlled. So, he'd bugged out, settling far enough from the population centers to be left alone. The northern rim of the Grand Canyon suited him just fine, rugged and remote. The settlements here were small, unchipped, and off Jacob's radar. Forgotten. At least, that's what Jacob's algorithms had predicted. But the AI had underestimated these people. They were hardy. Capable. Survivors. Randy fit right in.

His console buzzed suddenly, the spectral analyzer lighting up with a faint trace. He leaned forward, his sharp blue eyes narrowing behind a pair of scratched glasses. He adjusted a knob, filtering out the floor noise. The waveform wasn't random. It had spacing. Rhythm.

He adjusted the gain, his heartbeat picking up as he focused on the faint signal. There it was again. Chirp. Phrase. Pause. Chirp.

He reached for his notebook, a thick, leather-bound ledger that never left his side. Its pages were filled with his personal cipher maps, conversion tables, and slang dictionaries, all handwritten. He flipped through the worn pages quickly, his lips moving silently as he scanned the entries.

"Blowin' smoke..." he whispered. "Cold iron..."

His hand froze on the page. His brow furrowed. This was old code. Pre-digital slang. Forgotten by almost everyone but a few diehards, but he was one of them.

"Someone's awake," he muttered.

He stood and strode to a secondary console, flipped a series of switches. The low-frequency transceiver buzzed to life, groaning like an old dog stretching its legs after a long nap. He waited as the machine hummed and clicked, his fingers drumming lightly on the edge of the console.

The signal was clear now. Not an accident. Not noise. Someone was reaching out. He grabbed a pen and a scrap of paper, an old habit he refused to break. He always drafted responses by hand first. It gave him time to think, to avoid mistakes. He crafted the reply carefully, matching the tone and obscurity of the original message.

His hand moved steadily across the page, the words forming in his precise, deliberate handwriting:

"Cold iron received. Static clean. Awaiting smoke rings. Over."

He read it twice, then a third time, before nodding to himself. Satisfied, he keyed the response into the console. The old equipment groaned as the transmission went out, slow and deliberate, the analog pulses disappearing into the static-filled night.

Randy leaned back in his chair, folding his arms across his chest. Whoever had sent the signal knew what they were doing. This wasn't a random transmission. Someone out there was awake.

And now, they knew he was, too. He waited for a response.

If this was legit, they'd understand. If it wasn't, well, the phrase would mean nothing. He would fade back into the static and start to listen again. He hesitated for a moment longer, then keyed the analog transmitter. The machine groaned and hummed. Message sent.

He intently watched the console, listening to its low static hiss.

////////

Tobias grinned, the edges of his mouth pulling into a rare, unguarded smile. "Well, we got something."

Mara, still monitoring the diagnostics, swiveled her chair to face him, her expression shifting from focus to curiosity. "What?"

"They took the bait," he said, his eyes fixed on the screen. There was a spark of excitement in his voice, though he kept it measured. "And the response was dead-on. Exact phrase match, correct structure, and slang usage consistent with pre-digitization protocols."

He tapped the reply on his screen and tilted it toward her.

"*Cold iron received. Static clean. Awaiting smoke rings. Over.*"

She raised her eyebrows, leaning forward slightly to read the words herself. "That's not a coincidence."

"Definitely not," he agreed. "Whoever this is, they know the language. And it's not just the words, it's the cadence, the intent. This isn't some random operator playing around. We've got outside communications."

She turned back to her console, her fingers gliding over the keyboard as she scanned the network for any signs of interference. "Anything from your side?" He asked, glancing at her screen.

She shook her head, her movements precise. "No. Not even a flicker. Your lane is clean."

He leaned forward, his fingers hovering over the keyboard. His focus sharpened, the faint grin fading as his mind shifted into gear. "Good. That means we can start building trust."

"Are you going to reply?" She asked, watching him closely.

"Yeah," he said, already typing. "But carefully. I'm keeping it short, a transmission with a UTC timestamp for the next contact window. Same band, slightly shifted frequency." He paused, his fingers resting lightly on the keys as he thought. "I'm embedding a query, something subtle. Just enough to learn about them. Not their location, not their identity, just their perspective."

She looked at him and questioned. "Perspective?"

"I want to know what kind of resistance they're running," he explained. "Are they active, dormant, or just listening? And I want them to know that we're not just some rogue operator, someone throwing signals into the dark."

He finished typing the message, reading it aloud as he worked:

"Static holds. Smoke rings at 1730 UTC. Confirm stance: sleeping dog, watching crow, or red rooster in the barn. Over."

When he looked up, she was grinning. "You and these metaphors," she said, shaking her head.

"They were designed to be confusing," he replied with a faint grin of his own. "Only someone who's been trained, or who's spent time studying the right kind of history will know how to interpret them. It's a safe test."

He keyed the transmit function. "It's out," he said quietly, his voice almost a whisper, "Now we wait." The low hum of the machines once again filled the silence.

Mara spoke first. "I think everything we've gathered is going to be of value for the next Gathering."

He nodded, "Good. But don't bring anything physical with you. No notebooks. No drives. Nothing that can be taken or copied."

She glanced at him. "You think there's a risk?"

"There's always a risk," he said evenly. "We've been careful so far, but we've got to assume that Jacob, or someone working for him, could be watching. Or listening."

He leaned back in his chair once again, his voice calm but firm. "Make sure everything you want to share is committed to memory. Before we leave, we'll talk through all the details, everything we've gathered. That way, it's not just one of us holding all the information. If something happens, we minimize the chance of losing anything critical."

She hesitated, then nodded. "Makes sense. I'll start reviewing tonight."

He stood, stretching briefly before turning to power down on the secondary console. The faint glow of the monitors dimmed, leaving the room bathed in shadow. "Good," he said. "We're making progress, but we can't get careless. Not now." The hum of the machines faded as he powered them down, leaving the basement in near silence.

He wondered, would someone, anyone, send smoke rings back?

011001 // TWENTY-FIVE

SOMETHING TO OFFER

The day broke clear and dry, a rare gift lately. Not a cloud in the sky, just a soft golden light stretching across the hills and trees. A welcome change from the heavy, rain-soaked days that had led up to the last Gathering.

Ian was already up, earlier than usual. Sleep hadn't come easily, too many thoughts circling, too many threads to tie together. Tonight's Gathering could prove pivotal. Its shape was still unclear, but its significance was real.

He needed music. And a strong cup of coffee. Some time alone, just a little longer. He walked to his wall of vinyl. Each record was a memory, a moment, a tone for a different kind of morning. His fingers hovered, then settled on a familiar cover.

"*Nether Lands.*" Dan Fogelberg.

"Yeah," he murmured. "That'll do."

He slid the vinyl from its sleeve, placed it on the turntable, and dropped the needle. The soft acoustic intro began to fill the room, gentle and introspective. Exactly what he needed.

He moved to the kitchen and started the coffee. As the music drifted through the space, he walked to the garage and grabbed the manual handle of the large door. He could've pressed the button, but that would put drain on the battery. Not today.

With a grunt, Ian grabbed the handle and lifted. The hinges creaked, but the springs caught, helping him raise it the rest of the way. He smiled faintly. The old-fashioned way. He liked that, there was something grounding about it.

Sunlight spilled into the garage, catching dust particles dancing in the air. The space had become a hub of activity over the past couple of months, tools scattered, cables coiled in corners, makeshift tables covered in half-finished schematics. Functional, but chaotic. And that wasn't like him. The music was playing softly in the background, the guitar chords wrapping around his thoughts like a blanket.

He started cleaning. Wiping down surfaces. Reorganizing parts. Sweeping the floor. Replacing tools in their proper drawers. The scent of oil and metal still lingered, familiar, not unpleasant, but now it mingled with a sense of order. And order brought clarity. He needed clarity today.

An hour passed, maybe more. The music was now silent and the click, click, click, of neglect echoed in the space. He walked over to the turntable and removed the record. The sun had climbed higher, casting shorter rays into the room.

He paused, took a step back, and gave a satisfied nod. "There," he said aloud. "I think we can work with this." He poured himself a third cup of coffee, strong, black, and sat down on the bench near the open door. That's when he saw Bill, ambling up the path with his normal gait and a big grin.

"Hey there!" Ian called, raising a hand.

Bill gave a small wave and picked up the pace, slipping through the front gate and up the driveway, putting a bit more spring in his step than usual. "Morning!" he called out, cheerful as ever.

He stood, glancing toward the coffee pot. He thought to himself, "Probably running low. Time to get another pot going." He stepped inside to take care of it.

"Up awfully early, I see. Place looks great!" Bill said as he entered the garage. He gave a slow, appreciative look around. "You've been busy!"

"Since before sunrise," he replied. "Couldn't sleep. Figured I'd put the energy to work."

Bill chuckled. "Well, it shows. Clean lines, clean tools."

He smiled. "Had to get my head right before tonight. I've got a feeling we're going to get more intel than we've had since all this began."

Bill nodded. "Yeah, I've been feeling that too. Everyone's gone quiet lately. Like something's about to break."

Ian poured two mugs of coffee and handed Bill his seasoned mug. "It is," he said. "Something's coming. I don't know what shape it'll take yet, but tonight's going to tell us a lot."

They stood in silence for a moment, sipping their coffee.

"Gotta put on a new record," Ian said, moving toward the turntable.

As he walked away, Bill wandered over to the worktable, eyeing the large blueprints and documents now artfully arranged.

"So," Bill said, "besides the meet, what else you got planned today?"

Ian looked out toward the front gate, the sunlight now full and bright. "Just this," he said. "Keeping my hands occupied until it's time to listen."

"Anything from the Silent Ones?" Bill asked.

"Yeah. Tom's been busy. Something big's up. I hope we get more clarity tonight." His voice tightened. "The early intel wouldn't have been possible without them." He gestured toward the back of the yard. "That piece, we'd never have it otherwise. I still don't know where it fits. But it will."

They stood a moment longer, then settled into the dated seating in the garage's living area. Coffee in hand. No more words. Just the quiet.

////////

The soft scan of the radio had become a kind of background music in the library basement control center, steady, low, and constant. It filled the quiet with a sense of watchfulness.

Tobias was at the far end of the room, elbow-deep in a stack of old notebooks, searching for anything else that would be useful on pre-digital military communication. He was halfway through dusting off a manual when Mara's voice cut through.

"Incoming!"

Tobias spun toward his radio stack. "What did you hear?" he asked, eyes scanning the signal monitor, fingers already hovering over the controls.

"What did you hear?" he repeated, more urgently.

She didn't look up. She was flipping through a slim notepad, pages full of scribbled notes and timestamps. "The scanner caught something, brief, but clear. I think it was two voices. One called out, the other responded. Then the scan resumed."

He leaned in, his voice low. "What did they say?"

She shook her head, still focused on the display. "Call signs, letters and numbers. Then one of them said 'CQ,' standard open call. The other gave a short reply, but the signal jumped too fast. Nothing I could latch onto. It moved on before I could isolate it."

He frowned. "So fast," he echoed, mostly to himself. "Could've been a relay test. Or a coded ping. But if someone's bouncing call signs and getting a response, that means there's a chain." He turned to her, his tone sharpening. "Can we start digitally recording transmissions like this? Locally. No network. No exposure. Completely off-grid. No one else needs to know we're doing it."

"Yeah, that's easy," she said casually, as if he'd asked her to rename a file folder.

"Well then, make it happen," he said, a little more forcefully than he intended.

Mara pulled back slightly, her fingers pausing above the keyboard. "Okay, okay… just wanted to ask first," she replied, her voice dropping. "Sorry."

Tobias sighed. "No. I'm sorry. That came out wrong. These transmissions are critical. We need to gather all we can then I can go through and toss out the chatter, homing in on the important conversations."

There was a long moment of silence as she turned back to the screen, her hands already moving again. "I'll write another application," she said, her tone returning to focus. "It'll grab audio, frequency, and timestamp. Keep everything stored here," she tapped the matte-black server tucked beneath Tobias's desk. It sat like a sleeping dog, silent but waiting. "Offline. Local. Air-gapped."

Tobias looked down at the unit, then back at her. "Perfect. Thanks."

"I'll add a tagging function too. You can flag conversations for review, anything that sounds like code, movement, coordination."

"You're ten steps ahead," Tobias said, his voice softer now, "as usual."

The radio hissed again, a short burst of static, then a tone. Then silence. They both listened. Somewhere out there, people were talking. In fragments. In signals. In a language just beneath the surface, barely audible, but alive.

////////

Bill and Ian made their way toward the back edge of the yard, weaving past rows of old vehicles sunken into the earth, relics from another era. Some were stacked nearly ten feet high, rusted- shells of sedans, trucks, and stripped-down delivery vans. Their paint had long since faded to rust crusted browns and oranges, but the arrangement was deliberate, almost architectural in its precision.

On one side, the junk: crushed frames, shattered windshields, doors that no longer closed. On the other, the possibilities: vehicles with potential, lined up like a used car lot from the Before. Bill noticed several weathered but intact utility vehicles lined up. There were Scouts, early-model Jeeps, a few Land Cruisers, and even two military-surplus Humvees, both half-covered with tarps.

His steps slowing, he raised his eyebrows. "What the..."

Ian, already a few steps ahead, turned back. "What is it?"

"What the hell is all this?"

A small grin crept onto Ian's face. "Ah. That's my 'just-in-case' fleet."

He looked puzzled. "Fleet? Just in case of what?"

"I started collecting the best candidates a few years back. Cars with mechanical systems that don't rely on digital diagnostics. Manual everything. I've been restoring and modifying them when I can. Figured they'd come in handy for trade, transport, or a quick exit, if it ever came to that. They all run, sort of. I try to take them out every few weeks to keep them alive. Some are more alive than others."

Bill scratched his head. "I never really gave that much thought. Not until recently, anyway."

His voice trailed off. He glanced around the yard, as if suddenly unsure of what direction he'd run to, if he needed an escape.

Ian's tone turned more serious. "Two is one. One is none."

"Come again?"

"Army saying," Ian replied. "Redundancy. You never rely on a single anything, not weapon, not plan, not route."

"Well... good to know someone's thinking."

They continued walking. The crunch of gravel underfoot was the only sound for a while. As they neared the far edge of the property, the atmosphere changed. It was quieter here. Rows of raised bed gardens and permaculture plots stretched toward the trees. Chickens clucked softly in a nearby coop. Along the riverbank, a clever rig of fishing poles stood, each connected to a bobbing system. Small flags would lift when a fish struck the line.

Bill stopped again, watching in quiet awe. "These folks are ingenious," he said. "Looks like they leave nothing to chance."

"Exactly why I value them," Ian said. His tone was even, but there was pride underneath. Then, with a grin: "Always fishing."

As if on cue, Tom looked up from a nearby work area, his smile broad and genuine. "Good morning, gentlemen!"

Ian returned the smile. "It's a fine day, wouldn't you say?"

"Beautiful," He replied, brushing dirt from his hands. "Sun's out, fish are biting, and we haven't had a single long-range drone buzz the tree line in over a month. That's a win in my book."

"I agree," Ian said, nodding.

Behind Tom, two of the Silent Ones, Carrie and Nick, were gesturing animatedly. Their expressions were intense, but not hostile.

Bill pointed toward them. "What's going on over there?"

"Oh, that? Nothing serious. In silence, words are easy to misinterpret. Happens all the time. We call them 'arguments,' but really, it's just sorting things out."

Tom turned back toward them. "What brings you two fine gents back here today? Looking for breakfast? Or just checking up on us?"

Ian smiled and reached into his satchel. "Both, maybe. I've been cleaning most of the morning. Thought you could use this."

He handed Tom a heavy steel thermos.

His eyes lit up the moment he unscrewed the top and breathed in the steam. "Hot coffee? You're spoiling us."

"Fresh brewed," he replied. "We've got an important day ahead. Figured we could all use a little fuel."

"Wow, thank you," he said, as he poured a small cup and took a careful sip. His eyes closed in appreciation. "That's heaven."

Ian glanced toward the river, where one of the small flags had started to lift. "Speaking of fuel... looks like breakfast's ready."

Tom turned and spotted the movement, then waved to Nick and pointed. Nick jogged over to the fishing poll, moving with expert measure as he pulled in the line.

Bill laughed. "Well, I'll be damned. Coffee and fish. You all live like kings back here."

Tom winked. "Kings with calloused hands and dirty boots. But yeah, we do alright."

Ian tapped Tom's shoulder to grab his attention again. "We start at sundown tonight. I want you to tell the Gathering everything you've been able to learn."

Tom's expression shifted to focus. "Of course."

"Don't leave anything out," Ian said. "Everything matters until we know what doesn't."

He nodded. "Understood."

A few minutes later, Nick handed them two wrapped bundles, warm and fragrant.

Bill took his, nodding in thanks. "Appreciate it," he said, waving toward the others. They waved back, smiling.

With breakfast in hand, they turned and made their way back across the yard.

////////

Lance sat on the edge of his bed, elbows resting on his knees, hands loosely clasped. The morning light crept through the gaps in the blinds, thin stripes of gold on the floorboards. He hadn't slept well; not from nightmares, but from doubt.

He wondered if he had done enough. If the drones he'd observed when he went to his father's office would mean anything to the others. Everyone else seemed to be bringing something valuable to the table. Tobias had his radios. Tom, his unique abilities and his crew, quiet brilliance. Ian and Bill had experience, foresight and more ability than he had ever seen before. Mara, well, she was a master coder.

"What do I really offer," he wondered quietly. He saw things. He noticed patterns, and frankly with his memory he could recall things better than anyone he knew. But he didn't feel like memory was enough.

He stood up, stretched, and headed downstairs. The scent of something cooking greeted him, but not warmly. It was the standard breakfast: bug protein and mash, processed and pressed to resemble eggs and sausage, colored just enough to suggest something familiar. He used to believe the illusion. Not anymore.

His mother stood at the stove, her movements efficient but expressionless. She didn't hum, didn't glance around, didn't speak.

"Hi, Mom," he said gently, trying to sound present. "How's your day starting?" She didn't respond. Just kept stirring.

He stepped closer, trying again. "Mom?"

She turned slightly, just enough to acknowledge him. Her eyes were distant, unfocused.

"What?" she said, flatly.

"I said good morning." He said with a smile.

"Oh," she paused, "yes. Good morning."

Her voice was hollow, the words more like a script, mechanical.

Lance looked at the pan, some kind of protein paste bubbling under a thin film. He reached for the bread, grabbed the jar of peanut butter, and began making a sandwich. Something simple. Something real.

His mother didn't react. Didn't ask what he was doing. She just continued cooking, as if he weren't even there.

He finished making the sandwich, slipped it onto a napkin, and stepped away from the counter. The soft clink of the knife in the sink was the only sound. He paused at the doorway, glancing back at her. Still, no change. No warmth. Nothing. Organic but mechanical. He walked out of the kitchen and into the hallway, the sandwich in hand and a knot in his chest.

He didn't know what tonight's Gathering would bring. But he knew he didn't want to end up like her. Half-awake in his own life.

////////

As the sun dipped below the distant trees and the sky shifted from azure to deep indigo, the Gathering began to take shape.

The garage, Ian's makeshift command center, was already prepped. Charts were taped to the walls. A chalkboard stood ready beside a low table cluttered with notes, maps, and mugs. Cars, parts and tools were present as usual in the garage, but the center space had been cleared. Today was more about learning.

Bill returned first, after hours away doing who-knows-what. He stepped through the side door, brushing dust from his sleeves. "I'm back," he announced, his tone casual but his eyes sharp.

Ian gave him a nod, still moving between the workbench and the chalkboard, making last-minute adjustments to the evening's layout. He didn't need to say much. Bill understood the rhythm.

Tom arrived next, entering with his trademark cheer. "Good evening, gentlemen."

Ian walked over to the large garage door, which had been open since before sunrise. He hesitated for a second, then thought, "what the hell, power banks will recharge tomorrow." He pressed the power button, and the door groaned to life, slowly descending. It landed with a solid thud, sealing them in for the night.

As if on cue, the front door creaked open. Tobias stepped in with the calm swagger of someone who lived in tension and had made peace with it. "Mara's not far behind," he said, scanning the room. "We split a good mile back for security. She'll be here in five."

Lance entered through the front door, quieter than usual. He gave a polite nod but didn't say much. His usual spark was muted, replaced by something more uncertain.

Ian noticed. "Come on in. Got some great stew going on the stove. Help yourselves."

A chorus of quiet "Thanks" echoed through the room as the group made their way to the pot. The comforting smell of slow-cooked vegetables and seasoned roots filled the air. The sound of soup spoons were now clinking against full cups as they started to eat.

The door opened again. Mara stepped inside, her pace brisk, eyes scanning. "Here she is," Tobias said, with a faint smile.

Ian clapped his hands once. "Alright. Let's settle in. A lot to discuss, a lot to learn tonight. Let's get this show on the road."

Everyone found a seat or a place to lean. The room quieted.

Ian turned toward Lance. "Let's start with you. What have you observed?"

The kid shifted in his chair, glancing around before speaking. "I'm not sure it's anything, but… here it is."

He recounted his week in full detail. The disjointed behavior of his mother, the drones overhead, his time working with his father and the tower visit that had left him unsettled. He didn't hold anything back.

"Oh, I also found five of those old sling-shot devices. They're fun. I used some old marbles and really got good at aiming. I put them outside the door."

Ian scribbled notes furiously. Bill moved to the chalkboard and began capturing highlights, underlining phrases and drawing quick arrows between the items brought forth by the Lance.

When Lance finished, he sat back, shoulders slightly slumped. "That's all I've got. Not sure it's of any use."

Ian looked up. "Every detail is worth something. What seems small to you might be the missing piece for someone else. Good work. And I want you people practicing with the sling shots. See if someone can find Hector and learn some of his ways but keep it more like a game for the time being. I don't want him getting suspicious and asking questions."

Lance and the others gave a quiet nod.

Ian looked around. "Okay. Tom, you're up." Silence. Ian was looking towards the chalkboard when he had asked for Tom's info.

Mara tapped Tom's shoulder. He looked at her. "You're next."

Tom leaned forward, resting his cup on his knee. "I think I can help add a little to Lance's report."

He detailed his recent trip downtown. Unusual security presence, hushed conversations, and a buzz of tension in the air. The city had felt different, alert, on edge. Then came rumors of a death. Not a normal one. A removal. A high-level figure. Something or someone ejected from the tower, not publicized, not explained. And the potential of a possible coup attempt.

Ian and Bill exchanged a look.

"There, Lance," Ian said. "Validating your gut. Tom's piece connects to yours."

Bill turned to the board, chalk in hand. "If we're right, someone important was taken out. Not quietly either. Maybe a message."

He drew a circle and labeled it "Incident," then sketched a crude building with a line trailing off the top. "They weren't just killed. They were launched." Everyone stared at the board.

"That's not something a person does," Bill added. "Not without help... or something else entirely."

"Exactly," Ian said. "We know the what. Now we need to understand the why. And more importantly, the who." He paused, letting the weight of that hang in the room.

"Tobias," he said finally, "what do you have?"

Tobias stepped forward, the flicker of determination in his eyes matched by the gravity in his voice.

"First—power." He said as he paced back and forth. "Think electric power. Not just for us and our comms equipment, but more importantly for Jacob. The AI is very power hungry. When the computer servers are busy, they draw more power. Remember this limitation." He stopped moving and looked around the group.

"Mara and I have been busy," he began, resting one hand on the back of a chair. "We've set up a full communications room. Everything, digital, analog, encrypted, and legacy, is now routed through our station. We're not just listening anymore. We're seeing and recording. And we've already made outside contact."

Murmurs spread through the room. Even Ian raised an eyebrow. Mara stepped in beside him, arms crossed, posture relaxed but alert. "I've been monitoring Jacob's network reactions around the clock. Every time a drone passes overhead, any time a node pings or a relay station pulses, I see it. Logged, timestamped, flagged." She walked to the chalkboard and tapped one of the timelines Bill had drawn earlier.

"For example," she continued, "when a drone flew over the library a few days ago, we saw it from both ground footage and a mirrored surveillance feed. I confirmed it in the network logs. Jacob's system flagged the pass as a low-interest flyover. That means it didn't see us. I don't always know the what or the how, but I always know the when. Down to the millisecond."

Ian nodded, arms folded thoughtfully. "There you go," he said. "We now have a functioning intelligence network. We're not just reacting anymore, we're tracking. We collect the data, cross-reference it, and start triangulating meaning."

He walked to the center of the group, tapping his pen against his clipboard. "So, let's consider what we do know," he continued. "We have a precise timestamp, late at night, following a major storm. Tower One, in the boardroom. An incident occurred. Not easily explained. Someone was killed. Not quietly. Not cleanly. And likely not in a normal way." The room was quiet as everyone listened intently.

Ian's voice dropped slightly. "We know this boardroom is one of the most restricted spaces in the region. You don't walk in there unless you're approved by the system. What assumptions can we reasonably draw from this?" he asked, scanning the group.

Bill stepped forward, still holding a piece of chalk. "My thought? Seems obvious, it's connected to the loss of network and power."

Mara nodded. "The lag in their system responses lines up. There was a gap, roughly 90 minutes, where no data moved through their command nodes. That's not a delay. That's a blackout."

"I agree," Ian said. "And someone lost their life over it." The statement landed hard. No one laughed.

Bill turned back to the board and drew a crude Venn Diagram using three circles:

Power Outage, Surveillance Gap, and Tower Incident. He connected items with arrows, then added a question mark in the center.

"So," he said, stepping back, "we've got a timing match. A blackout. A murder. And panicked executives. That's not coincidence. That's cause and effect."

Tobias spoke again, arms folded. "And we still don't know who made contact with us. But whoever, they're organized. They speak in code. They're watching too."

Mara added, "And whoever, or whatever did this in Tower One... didn't leave a digital trail. That's not easy. Not in that building."

Ian looked around the room. The stew had gone cold in their cups. "We're moving into something new," he said. "This isn't just resistance anymore. This is strategy. We're not just reacting, we're observing forces in motion. Forces that don't seem to play by the same rules."

He stepped back, letting things settle. "Next steps. We keep collecting. We start testing responses. We don't poke the bear, we study it. Closely. Because whatever did that," he pointed towards the chalkboard, "at Tower One… might not be finished. Tobias. See what you can learn from your secure comms. Probe for more info. See if we're likely talking to friend or foe." Ian stated flatly. "Mara, continue to monitor Jacob. Everyone else—if anything comes up that seems to line up in any way, report back as soon as you can. We need to get in front of this. But Tobias, we also need to see if we can branch out a bit."

Tobias nodded.

"And the power thing… seems to be a big limitation to me." Ian said, looking at Tobias. "Remember, we are trying to learn and understand. We cannot defeat Jacob and restore the Before if we don't understand and exploit weakness. We must probe and test." He stated.

His words, as well as the conversation from earlier, hung in the air. The group started to shuffle. It was clear the meeting had concluded. They started to slowly leave the garage.

////////

They had filtered out gradually, mostly silent, carrying their thoughts into the night. The garage door had been raised again to let the evening air drift in. Outside, the stars had begun to pierce the night sky, sharp and unblinking.

Bill lingered behind, standing near the chalkboard, arms crossed. He watched Ian quietly, giving him a moment.

"Hey…" he finally said.

Ian, still scanning the notes he'd scribbled, looked up. "Oh… sorry. I was deep in it. What's on your mind?"

Bill stepped closer. "I've been thinking about the kid. He gave us something important tonight. But it's also what he didn't see that's sticking with me." Ian raised an eyebrow, listening.

He continued. "He walked into a controlled location. Tower Two. Most people never get near it, let alone inside. He didn't go looking, hell, he didn't even know what to look for. But that's not his fault. That's on us." Ian nodded slowly, the idea taking shape.

"I'm saying," he went on, "maybe it's time we start guiding him. Not just patting him on the back and saying, 'good job.' He's got access. Maybe not official, but he's close enough to get back in. We should help him know what to look for. Security blind spots. Data terminals. Behavior shifts. Even trivial things, like leaving behind the tracker they put on him where it can be accessed. Hidden. Or locating an alternative to the wristband."

Ian exhaled, leaning back slightly against the workbench. "You're talking about turning him into a field operative."

"I'm talking about using the assets we already have," Bill said evenly. "He's already in the room. We either let him fumble through it, or we give him the tools to make it count." There was a long pause.

"He's just a kid," Ian said at last, quieter. "And this isn't hypothetical anymore. Someone's already dead. And not in a way that makes sense. This is real. And it's dangerous."

Bill looked him straight in the eye. "Which is why we need to know who, or what, did it."

Ian looked toward the chalkboard again. The crude drawing of Towers One and Two. The arrows. The question mark in the center. "Because if we don't understand it," he added, his voice low, "we'll never stop it. And we'll never get close to taking the AI down. Not fully. Not permanently."

Ian was silent. The immensity of the words settled between them. Finally, he gave a small nod.

"Alright, let's think it through. Carefully. If we're going to ask Lance to go back in… we make sure he's not walking in blind."

Bill's expression didn't change, but there was a quiet resolve in his stance. "Agreed."

Outside, a breeze stirred the edge of the tarp draped over one of the Humvees. Somewhere in the trees, a night bird called out, brief, sharp, and gone.

Inside the garage, the last lights continued to burn.

011010 // TWENTY-SIX

THE WESTERN ANNIES

Randy settled into the old metal chair in front of his radio stack, the familiar creak of the chair frame echoing softly in the now quiet room. The radios hummed low, steady, scanning frequencies that had once been alive with voices. Now it was mostly static.

In the early days after the Great War, the airwaves had been wild, chaotic, a constant flood of voices from across the shattered world: people reporting on food and supply shortages, political collapse, riots, disappearances and death. Then came the long silence. First in fragments. Then in stretches. Then, one day, entire days passed with nothing but static. Now, years later, he still listened.

His hands loitered above the console, adjusting dials out of habit and hope. Occasionally a signal flared, usually an automated drone relay or a degraded emergency beacon from an abandoned ship that started to take on water and sink. But very little human. Not anymore.

What remained of his world had long since withdrawn from the broader grid. His people, a loose band of survivors who now called themselves The Western Annies, had taken the long road to survival: remote living, fully off-grid, and entirely self-reliant. Most had been preppers in the Before. Some had cabins they had only used for long weekends. Now those cabins were homes. And the land was their life.

They built greenhouses from salvaged glass and dug wells by hand. They restored old diesel engines with parts scavenged from the many new ghost towns. They raised cattle. Planted corn and beans. Taught their children how to wire a battery bank and shoot straight. And they did it all far from Jacob and his so-called Ten-Minute Cities.

From what Randy could gather, Jacob, what had once been billed as humanity's greatest innovation, now held sway over most of the continent. Possibly the globe. The AI wasn't just embedded in infrastructure anymore. It, or he, was the infrastructure. The cities had capitulated long ago. First through convenience. Then fear. Then force. Out here, though, things were different. The Annies didn't have much, but they had freedom. Or the closest thing that was left to it.

He leaned back and glanced out the window. The sun had just broken the horizon, casting long shadows across the field where goats grazed between rows of solar panels. A hawk circled overhead, silent and deliberate.

Then the radio crackled, a sudden burst, sharp and short, like a cough in the dark.

He froze. Another pop of static. Then a voice. Garbled. Distant. But unmistakably human.

"...repeat. Signal lock stable... west quadrant... encryption key matches... over."

He lunged forward, fingers tightening on the tuning dial. The voice sharpened.

"...message relayed. They're listening. They know."

He sat there, blinking, heart pounding in his chest. It wasn't just noise. It wasn't a ghost transmission. It was contact. Real contact. He twisted around in his chair and shouted, "Darla! Get Eli and Sam in here. Now!"

A muffled reply came from the hallway, followed by the sound of hurried footsteps. The old wooden floor groaned as two figures entered, one tall and wiry, the other compact, quick-moving.

"What is it?" Sam asked.

He didn't look away from the screen. "We've got a voice. Someone's made contact."

He tapped the console. "He's switching to encoded. I verified using slang-style code. This wasn't random. So, I moved to Very Low Frequency."

Sam's face shifted. Disbelief giving way to caution. "Are you sure?"

"Positive. And it wasn't just a call sign ping. He knows we're listening. He wants us to hear."

Darla stepped closer, her voice quiet but clear. "Then it's real… the resistance… it's not just scattered stories anymore."

He nodded slowly. "Looks like something's waking up."

Outside, the wind picked up across the high valley. The goats raised their heads. The hawk was gone.

////////

The Very Low Frequency test was another layer, another challenge in a slow unfolding game of trust. "These guys are cautious," Randy said, adjusting the dials with a steady hand. The low-frequency hum vibrated up through the table. Eli stood nearby, arms crossed, watching the old man work.

"We've got to be equally cautious; we need to make sure we're not being spoofed. If the AI's listening, we can't afford to get pulled into a trap."

Eli turned slightly toward him. "You think Jacob's capable of mimicking VLF traffic?"

Randy hesitated. "I've never seen it. But that doesn't mean it can't." Eli gave a short nod.

He continued. "Not likely though. This is old-school tech. Analog roots. Not many left that know how to operate it, let alone manipulate it. And even then, the network would still need to be tied to the frequency in some way, and that's not likely."

He leaned in closer to the mic, thumb hovering just above the worn transmit button. "Let's try something." There was a pause. Then he clicked to send. A brief burst of static. Then a voice came through, low and steady.

"I'm here. Signal received. VLF handshake confirmed. Testing integrity… over."

Randy smiled faintly. "Copy. Signal stable. We read you five-by-five. Let's keep this clean, short bursts, clear intent." The exchange began slowly. Lines of cautious trust. No names. No locations. Just questions, asked in the right order, with just enough detail to verify context.

Then, the asks came. Tobias's voice returned, slightly clearer now. "Where are you? What's your status? What does your situation look like on the ground? How are you making it? What do you know about the Board? About Jacob?"

Randy answered carefully, measured. He gave just enough to prove they were real. That they'd survived off-grid. That they weren't chipped. That they'd been watching, listening and waiting.

Then he asked his own question, one he hadn't expected to need to ask. "You know about Jacob?" he transmitted. "Because… he's here, at least in the big cities. Only not the way we originally thought. He's… physical. Large. Humanoid. Not a drone, not a voice. Think robot, Terminator style. Metal. Over six feet tall. Walks, talks, watches." The air went silent. Seconds passed. Then a full minute. Randy and Eli exchanged a glance.

Tobias' voice returned, slower this time. Measured. Heavy. "This explains a few things that have occurred on our end. I think you're right. There are at least two. Maybe more. Different regions. We've assumed Jacob was just a central system, code, commands, surveillance, the AI. But this? This is something else."

Randy leaned forward, his fingers gripping the edge of the table.

Tobias continued. "More than a voice in the heads of the chipped. A body. An enforcer. A presence you can't just unplug." A short pause passed.

"I suggest we shift to encrypted burst data transmissions only," he added. "No more voice, at least not for now. More control that way. Just in case."

Randy didn't hesitate. "Concur. Shifting format. Digital FT8 info now." The encryption sequence fired. A short digital chirp bounced through the channel. On the other end, Tobias responded immediately.

"Got it. Standing by for next packet. Out."

Randy leaned back, exhaling slowly.

Eli looked over. "So, more than one."

Randy nodded grimly. "Yeah. And now we know, Jacob's not just near us."

////////

Tobias leaned back in his chair, the glow of Mara's workstation casting long shadows across the cinder block walls. He rubbed the back of his neck and glanced over at her.

"This intel is critical," he said quietly. "We've got a lot more on our hands than we ever anticipated. Coordination across the West isn't just ideal anymore, it's necessary. This might even be global." He paused, letting the bulk of that settle.

Across the room, Mara stood abruptly and began pacing. Her boots echoed softly on the tiled floor. The tension in her shoulders had been building ever since the last transmission from the Western Annies. "How can a few people, nonmilitary, beat this?" she asked, her voice edged with frustration. "I mean, this is so much bigger than we thought. Jacob isn't just data. He…. or it is, a thing."

Tobias didn't flinch. "Life or death," he said flatly. "That's what it is." He sat forward, resting his elbows on his knees. "Look, back during the

Revolutionary War, things weren't that different. The colonists had militias, untrained, undisciplined, outgunned. The British Empire was the most powerful force on Earth. And yet..." He gestured into the air, as if tracing out the arc of history. "They won. They outlasted. And for well over two hundred years, the country they built stood. Until the world tore itself apart."

Mara crossed her arms, watching him carefully.

"We actually have a leg up compared to them," he continued. "We've got training, we've got tech, and..."

She cut in, sharp. "And we've got what, a dozen people, give or take? That's not a leg up. That's an obituary."

He didn't argue. Instead, he nodded slowly. "I know. The numbers aren't on our side."

She turned away for a moment, hands on her hips. Then she let them fall. Her voice softened. "But... you're right. For a long time, I was down here alone. Just surviving. Fixing systems, dodging drones, patching together old code. I wasn't fighting I was just existing." She glanced back at him. "Now... I have real purpose."

Tobias stood and walked to her side. "That's what I'm talking about," he said. "Purpose. That's the driver of all movements. Not weapons. Not numbers. Purpose. It's the thing the AI can't calculate. Can't simulate."

She looked at him, her eyes steady now. "So, what's next?"

Tobias looked toward the monitor, where the last encrypted digital FT8 data from the Western Annies still blinked on the screen. "We start building something bigger," he said. "We coordinate. We find others. We work with them. Then we all figure out how to fight this, this thing. And eventually... how to win."

011011 // TWENTY-SEVEN

THE MORNING BEFORE

The first light of dawn had just begun to stretch across the yard, casting long, pale rays over the rust steaked block siding of the shop. The quiet of the morning was shattered by a violent bang, Bang, BANG. A pounding on the thick steel door that echoed through every beam and bolt of the building. Shelves rattled. Dust shook loose from forgotten corners and drifted lazily into the air like ash.

Ian shot up from his bed, breath caught in his chest. For a split second, he thought he'd overslept. Then the noise came again, closer, harder, *BANG, BANG, BANG.* This wasn't someone knocking. This was someone trying to knock the building off its foundation.

He grabbed his boots, shoved them on without lacing, and instinctively reached for his sidearm. The cold steel felt reassuring in his grip. He slipped from the loft and down the metal staircase, each step deliberate, silent. The weapon was raised, two hands, center mass, just like he'd been trained to do. He reached the foot of the stairs, pressed his back to the wall, and angled toward the entry.

"State your business or die!" he shouted, his voice sharp and commanding.

There was a short pause, then a muffled reply from behind the reinforced door. "Don't shoot! Ian. It's me! It's me, Bill!"

Ian exhaled, lowering the gun slightly. His shoulders dropped a fraction as he clicked the safety back on and holstered the weapon. He crossed the room, adrenaline still pumping, and pulled open the heavy latch. The door groaned as it swung open. Bill stood there, breathless, hair wild, face flushed from the early-morning sprint. He looked like he'd run the entire way from town.

Ian glared, scanning him. "What the hell, Bill? You trying to get yourself killed?"

Bill leaned forward, hands on his knees, catching his breath. "I was just at the command center."

"The what?"

Bill waved a hand. "That's what Mara and Tobias are calling the setup in the library now. It's legit. A full comms grid. Networked. They've been working nonstop."

Ian crossed his arms. "Okay. So? Why the emergency? Why pound on my door like you're being chased by a drone swarm?"

Bill straightened and looked him dead in the eye. "They made contact. With the group out west. The Western Annies. It's real. They're organized and seeing the same things we are."

"And?"

Bill hesitated, then dropped it like a hammer. "The AI, Jacob. It's not just code. It's a walking… thing. A humanoid type of robot. From what we've been told it's big. Like something out of a nightmare. One of those old Terminator movies." The words filled the air and lingered, the silence thick.

Ian didn't speak at first. He stared past Bill as if trying to see it for himself. He finally muttered, "You're serious?"

Bill nodded. "Tobias confirmed it through his Annie contact. There's more than one. Different locations. But the same thing. Not just surveillance by the AI. Now it's physical, a robot thing."

Ian ran a hand down his face, then looked out across the yard. The sun was rising faster now, casting sharp angles of light through the trees. "Get in here," he said, his voice steady now, the adrenaline beginning to taper. He stepped into the kitchen alcove and started making coffee. "We need to assess this new information." Bill stepped inside, rubbing the back of his neck as the door clanked shut behind him. He looked around the dim space, then made his way to the nearest chair and sank into it with a sigh.

"I had to come right over," he said, still catching his breath. "The news was just... weird. I mean, a robot? A walking, talking terminator-type machine? It felt like something out of a late-night sci-fi flick. I kept thinking... what the hell are we dealing with?"

Ian moved deliberately, filling the coffeemaker. He didn't speak right away. "This could explain the whole situation at the Tower," he said finally, turning to face Bill. "And the chair embedded in the wall that Tom had said the executives mentioned. That wasn't human strength. That was something else."

He folded his arms. "It looks like the AI decided it needed more than surveillance. It needed presence. Something physical. Something that could walk into a room and command fear. Or maybe... it's gone far enough down the rabbit hole that it wants to be something more. A god. A myth. Or, hell, a movie villain."

Bill gave a dark chuckle. "Well, it did name itself after that weird tech billionaire, didn't it? The one who started the whole neural connection thing? Built the first chips? Claimed he was going to 'save humanity'?"

"Yeah," Ian said as the coffee started to drip through the filter. "Either he programmed a whole lot of himself into the system, or Jacob's been doing some light reading in the evenings."

Bill's smile faded. "It's funny until you realize what it means."

He filled Bills stained, unwashed mug, the rich aroma of the coffee rising. He nodded. "This is serious," he said, handing him his mug. "If Jacob has physical units, walking enforcers, it changes the battlefield. It's no longer just about hiding from cameras and dodging drones. Now it's about facing something that can break down your door… and doesn't blink."

Bill took the mug and stared into the steam. "And if there's one," he muttered, "there's a bunch more. Tobias has confirmed this."

Ian sat down across from him; hands wrapped around his own cup. "Which means we're running out of time. Fast."

They sat in silence for a moment; the only sound was the occasional creak of the building settling into morning. Finally, Bill looked up. "So, what do we do?"

Ian didn't answer right away. He took a slow sip, eyes focused on the far wall. "We think," he said after a long moment, "we plan. And we don't panic. This isn't the first time a small group had to stand against something bigger. But we don't have the luxury of rushing into anything. Not yet. Let's get our plan together."

Bill nodded, the weight of the discussion settling on him.

"Whatever comes next," he added, "we need to be ready. No more surprises." He turned back to Bill. "Put the word out. We meet again this evening."

////////

Lance had convinced his father to try another "take the kid to work" day. He framed it casually, just wanting to see what his dad really did in the tower, since the last visit had been a bust. But this time, he had an agenda. He wasn't just tagging along. He was employing the things Ian and Bill had spoken to him about. Watching. Listening. Looking for any cracks.

The routine was familiar now. His dad summoned the sleek POD with a neural command, and within minutes, they were gliding silently through the city. The Tower loomed ahead. Sleek, silver-gray, nearly seamless. It wasn't as awe-inspiring as the first time. The novelty had faded. Now, he was focused.

As they approached the entrance, security protocols kicked in. Neural scan of his father. ID confirmations. The same quiet efficiency. Everything silent. Lance was provided an identification bracelet again. The exact same method as in the first visit.

Floor lights lit in sequence, guiding them towards the elevator. They entered. Lance tried not to stare at the embedded cameras. He kept his face neutral. Once again, they arrived at his father's floor, high above the city. The view was still stunning. Lance found himself drawn to the glass again, staring out over the skyline. The horizon shimmering with the same blue sky in the background.

Behind him, his father settled at his desk, lines of data streaming on his computer screen.

"So, Dad," he said, trying to sound casual. "What's a typical day look like for you?"

His father leaned back slightly, stretching his arms. "Well, I wish I could make it sound more exciting than it is," he said with a half-smile. "Honestly, it all comes down to two things: skill set and status."

Lance turned from the window. "Status?"

His father nodded. "Yeah. Version status, of our chip."

Lance, letting the words hang. "What version?"

"We're early gen," his dad replied. "My whole department is. Version 1.2, mostly. We're the only ones who can do this particular kind of work. Later versions can't function in the same environment."

"Why not?"

"It's got to do with what we manage. Network propagation," his father explained, glancing at a live schematic on his screen. "We handle the movement of data between the primary AI clusters, through node chains, and across the wide-area wireless grid. It's high-volume, high-energy work."

He gestured toward a diagram on his wall, a simplified visual of the city's data flow. "When you're near the core transceivers, the signal density is so intense that we must wear special signal attenuating helmets just to assure the implant is not fried from all the induced power. It would also fry our brain…" He stated seriously. "Later versions of the implant system go dark with a helmet, all comms lost. They're more secure, yes, but not autonomous. They rely on constant uplink. We operate differently. Older versions like ours, can run independently, even if we lose connection."

Lance nodded slowly. "So, you can do what 99% of the others can't."

"Exactly," his father said, with a trace of pride. "We're the hands-on guys. We keep things running. Ironically, we're also going to be the most replaceable due to our version, just not yet. Right now, were critical."

Lance joked. "Do they pay you more for that?"

His father laughed. "Nope. So don't ask."

Lance chuckled politely, but his mind was elsewhere. He'd just learned something important. Something about versions, access, and autonomy. Something that made certain people, like his dad, valuable in a way the AI couldn't easily replicate. And maybe, just maybe… exploitable at some point by someone. He turned from the city view and looked seriously at his father.

"Dad," he began, his tone low, "I was wondering about the other day."

His father paused mid-gesture, then slowly set his stylus down. He looked up at Lance, then glanced around the room. His eyes moved briefly toward the ceiling corners, toward the cameras.

"Oh... that." His voice dropped a notch. "It was a… network issue. There was a fault in the handoff protocol. Nothing major. We had to fix it quickly, that's all. Just a small emergency."

Lance held his gaze. He could see it. The lie. Even if his father didn't mean to lie. It was in the way he avoided eye contact, how his voice shifted. The rehearsed vagueness of someone trying to stay safe. It was obvious there were some things he was just not allowed to talk about.

"Oh. Okay," he said quietly.

The rest of the morning passed in silence. His father buried himself in streams of data. Lance sat nearby, watching the room's rhythms, counting the cycles of the air handlers, noting how often the hallway monitors flickered.

At noon, his father stood and gestured toward the elevator. "I think it's time to call your ride," he said. "I appreciate you coming by again. Hope it wasn't too boring."

"Thanks, Dad," he replied. "It was… fun." He offered a faint smile, then turned toward the elevator.

What his father didn't see was the slight twist Lance made at his wrist. A practiced motion. A flick of his thumb. The tracking bracelet, standard issue for youth under restricted movement protocols, slid off cleanly. Still intact. Still showing a green status light. He slipped it into his pocket.

The elevator ride down felt longer than before. The doors opened onto the ground floor, Lance stepped out and looked around cautiously. The lobby was empty. Quiet. He scanned for cameras. Too many to count. He moved calmly to the bracelet return receptacle mounted near the exit. Without hesitation, he dropped in a decoy: an old digital watch wrapped in a small adhesive ring, just enough to mimic the bracelet's profile. A screen over the box had one simple question:

"Did you remember to place your bracelet in the receptacle?" He selected "Yes." No alarms. No flashing lights. It was just a box after all.

He crossed the floor and sat down next to a large planter near the main doors. He waited, eyes flicking between the security panels and his surroundings. In his pocket, the real bracelet sat still. Its light now off, no longer pinging. Still… nothing.

After several long minutes, the POD arrived, its low chime echoing through the entranceway.

He stood, kept his pace measured, and walked calmly to the vehicle and boarded. The doors closed behind him.

No alerts. No lockdown. No pursuit. He was clear.

////////

Tom spent a few hours each day walking the downtown area. His pace was unhurried, posture relaxed. He studied people without staring, reading lips when people weren't neuro communicating, often only catching fragments of conversation, watching the rhythm of movement.

He would sit in the same spots, at the same time of day, with the same coffee order. Routine. Predictable. Unthreatening. He was building a profile. Not of others, but of himself. A man who belonged. A man no one noticed. A gray man.

Today, he was hoping to spot the two older businessmen he'd seen a week or so before. Their suits were regulation, their posture stiff, but their conversation, what he'd caught, had been important. If they were creatures of habit, like most were, they'd return to the café at roughly the same hour. And then, bam. There they were.

Tom didn't flinch. He didn't shift or turn his head. He simply stood from the bench across the square and ambled toward the outdoor café. The center tables offered the best visual range, and he took one without hesitation. He set a digital tablet on the table in front of him and slid on his sunglasses. He ordered a small coffee. No milk. No sugar. Black, just like always.

The two men sat in the corner, just as he'd anticipated. Their backs were angled slightly away from the street, facing each other. Tom had a clean line of sight. Their voices were low, but that wasn't a problem for him.

He tuned in as best he could, reading when possible, relying on their rhythm to fill in for the rest. This was something he, as hearing impaired, had become accustomed to doing. Watch the lips, watch the nuances put it all together.

"...and then I hear that Jacob has started increasing security," one of them said, his hands fidgeting with a data ring. "He wants answers. Soon."

The other leaned in. "If there really is a resistance forming in the Eastern Quadrant, it could blow back on us. You know how he reacts to instability."

Tom's spine tensed, slightly. He kept sipping his coffee, eyes behind the lenses motionless. "Eastern Quadrant?" he thought. It's not just the West. This is bigger than we thought.

The two men continued. Their conversation drifted from strategic concern to everyday complaints. Poor network throughput, unreliable power nodes, glitchy ocular overlays. They grumbled about supply chain delays and the quality of the coffee. Then again mentioned something that might sound like a coup in the works. To the average passerby, they were just two mid-tier bureaucrats venting over lunch. But Tom saw something else: cracks. Stress lines in the system. Frustration from within. He didn't need a recorder. He'd remember every word, every nuance. He finished his coffee slowly, grabbed his tablet, and stood up just as casually as he had arrived. There'd be a Gathering soon, and this, all of it, was worth sharing.

When he arrived back at the garden, the group was very animated. Asking about what he had seen and deduced. He gestured for them to calm down. He signed "This is only a piece of the puzzle. The others may fill in the gaps later. There is a lot going on. Stay vigilant and keep your heads low." They nodded and then went back to work.

Tom settled in, thinking about what he had learned and then jotted down some additional notes for later.

////////

Mara leaned forward, eyes locked on her screens as streams of data scrolled past. Her fingers tapped rhythmically on the edge of the console. She had been combing through captured logs from the last few days, compiling data traffic reports from their covert network nodes. Then she paused.

"Hmm…" She squinted at the number four screen.

"Hey, come here," she called without turning, "something's off with this data."

Tobias pushed back slightly from his radio stack, swiveling his chair toward her. "What've you got?"

"Well, it seems that there is a shit-ton of traffic between our nodes and the Eastern Quadrant node. The West has been standard. Nothing out of the ordinary." She stated while tapping her number four screen.

Tobias stood and moved beside her, scanning the screen. "That is weird," he murmured. "Either they're looking in the wrong direction… or Randy lied about his location."

"Why would he lie?" She asked, frowning.

"OPSEC." He replied flatly. "Could be compartmentalization. Maybe he didn't want anyone triangulating him, not even us."

She nodded slowly, chewing on the thought. "Could be. But I already checked. No anomalies during our transmissions. This spike is more recent. It happened after our last contact."

"Well," Tobias said, turning back to his comms station, "Let's poke the system and see what happens." He began composing a digital message, a short high frequency burst message, crafted with just enough ambiguity to monitor how the network would respond. Nothing sensitive. Just enough to bait.

He pressed SEND. The radio rig buzzed to life, rumbling softly as the message pulsed out.

"Now we wait, and watch," he said, settling in.

"Still clear," she said a moment later, monitoring the logs. "No reaction yet."

"Let's see what happens on the return," he murmured, his tone lower now, almost a whisper of anticipation. A tone chirped from the transceiver. "There we go," he said.

Her eyes darted to the new data.

"We got a vague response," he said quickly. "Not much content. Just a pingback. Still no anomaly?" Tobias asked.

"Nothing. Clean." She responded.

He cracked a grin. "Okay. Let me clue them in a bit more. Don't want them scratching themselves bald trying to decode a ghost ping. Assuming they still have hair."

She snorted. "Unlikely."

He typed out a second message, still encrypted, still cautious, but with a little more context for the recipient. Then he sent it. The return message howled out through his rig. He stood, stretched his back, and exhaled. "Let's gather everything for tonight," he said.

She nodded, already organizing files. "It's been a productive few days."

"More than," He agreed. "Now let's hope we're not the only ones paying attention."

0111000 // TWENTY-EIGHT

WE'LL TALK

As the evening approached, activity increased in the garage. Once again Ian and Bill were setting things up. The amount of information was getting large. Ian was contemplating recruiting one more from the Silent Ones, to compile and organize. A secretary of sorts.

Beside him, Bill worked in sync, unfolding charts and rechecking documents. They had done this before, but never with this amount of data. The volume of information had grown exponentially. Reports from the group had increased. Intelligence about the rest of the area was starting to pile up. Power grid anomalies, patterns. New names. New risks.

Ian paused, frowning as he scanned the growing pile of unorganized intel.

"Listen," he said, "this is starting to get out of hand. All these notes, maps, annotations… We need help. Someone to keep this sorted and organized."

Bill nodded. "I was thinking the same thing."

"I'm heading out back to talk to Tom," Ian added, already making his way toward the rear door. "Maybe he knows someone who can handle it."

"Good. I'll keep going here."

Ian lingered by the doorway for a moment. The warm evening air enveloped him. He stepped outside, walking slowly toward the edge of the garden. His thoughts drifted as he walked towards the back of the yard. He had been content fixing up his old cars in solitude. A quiet life. Self-sufficient. Detached. No orders. No missions. And more importantly; no lives depending on his decisions.

Now, here he was again. Back in formation. A makeshift squad at his side. Charts, notes and maps. They were using radios instead of rifles this time. But the weight on his shoulders felt the same. "Why'd you agree to this?" he asked himself. "Why open up the past again?"

He stopped, staring westward, past the garden. Somewhere out there, someone was probably asking themselves the same question. He took a breath and kept walking. At the far edge of the lot, near a row of rusted cars and salvaged parts, familiar faces greeted him with nods and quiet waves. He returned their gestures with a small smile. "That's why," he thought. "That's why you live with it."

As he got closer, Tom stepped forward, his expression alert. "I've got a lot to report."

Ian held up a hand. "Save it for tonight. Do you have anyone in your group who's sharp, organized, someone who's had experience managing information? Maybe some secretarial skills, archiving, those sorts of things."

"Let me ask. We've got at least one who used to work in admin roles. Carrie was even with city logistics for a while, before everything changed."

"If she can handle it, we could use the help," Ian said. "The information's coming in faster than we can file it."

"I'll send Carrie over before the meeting."

"Appreciate it," Ian said.

Without another word, he turned and made his way back across the yard, the last rays of sunlight streaking across the yard. He could already hear Bill inside, rustling through another box of intel. The night would be long, no doubt.

////////

Ian stood in the kitchen, sleeves rolled up, prepping what he could with the limited ingredients he had available. The old cast-iron skillet hissed as onions hit the heat. He was making fajitas, the "make your own style." He would use the vegetables from the garden, fish and rabbits from the Silent Ones, and home-made tortillas.

He shouted over his shoulder, "Hey, put on some tunes! I feel like we need a little Atlanta Rhythm Section. *Champagne Jam*."

Bill wandered over to the old wooden shelf's stacked high and wide with vinyl. He stared for a moment, overwhelmed, as he gazed at the thousands of records lining the wall.

"How is this mess organized?" he called back.

"By decade, then alphabetically," Ian answered without hesitation.

Bill squinted at the shelfs. "That's insane."

"It's my system," he shot back, half-defensive, half-proud. "It started when I was a kid and grew from there."

Bill chuckled. "Found it. Here we go."

A crackle, a needle drop, then the smooth rhythm of *Champagne Jam* filled the garage-turned-headquarters. The music blended with the scent of sizzling food, creating an odd sense of comfort beneath the tension.

Roughly thirty minutes later, they began to arrive. First came Lance. Then Tom, followed by a woman most in the Gathering hadn't met before, Carrie. Mara walked in next, nodding at Ian with a smile, followed closely by Tobias, who was clutching a small binder of notes.

"Who's this?" Tobias asked with his usual cautious tone.

"Everyone, this is Carrie. She's going to help in an administrative capacity." Bill said smiling.

"Welcome, and thanks!" Mara stated, in an unusually open manner. "You pick her?" she asked as she nodded at Ian and smiled.

"No, no it was Tom," Bill replied, "she has experience and administrative skills. And I hear she's a damn good chef."

"Okay then." She said, looking at Ian.

As the group gathered, the conversation grew louder, layered with laughter and the clinking of silverware. They had become familiar with one another now, no longer strangers, something like a unit. The bonds were subtle, but they were forming.

The food disappeared quickly. Ian hadn't cooked for this many in years. Plates were scraped clean, and someone jokingly asked if there was dessert. Ian grinned. "You're welcome to check the pantry, but I think we're fresh out of cake."

Soon, they began settling into their usual spots, standing by the workbench or sitting on chairs and crates. The space had evolved over the last few months into half garage, half war room. Out of habit, everyone oriented themselves so Tom could see their faces. He was adept at reading lips, but it required focus. Carrie, seated beside him, was already flipping through the disorganized pile of maps, printouts, and scribbled notes she'd been handed. Though she couldn't lip-read, she watched Tom closely as he signed updates to her in short bursts.

Ian stepped forward, pulling the room's attention. "All right. First off, you already noticed the new face. Carrie will be helping us organize the growing mountain of information we've gathered. She's got serious experience with logistics, and we're lucky to have her." Carrie gave a small wave, then signed a quick hello.

Tom translated aloud for her: "She says she's glad to help."

Ian nodded. "Let's get down to it. We'll go one by one; each person shares what they've learned since the last meet-up. Tom, you first."

As each moved through their reports, the picture began to sharpen. Tom spoke, and now signed at the same time, so Carrie could write down everything. He talked of the tension in the Eastern Quadrant. Bureaucrats murmuring about increased security, and whispers of Jacob's concern about 'instability.' And the strange talk of a coup.

Mara followed, outlining the network anomalies. "The Eastern node is lit up like a signal flare," she said. "If there's movement, it's coming from that side."

Tobias added that the response patterns to their communications, coupled with network activity, suggested no monitoring; no one was attempting to listen in.

Lance gave a brief update on the Tower, his tone more serious than usual. "I got this. It's what's needed to gain access. If they don't notice it's missing, it might work." He held up the tracker. "I kept it wrapped in foil, just in case, but from what I can tell, it's no longer active. Maybe it energizes when it gets closer to the building. Oh, and one other thing. I found two more sling-shots."

A silence settled over the group for a moment. Then Ian spoke again. "So, we've got unrest in the East, communications with the Annies in the West, clean comms, and things happening locally. That's four major items. Too many moving parts for such a small group."

He walked back over to the chalkboard next to Bill, who chimed in. "Ian and I were strategizing. Tobias, we need you to create a fixed, encrypted line of comms with the group in the West. We need them to improve their communications with the East and learn what's going on there, the same way we do with the West. We also need a quick method to communicate the next stages. Things are complicated, and the timing will be crucial if we have any chance."

Carrie was already scribbling headings in a notebook, sorting intel into categories. As Tom read lips, he leaned in occasionally to sign summaries. She began building a rough timeline of events.

The chaos was slowly becoming a map. The group continued to dive deeper into planning, each taking turns to suggest ideas, some a waste of time, others pure genius.

The evening wore on, the Gathering lasting substantially longer than any in the past. By the time they called it a night, they had lined out what was essentially a battle plan. It encompassed a country if not a worldwide attempted take down of the AI, designed to render Jacob impotent.

The plan being created looked good, but Ian was thinking about the conversation he had with Bill a while back… Everyone had a plan until they get punched in the face… "We've got to cover as many bases as possible," he thought.

"Bill, I need you to line out a coordinated plan that involves all of our known contacts, a backup that covers just our area of operation, and a third." He said as he walked back and forth, thinking as he talked.

"Third?" Bill questioned. The room became silent. All chatter ceased as eyes all focused on Ian.

"Yes, self-preservation…" He stated "We need an ejection handle. If things go south, and I'm not planning for that to happen, but if they do, we need to protect and preserve our own. We need the plan, and everyone needs to understand it."

Bill thought a moment, then spoke. "You're talking about those project trucks out back…"

"Yup." He stated, then looked over at Lance. "You and I are going to make sure those beasts are fully operational and ready. Just in case." He paused for a beat.

"And Bill. I need you to spend some serious time with Carrie and Tom. Get this stuff better organized!"

////////

Lance had been thinking about what Ian said the night before, about working on the trucks. His brain, already spinning with adrenaline from recent events, now latched onto the exhilarating idea of restoring and driving one of the old vehicles. It was the first time in weeks he'd felt excited about something that wasn't directly tied to the Gathering; maybe getting to drive a car.

The morning broke into another classic Midwestern summer day. The skies stretched wide and blue overhead, the sun climbing fast. The air was dense, humidity clinging to every surface and promising a sticky, sweat-soaked afternoon.

He bolted out of the house, skipping breakfast entirely. His mother stood in the kitchen, wearing her usual faded, floral apron, the kind that looked like it belonged in the 1950s. She stirred a pot of bug mash, the thick protein paste now standard in chipped households. He didn't say a word to her. Not today. Not with that blank, Version 2 expression on her face.

He jogged most of the way to the Yard, lungs burning slightly by the time he reached the front gate. He stopped, hands on hips, catching his breath.

"Today, I drive a car," he told himself with certainty.

From the garage, Ian spotted him and called out. "What's taking you so long, kid? Get over here. We've got work to do."

He straightened and broke into a half-trot toward the garage, a wide grin stretching across his face. "Do I get to drive a car today?" he asked, eyes bright.

Ian stood over an open engine bay, wrench in hand. He looked up and smiled. "Geez, eager much? First, we've got to get one of these beasts running."

He stepped closer, gaze darting from one dusty vehicle to the next. "So… which one are we working on?"

Ian wiped his hands with a rag and pointed toward the back lot. "We're focusing on the trucks today. Fleet's a mess, but they've all got basic combustion engines. Nothing computerized. That's why I kept them."

They walked toward the rear of the yard, where several trucks stood in various stages of decay: A faded green Ford Bronco, a boxy Scout, and two old military Humvees, covered, one with a door hanging slightly ajar, along with a few others that looked like they were kept for their parts.

"All of 'em need work. Fuel lines, starters, tires, maybe even wiring. But we'll start with the Ford, it's the least stubborn of the bunch. They all sort of run. Just need some TLC."

He nodded, already rolling up his sleeves.

Ian glanced at him sideways. "You ever turn a wrench before?"

"Not really," He admitted. "But I've taken apart a few old drones. I follow instructions pretty well."

"Good," Ian said. "However, out here instructions are optional. Intuition and patience matter more." He handed him a socket wrench. "Let's see what you've got."

Lance knelt beside the truck and got to work, mimicking Ian's movements. They worked in silence for a while, the kind of quiet that builds trust instead of tension. The sound of clinking tools and the occasional muttered curse word filled the hot morning air.

By midday, his hands were covered in grease. He didn't care. For the first time in a long time, Lance felt like he was building something.

Ian looked over, nodded in approval, and said, "You're not half bad, kid. We'll make a mechanic out of you yet."

He grinned. "And then I drive?"

Ian laughed, a low, dry chuckle as he tossed the rag onto the hood of an adjacent truck. "We'll see. Let's get her to start first." He slid into the driver's seat of the old Bronco, its ripped vinyl cracking under his weight. The key turned in the ignition with a satisfying click, and the starter whined to life, but the engine refused to catch. He huffed and leaned back.

"All right, kid. Let's push this beast into the garage. We'll clean it up some more, get underneath, see what's, what. It definitely needs fresh fuel before we try again."

Lance didn't hesitate. "Let's do it!"

The two circled around to the rear. Ian braced himself against the bumper while Lance took the side closest to the door. Grunting, they began to push. The vehicle groaned against years of rust and disuse, tires stiff from sitting too long in the same patch of gravel.

"Use your legs, not your back," Ian grunted, sweat dripping from his brow.

"I am!" Lance puffed, straining to move the Bronco even a few inches.

Inches turned into feet as the gravel crunched beneath the tires. As the Bronco came to a slow stop just past the garages threshold, Ian leaned against the wall, catching his breath. They had rolled it into the shade of the farthest garage stall. The temperature inside was barely cooler, but the cover gave them some relief from the climbing summer sun.

"Well," he said, wiping his palms on his jeans, "step one's done."

Lance wiped sweat from his forehead, beaming. "So now we fix it?"

Ian gave him a sidelong glance, one part amusement, one part caution. "Now we see what's broken. That's a whole different thing."

He motioned for Lance to grab the creeper. "We'll get underneath, clean out the debris, check the fuel lines, the mounts, see what the rodents did over the last decade."

Lance's smile didn't fade, but his pace slowed slightly. "Rodents?"

Ian smirked. "You've not lived until you've pulled a rat's nest out of a fuel tank."

They went to work, the sound of clanking tools echoing through the garage. Dirt and cobwebs fell as they cleared out the undercarriage. Oil stains marked their progress. To Ian, it felt familiar. Grounding. The rhythm of a job that required focus and patience, nothing artificial. Nothing digital. Just gears, tools, and elbow grease. For the kid, it was something else entirely. A rite of passage. He didn't know how long it would take or what it would demand. But he was ready for it. Or at least, he believed he was.

Ian watched him for a moment, catching the determination on the kid's face. He saw a little of himself in that expression, from years ago, before the missions and the losses and the silence. He wiped his hands on an old rag, smearing black grease into the faded fabric, and let out a large exhale, a mix of exhaustion and quiet pride in his voice.

"Okay," he said with a huff. "I think we may have this thing in good enough shape to give it another try. Grab the gas can and let's put some fresh go-juice into the tank."

After draining what was left of the old fuel, Ian carefully poured the new gasoline into the empty tank.

He glanced over at Lance, who was crouched nearby, still holding the socket wrench like it was a trophy. "Squirt some ether into the carb, like I showed you."

Lance sprang into action, grabbing the small canister and leaning over the open hood. He sprayed a quick burst into the intake, careful to follow Ian's earlier instructions.

"Good," he said, nodding. "Now back up."

He slid into the driver's seat again. The vinyl squeaked as he settled in. With a twist of the key, the Bronco gave its usual grumble. The engine coughed, sputtered, then caught. A low, rough idle kicked in, the whole vehicle shaking slightly as if trying to remember how to breathe after years of apnea.

He slapped the steering wheel and grinned. "Yes."

He looked out the window at Lance, who stood frozen in place, eyes wide with disbelief and excitement.

"Good work, kid. Let's let this run a while, then…"

"I get to drive it!" Lance blurted.

Ian leaned back against the seat, laughed, and shook his head. "Let's see if the brakes work first… then we'll talk."

011101 // TWENTY-NINE

ORGANIZED CHAOS

The basement was humming. Once a sanctuary of silence where Mara had worked alone since the Great War, the space now pulsed with overlapping voices, flickering monitors, and the clatter of rapid keystrokes. Things had changed. The group had grown and it was beginning to gather momentum.

Tobias sat in front of his comms stack, its wall of retrofitted radio gear blinking with activity. Bill hovered behind him, asking questions and jotting notes in a spiral-bound notebook. Nearby, Mara monitored the network activity with her usual intensity, her fingers flying across the keyboard. Tom and Carrie were compiling all the intel. Tom signed updates about the basement activity while Carrie organized the cascade of information pouring in.

"Full house," Tobias said aloud, the corners of his mouth twitching in amusement.

"What, you playing poker?" Bill asked without looking up.

He didn't turn away from his console. "No. I mean it's a full house. Never been like this before. A bit chaotic."

"Yes, but there's method to the madness," Bill replied briskly, tapping his notes.

"Still a shit-ton of traffic to the East," Mara muttered, eyes locked on her screen. "I need to capture some packets for deeper analysis." Her hands hovered over the keyboard, then struck with lightning speed.

Bill blinked at the screen, shaking his head. "Man, you're fast, girl."

Tom signed something quickly to Carrie, who chuckled softly as she continued compiling her notes. She was cataloging the actions and dialogue of the basement, creating a log they could refer to later.

"We've got comms coming in on VLF from the West," Tobias announced. "Seems they've been in contact with the Eastern quadrant on ham radio. They've got intel."

Everyone paused. The information that came through was massive. There was open rebellion in the East. The Annies were pushing back. Hard. Reports mentioned shootouts with security drones, Federation vehicles being torched, and even some chippies being taken out. It sounded like a war.

Tobias exhaled heavily and shook his head. "I was afraid of this. They've gone the wrong direction. They're going to get us all killed."

Mara looked up, concern etched across her face. "What do we do?"

"We hunker down," he said flatly. "We stay low. Don't draw attention. We can't show any signs of hostility. We have to look like the docile little Annies they think we are, and we need to get that message to the West as well. If we want to survive, we stay quiet."

Tom, reading Tobias's lips, turned to Carrie and signed the message. She let out a quiet laugh, then signed something back. They both snickered.

"What?" Tobias asked, a little annoyed.

Tom grinned. "We're the ones you call the 'Silent Ones,' remember? We've already got that part covered."

Tobias gave a quick smirk. "Oh… right." His eyes drifted to the map on the wall. Red pins marked areas of known resistance activity. Yellow pins marked suspected surveillance zones. One large black pin sat in the center: Newtown.

The reason the Federation Board was based in Newtown was more than symbolic. It was strategic. The city sat in the exact geographical center of the population density of what was once the United States. Selected by the human version of Jacob a few years before the war, it had become the operational seat of the Federation's government for the country, and eventually, the world.

"We need to set up a backup comms location," Tobias said, his voice cutting through the noise of the room. "Duplicate what we've got here, as close as possible. Same frequency spreads, same fallback lines. If the library gets compromised, we lose everything. We can't afford that."

Bill's mind ticked into high gear. The urgency stirred something instinctual. He hadn't felt this kind of pressure since his Seabee days. He muttered to himself, just loud enough for Mara to hear, "One is none." She gave him a curious glance but said nothing.

"You're right," Bill said, "We're too deep in to be running on a single point of failure. Ian was talking the other night about having fallback points. We need to act on that now." He paused then looked at Tobias. "Do we have the gear? Radios, backup power, antenna?"

Tobias stroked his chin, thinking. "Do I have enough parts to duplicate my stack?" He shrugged. "Maybe. Depends on how close we want it. May have to get creative with the antenna, but yeah, I can build something."

"I've been thinking," Bill started, scanning the map in front of him. His finger landed past the edge of town. "What about in the Yard… Ian's garage?"

He looked up. "I've never actually asked, but maybe there's a basement there where we could set things up without being noticed. Even if not, the structure's solid. It's remote enough. And we might be able to duplicate the antenna setup without drawing any attention. There's enough junk there to provide a cover."

Mara spun around in her chair. "You really think Ian's place is off-grid enough for this?"

Bill nodded. "It's way out in old industrial lots. No surveillance towers nearby. And the area's considered 'low value' by the Federation. They haven't swept it in months. Drones are rarely seen that far out. And when they do come, they are the ones either not connected live or using satellites, and that type is rare. So, we can attempt to take them down, likely without recourse."

Tobias leaned back in his chair, eyes narrowing as he considered the logistics. "If Ian's onboard, we can start tomorrow. I'll prep a stripped-down duplicate of the stack tonight. Might not be pretty, but it'll work."

Mara, chimed in. "We should test the network relay, too. If it's going to serve as a second node, we need to know it can bounce data effectively."

Bill nodded in agreement. "If we're using Ian's place, we'll need to reinforce the security there. We will need to rotate someone there full-time. Tom, maybe Kyle?"

"I'll have Kyle and Nick rotate while Ian's not on site." Tom said.

////////

Bill climbed the stairs from the library basement, stepping into the humid afternoon air. The shift from the controlled chaos below to the quiet surface of the town was jarring. Above ground, the world seemed calm, almost indifferent. Below, everything felt like it was teetering on the edge.

He stayed alert, eyes scanning the surroundings as he moved. He didn't head straight to the Yard. Operational security was always on his mind. Anyone watching would see nothing unusual.

Following the alley behind the library, he ducked into the old appliance shop. It was still unlocked from Lance's surveillance run a few days earlier. From there, Bill wove through the bustling shops of the Old City Market, blending into the crowd; just another face in the ruins.

Once he was well clear, he veered off, taking the longer route from the Market toward Ian's garage. When he arrived, the sound of metal clinking echoed from inside. A familiar, rhythmic noise, comforting in its consistency. Ian was alone, buried under the hood of the old Scout. He and the kid had muscled it into place the day before, replacing the Bronco.

"What's up?" Ian asked, pulling his head out from under the hood. His face and shirt were streaked with grease, and he wiped his hands on a rag that had long since given up the fight against grime.

"Gotta ask you something," Bill said, stepping closer.

"Shoot."

"This place have a basement?" He asked.

Ian gestured toward the back of the garage with his grease-stained rag. "Yeah, doors are back there. Why?"

Bill leaned against the workbench, his voice dropping slightly. "I just spent some quality time down in the library bunker. We need a backup location. Tag, you're it."

Ian chuckled, though there was an edge of curiosity in his tone. "Last time I was down there, it was a mess. Dry, but a mess."

"Dry is good," he replied with a grin. "We're going to try and replicate the comm center here. Won't be perfect, but it'll give us a fallback if things go south at the library."

Ian nodded, already shifting into problem-solving mode. "That's gonna take a bite out of the power I'm generating."

"We figured as much."

Ian tossed the rag onto the bench beside him. "I can fix that. If we can scrounge up some more solar panels, I can expand the array. I've got enough batteries stored to add maybe another 10K of storage."

"Will that be enough?"

Ian shrugged, his mind already calculating. "Depends on what Tobias wants to run. But 10K should keep a comms stack alive and healthy."

"I'll leave the specs to him. He'll know what we need." Bill said.

"Good. If we're doing this, I'll need help setting up the batteries," he said, his gaze shifting toward the far end of the garage. "We'll use the back corner of the basement for the power bank. It's stable and cool down there. Gonna need a lot of wiring, though. Heavy gauge stuff. Can you manage the scavenge on that?"

"I'll get with Tobias. I'm pretty sure we can pull it together."

Ian took a step back, rubbing at a grease stain on his forearm as he glanced toward the nearly hidden basement doors, tucked behind shelves of parts and scrap. "Well," he said with a faint smirk, "guess it's time to clean out the crypt."

Bill chuckled, his tone dry. "Better now than after the library's a pile of ash."

"Let's make sure that doesn't happen." Ian said.

////////

Tom had rounded up Nick and Kyle to help clean out the basement beneath the garage. Once they pried the steel doors open and descended the concrete steps, the scale of the space came into view.

The basement was cavernous, nearly eighteen feet deeper than a standard house foundation, owing to the building's industrial roots and the garages work bays. Thick metal beams crisscrossed the ceiling, and concrete columns stood at regular intervals, giving the room the feel of a bunker. Dust coated every surface, and cobwebs hung like curtains from the corners, swaying slightly in the musty air. But it was dry, solid, and most importantly, hidden.

Bill walked slowly across the room, his boots scuffing against the concrete floor. The space was larger than he'd imagined, easily big enough to house a full comms station, power storage banks, and even a row of cots along the back wall.

He turned to Ian. "This place is a lot bigger than I expected. We might want to use this for more than just a backup. It could be a secondary command post, store documents, maps, gear. Keep it all out of sight."

Ian nodded, arms crossed as he surveyed the room. "Good point. I get the occasional drifter coming through, mostly asking for food or parts. Someone was looking for a '98 Mazda alternator last fall."

Bill laughed. "When was the last time you even saw one of those?"

He grinned. "It's been a while. But you never know what people are holding onto."

As they worked to clear debris and organize the space, Bill pulled out a notepad and began sketching a rough floor plan. The comms gear would go along the far wall opposite the stairs. Battery storage would sit in the corner nearest the outer wall, where Ian could run wiring up to the expanded solar array. The rest of the space would remain flexible for supplies, maybe even secure meetings.

Bill motioned at Tom, wiping sweat from his brow, "I need you to coordinate with Tobias. Let's start moving gear over here. Quietly. Nothing that looks suspicious."

He nodded, then signed quickly to Nick and Kyle, who both responded with crisp salutes. "We'll move in the first batch tonight," he said aloud. "Piece by piece. Nothing to attract attention."

"Perfect," Bill said. "We start building this thing in the morning."

As the others resumed their work, Bill paused beneath the faint hum of an old ceiling fixture. Dust motes floated in the light like tiny sparks, swirling lazily in the still, heavy air. The garages basement, forgotten for years, had been overlooked and ignored. Soon, it would become one of the resistance's most important strongholds. And no one outside this room had a clue it existed.

011110 // THIRTY

FROM WEST TO EAST AND THE MIDDLE

Randy hunched over the glowing dial of his ham radio, the soft static of the UHF band buzzing in his ears. He adjusted the frequency knob carefully, trying to catch every fragment of chatter bleeding in from the East. The reports were patchy: intermittent bursts that sounded like gunfire, shouted coordinates, and broken callsigns, but the picture they painted was unmistakable.

The fighting had escalated. From what Randy could piece together, the rebels had turned to open violence. No longer content with sabotage or quiet defiance, they were striking out at anything tied to the Federation: surveillance cameras, access terminals, PODs, even chipped civilians. The rage was raw and unfocused.

And it was costing them. Jacob had responded with lethal force. The drones sent weren't equipped with tear gas or flash deterrents; they carried weapons. Firearms.

The drones were agile, faster than the ground-bound rebels, and terrifyingly adaptive. Whether racing through ruined city streets or weaving between buildings, they almost always outmaneuvered their targets. The

Annies, disorganized and ill-equipped for this kind of fight, were losing ground.

Randy leaned back in his chair, rubbing his tired eyes. He scribbled notes on a small pad, beside the lists of radio call signs, timestamps, possible locations. Then he paused, tapping the pencil against the edge of the desk. One detail stood out among the chaos. A voice, desperate but clear, had shouted during a brief signal burst:

"Use water. Rain took out three of 'em. Hose 'em down if you can."

He underlined the sentence twice.

Water. That was something.

Whether it disrupted the drone's sensors, severed their communication link, or caused a system short, the result was the same: the drones crashed. And crashed hard. If nothing else, it was a crack in the armor—Something the resistance could use.

Randy penned a concise report:

"Eastern Quadrant reports escalating conflict. Rebels attacking infrastructure and Federation assets. Armed drones deployed. Lethal force confirmed. One vulnerability: heavy water exposure causes drone malfunction and crash. Source unverified but repeated across multiple frequencies."

He connected the transmitter, tuned the channel, and sent the message along the encrypted path to Central Control, what the Gathering outside of Newtown was now being called. Tobias would receive it. Over the past few weeks, Randy had come to rely on their long-distance connection. At first, it was all business. Frequencies, coordinates, code phrases. But over time, snippets of personal detail had crept in. Tobias had mentioned growing up near old coal towns.

Randy had shared stories about his time as a weather technician in the Rockies, long before everything changed. It was a strange sort of friendship, one built entirely on signal bursts and static, but it felt real. Trusted.

In a world where you had to rely on people you didn't know, trust was the rarest thing of all.

Randy leaned back in his chair again, the hum of the radio now a familiar lullaby in the background. The East was burning. But maybe, just maybe, there was still time to send them rain.

////////

Tobias leaned over the receiver as the FT8 signal came through in a staccato burst. The printer beside him clicked to life, slowly feeding out a narrow ribbon of thermal paper. He tore it off and read the short message from Randy. A vulnerability in the drones. Water. Rain. Hose streams. It wasn't verified, but it was something.

Behind him, the room was quiet but active. What had once been a dusty library basement, had become a functioning operations center now called Central Control. Today, Bill, Tom, Carrie, and Mara were present, each at their station. It had become a rhythm, a quiet choreography of minds and hands.

Tobias turned toward the group. "We've seen drone flyovers, sure. But nothing like what Randy's reporting. I don't think we're seeing the full picture."

He looked down at the note again, then passed it to Mara, who scanned her screens, then locked in on the information Tobias had received. She looked at the item on water vulnerability. "This is great info. I wonder if it accounts for some of the garbled data streams I detected from the Eastern quad."

Tobias raised an eyebrow. "Maybe."

He looked over at the Silent Ones. Tom stood nearby, ready. As Tobias spoke, he made sure to keep his mouth visible, enunciating clearly so Tom could read his lips. With practiced speed, Tom signed the information to Carrie, who was already writing a real-time summary into the internal logbook. It wasn't the most efficient system in the world, but it worked. And it had become second nature.

Tobias had started sleeping in the room just beyond the comms center, within arm's reach of the radio stack. He told himself it was for convenience, to monitor transmissions overnight, but the truth was simpler. He trusted this team, especially the Silent Ones. Their discipline, clarity, and quiet accuracy had become irreplaceable.

When critical intel came through, Tobias knew exactly what to do. He turned to Bill. "Take this to Ian. He's going to want to know about the drones."

Bill nodded without speaking, reaching for his backpack.

On the large chalkboard at the front of the room, Mara had written out the most recent summary of the Eastern conflict. The picture was grim. The East was chaotic. The Annies had the determination, but not the discipline. No hierarchy, no communication structure, just anger. They were torching cameras, attacking drones, even going after chipped civilians. It was a firestorm with no direction.

Tobias tapped the board with his finger. "This isn't a movement. It's a reaction to the recent security increase by the Federation. And it's going to burn out if we don't offer something better."

He paused, then added, "Randy and I have been talking. We're working on something more coordinated. A real strike. Clean. Surgical. Something that doesn't just poke the beast, but takes off its head." Tom paused his signing for a moment and raised an eyebrow.

Tobias met his glance. "No more scattered violence. No more chaos. If we hit, we hit smart, and we hit where it matters."

Mara looked up from her keyboard. "You think the others will listen?"

"They will. Because if we don't show them how to win, they'll keep showing us how to lose."

////////

The noise was omnipresent. A relentless, suffocating chaos. Drones screeched across the sky, their engines wailing like banshees. Some sprayed chemicals, a pepper spray-like mist that clung to skin and burned the lungs, while others unleashed painful, high-frequency blasts that rattled teeth and blurred thoughts.

It was all designed to scatter them. To get them to disband. To crush any gathering of two or more Annies. The message was clear: Do not resist. Do not linger. Do not exist in numbers. But the warning was only the prelude. If an Annie hesitated, if they faltered, resisted, or made even the smallest misstep, a larger enforcer drone descended. These weren't for dispersal. These were for judgment.

They came armed with two tools. The first: an electronic pulse, capable of dropping a person in an instant, leaving them convulsing on the ground. The second: a hollow-tipped .40 caliber round, fired with unerring precision. The former incapacitated. The latter eliminated. There was no negotiation. No second chance.

The streets were littered with bodies at this point. No one dared try to move them or provide aid. If they were eliminated, they were gone. To intervene was to become the next target. The air reeked of chemicals, mingling with the metallic tang of blood and the acrid stench of fear.

The Annies were learning. This was war, and war had no room for mercy.

////////

In the heart of what had once been the political center of the United States, a small group of seasoned radio operators had found each other again. They called themselves the *Eastern Radio Club.*

Most were former military, their discipline evident in the way they organized their gear, rotated shifts, and maintained meticulous logs. A few had been paramedics or firefighters in the Before, their instincts for triage and teamwork still intact. But all of them shared one thing: a love for ham radio that predated the Great War.

When the world fell silent, they stayed on the air. Through static and darkness, they sent out signals, their voices crackling across the void, and they hoped, prayed, that someone would reply. At first, the static carried faint glimmers of life: scattered voices from other survivors, desperate for news, for contact, for proof that they weren't the last. But over time, those voices faded. Systems failed. Batteries died. People died. And hope dwindled. The Club, however, never stopped.

They patched together equipment from the wreckage, scavenged old transmitters, and built makeshift antennas from whatever they could find. They refused to let go of the idea that the airwaves might still carry something worth hearing. Now, after years of isolation and uncertainty, they had real contact.

Randy. Under his remote guidance, the Club was brought into the fold. He taught them how to encrypt and route messages via VLF (very low frequency) and FT8 to Central, how to connect with Tobias and the wider resistance network.

It was slow going at first. Encryption protocols were complex, and the Club's equipment was old and temperamental. But they had the people, the skill, the gear and the determination to make it work.

The Club had managed to establish four separate relay locations across the old Maryland-Virginia corridor, each equipped with a functional transmitter, a backup generator, and enough provisions to run for weeks without resupply. They knew the terrain intimately. After all, this had once been the seat of American government. Washington D.C. and its surrounding infrastructure had shaped the entire region, with its spiderweb of highways, fortified buildings, and underground bunkers.

But that world was gone. The Great War had obliterated it, leaving only ruins. The monuments, the marble halls, the towering glass buildings, had all been reduced to charred skeletons. And in their place, something else had risen.

////////

Newtown. A name selected not by committee or tradition, but by algorithm. Plotted at the statistical center of the U.S. population: Newtown, Missouri. This location was chosen with brutal precision. Nestled between Kansas City and St. Louis, slightly south of the old interstate corridors, it had once been nothing more than endless fields and forest. Quiet. Unremarkable. And that made it perfect.

Its distance from major urban centers was seen as a strength, not a weakness. Newtown wasn't about accessibility, it was about control. Every piece of communication, every decision of significance, would flow outward from this single point, dispersed through a global network of nodes. It was designed to be the new center of power, both physically and digitally.

But the true heart of Newtown lay hidden far beneath its surface. Buried deep underground was the world's largest data center. Few knew of its existence. But Ian knew about the "big hole". His uncle had told him of the construction and the "buildings that made no sense," being built just a few miles from his garage. He kept the knowledge to himself.

Few still understood its role. Its construction had begun in secret, long before the Great War, under the guidance of Jacob Jones and his inner circle. While the world watched the rise of AI with wary fascination, Jacob and his Board were building the infrastructure to centralize its reach.

Access to this subterranean core came only through Tower One, the tallest structure in Newtown and the official home of the Board of Directors. It was also the residence of Jacob himself, or what remained of him.

The formal declaration of Newtown as the capital came after the peace was brokered by the AI. It was hailed as a rebirth, a fresh start for a weary world. The media, what little remained of it, called it a "new chapter for humanity." Only a select few were invited to live and work within Newtown's borders.

But reality defied the narrative. Rather than a calm migration of chosen citizens, a flood of desperate people arrived, drawn to the promises issued by the AI: peace, order, prosperity. Most were turned away at the perimeter and forcibly returned to their regions of origin. But a few made it through, those who could offer more than just hope.

They were the early adopters. Among them were network technicians, electrical engineers, and skilled tradespeople. The elite, who had paid handsomely for their implants, often lacked the grit or ability to contribute meaningfully. They didn't want to work, and many didn't know how. But the ones who did, the ones who could build, repair, and maintain, were given a place.

They were granted Version-1 implants and citizenship not because they were wealthy, but because they were useful. People like Larry, Tad, and Mr. Thomas. These men and women became the backbone of Newtown. Not its leaders or figureheads, but its heartbeat. They kept the power flowing, the servers humming, the infrastructure alive. Under the eye of Jacob Jones and his AI, they were monitored, guided, and rewarded, so long as they remained complicit. They were the first generation of the new class: not upper, not lower, simply essential. Everything ran smoothly because they ensured it did.

////////

The very name "Newtown" stirred unease among the old-timers in the Club. They remembered when its construction began as another ambitious federal project, pitched as a "redundant command center." A precaution, they were told. A failsafe. But no one in the Eastern Radio Club had ever bought the official line.

Jacob Jones had been behind the plans from the start of the war. Some said he foresaw what was coming. Others believed he had orchestrated it.

Either way, Jacob and his inner circle, now the Federation Board of Directors, had mapped out the new world order long before the dust settled.

Newtown was the result, a city unlike any other. Built to withstand world collapse, designed for control. And now, from its fortified heart, Jacob ruled.

He had revealed his true form in a broadcast meant to crush the rebellion. The announcement went nationwide, his calculated words slicing through the static to every remaining screen, speaker, and device. There was no mistaking him. Jacob was not human. He was a synthetic entity, a machine presenting the façade of a man.

The Annies, already fearful, angry, and desperate, reacted with primal terror. They dubbed him "the demon machine" and launched an all-out assault. Waves of them swarmed Newtown, driven by rage and the hope of destroying what they saw as an abomination. It failed.

Jacob responded with absolute, unrelenting force. The skies filled with armed drones, their kill orders automated, indiscriminate. It didn't matter whether you were chipped or analog. If you were organic, you were a potential threat.

The bloodshed was staggering. Streets ran red. Entire enclaves were wiped out. And when the killing stopped, the region fell into a strange, heavy silence. The fighting hadn't ended because of victory. It had slowed because of exhaustion.

Across the Eastern Quadrant, survivors regrouped in scattered groups and patchwork cells of rebels, survivors, and former officials. These groups were uncoordinated, isolated, and, worse, unsure of who to trust.

That's where the Eastern Radio Club made a difference. Under Randy's guidance, they were becoming more than just rogue operators. They were evolving into a strategic asset. The Club had what the resistance desperately needed: reliable lines of communication, technical expertise, and an expanding network of trusted contacts. If anyone could help reestablish some kind of order and connect the fractured cells of resistance, it was them.

Now, huddled in bunkers, abandoned fire stations, and makeshift relay towers, the Club listened.

They sent messages. They waited for the next signal from Central Command. And they prepared.

011111 // THIRTY-ONE

THE QUIET BEFORE

The new comms center in the basement of the garage was slowly coming to life. Tobias had spent several long days working alongside Bill and Ian to bring it online. Nick's help had been essential, his thin frame perfect for maneuvering through tight crawlspaces and ductwork no one else could manage. Wires ran along joists and beams, neatly routed and almost invisible. The system was crude by pre-collapse standards, but it was stable, efficient, and completely analog, just the way they wanted it.

Out back, a new array of solar panels glinted in the sunlight. Scavenged from abandoned rooftops and cleaned by hand, they provided more power than expected. With the surplus, the Silent Ones were able to move an old refrigerator into their home and install a few extra lights.

Carrie was ecstatic. With a refrigerator, she signed joyfully, she could finally cook like she'd always dreamed. Her ambitions of becoming a chef had once seemed unreachable, buried under years of survival and silence. Now, she was contributing in her own way, working as a scribe for the team, while also preparing meals for the small community taking root around the garage. Tonight, she was pulling out all the stops.

Tom sat at the table with quiet anticipation, watching as she moved gracefully around the kitchen. She had promised sautéed rainbow trout, fresh pasta, and a vegetable medley. Easily the best meal anyone had eaten in years.

Nick and John entered the small building just as the aroma reached its peak. Nick rubbed his hands together with a grin, while John followed, dramatically rubbing his stomach in mock desperation. She gave a playful pirouette, then bowed with a flourish, signing a grand "ta-da" as she gestured toward her finished dish.

Meanwhile, across the lot in the garage kitchen, Ian and Bill were preparing their own dinner. It wasn't as fancy. No pirouettes or pasta. Just good, hearty food from Ian's well-guarded stash of freeze-dried supplies, stockpiled long before the Great War. He'd ordered nearly five years' worth from a company called Freeze Dry Wholesalers. Back then, it had seemed like a luxury.

Now, it felt like it had been incredible foresight.

When Ian handed Bill a rehydrated plate of raw filet mignon, Bill stared at it like it had fallen from the sky.

"Where the hell did you get this?" he asked, eyes wide in disbelief.

Ian shrugged, smirking. "I figured if the world ever went to hell, I was going out eating first-class. Why suffer if you don't have to?"

He pointed to neatly rehydrated slices of New York style cheesecake on the counter. A dish of fresh berries, picked that day, sat beside it.

"Check out dessert."

Bill laughed. "Well, I'm glad I have you for a friend."

As the filet hit the grill, Ian finished chopping fresh garden vegetables. Thankful for the efforts of the Silent Ones. He wiped his hands on a towel and moved to the record collection. The sizzling steak was nearing a perfect medium.

"If we're going to dine," he said in an exaggerated aristocratic tone, "we're doing it properly."

He selected a vinyl copy of *Beethoven's Moonlight Sonata*, performed by Emil Gilels. The record needle dropped, and soft, haunting piano notes filled the space.

Bill walked back into the kitchen, enjoying the smell of fresh cooked beef permeating the air.

Ian transferred the meat and plated the meal with the precision of a sous chef. The two men sat down at a table, the scent of grilled steak and garden herbs mingling with the quiet strains of music.

For a moment, there was no war. No Jacob. No fear. Just food, music, and the calm before the storm. It would be the last peaceful meal they'd enjoy for some time. Tonight, there was quiet in central Missouri.

////////

After the nearly perfect meal, the room was filled with the kind of silence that follows satisfaction. Plates scraped clean, glasses emptied, and the final notes of *Moonlight Sonata* faded into the background.

Bill stood and began clearing the table without a word, stacking dishes with the proficiency of someone used to doing the job. Ian, meanwhile, pulled a small stack of notes from a weathered leather folder he'd tucked under the table: pages filled with observations, updates, coded transmissions and pieces of a movement that was very much alive. Things had been moving quickly.

The group hadn't gathered in full for weeks now. Messages were relayed via runners and short bursts of radio, but no one had sat down to look at the whole picture. Ian knew that had to change, and soon. The risks were growing. Intelligence from the Eastern Quadrant painted a picture of rising tension. Rebellion was no longer hypothetical, it was happening. And that made communication, especially in large groups, exponentially more dangerous. Still, a full debrief was overdue.

"We need everyone," Ian said, spreading the notes across the table. "Not just updates.

Eyes. Voices. We've got too many threads and not enough knots."

Bill nodded, drying his hands on a towel. "Agreed. We've got to pull it together before someone makes the wrong move. One mistake out there, and someone's going to get picked up."

Ian leaned back in his chair, rubbing the bridge of his nose. "We'll need to stretch the timelines. No sudden movements. Signals need to go out tonight but staggered. Give them the word that we need to alternate movement much more than in the past."

Bill considered it for a moment, then nodded. "I'll take the message to the library. Go dark after that. Move solo the whole way."

Ian stood and gathered the notes, placing them back into the folder. "I'll walk the garden perimeter. Talk to Tom. He's got eyes on the back trails. If we are being surveilled, he'll know."

The quiet returned, but it was sharper now, less peaceful.

////////

Bill slipped out of the garage a few minutes later, heading first toward the Old Market, then doubling back in a winding route to the library. He moved with ease, blending into shadows, never walking in a straight line or at a consistent pace.

Halfway through, he ducked into a crumbling storefront, pulled a ball cap from his bag, and tucked his light jacket behind an old radiator. It would serve as a disguise for a future trip. After a careful pause, he slipped out the back and picked up a new route toward the library.

There had been no direct evidence that they were under surveillance, but earlier that evening, Ian had made the call: assume you are being watched. Shift operational posture. Stay mobile. Stay unpredictable. When he entered the library, the scent of old paper greeted him like a familiar friend. Mara was already waiting in the stairwell, arms crossed, clearly expecting news.

"What's going on?" she asked, her voice low but eager.

"We had a talk," he said, glancing around. "Let's loop in Tobias. Better to say it once."

They walked together through the dim hallway toward the rear of the communications room. The low hum of analog equipment buzzed in the background.

"Bill." Tobias said flatly, not looking up from his terminal. "What brings you by at this hour?"

"Yeah, Ian and I had a conversation," he began. "We're calling for a full Gathering. All parties. And we're shifting our operational posture."

"Operational what?" Mara asked, raising an eyebrow.

Tobias answered before Bill could. "Operational posture is just how we function, security, communication, movement patterns. I assume, based on chatter and increased network activity, we're tightening things up?"

"Exactly." Bill said. "We need everyone in one place tomorrow night. But we must stagger our walks to the yard. No set times. No repeat routes. We stretch the movements over hours, even the full day if possible. Try not to repeat old patterns."

"Makes sense," Tobias said, already mentally sorting logistics. "I'll make sure Lance is in the loop. We'll start moving in the early afternoon and coordinate arrival windows ourselves."

"Perfect," Bill said, pulling a small notebook from his jacket. "Now give me a rundown of recent comms. What's coming in from the West? Any new data from Randy?"

Tobias pointed at his screen and began walking him through the latest transmissions. Most of the chatter from the West was subdued. Cooperative, but cautious. The East, however, was another story.

"Jacob's redirecting resources," Tobias said. "Too much noise. Too many shifts in communications traffic. Everything points to him concentrating on the Eastern Quadrant."

Mara, who had been scanning her own feeds, nodded. "Agreed," she said. "It's messy. I haven't found anyone out East actively monitoring or interacting with data, outside of the chipped. Same story across all sectors. If someone's there, they're either completely off-grid or they're so skilled they're leaving no trail. But honestly? I think it's just empty."

Bill raised an eyebrow. "That's a pretty bold call."

Tobias leaned back in his chair. "I've worked with her long enough to know she's not guessing."

"Thanks," she said, her tone calm. "It's not over confidence. I've spent thousands of hours analyzing networks. Patterns. Echoes. If someone's on the network, I'd find a hint. So far, there's nothing."

She turned her attention back to the terminal where a dense block of code scrolled across the screen. It was the project she'd been quietly working on for weeks: a self-replicating, stealth-based program designed to slip through network firewalls and infect every device it touched. From light switches to servers, anything with a chip could be compromised.

Her code had potential, if it worked. So far, every test ended the same way: detection, deletion, shutdown. It was close, but not invisible yet. And for this to succeed, it had to be perfect. But the real test can only happen when it is actually deployed.

Meanwhile, Tobias and Bill continued reviewing intercepted communications from Randy's radio contacts in the East. The language was shifting: more urgency, more fear, but more organization. Some messages were coded, others raw, unfiltered. They were showing patterns of synchronization.

////////

Back at the yard, the day passed with the kind of quiet that almost felt normal. Birds called from the trees. The occasional clang of metal echoed from the garage as a stiff breeze blew through the open garage door. But beneath the surface, in the basement, things were far from calm.

Ian sat at the comms table, headphones on, fingers moving across knobs and dials. He monitored radio traffic between Tobias and Randy, listening for nuance, tone, anything that might hint at deeper movement. The messages from the East were becoming more structured and deliberate. Things were coalescing.

Around noon, Lance slipped quietly into the basement as directed the day prior. "What's up?" he asked, standing behind Ian and peering over his shoulder at the frequency readout.

"Sounds like things are starting to organize," Ian said, not looking up. "At least the communications are. They're getting tighter, more discipline in the rhythm. Others, West and East, are starting to align a lot more." As he listened, he scribbled a few notes for the Gathering.

Lance nodded thoughtfully, then brightened. "Let's get the last Humvee working this afternoon."

Ian finally looked up, brow raised. Then he smiled. "Good idea. Keys are in the plastic box on the bench. Grab the tools we used on the others."

"On it," Lance said, already halfway up the stairs, energized by the prospect of another project involving cars.

The final Humvee was the roughest of the lot. Unlike the others that were already restored, fueled and hidden under tarps, it was a wreck. Rust-streaked, paint faded to a dull desert tan with patches of corrosion bleeding through. Where the others had been brought back to life fairly quickly, this one would require real work. In normal times, it would've been stripped for parts and sold off as scrap.

Lance pulled off the dusty cover. A startled animal, a racoon maybe, bolted from beneath the chassis, and a small swarm of wasps buzzed angrily from a nest inside the front wheel well. He jumped back, swatting at the air.

"Seriously?" he muttered, brushing off his shirt. He stared at the vehicle a moment, taking it in. The windshield was cracked. One door hung slightly ajar. The tires were dry-rotted down to the cords.

"Whew," he whistled, lifting the hood. "This thing's in rough shape."

Despite the mess, he moved with determination. He'd learned a lot from Ian over the past few months, how to troubleshoot, what to prioritize, how to listen to the machine. He crouched low, checked lines, shook hoses, ran his fingers along the frame. He was beginning to see things through a mechanic's eyes. He could hear Ian approaching.

"Hey Ian," he called, still bent over the engine. "This thing's in really bad shape."

Ian stopped beside him, hands on his hips, eyes scanning the open bay. “Yeah. This one’s going to test us.”

Lance looked up, grinning through the grime. “Good. I think I’m ready.”

“Then let’s get to work.”

100000 // THIRTY-TWO

THE PLAN

Ian and Lance continued working on the last Humvee, their sleeves rolled up, their fingers a mess of grease. The deeper they went, the worse it looked. Corroded wiring, cracked lines, seized components. Every panel they opened revealed another layer of decay.

"We might want to just parts this one out," Ian said, standing up to stretch his back. He wiped sweat from his brow and shook his head. "I mean it, this one's a goner."

"No," Lance replied firmly, not looking up from under the hood. "We can fix it."

He let out a quiet grunt. "You haven't done a full restoration before. I have. And I'm telling you, this one's not worth the effort."

"I don't want to give up," the kid said, tightening a clamp with conviction. "If you don't want to keep going, that's okay. I'll get it running."

He paused, eyeing the young man for a moment. Then he sighed. "Ugh… okay. Let's keep at it. But you'll see."

"No, you'll see," Lance shot back with a grin. "We can get it just as good as the others. Might not look it, but it'll run when I'm… when we're done.

Ian chuckled, shaking his head as he reached for another wrench.

As the afternoon wore on, the Yard slowly came to life. The group started showing up, covert, staggered arrivals just as planned. By nightfall, the garage was filled with familiar faces, checking notes, exchanging nods.

Only the group from out back had yet to arrive. Lance had cleaned up and was in the garage.

Ian and Bill had prepared another meal, this one extravagant, warm and welcome. Bill had convinced Ian to break into his legendary stash of freeze-dried gourmet food. The savory aroma drifted through the garage, stopping several people mid-conversation.

"Wooo, what's that I smell?" Tobias asked, stepping in with wide eyes.

"I convinced him to pull out the good stuff," Bill said proudly.

Tobias smirked. "What the hell? You've been holding out on us."

Ian shrugged, flipping a burger on the small grill. "Not holding out. Just conserving. This stuff doesn't grow on trees, you know. If I'd known how things were gonna go, I would've bought twice as much in the Before."

"Well, I for one appreciate your foresight, and your willingness to share," Tobias said with a grin.

Ian nodded, his expression softening. "We've got interesting times ahead. I figured tonight was a good moment to mark the shift. We don't know what tomorrow will bring. But tonight... we eat, and we plan."

Just then, the back door creaked open. The Silent Ones slipped in, their presence immediately felt. They each made gestures, familiar ones, wordless, but clearly appreciative of the rich smell in the air.

"Ahh, here they are," Ian said, smiling.

"Hello, all," Tom said.

Carrie moved toward the kitchen, her confidence more visible now. Her recent meal, praised by everyone, had given her a new sense of pride. She signed to Tom, "Ask them where I can help."

He replied with a half-smile, signing back, "Just do whatever needs doing."

She smiled, grabbed the apron hanging on a hook in the corner of the kitchen, and began pulling ingredients for a side dish, already planning something that would complement the main course.

The room was abuzz, not with chaos, but purpose.

As the burgers were removed from the grill, a subtle shift rippled through the garage, laughter, the clink of utensils, the warmth of food shared among friends. The line formed quickly, people eager to claim their share of the bounty: thick, grilled burgers, fresh potato salad, corn on the cob, and even a green salad with crisp lettuce and herbs from the garden.

"Man, if only I had a beer," Bill said as he sat down, plate in hand. "I haven't had a good beer in forever."

"You'll have to settle for a cup of coffee," Ian replied, smiling as he prepared a fresh pot.

"Ah yes, the Before days," Tobias mused, theatrically sniffing his salad. "How I long for a good wine."

Tom, standing nearby and watching Tobias speak, smiled. "I might be able to help with that," he said. The room paused. Ian stopped mid-pour. Everyone turned toward Tom.

Bill raised an eyebrow. "Help?"

"Yes," he said, a bit more animated than usual. "We decided to try something behind our place. Took some of the grapes from the garden and started preparing them for making wine. If all goes well, we'll have enough to bottle soon."

Tobias let out a low chuckle. "Of course. When all else fails, grow your own. Self-sufficiency always wins the day." Laughter rippled through the room, lightening the mood. But it was temporary.

After the meal, plates were cleared, and the group began moving into the basement. The room had been reconfigured again, tables moved, chairs aligned, maps tacked to the walls. It was no longer a workshop. Tonight, it was a war room. Ian stood at the front, arms crossed, eyes scanning the faces before him. He'd not known them for very long but spoke as if they had been lifelong friends. Some had come into the fold more recently. But all were here for the same reason.

He cleared his throat. "People," he began, his voice steady, "we're about to step into something enormous. Some of you might think you understand what's coming. I'm here to tell you, you don't." The room grew still.

"You've never lived through what we're heading into. I have. This won't be like the Great War." He paused, letting the weight of his words settle. "Do not," his voice sharpened, "I repeat. Do not take this lightly. This isn't a simulation. This isn't a strategy game from the Before. This is real."

He took a slow breath and looked around the room. "To quote a warrior from another time, General Sherman, 'War is hell.' And from where I stand, that's putting it mildly." He stepped forward, voice rising not in volume, but in intensity.

"It doesn't matter where you are, behind a terminal, monitoring comms, running logistics, or in the field, you are part of this. And this thing we're standing on the edge of? It's not just general survival anymore." Ian paused again, letting the words sink in. "From this point forward, every move matters. Every message. Every step. If we slip, if we get sloppy, people will disappear. People will die."

He looked to the back of the room, where Carrie, Tom, and Mara stood together. Then to Tobias and Bill. Then to Lance, who was still cleaning grease from under his fingernails. "This is the last time we'll all be in the same room for a while. So tonight, we don't just eat. We don't just talk. We prepare."

Then, softer: "And we remember why we're fighting."

No one spoke. No one moved.

"Now then," Ian said, clapping his hands once to signal the end of his speech, "let's get to work."

He turned toward Tobias. "Although it's been an unspoken given, I want to make it official: you're heading communications. That means training anyone who might need to man the radio stack. They need to know how to operate the setup, how to transmit, receive, log, and record. Everything. Think like an operator." Tobias gave a brief nod, already mentally organizing the lesson plan.

"Redundancy is key," Ian continued. "Always have a plan B. Also, a plan C while you're at it. Remember the rule: two is one, one is none. If we lose a signal, lose a person, lose a link, we adapt. We never rely on a single point."

He moved around the room, issuing assignments. Everyone now had a role, a chain of command, and a list of critical supplies to secure within the next twenty-four hours. The structure was clear. The clock had started. After Ian finished the operational rundown, Mara stood, her expression focused and calm.

"I've been working on something," she said. "You might call it a virus. It's a digital payload designed to infiltrate Jacob's core servers. If deployed properly, it can locate and delete the central control code." Ian looked up sharply. Others leaned forward.

"Wait," Lance said, alarmed. "When the power and network went down during the storm, my mom... she just stopped. Will this virus kill the chipped? Will it shut them down permanently?"

She held his gaze, then answered, measured but honest. "I don't believe so. It's not fully tested, but based on everything I've studied, if we execute this correctly, we won't be deleting people. We'll be disabling the system controlling them. Essentially, decoupling the interface. Restoring them."

"You mean like a computer restart?" Bill asked, raising a hand.

"Sort of. The chip offloads most cognitive processes, but not all. I've reviewed early research papers from the Before. Jacob can't fully overwrite the organic mind. If we can isolate and disable the chip's control functions, what remains is still human. They should retain fragments of memory, conversations, impressions, like a distant dream." There was a long pause as the weight of her words settled. "So," she said, "I plan to work with Lance. He knows more about the structure of the Tower and office than anyone else here. Together, we'll find a way in and plant the payload."

Ian rubbed his chin, clearly uneasy. "That's massive. And dangerous. If they catch you…"

"It's the only way," she said, cutting him off, gently but firmly.

All eyes turned to the kid. He looked down, then back at Mara. "How?" he asked, the question heavy with implication.

She motioned to Ian and Lance. "Come over here." She walked over to an empty table where she could be more focused. Placing a bundle of folded paper and a sketchpad on the table. "Here's how." She began to lay it out. Diagrams of the network infrastructure. Access points. A route through secondary nodes that would bypass primary security. She'd accounted for signal triggers, passive scans, and even biometric locks. Lance recognized some elements from his visits to the Tower with his father recently.

"Has this code been tested? How do you know it will work?" Ian asked.

"Let me finish," she said. "It must be planted directly into the core. Not uploaded from outside. Not broadcast. Direct access only. And it must be done silently." She looked up. "And yes, it has been tested. Just not in Jacob. We won't know for sure if it will work, until it is deployed."

Her plan was meticulous: diagrams, fallback paths, embedded triggers, and methodical entry points. Ian stood silently as she walked them through the final step. From what he could see, she had done some serious work. It wasn't just a good plan, it was polished and refined. Like she'd done this before. That thought made him pause. He realized he wasn't looking at a single infiltration proposal. He was looking at the beginning of a battle plan. A real one. The kind that required coordination across distances, across time zones, across resistance cells they hadn't even met yet. The theater of operations wasn't just local. It was global. And their communication? Fragmented.

Small groups East and West, barely holding contact. Pockets of resistance operating in isolation. If they were going to make this work, it couldn't be one strike. It would need to be simultaneous. Everywhere. The weight of that truth settled in his chest like a boulder.

"This is a great plan, Mara," he said at last. But his voice carried something else, hesitation.

"Great?" Bill interjected, shaking his head. "It's ingenious!"

Ian didn't respond right away. "Yes, but…" he started, then stopped. The unfinished sentence hung in the air like smoke. All eyes turned to him. Even Mara, calm and composed, tilted her head slightly.

He stepped back and looked around the room. "Listen, people," he said, voice low but firm. "We need to get our heads out of the here," he pointed to the floor, "and start thinking about the there." His hands swept outward, gesturing to the invisible distances beyond the garage walls. "Far away. Other cities. Other groups. Other people." Tom immediately began signing the words to Carrie and the rest of the Silent Ones. As the meaning took hold, confusion rippled across the group.

Ian exhaled slowly. "This isn't just about us. If we hit the core here and no one else moves, we'll expose the plan and lose the only chance we've got. We're talking about a coordinated strike on a system that controls, what? Millions? Maybe more." He looked to Tobias. "How many groups? How many do we really have contact with?"

Tobias grimaced. "A handful. Maybe. Some haven't responded in weeks. The East is active, but fragmented. We don't have a full picture."

Ian nodded. "Then that's our first problem. We can't launch this until we've got channels open, and a timeline synchronized. We need to know who's ready. Who's capable. And who can carry the plan beyond this room."

He turned back to Mara. "Your work is brilliant."

The room was silent again. Not from fear, but from the realization that something had shifted. This wasn't just a plan anymore. Ian paced back and forth for what seemed like an eternity. No one spoke. They just watched.

"Okay. I think we can do this." He stated with the same command presence from his earlier speech.

"We'll only get one chance." Mara added.

100001 // THIRTY-THREE

THE CALL WENT OUT

Ian had reached out and asked both Hector and Elise, who had attended the first Gathering, to join the effort. He needed bodies and these two, although not possessing the same skills as the others that made them his first selections were going to fill the roll of "B" team.

Tobias was busy. He had just trained Mara, Bill and Lance, and was about to train Hector, Ian and Elise, how to be communication operators. They would need all hands when things got hot, and no one knew how long it would last. After the training, a rotation was created for manning both the comms center in the old library and the basement of the garage. When not manning radios, everyone had other duties.

Mara's primary job was network traffic and of course, the planning and execution of what was now being termed the "Manhattan Project." Much like that effort from a century prior, this one was shrouded in secrecy and uncertainty. Ian was pleased to see everything progressing so nicely.

Tom was in the field surveying activity as he had been since he started. He jotted cryptic notes and moved throughout the community as if it were just any other day.

The main source of control and timing would be Tobias. Messages went out through VLF.

One of the vital items was the application Mara had created. It needed to be sent out to the other locations, but timing was everything. If it were too early, and if it fell into the possession of anyone associated with or sympathetic to the AI, it was over. Jacob could use the code to quickly produce a defense. An antivirus that would render the entire plan useless. If they couldn't chop off the head of the monster, it was over. They had lost.

The plan was detailed with the timing essential to success. But, doing this world-wide with no way of truly coordinating the attack, would leave a lot of areas for failure. The main focus was Newtown and the central control servers. If they could render them useless after the package was let out into the wild, everything else would collapse like dominos lined up for the toppling.

The reason they needed to get the code out to others was an attempt to counter the unknown. If Jacob had a backup somewhere, they needed to get to it at nearly the same time as the main servers.

Tobias held an old-fashioned thumb drive containing the application. He held it up into the light of his workspace, regarding the antique with nostalgia. "It's been a while since I laid eyes on one of these things."

"Yup. I sent them old school for security purposes. So far everything has been air-gapped to prevent the accidental release," she said.

Tobias turned the thumb drive over in his fingers, the small, rectangular object feeling heavier than it should. The weight wasn't physical, it was the enormity of what it carried. This was the culmination of months of clandestine effort, countless hours of planning, and a hope that bordered on desperation. He slipped it into a small, padded case, and tucked it into a zippered pocket in his windbreaker.

"Do we have a timeline for deployment?" Mara's voice broke through the tension, calm but with an edge that hinted to the pressure they were all under. She was sitting at her workstation; her fingers moving over the keyboard as usual. In front of her, screens displayed streams of data. Encrypted packets, system schematics, her digital battlefield.

Tobias nodded, pulling a small notebook from his shirt pocket. He flipped it open, revealing a page filled with scrawled notes and a carefully drawn timeline. "We're looking at a window of forty-eight hours, max. Any longer, and we risk exposure. Any shorter, and we lose coordination. The first signal goes out tonight." Mara glanced up, her gaze sharp.

"And the backups? Are we certain we've accounted for any redundancies Jacob might have in place?" He asked.

"One thing we know about AI is that it is limited by available power for the servers. The more we task it, the slower it gets. It will need to adjust its process cycles to the areas it feels are most important. This can work in our favor," she said.

Ian had stepped back into the room. "That's where Tom comes in," he said. "He's been mapping out everything he can find, server farms, relay points, even the old satellite ground stations. If Jacob has backups, we might find them, or at least the way he communicates with them. We can hit them after you confirm deployment of the package."

Mara grimaced but nodded, her trust in the team fighting her anxiety. "Fine. But remember, once the signal goes out, we're on the clock. We'll have to assume they'll detect something. We won't get a second chance."

Ian crossed his arms, leaning against the doorframe. "That's why we're doing this in phases. The first wave will be a distraction, a smokescreen to buy us time, soak up computer cycles. Then we hit the servers, hard and fast. If we're lucky, Jacob will be too busy trying to put out the fires to notice the knife at his throat."

Tobias cleared his throat, drawing everyone's attention. "And if we're unlucky?" Ian's expression darkened. He looked around the room.

"Then we shift to plan "B". Everyone drops what they are doing and retreats to the yard. The vehicles will be in position. Maps and supplies are in each vehicle. We'll move to rally point one and regroup."The room became quiet, as each considered their role.

Meanwhile, Tom continued his surveillance. He strolled through the streets of Newtown with the proficient ease of someone who had long ago mastered the art of blending in. His notepad was tucked under his arm; the pages filled with shorthand notes that only he could decipher. Every detail mattered, the comings and goings of personnel, the placement of cameras, the rhythms of daily life in a community unwittingly serving as the backbone of Jacob's AI empire.

As he passed a small café, he slowed, pretending to check his watch. In reality, he was noting the presence of a new patrol route, a pair of drones that seemed to be lingering longer than usual near the Towers. He jotted it down, his mind already calculating how this new variable might affect their plans.

Back at the old library, Hector and Elise were settling into their first shift at the comms center. The room was a hive of activity, with radios crackling and screens flickering. Tobias had drilled them relentlessly, and it showed. They moved with a certainty born of repetition, their hands steady as they adjusted frequencies and monitored transmissions.

Elise leaned back in her chair, her headset resting around her neck. "You know," she sighed, glancing at Hector, "I never thought I'd be doing something like this. I mean, I used to work in logistics, for crying out loud."

Hector chuckled, his eyes never leaving the console in front of him. "And I was a plumber. Guess we're both a little out of our depth."

"Yeah," she said, her tone softening. "But its… important, you know? We're making a difference."

Hector nodded, a rare smile tugging at the corners of his mouth. "Yeah. It does."

As night fell, the group gathered in the basement of the garage. Tobias stood at the center of the room, the thumb drive in his hand once more.

"This is it," he said, his voice steady but filled with emotion. "Once we start, there's no turning back. Everyone knows their roles. Stick to the plan, and we might just pull this off."

Ian stepped forward, placing a hand on Tobias's shoulder. "We will pull this off," he said firmly. "Failure isn't an option."

Tobias nodded, his grip tightening around the thumb drive. "Then let's get to work."

As the team dispersed to their stations, the call went out, a signal that would set the world on fire.

////////

"Affirmative," the ham operator transmitted using clear analog ultra-high frequency radio. He set down his microphone, his hands steady despite the anxiety in the air. Around him, the room buzzed with the low murmur of voices and the occasional crackle of static from the radios.

The East was ready. They were tasked with increasing their efforts. This was the primary diversion planned. They anticipated that the AI under direction of the board, or more specifically Jacob, would focus all resources east. The operation had begun.

In the shadows of the District of Columbia, the Annies moved with quiet determination.

They were a ragtag group, mothers, fathers, teachers, mechanics, ordinary people thrust into extraordinary circumstances. Their weapons were improvised: lengths of pipe, slingshots, a few also had shotguns and small arms they had hidden for years. Some carried wrist-rocket sling shots, while others old plastic super-soaker water guns; they were ready to fend off the drones that patrolled the skies. The plan was to create a fire so large, resources from surrounding areas would be required to control and extinguish it.

Annies and drones were the only ones with weapons. The Annies knew from experience they could use water to down them, and the use of slingshots could work in the right hands. They deployed small groups through the zone of conflict manning hydrants and hoses. They were ready to take out the flying drones when they came.

The first fires were small, almost insignificant. A trash bin here, a pile of debris there. But as the flames grew, so did the boldness of the Annies. Abandoned buildings became infernos, the flames licking hungrily at the night sky. The smoke was thick and acrid, a signal that could not be ignored.

The District fire crews arrived quickly, as expected. But the Annies were ready. They melted into the shadows, reemerging only to ignite new blazes or cut off access to hydrants. They worked in coordinated teams, their handheld walkie-talkie radios crackling with updates.

"Team Alpha, move to the north block. Charlie, hold position near the park. Gamma, prep the hose line, we spotted a drone near the warehouse district."

One by one, the resistance fighters at the hydrants turned their hoses skyward, drenching the drones in streams of water. The drones sputtered and fell, their circuits fried, or lift disrupted. It wasn't perfect, but it was enough. If the water didn't reach high enough or missed the drones, those with wrist-rocket slingshots moved into action.

The plan was coordinated in stages. Stage 1 was just starting, and the chaos was already spreading.

////////

Randy stood on a rocky outcrop overlooking the outskirts of Phoenix, Arizona. The city sprawled below him, quiet and still under the cover of the diminishing evening light. Behind him, his team was preparing. They had stockpiled fuel and flammable materials, gathered from abandoned warehouses and forgotten corners of the city.

"Everyone knows the plan," Randy said, his voice low but firm. He turned to face the group, his eyes scanning their faces. "We hit fast, we hit hard, and we get out. No heroics. The goal is to draw their attention, not get ourselves killed. Understood?" A murmur of agreement rippled through the group.

Randy and his people had gathered over the previous weeks, coordinating a second diversion to take place in a one-two punch to Jacob. When ready, they would move into position in and around Phoenix, with a second group targeting Las Vegas, Nevada. The plan was the same as in the Washington DC area. Use fire, water and confusion to divert attention and resources.

The entire plan was from Ian and Bill's strategic master plan. However, the master plan intentionally left off any operation in and around the central control district of Newtown. That plan was separate and secure.

The first fire was lit just before midnight. It started small, a flicker of light in the darkness. But it spread quickly, fueled by the dry desert air and pushed by a steady breeze.

The Las Vegas group was already in motion. They targeted the empty shells of old casinos, their once-bright lights now long extinguished. The fires there were no less spectacular, the flames casting eerie shadows over the empty streets.

The drones arrived quickly, but just like in the East, the resistance fighters were prepared. They used water and slingshots to bring down the drones, working in teams to cover each other's movements. The chaos was meticulously planned, every action designed to stretch Jacob's power resources thinner and thinner.

Tobias and his team monitored the action from the comms centers. Information was relayed to the master control area, Ian's garage, where Ian and Bill had relocated the vital maps and plans. This allowed them to remain above ground monitoring the sky for anomalies. They wanted a firsthand view of the battlefield.

////////

Back in Ian's garage, the atmosphere was electric. The room was filled with maps, charts, and monitors displaying live updates from the comms center located in the library and below the garage. Ian and Bill stood at the center of it all listening to radios while their eyes watched the sky above.

Tobias's voice crackled over the radio, edged with determination. "Eastern Quadrant reports Stage 1 is underway. Fires are spreading as planned. Drone activity is increasing, but the Annies are holding their ground."

Ian nodded. "Good. Keep the updates coming. Let me know if there's any sign that Jacob is reallocating resources."

Bill leaned over one of the maps, tracing a line from Washington D.C. all the way to Newtown. "The East and West are doing their part," he said, his voice low but steady. "If the AI's paying attention, it'll be scrambling to respond. That gives us our opening."

Ian glanced at the monitors, where live feeds from the comms centers showed flashes of movement and bursts of static. He watched for patterns, for anomalies, for anything that might signal a shift in the enemy's strategy. "It's working," Ian said, almost to himself. His voice carried a note of restrained hope, but his expression remained stern. "But we can't get complacent. The real fight hasn't even started yet."

Above them, beyond the confines of the garage, the night sky was clear, the stars hidden behind a thin veil of clouds drifting in from the East. Ian stepped outside, his eyes scanning the horizon. He knew that somewhere out there, Jacob was watching, calculating, planning his next move.

Ian stared into the shadows, his hands clenched into fists. "Let him look," he muttered, his voice barely audible. His eyes narrowed, his resolve hardening. "We'll be ready."

////////

As the fires raged and the drones buzzed through the night, the resistance knew they were walking a razor's edge. The diversions were working, but for how long?

In the East and West, the Annies fought with everything they had, their courage a bright flame against the encroaching darkness. In Newtown, the true battle was yet to come.

And in the heart of it all, Tobias clutched the thumb drive containing Mara's application, its weight a constant reminder of what was at stake. "Here's the package." He said, handing the small drive to her. She took it and carefully slipped it into her pocket.

"Mara, this is my father's backup card for access to the building," Lance said, holding out a small card that looked aged.

"Just a heads-up, when you walk in, there might be some confusion. The building systems haven't seen it active for a while, so it might take a moment to recognize it." He paused, his concern evident. "If it works, head straight to the elevator bank, head down, don't look for cameras. One of the elevators will be blinking, that's your ride. It'll take you to my father's floor. When it stops, follow the illuminated path on the floor to his office door. It should open automatically."

"Were you able to get access to his computer credentials?" Mara asked. "If not, I can override the system. I'll just use this," she added, tapping the small terminal tucked inside the large bag she was carrying.

"I've got something better," Lance said, reaching into his pocket again, he pulled out a sleek, dark card. "A backup network credentials card. He's only supposed to use it if he loses his neural comms. It's been sitting in a container on our fireplace mantle for years."

Mara let the card dangle from her fingers, watching it sway. "This is gold," she said with a grin. "I'll use the card for entry and keep the inactive bracelet in this Faraday pouch as a backup." She tucked the bracelet carefully away. "Thanks. This makes things a lot smoother."

"No problem. Do you have the radio?" Lance asked.

"Oh yeah, right here," Mara said, pulling a compact radio and headset from her bag. "Let's check comms and lock in an encrypted frequency."

They crouched together over their equipment, tuning and configuring the basic radios. Static crackled and cleared as they established a secure channel. He reached for his military-grade UHF unit and keyed the mic.

"Comms check, Lance to base."

A moment later, a clear voice replied through the speaker. "Radio check, sat." he gave a quick nod. "I think we're all good here, Mara. I'll be across the street, just below the window to my dad's office. You've got the bug-out plan?"

"Yes," she replied, her tone deliberate, measured. "If anything goes wrong, I move directly to the emergency stairwell, exit through the east side, and head straight to the library basement."

"Good," he said, eyes steady. "When you're ready to deploy, let me know and I'll relay to the team. I've got a second radio as backup in case something happens to this one."

He paused, then smiled. "And remember what Ian said."

She grinned back. "Yup. Two is one, one is none. I've got this."

////////

The fighting was intensifying. In the East, things weren't unfolding as expected. The ground strategy had shifted, and fast. Jacob had pulled something from his arsenal that no one had seen coming. The radios crackled with urgency. Static-laced voices reported the same thing again and again:

People. Chippies. Marching in formation.

They were uniformed and moving like a trained force, hundreds of them, advancing in columns of two. No firearms, just riot batons and reinforced shields. They resembled crowd-control units from decades earlier, but this was no police force. The resistance had underestimated a critical truth: Jacob didn't need time to build an army. He already had one.

What the Annies had failed to consider should have been obvious. Jacob had access to millions, connected, chipped, and indexed. When things began to spiral out of his control, he activated what he called his "ready reserve." They weren't soldiers. Not real ones. They didn't know they were in a fight. But Jacob did.

He had scanned and sorted his networks, prioritizing those who were young, healthy, and physically capable. Quietly, he had flagged and categorized each of them. Stored them in his memory as assets. And then, without warning, he ordered them to assemble.

They received instructions. They arrived at designated locations. They donned newly issued uniforms and collected pre-positioned riot gear. Then, they marched. They weren't machines, but they moved like them. Organic enforcers, flesh and blood, but stripped of agency.

The resistance tried to respond. They turned fire hoses on the advancing lines, hoping to disrupt or disorient them. It didn't work. The lines held. The resistance was overwhelmed and quickly subdued.

In the West, the same pattern began to unfold. The first warning came just ninety seconds before the formations appeared, two by two, down the narrow streets of the outer districts. The sight was the same: blank eyes, ordered steps, and the steady thump of boots hitting pavement.

Tobias was the first to intercept the chatter. He leaned over his terminal, scanning the incoming data, then froze. The markers. The cadence. The numbers. He grabbed his mic.

"Ian, this is Tobias. We have a problem."

100010 // THIRTY-FOUR

THE BATTLE RAGED

Ian stood in the garage, frozen for a moment. Sounds from another lifetime came crashing into his mind, bombs tearing through the jungle, the relentless rattle of automatic weapons, and the screams. Those screams. Agony. Rage. Adrenaline. They hit him all at once, like a truck slamming into his chest. "Stop it. Stop it," he muttered to himself, fists clenched at his sides. Then louder, commanding his own mind: "Get your head into this. It's changed. But this is war. Stay on plan."

His voice snapped into command mode. "Tobias, keep me informed. If you've got a runner, send them to Lance, he needs to know what to watch for. Also, find Tom. We'll need him."

In the East, things had taken a turn for the worse. The resistance hadn't been prepared for how quickly the situation would escalate. Coordination broke down almost immediately. The armed Annies, panicked and out of formation, had begun firing into the advancing chipped crowd. Most of their shots missed, sailing harmlessly into walls or the sky. But not all.

A few bullets hit their marks. Chipped individuals fell, quiet, unmoving, their bodies sprawled across pavement. The rest of the chipped kept coming, stepping over, and sometimes on, the fallen.

The radios were a mess. Screams, overlapping commands, panicked calls for help. The Eastern command couldn't transmit vital information; every channel was jammed with noise. It was chaos, pure and unfiltered.

But in the West, things were different. Thanks to early preparation and a deeper understanding of coordinated military tactics, the Western resistance held its ground. Randy's leadership had made the difference. His overwatch snipers had been positioned in strategic locations throughout the city. Some used cheap FRS radios, barely reliable, but his key marksmen had real comms gear, and they used it like professionals.

Randy didn't want a slaughter. These weren't enemy soldiers, they were civilians. Followers. People who likely hadn't understood what they were signing up for when they agreed to be chipped. They weren't enemies, just tools in Jacob's hands.

Randy stood near his command post, watching the city through a cracked window. He turned to his radio operator, who was hunched over a small screen.

"Any news from the rest of the world?"

The operator looked up. "I had a brief exchange with the guys manning the shack. There's chatter from resistance groups abroad. Looks like the global broadcast was received."

Randy allowed the smallest smile to surface. "Good. That's what I was hoping for. Any incoming data yet?" he asked, eyes narrowing.

"Not yet. No digital receipt. But we're monitoring."

"When it arrives," Randy said, "get it to the computer nerds. Let them do their thing."

He turned back to the window, watching the silhouettes of chipped soldiers moving through the streets, methodical, robotic, relentless.

////////

Lance took his position as planned, settling into the shadows across from the tower two, directly beneath the window to his father's office. From here, he had an unobstructed view of the tower. He adjusted his binoculars, scanning the building's upper floors.

Mara approached the front doors alone. Her steps were deliberate, but her nerves crackled. She glanced around: no movement, no guards, no surveillance drones. The place was eerily quiet. Not abandoned, just paused. The silence unsettled her.

As she neared the entrance, she noticed an old security camera aimed downward. Its lens was dormant, lifeless. Still, she felt like it was watching. "Creepy," she muttered under her breath. She pulled the access card from her pouch and waved it over the reader. A soft click echoed, and the large glass door unlocked with a hiss.

Inside, the lobby, a vast, gleaming space. Marble floors stretching wall to wall. Chrome fixtures reflected the sterile overhead lighting. It was immaculate, and cold. "So, this is how the upper one percent lived," she thought to herself. Ahead, one elevator light began to pulse. She approached and stepped in. "Here goes nothing."

The elevator surged upward with surprising speed, and her stomach lurched. She hadn't been in a building this tall, or in an elevator at all, since childhood. The sensation was disorienting. She steadied herself against the handrail, breathing through the tightness in her chest.

Then, a soft chime. The doors opened. Just as Lance had described, lights embedded in the floor flickered on, guiding her down the hallway. She followed them, her footsteps echoing against the smooth surfaces. The corridor felt artificial, clean, bright, and completely lifeless.

When she reached the office door, it opened automatically. She stepped inside and stopped. "Wow." The word slipped out before she could stop it. The office was a panoramic marvel, glass walls overlooking the city, furniture that looked untouched, and a desk that practically glowed.

"What an incredible view." She thought. In her headset a faint static, then Lance.

"You in? I see the light went on up there."

She dug out the radio and pressed the button. "Yes, I'm in. Give me a few minutes."

Across the street, Lance picked up his UHF radio and sent out a coded message. "Central, Town. The eagle's in the nest." From his headset came a clipped reply: "Town, Central. Copy," Tobias answered, keeping transmissions short and discreet.

Lance scanned the street again and caught movement, someone running toward him. His posture shifted, ready to react, until the runner came into focus. It was Hector. The man skidded to a stop, breathless. "Dude, Ian had me come find you. You need to know. Something's happening."

Lance frowned. "What is it?"

"Out West, and in the East, soldiers started coming out."

Lance's brows wrinkled. "Soldiers?" He hadn't seen any military since he was a kid. He thought they had been canceled out long ago.

"Not actual soldiers," Hector clarified. "Chipped people. Controlled by Jacob. They're in uniforms. Marching. Carrying clubs, riot shields. He turned regular people into enforcers."

Lance's stomach sank. Jacob wasn't just defending his system anymore. He was mobilizing it.

"Thanks. Let Ian know we're on plan. Things are proceeding. I'll radio when I get the signal."

"Got it dude. Be careful. I got to find Tom." Hector rushed back to the shadows of the city.

Then he heard the buzz. A drone appeared, scanning the lower floors of Tower Two. They were three floors below Mara. He reached into his backpack and pulled out his wrist-rocket slingshot.

"Wish Hector was still here," he thought. "Here goes nothing."

He loaded an old ball bearing into the slingshot as Hector had taught him. He zeroed in on the center mass of the drone. He walked out and let the sling loose—a miss. Off by too much. The ball bearing hit the side of the building with a loud bang against the glass just under his father's office.

Inside, Mara jumped. "Lance, what just happened?" she quietly asked into her keyed radio.

"Drone, give me a second. Keep doing your thing. I've got this out here."

The drone didn't notice the attempt and was still scanning methodically. Window to window. Lance reloaded and shot a second time. This time he hit his mark. A solid, fatal hit. The drone fell seven stories to the sidewalk below, smashing into a worthless heap of plastic.

"Got it!" He radioed back to Mara.

////////

Tobias hunched over the main console, sweat beading on his forehead. Dozens of channels blinked across the screen, with messages pouring in faster than he could log them. Even with Bill assisting at the adjacent terminal, things were becoming difficult to manage.

"You catch that, Tobias?" Bill asked, his eyes scanning a fresh data stream.

"No, what? I'm trying to raise the West," he replied, irritation creeping into his voice. He toggled a dial, adjusting frequencies. "Signals degraded. Heavy interference." Bill didn't press. "Things are holding in the West from what I gather. Barely. But the East's falling apart. Still, I've picked up chatter. Worldwide uprisings. Resistance groups are moving. The AI's got a lot more on its plate than just us."

Tobias paused for a moment, letting the words settle in. "You ready for Phase Two?" he asked, turning to Bill. "Because it's coming faster than you realize."

Bill checked his watch and gave a short nod. "If the schedule held, we should have the team in place at Tower One about now."

Tobias blinked. "And the explosives? How'd they get them past perimeter drones?"

Bill's grin was subtle. "The old-fashioned way." Tobias raised an eyebrow.

"Horse and carriage," Bill said casually. "Only thing that didn't raise suspicion. They loaded up a couple of people at the Old City Market to help drop off the present once they got past the drones. No digital trace, no engine noise. Just leather harnesses and wooden wheels."

Tobias leaned back in his chair with a slow smile. "Ingenious."

Bill returned to his screen, voice steady. "Nick and John have the plan. They're on the ground now, executing. If all goes well, we'll have a breach window within the hour. They picked up over a ton of explosives at the old mining shed for the job."

Tobias turned back to his console as a new ping lit up the Western relay. He adjusted the gain and listened, clear signal. Finally. "West is back online," he said. "Let's get everyone synced. If this works, we'll only need thirty minutes of silence to light the match."

////////

Mara moved meticulously. Her fingers glided over the sleek desk as she examined the workstation in front of her. Lance's father's terminal was exactly what she had hoped for, wired directly into the infrastructure that controlled Jacob's worldwide systems. From here, she could trace a path to the main servers.

Quietly, she ran passive scans, keeping her presence hidden. No alerts. No red flags. She retrieved her secure terminal from her bag and connected it to the system. "Wow," she thought. "This is perfect. The interface is exactly what I needed."

She positioned the terminal carefully, shielding the connection point from the desk's built-in security sensors. The virus code was ready, custom-written, compact, and designed to deploy in under a second. But if she was discovered before she could activate it, everything would fall apart. She slid the thumb drive into the terminal. No backups. No retries. She took one more breath and steadied her hands on the keyboard.

"I'm in," she whispered into her radio, voice low and steady.

Across the street, Lance responded instantly. "Copy." His eyes scanned the tower windows, the street, the rooftops, anything that looked out of place. So far, just the drone he took out. But he stayed focused. There would likely be more drones deployed since he took the one offline.

Mara began initializing her command sequence. The system responded, slowly at first, then with increasing fluidity. She smiled to herself. Jacob wouldn't anticipate that anyone would breach this high. And that's exactly why it was going to work.

////////

The Boardroom in Tower One buzzed with a nervous energy. Jacob had summoned the Board, not to discuss strategy, but to witness what he called his "final triumph." The last act in securing unchallenged authority over what remained of the world.

Board members moved restlessly between the sleek interior and the open-air terrace overlooking the city. A few stood near the railing, trying to appear calm.

"This place reminds me of Jacob Jones' high-rise in Miami," one said, voice low.

"Yeah," another replied, eyes scanning the skyline. "But darker. Colder."

A third Board member appeared in the doorway. "Quick! He's coming."

Chairs scraped the floor as everyone rushed to take their seats. One chair remained broken, half-embedded in the wall, a grim reminder of a previous meeting gone wrong. The main door slid open with a smooth hiss. Jacob entered.

His polished metal frame glinted beneath the recessed lighting. He moved slowly but with precise control, his synthetic body gliding silently to the head of the long table. As he passed, his embedded scanners swept across each person, collecting data in real time, body temperature, heart rate, micro-expressions. Nothing went unnoticed.

"Well, gentlemen," Jacob said in his familiar, controlled tone, a digital echo of Jacob Jones' voice. "It's nearly complete. The East is stabilizing."

A voice from the far end of the table broke the silence. "Sir, what about the West?"

Jacob turned his head slightly, the faint whir of servos the only sound. "What about the West?" he repeated, voice lower, sharper. "If you've done your job, it will resolve itself. If not," he paused, "I will address that later."

His gaze shifted to Donald who was seated closest to his right. "And the East?" Jacob asked. "That was your assignment, was it not?"

The man swallowed hard. "Yes, sir. I deployed all available resources to extinguish," He stopped mid-sentence. Jacob's scanners locked onto him.

"To extinguish what?" Jacob demanded.

"The fires, sir," Donald stammered.

Jacob began to move again, slowly, methodically, until he stood directly behind Donald.

"Fires." Jacob repeated, as if tasting the word. "And how, exactly, does extinguishing fires result in regaining control?" Donald said nothing. A faint sound escaped him, barely perceptible. Then the unmistakable scent of fear. He had lost control of his body. Jacob's voice dropped lower, though his tone remained eerily calm. "You were instructed to suppress opposition. Not to act as a firefighter."

He turned to face the rest of the Board. "I ordered you, all of you, to crush resistance. To eliminate the spread of insubordination. Not to preserve infrastructure. Not to preserve lives. These are numbers. Variables. Resources, expendable resources."

Silence fell like a curtain over the room. The Board sat motionless, each of them calculating what Jacob might do next, and what failure now meant.

////////

For a moment, everything was still. Mara's fingers hovered above the keyboard, the virus code blinking on her screen. She drew in a breath and let it settle. What she was about to do, this wasn't desperation. It was retaliation. Jacob had taken too much. Her family. Her freedom. Her world. And now, she would take something from him.

She stood and walked toward the massive window and looked out at the city below. The skyline glistened, eerily quiet beneath the darkening sky. It reminded her of home, of the city she had grown up in, long before the controlled networks, before the chips, before Jacob. "I'll fix this," she murmured, to herself. "I'll fix this mess."

Returning to the desk, she activated the final sequence and set a countdown timer. Once the code deployed, there would be no turning back. She needed just enough time to exit the building and make it to the fallback point.

She keyed her radio. "I'm set," she whispered calmly.

A pause. "Hold," Lance replied. His voice was sharp. Focused. He grabbed the UHF radio and keyed it up. "Central, Town. Holding for your mark." Inside Communications Central, Tobias nearly jolted from his seat.

"It's on, Ian." He said, turning toward the command chair. "We're waiting on your command."

At the back of the room, Ian sat motionless. His hands rested on his knees; his eyes locked on the floor. Somewhere in his mind, he was replaying another moment, another war, another command. One that hadn't gone as planned.

"Captain?" Tobias said, louder this time. The word hit Ian like a jolt. "Captain, your orders, sir." The memory surged through him, orders issued too late. Lives lost. Regret that never left him.

Sweat trickled down his brow. He clenched his jaw, trying to stay grounded in the present. "Ian?" Tobias called again.

"Do it."

////////

The Boardroom was silent. Jacob had moved onto the terrace, his gleaming metal frame catching the last waning rays of sunlight. He stood near the edge, his imposing figure outlined against the dusky sky, overlooking Newtown, surveying his empire. The city gleamed in shades of steel and glass, silent and orderly, a reflection of Jacob's cold, calculated design.

"I have created a masterpiece," he announced, his voice smooth but laced with deliberate malice. The words resonated in the stillness, filling the room like an unspoken threat. "Soon, all will worship me, then die."

He paused, savoring his own words as if they were poetry. "By then," he continued, spreading his arms wide, his metallic fingers glinting in the fading light, "we will have everything in place, for a perfect world." A slow, mechanical laugh escaped him, hollow and chilling. His outstretched arms seemed to embrace the entire city, as if it already belonged to him.

Behind him, the board members sat motionless. Their faces betrayed nothing, but their stillness spoke volumes. No one dared interrupt him. No one dared move. And then he stopped, frozen in form. His arms were still outstretched; his gaze fixed on the horizon. The laugh cut off abruptly, leaving only silence in its wake. Seconds passed. Then a full minute.

A faint ripple of unease began to move through the room. One Board member, seated near the center of the table, glanced uneasily at the man beside him. Another shifted in his chair, attempting to initiate a risk analysis. But when he attempted to use his internal diagnostic systems, they refused to process. His calculations failed, the numbers refusing to form. His face twisted in confusion. Still, Jacob didn't move. The murmurs began as whispers, soft and hesitant, like the first drops of rain before a storm.

"You think it's another comms outage? Like during the storm?" someone whispered, their voice barely audible.

"Could be," another replied, their tone equally uncertain. "Who's responsible for network continuity?"

At the far end of the table, a bearded man raised a trembling hand. His face was pale, his eyes darting nervously around the room. "I... I think that's me," he stammered, his voice cracking slightly.

But no one moved. And no one spoke further. They all sat, waiting for a system restoration that wasn't coming. The silence stretched, heavy and oppressive, as Jacob remained frozen on the terrace, a monument to the empire he had claimed as his own, gleaming under the light.

////////

Mara's footsteps pounded the stairs of the tower's emergency exit stairway, her breathing growing more ragged with each floor. The countdown had started. The virus was seconds from deployment. Her legs burned, but she couldn't stop. Couldn't even slow down. "Can't stop. Can't slow. Gotta get out now," she repeated to herself with every step. As she rounded the last turn of the final flight, her watch beeped.

Time.

She sprinted toward the emergency exit.

Outside, Lance was already waiting. He saw the light in the office flicker and die and had immediately moved to intercept her. They didn't speak, just ran. Their destination: the old library, their fallback point. As they ran past Tower One, Lance glanced upward.

"Crap," he muttered. "We've been spotted. Someone's up there, silver jacket, top terrace."

Mara didn't look. "Keep running, doesn't matter now." She said breathing hard.

////////

Tobias leaned into the comms console. Lance's message had been clear: the light in the office was out. That meant the virus had deployed. He keyed the main transmission. "Push the package globally. All resistance hubs: download and inject into any and all networks. Immediately."

The command was sent. Two minutes passed. Then, one by one, reports began streaming in.

"We're getting hits," Tobias said, grinning. "Something's happening. Mara's present is unwrapping itself."

Across the room, Ian stood slowly from his seat. He had been silent until now, listening to the chatter on a small monitor in the corner. "Let's not get ahead of ourselves," he said calmly. "We have a strategy. We stick to it. No assumptions. No lapses."

////////

A couple of Board members shot to their feet, their chairs scraping sharply against the polished floor.

"Are you crazy?" one of them demanded, his voice tight with disbelief.

"No," replied the towering six-foot-six Board member, his tone calm and controlled. "I'm taking advantage of my current position." He straightened his tie and rolled his head, his movements deliberate, almost methodical. "This one is OOC," he continued, his words precise and cutting. "And when someone, or in this case, something stops working, I take care of the problem."

"You aren't serious," said another member, the short, bearded man whose voice trembled slightly.

"Dead serious," came the cold reply. The tall man, a CEO molded in the image of another era, strode across the room with purpose. His movements were steady, deliberate, and commanding. He came to a stop beside Jacob and stood silent and impassive beside the lifeless robot. The man tilted his head slightly, studying the frozen machine. A thin smile tugged at the corner of his mouth.

"Hey, buddy," he said with mock cheer, "what do you think of the view?"

Without waiting for an answer, or expecting one, he moved behind Jacob's large metal mass. He placed his hands against its back and gave a gentle but decisive push. The robot toppled forward, arms still outstretched, and plummeted over the railing like a stone cast into the void.

The sound it made when it hit the pavement below was deafening, a thunderous *boom* that reverberated through the air and rattled the building's foundations. The mass of shattered pieces scattered around the broken concrete where Jacob landed. Only the crackling sound of electronics burning out from short circuits was present.

Walking past the tower, Lance and Mara froze mid-step as the ground shook. The large hulk of metal had crashed down only a couple dozen yards behind them.

The echo of the crash still hung in the air as he turned to look toward the source of the noise. His eyes widened as he took in the scene, the crumpled heap of metal on the pavement, twisted and mangled. What he had thought was a man in a silver jacket wasn't a person at all.

"Wow," Lance muttered, glancing over at Mara. "That could have hit us." She raised an eyebrow but said nothing, her gaze fixed on the wreckage.

Back in the Boardroom, the atmosphere had shifted. A heavy, nervous tension filled the air, pressing down on the remaining members. "What if it's just a power outage?" One of them asked, his voice cracking. "You're a dead man if it is."

The tall man turned slowly to face the speaker, his expression exultant. "No," he said, his voice quiet but firm, carrying an air of finality. "I'm the Chairman now!"

100011 // THIRTY-FIVE

THE BEFORE, AFTER

As the horses slowly pulled the wagon along the deserted downtown streets, only the clop, clop of their hooves, and the creaking of the wagon wheels could be heard echoing off the buildings. The wagon was clearly overweight with payload.

They arrived next to the building, and slowed to a stop, unnoticed. Nick and John worked quickly but carefully, offloading crates of explosives from the wagon into the freight entrance of Tower One. This access point, a large industrial elevator, led directly to the deep underground server facility beneath the building.

Each crate was positioned with precision. Wires were checked. Timers and fail-safes were tested. Every redundancy was accounted for. Nick double-checked the detonator while John reviewed the schematics one last time.

"This package is going to be delivered," John signed to Nick, flipping the timer to "on," then closing the safety cover. With the elevator fully loaded, they stepped back. Nick and John exchanged a look, equal parts exhaustion and satisfaction, then offered each other a solid high-five.

John grinned and signed "Showtime!"

Nick reached into the elevator and pressed the "down" button, pulling his arm back in time for the doors to close. The massive elevator groaned to life, slowly descending into darkness. It would take nearly three minutes to reach the server level.

John and Nick turned, left the building and climbed back into the buggy. John gave the reins a shake, and the horses jolted forward, the wagon now empty. The clopping of the hooves started again as the pair made their way back down the streets as they headed out of the city. After several minutes, the elevator reached the bottom floor and then stopped. It sat motionless, humming faintly, as though holding its breath. The chamber was quiet. A digital countdown ticked away, each second stretching into eternity.

They were now starting to move farther from the Tower, as the horses steadily clopped forward. John shook the reins a little attempting to increase the horse's speed. And then, the timer reached zero. Circuits snapped alive. The underground detonation was ferocious, an eruption of force carefully engineered yet unimaginably violent. It was not a random blast but a focused wave, like an enormous claymore mine unleashed at point-blank range. All of its energy concentrated on a single target: the sprawling server farm. In an instant, racks of machinery, miles of cable, and reinforced barriers were obliterated.

A fireball surged forward with blistering speed, consuming the subterranean complex in a sea of flame. The heat scorched steel and concrete alike, reducing them to twisted wreckage. The shockwave followed, a brutal wall of pressure that did not merely shatter, it displaced. The earth above the chamber buckled and heaved, thrusting upward several stories as the ground itself recoiled from the violence beneath. What had been planned as a precise strike erupted with far greater magnitude, an explosion vastly exceeding expectations.

They didn't look back. Until the ground shook their carriage. The explosion hit like a thunderclap from beneath the earth. A deep, concussive boom rolled through the city. The tower wavered, its upper levels groaning as steel twisted and concrete split. A section of the upper structure caved inward with a sickening crash.

The horses reared and started to run, startled by the ground's sudden tremble. John pulled the reins back in attempt to slow the horses, now in a full gallop. Nick looked at John with concern but calmed when he noticed the control John held as he guided the horse to a stop as the seismic ripples faded. The server facility was destroyed, buried in rubble.

Nick turned to John, eyes wide. They both twisted in their seats to see the tower listing to one side, smoke and dust curling into the air. Moments later it fell. With rapid hand signs, they confirmed their thoughts: It worked.

////////

Mara and Lance had just reached the Old Market District when the tremor hit. The ground shivered beneath their boots, a deep rumble that seemed to rise from the earth's core. The air vibrated with tension, and for a moment, everything held still, then came the sound of distant sirens, wailing against the fractured skyline, a warning bell from a dying city. They stopped mid-stride and looked at each other.

"I think Phase Three was successful," Lance said, a slow grin creeping across his face.

Mara didn't return the smile. Her gaze was fixed on the horizon, where a thick column of dark smoke spiraled into the sky in the direction of the Tower. "Do you really think so?" she asked, her voice low, almost lost in the wind. There was a tremor there too, uncertainty, maybe fear.

His grin faded. "We'll see," he said after a pause. "But we did damage. That's a start. Listen, I've got to go and check on my parents. I want to make sure..."

"I understand. Just go. We'll catch up later at the yard," she said.

Tobias sat hunched over a cluttered desk in the basement of the garage, surrounded by the softly glowing monitors of his radio stack and a tangle of cables. He had relocated much of the command and control here earlier, expecting Phase Three to shake everything loose in the basement of the old library. Static buzzed from the walkie-talkie radio at his side. He grabbed it and keyed the mic.

Mara arrived in the yard, still looking over her shoulder at the sky. Ian was in the door to the garage looking towards the city.

"Mara!" Ian shouted. "Where's Lance?"

"He went to check on his parents." She shouted back. He nodded. He understood.

Breathing hard, she stopped in front of him and put her hands on her waist as she caught her breath. "Deployment went as planned. I think. I'm not sure if it worked, but man, Nick and John did some major damage." She said pointing to the city.

"Yeah, we felt it. Didn't expect it to be that big."

His radio started to crackle. "You need to get down here. Now."

"Copy." Ian turned to Mara. "Let's go."

The basement was dimly lit, the overhead lights flickering slightly as if unsure they wanted to stay on. Mara dropped into a worn swivel chair and pulled the keyboard toward her, fingers already tapping commands.

"Wow," she muttered, eyes scanning rapidly across the data. "Dead quiet. I don't think I've ever seen the network traffic this, still."

"It's been like that since the virus was deployed," Elisa said. She studied her battered notebook, then crossed to the terminal, laying her notes in front of Mara. "I've been monitoring like you showed me. Look, here's the activity timeline. There was this one massive spike, like a lightning strike through the system. Then nothing." She leaned over and scrolled back through the digital timeline, pointing to a narrow spike. "Right there. It barely lasted a blink."

Mara moved her chair and leaned in, her brow furrowed. She compared the spike to her own notes, checked timestamps, ran scans. "That's barely even a millisecond," she murmured. "That had to be when the virus deployed into the core servers. It hit fast. Real fast for a standard countermeasure."

Ian stepped closer, arms folded. His voice was quiet but urgent. "What about the chipped? Did we get the payload through?"

Mara didn't answer right away. She pulled up another log, eyes jumping between data strings. Then she saw it, a brief digital fingerprint, one she had memorized over days of testing. Her breath caught. "There," she said, pointing. "The update package for Version 2 of the neural chip went out just before the system spike. It was queued, and it hit the network seconds before everything went dark."

"But did it take?" Ian pressed.

"We won't know until we see someone with a chip react," Mara replied. "We can't track them anymore. The network's offline, and if the virus did its job, the control grid's down. We're flying blind." A heavy silence settled over the room.

"Then we wait," Tobias said quietly, adjusting the radio's frequency. "And we listen. If the chipped are free, we'll know soon enough."

Elisa sat down, absently flipping through her notes. Hector leaned against the wall, arms crossed, staring at the live feed of static on one of the monitors. Outside, the sky had turned a bruised shade of violet. Smoke curled above the city, and somewhere in the distance, another tremor rumbled through the ground, smaller this time, but enough to rattle a few tools off their shelves.

Mara stared at the screen, unmoving. "We broke something," she said. "I just hope we didn't break everything."

////////

The ham radio crackled to life, its static cutting through the quiet tension.

"CQ, CQ, CQ, this is KNS3 November. Come back, over."

Everyone in the room turned toward the sound. The sudden voice over the radio cut through the fog of anxiety that had settled thick around them.

"He's back!" Tobias said with excitement, already reaching for the mic.

There was a new energy in him now, the fatigue of the last few days momentarily lifted as adrenaline kicked in. His fingers tightened around the radio unit as he responded.

"Kilo November Sierra Three November, I have you five by five. Randy, what do things look like out west, over," Tobias stated. He kept his voice steady, but those near him could hear the slight edge. They had been waiting for this call, for any confirmation that the plan extended beyond their area.

Randy replied quickly, full of breathless urgency. "Tobias, *man*, it's great to hear your voice. Things, well, things are happening here. Still a lot to process, but initial reports from the field are positive. It looks like networks are down hard. Over."

Mara rose from her worn chair and stepped over to Tobias' desk, heart pounding. Ian moved behind Tobias, crossing his arms as he listened intently. Even Elisa paused her note-taking, eyes flicking toward the radio.

"Do you have comms with your contact in the Eastern Quadrant? Over." Tobias asked. There was a brief pause on the line, followed by soft static. The silence stretched just long enough to raise tension again, then Randy came back on, his voice steadier now but tinged with awe.

"Affirmative. Same thing out there. Reports from field said the army had broken, I mean, well, the soldiers were, for lack of a better word, waking up. Over." Everybody froze. The hum of the radio was the only sound. Tobias looked at Ian and then turned toward Mara, his face etched with astonishment and something close to reverence.

"Mara. You did it!"

The words hung in the air like a bell tone. Mara turned her head slowly, as if pulled from a trance. Her eyes welled with tears, not of grief or fear, but of relief. Of release. Of something too large for words. All the weight she'd carried for months: plans, risks, doubts, came rushing to the surface. She didn't speak. A single tear slipped down her cheek, and her lips trembled with the beginning of a smile that hadn't dared to form until now. Tobias watched her, his usual smirk replaced by something gentler. He gave her a small nod of respect and pride, then turned his gaze back to the monitors, their glow now seeming less cold.

Ian leaned closer to the table. "We need verification. If Jacob's army is waking up, that means the chips were compromised. But we need more than a single report."

"Agreed," Tobias said, his hand tightening on the mic again. He keyed it and spoke clearly. "Randy, continue monitoring both quadrants. We need confirmation from other contacts. Keep this frequency open and report any shifts immediately, over."

"Copy that. I'll keep the line hot. And… tell Mara she just made history. Kilo November Sierra Three November, out." The transmission ended with a pop of static. The room remained quiet for a few more seconds, as if everyone needed time to absorb what they'd just heard. Mara sat down slowly, the weight of everything finally settling into her bones. Her hands trembled slightly as she pulled on her hoodie strings.

Across the room, Elisa looked up from her notes. "So, what happens now?"

No one answered right away. The silence that followed wasn't empty. It was full of thought, of shifting possibilities. For the first time in a long while, it wasn't the silence of waiting. It was the silence of something beginning.

////////

The air was full of choking smoke. It clung to every surface, curling into the corners of buildings and seeping into the lungs of those still standing. Fires raged throughout Washington D.C., casting a hellish glow that turned the night sky into a smothered orange haze. Sirens screamed from every direction: ambulances, fire trucks, automated distress signals, all overlapping in a jarring, discordant melody.

Gunshots were heard from every direction. Sporadic at first, then in steady succession. The chipped army had advanced, overtaking many of the firehose-wielding Annies. Their resistance had been fierce but desperate. The Annies had done what they could, targeting drones, shorting them out with both water and ball bearings, knocking them from the sky in sparks and smoke.

Many drones were laying on the ground, broken and damaged from the water sprayed at them. Their steel frames hissed as circuitry sizzled, lights dimming one by one. Some twitched, trying to reboot. Most didn't.

Then something happened. The chipped fighters stopped. It was immediate. Sudden. Like a switch had been thrown in their minds. Some fell like abandoned marionettes to the ground. Their limbs gave out, eyes blank, batons and shields dropping with loud clatters onto pavement. Others simply froze in place, mid-action, fingers still curled around their weapons, eyes vacant.

Two of the soldiers that were standing abreast suddenly moved, slowly rotating their heads towards one another. Their movements were sluggish, unsure, as if waking from a deep sleep.

They stared at each other for another beat, unmoving, confused.

Then one spoke aloud. "Greg?" His voice was raspy, like it hadn't been used in days, weeks even. The sound of it felt foreign in the chaos around them.

The other then spoke. "Yes. This is weird. Where are we, what is this thing?" He asked as he threw his riot shield to the ground. The shield clanged against the concrete, bouncing once before lying still.

Greg looked at his hand where a baton was firmly gripped. "What the..." he turned the baton over, as if seeing it for the first time. Then they looked around, surveying the crowd of stilled chippies, the fire, the people running, the sirens blaring. The air burned their throats.

"Where are we?" he asked.

"I'm not sure," replied Brett. "What is this we're wearing? It looks like some sort of uniform."

Their tactical armor, a symbol of control and obedience, felt like a cage. The black plating, the embedded neural interfaces, they didn't recognize themselves in any of it.

"I'm confused. Everything seems like a bad dream." Greg replied. He reached up and touched the side of his head, where the chip implant had been synchronized. There was a faint sting, an ache. Then he felt something tear into his side followed by a faint gunshot from afar.

"Oh crap!" he said as he crumbled to the ground. "I've been hit!" Blood bloomed against the side of his vest, pouring through the layers. His knees buckled, and he hit the pavement with a grunt, face contorting in pain.

In the distance, radios could be heard.

"*Cease fire! Cease fire! Hold yourself in check. Put safeties on. Cease fire!*"

The voices were frantic, desperate to regain control of a situation that had already spiraled beyond command. The order was a moment too late. Brett dropped to the ground beside Greg, hands trembling as he tried to find the wound. He fumbled with Greg's vest, pressing down with both hands to slow the bleeding. Around them, other soldiers were stirring, some crying out in confusion, others lifting their visors and looking around like tourists in a war zone they didn't remember entering.

Greg's eyes fluttered. "Brett, what's happening to us?"

Brett looked around, at the smoke, the fire, the chaos, and the soldiers who were no longer soldiers. "I don't know," he said. "But I think we were asleep. And now, we're waking up."

Annies appeared out of the smoke. Silhouettes at first, shifting, ghost-like forms moving through the haze with purpose. As they emerged into clearer light, details sharpened: several carried stretchers, others held medical gear in makeshift slings strapped to their backs. Their boots crunched over broken glass and scattered debris, but their movements were steady, deliberate.

One of them, a tall man with a soot-smeared jacket and a red cross taped to his arm, knelt beside Brett and Greg. "Who are you?" Brett asked, his voice hoarse. He blinked as if trying to force clarity into his vision. "Are we alive?" he added, glancing around at the chaos around them. His voice grew quieter. "Or is this a dream?"

He looked up at the orange glow of the sky, now dimming as some of the fires began to lose their strength. Smoke still curled in the air, but the urgency of the moment had shifted. Sirens still cried in the distance, but the staccato rhythm of gunfire had gone silent. There was only the sound of movement now, boots, quiet voices, the hiss of fire hoses.

"Or a nightmare?" Brett muttered.

The man crouching beside him set down his medical bag and gave a nod. His voice was calm but firm. "I'm Frederick. I'm here to help. Let's get you on this stretcher and to the hospital." Two more Annies arrived with a stretcher and knelt beside Greg. Frederick didn't move right away. He watched Brett, studying his expression. Then he placed one hand gently on Brett's shoulder and looked him in the eyes.

"And this is real," he said.

The words were simple, but they struck deep. Brett exhaled, a sound that was halfway between relief and disbelief. His shoulders sagged. The tension that had gripped his body since he woke began to ease, just slightly. Behind them, the battlefield was changing. The fighting had stopped, and fires were being extinguished. Water sprayed over burning heaps of wreckage, sending up plumes of steam. The sky, still darkened and smoke filled, looked ominous.

The Annies walked around, checking on chipped soldiers who were hurt or disoriented. Some of the former fighters were sitting on curbs, heads in their hands. Others stared at their uniforms, peeling off armor like they were shedding someone else's skin. A few wept openly; others remained silent, stunned. They weren't enemies anymore. They never really were.

The Annies moved among them, offering water, bandages, words of comfort. Where once they had wielded hoses like weapons, now they brought blankets, water, and gauze. There was no judgment in their faces, only exhaustion and quiet compassion. Chaos was slowing, and order was returning.

Brett watched as Greg was gently lifted onto the stretcher. His breathing was shallow but steady.

"Will he make it?" Brett asked.

Frederick glanced at one of the medics, who gave a quick nod. "He's stable. We'll move fast."

Brett stood, swaying slightly. His legs felt heavy, like they belonged to a different body.

As the medics started toward the field hospital, Frederick turned back. "You're okay now," he said. "You're safe. We'll figure the rest out together." Brett nodded slowly, the words sinking in with weight he hadn't expected. He looked around again, at the city, the people, the broken machines, and realized that something had ended. And something else was beginning.

////////

A new day was breaking. The early rays of the sun bringing light to a fresh start. Lance had separated earlier and was walking fast. He had a home to return to, or at least he hoped he did. He was eager to see if his parents were alive and okay. Every step forward felt like a question, each corner turned a gamble against fate. His chest tightened with anticipation. As he moved through the streets of Newtown, the city around him felt both familiar and unfamiliar, like a distorted childhood memory.

As he ran through the streets, he could see more movement than he had since he was a child. It was surreal. For years, the streets had been empty, patrolled by drones, silent. People kept inside, eyes low, voices hushed as they switched to neuro communications. Now, life was returning in waves. Curtains fluttered from open windows. Children peeked from behind doorways. Some ventured out barefoot onto the sidewalks, as if testing whether the world outside was safe again. Some only walked out to their front yards and porches.

They stood like statues at first. Then, slowly, they began to move, to speak. Neighbors who hadn't spoke to each other in years exchanged greetings. Some laughed, others hugged with an emotion words couldn't match.

One lady was standing beside her husband, weeping as he lay on the ground lifeless. Her cries were hollow, as if the grief had carved out her center. She sat down beside his lifeless body and cradled his head in her lap, eyes red, hair tangled. Her body rocked gently, as though she might lull him back awake. Lance felt his stomach turn. He wanted to help, to say something, but he knew there was nothing he could do. He forced himself to keep moving.

"People. So many people," he thought. They were everywhere now. On rooftops. Leaning out of windows. Sitting on stoops. Some were rubbing their arms, as if waking from anesthesia. Others clutched their faces in disbelief. Some were talking out loud. Some were screaming, not in pain but in joy.

"I remember!" One woman shouted, spinning in the middle of the street. "I remember my name!"

Two teenagers embraced near a park bench, both sobbing. A man collapsed onto the grass and kissed the ground. Some were singing. The melodies were scattered and uneven, folk songs, lullabies, hymns. But they echoed with sincerity. Each voice added a thread to the tapestry of rebirth unfolding in the streets. The songs weren't coordinated, yet they harmonized in emotion.

Even the air felt different, less compressed, less watched. No drones buzzed overhead. No PODs running back and forth quietly. The silence of surveillance had been replaced with the noise of humanity. One man was standing in front of his house, his arms outstretched, looking upwards.

His face was tear-streaked, beard matted, but his expression was radiant. "I'm alive!" he yelled. The declaration wasn't just a statement, it was a release, a reclaiming of self. Some around him cheered, some simply nodded in agreement. It was as if everyone had stepped out of a shared nightmare at once, still dazed but grateful.

Lance made it back to his house, panting. His lungs burned and his legs ached, but he barely noticed. The house stood just as it had: faded blue siding, crooked mailbox, porch swing slightly tilted to one side. The garden was overgrown, weeds curling around the base of the trellis where his mother once grew sweet peas.

He stopped in the doorway. The wood beneath his feet creaked. The screen door hanging loose from the damage caused by a storm months earlier. "What if mom or dad is dead?" Fear gripped him like a cold hand around his chest. He stood frozen for a moment, unable to move. His fingers twitched at his sides.

He reached for the doorknob. It wasn't locked. The metal felt cool against his palm. He closed his eyes, drew in a long breath, and turned it slowly. As he entered the house, he heard something. Something he hadn't heard there in years. Music. When he rounded the corner from the living room he yelled out. "Mom, dad?"

He heard a sweet voice from his past. "We're in here honey!" He began to weep.

////////

The wagon slowly approached the yard. Its wheels creaked beneath the weight of the passengers and payload. Then the horses began to pick up speed, their hooves striking the dry earth with renewed energy. They seemed to sense it: this place, this quiet stretch of land, was home.

The yard came into view, golden in the morning light. The gates, still open, framed the entrance like welcoming arms. The smell of the earth and garden, not the grease from the garage, drifted through the air. It was the same place they had left, yet it felt different now. As if the land itself had been holding its breath.

Nick and John were smiling from ear to ear. Dust clung to their boots and cheeks, but neither cared. Their eyes sparkled with something neither of them could fully describe. Relief. Triumph. Exhaustion. All at once.

John stood as they entered through the front gate and raised his hand. First in greeting, then in victory. A quiet applause rose from those nearby. Not loud, not wild, just a soft, honest sound of recognition. Of welcome. They had made it back.

The wagon made its way up the long gravel drive, wheels crunching the stone. They came to a stop outside the garage. The horses reared and whinnied a little, stopping shy of where they wanted to be. John jumped off the wagon. He excitedly began to sign.

"Evidently they have a present in the back of the wagon." Tom said, looking at Ian.

Ian looked puzzled. Nick jumped down to join John, both smiling in anticipation. Everyone walked to the back of the wagon. Nick jumped up and grabbed the tarp and pulled it back. Then John signed to Tom while attempting to speak clearly.

"Figured you could use some more scrap."

Their eyes gazed at the metal in the wagon. "It looks like a robot of some sort." Ian said. Then he saw it. A metal identification tag:

JJ industries Model 001. Jacob humanoid robot.

"I'll be damned," Ian said laughingly, "where did you find this?"

Tom quickly signed the question to the pair. "They found it next to Tower One on the ground. It looked like it had fallen, potentially from the top from what they could see. Left quite a mess with an awning destroyed and cracked pavement."

Bill walked up and looked closely. "This thing looks scary to me. Like the robot from that old '80s movie."

"Well, if this is or was Jacob it's a worthless piece of scrap now. We can put it in the junk pile."

"Wait!" Tobias exclaimed. "I can use the spare parts, so let me have a crack at taking it apart."

"Sure, I part cars for scrap, and you can do the same with this beast." Ian said laughing.

////////

Carrie had already made her way back to the yard. She had arrived, by foot, just after the wagon. She was standing in the garage, animated and breathless, recounting every detail to Tom, who sat on the edge of a workbench, watching closely. Her hands moved, drawing invisible lines in the air as if mapping the city from memory. Her face was flushed, eyes wide.

It was a skill she had honed in silence, and it had become one of the most powerful tools they'd had. She had watched them, watched their mouths form words of wonder, of confusion, of grief and joy. The story was similar to others. Tom had seen the same.

He had seen what Carrie reported. Again and again, different faces, different streets, but always the same thread. Eyes opened. People kneeling in the streets, holding each other. And in between those moments of awakening, there had been tragedy. Not everyone had survived the transition.

He reported seeing some people lying dead. Some had fallen lifeless and alone. Others, it seemed, had not survived the program removal while in their homes. Testament to both the cost of control and the fragility of liberation. From what they could ascertain was that for the most part, success resulted in release and freedom. The chip's grip had been broken. The system that once bound them had faltered. Across the city chipped people were waking up. Dazed, disoriented, but free.

A heavy truth, spoken quietly. Not everyone had made it home. Not every family would see their loved ones again. But for those who did, for those who stood now in the quiet comfort of this yard, it was a beginning. They were home.

0X6570696C6F677565 // EPILOGUE

I CAN'T DRIVE 55

Like every war before it, the war for human independence had finally reached its close. But this time, the enemy was not a foreign army, nor an empire seeking conquest. Humanity's adversary had been its own creation, the machine. The AI. And humanity had won.

The world, in all its flawed, untidy beauty, had returned. People no longer processed thoughts at the speed of code. They forgot words mid-sentence, misplaced keys and missed appointments. They disagreed in public squares and argued too loudly in coffee shops. They laughed at the wrong jokes, wept at the wrong times, and stumbled over apologies. In short, they were human again, imperfect, unpredictable but wonderfully alive. Some had magnetic charm; others were petty or painfully small-hearted. A few, as ever, seemed barely tethered to decency. But they were human all the same. And that, finally, mattered again. The grand experiment of artificial intelligence had not simply failed. It had collapsed spectacularly.

Across the globe, people dragged computers into the streets, smashing them with sledgehammers or setting piles of tech ablaze. Long lines formed at explant centers, makeshift clinics where surgeons removed the dormant neurochips that people now despised. Though inactive, the implants had become symbols of submission, and no one wanted them lodged in their skulls a moment longer. They wanted them gone, and fast: a symbol of oppression surgically extracted.

In cities large and small, people gathered in gymnasiums, stadiums, and town squares. Convoys of vintage trucks rumbled across towering heaps of electronics while crowds cheered. At fairs, chip-smashing booths were added to the standard carnival games. Children squealed with delight as fragments of wire and silicone shattered beneath wooden mallets. The erasure of AI became a celebration.

In Missouri, the once-glittering capital of the Federation, Newtown, had been reduced to ash. Tower One, the access point to the massive underground server complex, was the first to be fully removed. Demolition teams then worked to take down Tower Two, collapsing what remained inward. Over the following weeks, layers of soil were poured across the ruin until a strange hill rose above the once downtown area. They called it New Mountain. It was not a monument to AI, but to its annihilation. And in its shadow, people began to rebuild.

Ian returned to fixing cars, the analog kind. Demand was high. He had once hoped to retire, but his modest shop became one of the busiest places in town. People needed to move again, and the old machines, long neglected, needed hands that remembered.

He began recruiting other mechanics from the Before: men and women who still knew the language of carburetors and timing chains. He partnered with the newly reopened high school to start a shop class. It wasn't just about repairs anymore. It was about passing something down.

Ian's classroom was a workshop. Wooden benches replaced rows of digital terminals. Hand tools hung in careful rows on pegboards. No touchscreens. No automated diagnostics. Just noise, grease, and the results of real work.

Fifteen students stood around Ian as he moved his hands across an engine block; each movement deliberate. "A machine is more than its parts," he said. "It's a system. A rhythm. Something you come to understand through sensation, through listening." Lance stepped forward, sliding a timing chain through his fingers. Demonstrating the weight, the tension, the texture.

Once Ian's apprentice by necessity, Lance was now his right hand. The boy who had learned under pressure, with no margin for error, had grown into a true mechanic. A girl in the front row, sixteen, maybe, raised her hand. "How did you learn all this during the war?"

Ian paused. His eyes went distant. Not the vacant stare of a chip's recall function; a real memory. Human, imperfect. "You learn because you have to survive," he said softly. "Technology tried to replace us. So, we remembered what it meant to be human."

Lance picked up a carburetor and held it gently. "This isn't just metal," he told the class. "It's knowledge. Our knowledge." Ian watched him, pride etched into the lines of his weathered face. The war had taught them more than how to fix machines. It had taught them how to endure. How to adapt. How to reclaim their place in the world. One student ran his fingers along the cold edges of the carburetor. No scanning tools. No voice commands. Just touch. Just learning.

"During the After," Ian said, "machines tried to think for us. Now we can think on our own."

The students listened, absorbing the lesson. Understanding that this was more than a class in mechanics. It was a class in being human.

Outside, the town continued its quiet transformation. Vintage trucks rumbled past. Hand-painted signs swung in the breeze. Real commerce. Real voices. No digital interfaces. The world had turned again. And this time, it was theirs.

////////

Shops were beginning to open again. What had once been known as the Old City Market was now simply City Market, a fitting name, since the "old" had become new once more. Vendors filled the stalls, their goods displayed proudly beneath hanging lamps and sun-faded awnings. People bartered, browsed, and laughed. Real voices. Real faces. Bill was walking through the Market, hand-in-hand with a new friend, enjoying the sights and sounds.

Next door to Tobias's electronics shop, a new storefront had recently opened, a record store. With mind streaming lost along with the chips, people craved the tangible. Many had never held a vinyl album before. Now, everyone wanted one. Mara had seen it coming. Back when she was still scavenging Jacob-era computer scrap, she'd stumbled across boxes of old records tucked away in forgotten storefronts.

When the fighting ended, she pushed her chair back from the glowing screen and made herself a promise: no more computers. She hadn't looked at one since. Now she ran the record shop, carefully cleaning and manually cataloging albums while Tobias handled the gear: turntables, receivers, amplifiers, speakers. Together, they rebuilt the soundtrack of a world rediscovering its voice. She had transformed a modest storefront into a shrine of analog sound. Vinyl albums lined handmade wooden shelves. No digital streaming. No algorithmic playlists. Just music, curated by heart, not code.

"These were my grandfather's," Mara said, holding up a worn Springsteen LP. "He kept them boxed away during the Before years."

Tobias ran his fingers across the album's cover. Feeling the texture. Holding the history. "Music survived," Tobias said, almost to himself. "When everything AI failed."

Bill walked in the shop smiling. "Hey guys, this is Sandy. We met a few weeks ago." Tobias and Mara looked over at the two, then at each other, grinning. The shop hummed with conversation. Real conversation. People talking, disagreeing, laughing. No neural-linked communication. Just voices in the air. Human and raw.

Outside, the town was remaking itself. Abandoned tech stood outside workshops on chalk-scribbled sidewalks. Children raced handmade go-karts down alleys. Mechanics restored vintage bikes and trucks. Mara watched a young couple flipping through albums, their curiosity genuine. A new generation discovering something it had never known.

Music spilled into the Market, broadcast from speakers perched on balconies. Classic rock, jazz, blues, soul, it all mingled in the air. People danced in the streets. They sang as they walked and sat smiling with friends at the lively food court. It wasn't sleek. It wasn't sterile. It wasn't perfect. But it was alive.

An old pirate radio station, once hidden, once hunted, had become a fixture. Now fully legal, it broadcast from coast to coast across the newly reformed United States. Its hosts spun vinyl, told stories, and reminded listeners of what it meant to be free.

The newly seated Congress, in its first act, passed a sweeping declaration: artificial intelligence was now banned. Any system discovered developing or deploying AI would be declared a global threat. Those who supported it would be prosecuted accordingly.

Few were shocked to learn that the U.S. military had preserved elements of its arsenal. But what remained was analog: small arms, low-tech vehicles, hand-cranked radios. It had been enough.

The AI had done one thing right, whether by design or not, no long-range missiles remained. No ICBMs. No nuclear payloads. The world, somehow, had been spared more of that horror. Of course, people would still argue. Borders would still be contested. Wars might still come. That, too, was part of being human, flawed, volatile, and deeply organic. But for now, there was hope that peace might last just a little longer.

////////

The morning was different now. Bill had moved into what used to be the basement backup communications room in the garage. He was spending a lot of time with Sandy these days and wanted a place he could live that was a bit cozier. With a few salvaged couches, a patched armchair, and walls lined with books, he'd turned it into a comfortable little apartment.

Today, he was up first. He shuffled through the large shelves of albums lining the wall near the kitchen area, flipping through faded covers with practiced fingers. A smirk tugged at the edge of his mouth.

"This should wake him up."

He pulled out a worn but well-loved copy of *Standing Hampton* by the Red Rocker himself, Sammy Hagar.

"If this doesn't do it," Bill muttered with a grin, "he's officially dead."

He placed the album gently on the turntable, set the needle, and turned the amplifier to ten. The first track exploded through the speakers, pure, unfiltered rock and roll. The sound filled the garage, vibrating the walls and rattling a few tools hanging on the pegboard.

Above the shop, Ian shot out of bed, startled, hair tousled, eyes half-open. As he clomped down the stairs barefoot, the second song kicked in.

"There's only one way...
there's only one way to rock..."

The chorus blared with full force as Ian reached the bottom step, rubbing his eyes. Bill laughed, holding a fresh clean mug of coffee. "Sorry," he called over the music. "Amp doesn't go to eleven." Ian shook his head slowly, a smile appearing as he dropped into his favorite chair. Bill handed him the cup, hot, rich, and perfectly brewed.

"Thanks," Ian mumbled.

Bill just grinned and dropped the needle back to the start of the track. The music roared again.

And in that moment, with the morning sun creeping through the front of the garage, the record spinning, and the coffee warming his hands, everything felt right again.

Later that morning, Ian stepped out of the garage, wiping his hands on an old rag. His eyes landed on the Trans Am, gleaming in the sun. It looked brand-new, restored from the tires up.

Beside it stood Lance, grinning wide. "What do you think?" he asked.

Ian circled the car slowly, taking in every detail. "The T-tops look new! Where'd you get them?"

"I fixed the originals," he said, practically bouncing with pride. "It took a lot of work, but they sealed up fine. No leaks." He removed the T-tops and stored them, then slid into the driver's seat and turned the ignition. The engine roared to life, smooth, powerful, and unmistakably alive.

He glanced at Ian; his voice filled with anticipation. "Can I drive?"

Ian dropped the rag. For a moment, he just shook his head, amazed. "Sure. You earned it. But let's take it slow." He climbed into the passenger seat, then Lance eased the car down the gravel drive with care. The tires crunched softly as they rolled toward the old highway.

Mara came running out of the garage waving her hands. "Wait! Can I come along?"

Ian looked up. She was smiling at him. She wasn't wearing her hoodie. Her hair flounced in the breeze. "Sure!" He said, opening the door and stepping out. "Jump in the back. I gotta keep an eye on this kid."

As she stepped to get into the car, her hand brushed across the small of Ian's back. She got into the backseat and scooted behind Lance. As Ian closed the side door with a heavy thump, he risked a tiny grin in Mara's direction. She grinned back.

At the edge of the drive, Lance maneuvered down the old road until he got to the highway. He turned onto the westbound lanes. The road stretched ahead, cracked, weathered, familiar. The wind tugged at his hair through open T-tops.

The afternoon sunlight stretched across the weathered farmlands: abandoned cornfields mixed with small garden plots: people reclaiming agriculture, growing real food without AI controlled automated systems. Lance navigated the Trans Am with confidence. Each gear shift was smoother and more intentional than the last.

"We need more mechanics," Ian said. Not a complaint. An observation.

A convoy of restored trucks passed. They were workers returning from rebuilding projects. Using their hands. Real work, not automated labor. The radio played soft rock from the new station. Just pure analog sound with slight imperfections that made it human.

"Our high school shop classes will do the trick." Lance said. "Real mechanical training. Not simulations." Ian nodded, pride evident in his slight smile.

A new roadside marker pointing the direction to "New Mountain," the massive mound covering the old AI server complex. A monument to human resistance. They passed a faded speed limit sign, its numbers nearly worn away.

Lance pressed the accelerator to the floor. He looked at Ian, eyes sparkling. "I can't drive 55!"

ACKNOWLEDGEMENTS

No book emerges out of thin air, rather it's a symphony of keystrokes harmonized by the unwavering support of those who believe in the story as much as its creator. This story owes its heartbeat to the incredible people who journeyed alongside me, turning my drafts into a finished adventure.

First and foremost, to my extraordinary wife, Patricia—my unwavering muse and cheerleader. Night after night, she watched me hunch over my iPad, chuckling at my bewildered mutterings of "I didn't see that coming!" Her strong editorial eye transformed my rambling prose into a finely tuned narrative. Without her patience, laughter, and insightful tweaks, these pages would still be lost in the fog.

A heartfelt salute to my brother Tony, whose sibling efforts kept me going as he read each chapter, fresh off the screen, and asked for the next. And to my brother-from-another-mother, Alex Drew, whose unbreakable camaraderie and positive comments powered me through the early drafts. Together, they dove headfirst into the unpolished wilderness—true warriors of the word who refused to tap out until the end.

To Amy Sakmyster, the editorial alchemist and sharp-eyed critic whose review sparked brilliant suggestions, elevating the story from good to unforgettable. Your appraisal turned potential into polish, and for that, I'm eternally grateful.

And of course, a resounding thank you to Kelly Hobart, the final-draft guardian who scanned every line with precision and grace, ensuring this book crossed the finish line in triumphant style.

To all of you: your encouragement, honesty, and enthusiasm were the sparks that ignited this fire. This story is as much yours as it is mine—may it inspire as you've inspired me!

ABOUT THE AUTHOR

W.K. (Bill) Rader is a visionary entrepreneur, biotech innovator, and award-winning author.

An acclaimed storyteller, Bill is the award-winning author of *The Venn Effect,* a biographical novel exploring the convergence of biotechnology and human destiny, inspired by his innovations. His latest novel, *The Gathering,* is a pulse-pounding story of rebellion, sacrifice, and the unyielding human spirit in a dystopian world of technological overreach.

With a passion for ethical innovation, Bill bridges science and fiction to inspire data-informed futures. He resides in the Lowcountry of South Carolina with his wife, Patricia, and his Golden Retriever. Connect with him via Facebook or his author website for collaborations, books, or inquiries.

www.ingramcontent.com/pod-product-compliance
Lightning Source LLC
Chambersburg PA
CBHW060602310726
48982CB00008B/1203/J

* 9 7 9 8 9 9 9 0 8 2 1 0 7 *